Of
Perfect
Spirit

The story, all names, characters, and incidents portrayed in this production are fictitious. No identification with actual persons (living or deceased), places, buildings, and/or products is intended or should be inferred.

Of Perfect Spirit
a novel in
The Anthology From Föld

Copyright © 2025 by Erik Tucsok

All rights reserved.

Edited by Kristy Gibbs

Book Cover by Christian Hadfield

ISBN 978-1-0689686-1-7

First Edition: May 2025

Published by Erik Tucsok
London, Ontario CAN
www.fromfold.com

10 9 8 7 6 5 4 3 2 1

Of Perfect Spirit

a novel in The Anthology From Föld

By

Erik Tucsok

For those who sacrificed many hours waiting for me, and for those who knew there was a reason.

A special thank you to my brother, Jordan.
Whenever I can't, he can.

The Prologue

The wind cuts Rhein as he whips his head around to track behind him.

They haven't caught up yet, I might just make it.

His gaze crawls along the peaking edges of the shore-side cliffs. Rhein draws in two more deep breaths before returning his sights down. The iridescent blue wisps dancing along the back of the spectral hound he rides upon inadvertently lick the woven cover of the baby. His eyes lingering in a fatherly love while inspecting the infant. The fingers of his hand, already securing the bundle, tighten. Predatory snaps of his vision, to affirm the waterfalls remain in sight, fails to bring him any relief.

The wind cuts again. He yanks on the mound of spectral fur clumped in his other hand, urging the beast to accelerate. His breath quickens.

"Ani, my darling baby girl. The whole world waits for you, a world I so desperately wanted to share, but the Gods have other plans. I hope that the warm touch of summer fills you with the same joy it has for me. I pray that the goals you reach for are met, not with ease, but the long due satisfaction of work well rewarded. I know you will find love, be as beautiful as your mother, and lead your own kind of family. It brings me to my knees knowing that the people need you more than I do, or that what you need will mostly be overlooked, because I don't know if it's true. What I do know is that you will stand tall on your own. You will give the Gods a worthy opponent, and prove to everyone that you are more than enough. The strength inside of you will lift us all–"

A wild howl erupts behind Rhein. He swings his face to spy an encroaching band of riders upon true hounds.

"And I will not apologize for the choices I've made."

He returns his sights to the waterfalls lying beyond the cliff's edge and the trailing shoreline ahead. The distant spectacle, well into the alpine forest, is far outside of reach for the man and his hound. Rhein averts his eyes to land on the approaching city.

Carcras.

Making one more peak behind himself, Rhein's world grows smaller.

…It will have to do.

The man releases his grip of the hound to withdraw a leather belt from around his chest. He secures the bundle of Ani to the beast's neck with the strap. Carefully he lifts the isolated flap to reveal the delicate face of an infant girl. After a quick sniffle he closes and tightens it.

"You go as fast and far as you can, do you hear me? I will give you all the time I can."

Rhein forces out a snort, then pushes up from the hound to flip off and away. He lands on his feet, stirring up dust, before turning to face his coming enemies.

The spectral hound continues its charge. Its exaggerated stature aids the unnatural pace bringing the pair to the fair fields outside of Carcras. The thump of melodic running ceases. Blue wisps of spirit evaporate leaving only its potential to fling the bundle into a nearby dried-up creek bed. Rolling across the dirt, churning up dust, the tightly packed sack of linen lands under a grass-covered nook of soil. It rocks to a stillness. Every insect holds their notes for a moment before continuing.

An uncomfortable wailing echoes along the night-colored field. A man of significant stature moves like a shadow between the reeds and nettles. One heavy boot precedes another into the dusty creek bed. Two square hands wrap themselves around the source of infantile pleading. The flap opens with a gentle pinch as he investigates. Unsurprisingly he finds the baby culprit, along with a far more intriguing note nestled within the linen wrap.

ANI, FARMER'S DAUGHTER
WHEN SHE ASKS, IPITH WAS OUR HOME.

His warm breath cascades from him, along the crumpled note, and graces his fingers. He tightens his jaw while looking vastern, the direction he knows Ipith to be. Without another thought, he gathers the child. While abruptly standing up, he snaps his eyes to the vast wooden walls defending Carcras, then the fresh lights set within to fend off the night. One dusty boot crosses into reeds ahead. Two dry hands hold the bundle firm.

Chapter 1
The Youth

The air rests as flat and still as Tushma's mood this morning. His simple grunts, always one more than he needs to give, finally crack Ani.

"What?" the young girl spits out at the man.

He forces an extra grunt of disapproval towards the bundle of goods he wraps within the cloth container before him.

"You're looking old today," she jabs.

"Dealing with you hasn't been the rejuvenating experience I was promised," he replies heavily.

Ani watches as he finishes stretching the end of the knot he produced to be fully taut. He finally glances over to her, giving the light enough time to ignite the dark blue of his eyes. The illumination lightens the grey dominating his dangling beard. By pushing down on the treated wood table with the top of his fist, the man rises to his full height. She studies the leaves of the nearby hanging branch as they play with his short black hair.

Tushma's lip bulges as he licks the front of his lower teeth in his mouth. He then snaps a lively face to Ani before commenting, "You're going in that?"

The young girl looks down and assesses herself.

"It's not as if I'm wearing some burlap sack. I have padding, I have leathers, and I have my favourite pants on because someone told me that dresses aren't acceptable out in the wilds and I should–"

"Yeah, yeah," Tushma cuts her off while moving to an adjected bench. He reaches for a hunting bow reinforced by a pristine wrapping of cables along its length, though missing its string. "I also told you to pack for hunting and not flower picking. Lose the satchel."

Ani gives herself another look, this time focusing on the strap across her chest. "It holds my cheese. What if I get hungry while we're out?"

"Then, we will find something to eat out there. Or eat the cheese now so you won't be hungry."

"If I bring the bag then I can eat it when I want and fill it with more stuff," Ani argues.

Tushma tightens his face as he firmly answers, "If you give chase and a branch snags that satchel then you'll be something else's food, Ani."

That sounds like he knows what we're hunting.

"What exactly are we after in the wilds today?" the young girl inquires while moving a loose strand of hair behind her ear.

A small grin pulls on the aged face of the man. He plucks a string from the rack of the bench, then begins notching it while quipping, "Tired of arguing about cheese, are we?"

Ani furrows her brow. She rises to stretch her legs out before crossing her gaze over the open-air workspace. The mess of tables are covered in half-carved pieces of wood, just barely dry from last night's rain. Her eyes dart to the clouds, lingering in the bright sky, then drop to the organized pile of wood logs they called home. She inspects the crooked corner on the far side, the only part that the old man had let her help with. Ani smiles before tilting her head away from the mossy structure, towards the stream running down the gentle hill beyond. Leaning forward to propel herself from atop the rock she perches upon, she carefully picks rocks to hop from until she comes to the stream's edge. The smell of fresh water brings her nose up the natural flow where she gazes deep in between the alpine trees far into the vast forest.

I wonder what creatures we'll find out there today. The odds are pretty good we'll cross an arkölox or söcartya. Never together, obviously, the huge paws of the arkölox would rip a skinny söcartya to shreds. Though, I wonder which would win in a race. The arkölox have six legs, but... I bet the söcartya's lankiness would help it between the trees. It's so deer-like– Does it even eat meat? It must, otherwise why bother mimicking other creatures if not to lure them to their death...

Ani shudders at the thought.

"What's the matter?" Tushma asks from afar.

"Thinking about söcartya laughter..."

Her sights trail up to a stone frown.

"Hurry up, girl," Tushma growls out at Ani. "I need to go into Barrelwood for supplies as well. The day doesn't wait for anyone."

The young girl brings her eyes back to the running waters directly below her. She only takes the briefest of moments to look at her hair, the same colour as Tushma. The distorted set of puffy eyes staring back draws her attention. Raising one hand to slowly touch her skin, Ani feels the looseness on herself. A quick dive of her hands brings the refreshing liquid up into a splash upon her face.

As a small crouching creature would, Ani arcs her head over her shoulder to comment, "You mean, 'We'."

"Yes, yes. I can't go anywhere without you," he grumbles.

She returns her eyes to the flowing stream only for a harsh snap of wood to lure her focus back towards the man at the workbench. A darkness enshrouds Tushma while the masterwork of a bow hangs as limp as a dying fawn in his hands.

"And I believe that was my rule to begin with, little lady," he continues before letting out an exhausted sigh.

"I didn't like that bow anyways," the young girl jovially remarks.

Ani stretches her whole body long as she stands, then marches back up to the workspace outside of the cabin. She approaches the man and her broken weapon with an unsung grace as her hand reaches out to gently grip the nock. The half-hearted pinching of Tushma's mouth bothers Ani. She gathers the bow's remains and brings them to a rest upon the wooden tabletop. Her eyes track along the other bows gathering dust on the rack.

"They're too big for you," the old man states.

"You know, you make a lot of rules. Rules that make no sense. You should be thanking me when I bring reason to them." Ani spins around to face Tushma. His glare had been swept away and replaced by a beaming grin at her. "And! It looks as if I finally get to have that new bow I've been wanting for the last few seasons."

The gleam in his eyes fade.

"I know, I know. 'We don't have the coin'. 'This is why we hunt'." Her pitch rises into a sarcastic screech, "'But how are we to properly hunt without my'– 'No! None of that. We have plenty of weapons, tools.' Once again, I've asked myself why we need swords out here, but reason slinks its way up into… here."

Tushma's tilted expression barely cracks under the comedic assault from the young girl. Her eyes wander along the length of one bench to the next until they spot a spear resting at an angle against the weathered wood.

"Or, how about you let me use Foolish Tardy?"

The perky grin from Ani is too much, and the old man's eyebrows finally relax.

"You're too smart for your own good," Tushma utters, barely loud enough for Ani to hear.

"What was that?" She holds her hand behind her ear playfully. "I must have arkölox fur in my ears."

"I said, 'You go ahead'." The old man then shifts his gaze to a rack of unstrung bows before waving his hand in a flutter towards the forest beyond. "Let's see if you've learned anything about not being tracked."

A smile stretches across Ani's face from ear to ear. She gives him a short and fast barrage of nods before racing towards the leaning polearm. The silver, metal blade affixed at the end glints black as she comes around to reach for the weapon. Snatching the unnatural shaft of the spear sends a peculiar sensation up her arm. Molded with grooves to resemble a six-pointed star, it allows her hand to dig into the hollow recess of the shaft. Her nose gives a quick scrunch before she rushes off. With the spear in one hand, and her other securing her flailing satchel, Ani sprints past the set of chicken coops, then beyond the edges of their settled camp.

"Remember," Tushma calls out, "travel to the mountains, not to the seas."

A shrill 'Yes' bursts from Ani as she gallops away into the forest. She passes the usual route that she takes when wandering through the forest, passing the gigantic fir tree and not getting turned around at the tooth-shaped boulder.

Soon she finds herself at the trail that the two typically take when starting a hunt.

We don't always end up at the same place. 'Keeps the animals confused'. How does that make any sense, it just keeps them on their toes.

A pile of coloured mushrooms, growing in a snaking pattern through the short grass and mosses, brighten the greens and browns of the trail with their radiant hues. Ani stops to admire the diminutive sprouts, poking each of their blooming caps with the end of her spear.

Pink. Yellow. Even a big gangly green one. 'You're not to be touching them'. Of course, your old-ly-ness, I shall not touch anything that can kill me.

The young girl ceases her thought by kicking the nearest mushroom. She watches the helpless growth tumble onto the open trail. Her falling eyes then find a familiar set of tracks, along with droppings.

I'm not checking poop, but I think I'll follow this for a bit; see if Tushma can find me while I track a little on my own.

Ani slides her boot to move some fallen brush overtop of the droppings, then skips away into a dramatic pursuit. Quiet stalking brings her uphill where she slows for a moment to look out into the valley behind her.

I wonder if I can see the cabin from here.

Her spying eyes plunge into the distance, wandering along lowlands and plains before locating the wisp of smoke coming from their home. A coarse wind blasts upon the trees, bringing her focus to Lake Barrelwood before tracking up the footholds beyond, towards a darkened set of forest denser than the rest.

Glad I didn't end up over there, then I certainly would have been something's lunch.

After smiling to herself, she turns back to finish the final steps of her trail, reaching the valley's lowly peak. An abrupt gust of warm sea air smashes into Ani. Every hair on her body rises. She grabs a hold of the nearest tree trunk as she tracks the lessening vegetation from the breaching treeline to the craggy edge ahead of her.

What's the worst that could happen?

Impulsively, she creeps forward. Dust begins to plume with each supporting hit of the spear on the dry ground. Step after step brings her closer to the fringe. Her mind races between mystery and peril until what lies beyond the edge reveals itself. She can feel the gravity of the grotto as the depths below pull on her. Tiny shipwrecks litter the basin, trapping waves that harshly splash against the beaten vessels.

Oh, I'm not supposed to be here...

From top to bottom, the cliff walls are embedded with sunken holes housing some distant but resting terrors. The young girl's eyes widen while trying to comprehend the spectacle of a thousand monsters gliding from peak to rocky peak. Scales gleaming throughout bear vivid blues ranging from a soft sky to a midnight sea. She blinks rapidly, a natural reaction to the overwhelming sight forcing a decision upon her. Without warning, the fierce red of others vibrates through the sea of blues. Crimsons, a warning to all of the fiery power inside, break through the masses. They soar far into the sky, towards the bright yellow fila, before relaxing to plummet back from whence they came.

Ani's eyes struggle to not see purple in the absolute blending of brotherly scales. She abuses the moment to realize her hands are shaking like a calf. Melding both hands into a holding grip of her spear, she tries to gather some semblance of control. The moment is shattered as her senses are overtaken by a smell.

The forge… metal in the forge, but way more. Hundreds of ores burning.

A movement in the distance to her left brings her nose closer to the smell. A spiralling beast of iridescent orange displays a magnificent effort while its wings climb from a foggy prison. It rises until its four powerful legs grapple the craggy peak at the furthest opposing summit. Ani cocks her head as more plumes of smoke spew from the scales along the monster's body. The beast extends, then retracts its wings, in a satisfying stretch before drifting its gaze along the grotto at its kin.

Her long hair blows wildly, whipping across her vision. Sensations return to Ani, freeing her from the prey-like paralysis. With a gentle stride she slinks back from the grotto's edge to slip away from the den of beasts. Tracking her breathing keeps her focused on her steps and not the impending danger. Her eyes snap to the mountains in the filaash. As she gently spins, the dry soils extending from the dark forest release small crumbles that crunch, provoking attention.

That'll be it. Stupid little stone rolls too loud and I'm dinner. 'Quick and quiet', just like he said. Except this time, I'm being hunted.

She quickly checks over her shoulder to confirm her fear, only to be relieved that none of the nest had taken notice of her. Turning her head back, she finds her true fear.

Maybe… Maybe he doesn't see me.

The scowl of Tushma burns the boundaries of the young girl's mind. A firm and silent finger point tugs on her feet, bringing her from the plateau back into the forest.

"Are you okay? Did you hit your head?" he asks endearingly.

"Um... no?" Ani replies.

A swift thwap assaults the back of her head.

"Then why did I find you in the one place I told you not to be?"

Ani hesitates to answer for a second. "It was an accident."

Another swift thwap lands, sending a throbbing echo through her skull.

"What was that for?" she cries out.

"It was an accident," Tushma flippantly answers, then stalks deeper into the forest.

The young girl rolls her eyes before hopping ahead to catch up to him. They wander in silence, past fallen trees and blooming mushrooms, for some time before Ani finally breaks.

"What were those things?"

"What things?" Tushma replies.

"The flying things."

The old man itches his chin before responding. "That's vague, ask a real question."

A real question... What does he mean by that? That was a real question. I want to know what those things are. They are real, right? Was I imagining them? That would be crazy. Am I crazy? No, I'm just young. 'Full of silly ideas' he always says. Wait until I grow up, old man, then you'll have to answer all of my questions. I wonder what a young Tushma was like...

"What did you want to be when you grew up?" the young girl interrogates.

The old man cracks a smile before falling into a hearty chuckle. "Well, well, it seems I have raised you with dreams and whimsy. Little lady, boys where I come from don't have to worry about what they are going to become, because they know it the first time they set eyes on their father."

Ani shoots Tushma a sharpened glare. "That's no fun and you know it."

He looks off before sniffing hard, then explains, "You know, it's been so long since I cared to think about it, but I was rather fond of playing music. Not any metal contraption, don't care to waste my lungs like that, but I did have a drum when I was younger... much younger."

"Ba dum, ba dum, ba dum," Ani mouths while playing a phantom instrument. She loses herself within the play. Soon her sights drift back to find Tushma watching on. She slows down her beat. "I know, I know, we're hunting."

"Quick and quiet is best. I don't mind the idle chatter, but your lack of focus... it's going to take us twice as long out here."

"And what exactly are we hunting again?"

"Bear," Tushma promptly responds.

"Bear?" Ani cracks back. "What makes you think we're going to find a bear out here? Not at this time of year. We're better off finding a deer."

"You mean söcartya?"

"Absolutely not."

The old man shakes his head. "Don't worry, I can smell bear."

"Woah, maybe you should have been a professional smeller when you grew up."

Tushma closes his eyes tightly, only to re-open them while throwing a glare at the young girl. "Okay, fine. What is it you want to say?"

"Ah ha! I knew you cared." Ani squints out into the rising distance before them. She focuses on the swaying of the massive trees.

The trees – are – bigger on this side of the lake.

"Maybe I'll lumber," she continues. "From what you've been telling me about the Timber Drift they need all the people they can get. And then maybe I'll snag myself one of those floating planks from Drifton."

"You couldn't handle–"

She cuts the man off, "I so could handle chopping trees. You haven't seen me while you're gone, I cleared the whole vastern field. You think a bitterworm did that? Those little bear turds might be good at dissolving trees, but I put my back into–"

"I was about to say driftboard."

Ani throws her arms up in utter disbelief, "You have to be kidding me. Get out of here."

The old man stops in his tracks. Ani pauses, her smile fading away while eyeing him.

"What? I thought we we're kidding–"

"Shh," Tushma presses while throwing her a glare.

A heat cascades along the young girl as she tightens her mouth. Her eyes track across the visage of trees, spying for anything that would catch the old man's attention.

"I don't see it," she whispers.

His prodding finger guides her sight, leading to a well covered grove of brush hiding a hand-sized patch of brown fur.

A bear! We actually found one.

Ani doubles her stillness while allowing Tushma to initiate the hunt. His stance is wide, and footsteps muffled, as he strafes to broaden his vantage of the beast. With one wrong step, a dry twig crunches under toe. The patch of fur bolts away, causing its own noisy ruckus. Ani strengthens the hold on her spear before the pair give chase, darting ahead into the thickening forest.

The deep dark!

"Tushma, we can't go this way!" she calls out.

His continual heavy breathing informs the young girl that her words have fallen on deaf ears. She avoids hesitation, sprinting to catch up. Amid a bright clearing, she finds Tushma crouching. Ani joins him in time to hear his usual grumble before words.

"I knew I smelt one," the old man mutters out.

Ani sharpens her gaze through the trees ahead to spy a large stone bobbing up and down. While passing Tushma to gather a clearer view, she catches sight of the brown fur before hearing the struggling cries of the majestic creature. Her shifting head reveals the source of the scuffle. A glare of white teeth sinking into a bear carcass sends her body into a state of panic.

Wait, wait, wait, that's not stone!

"Tushma!" the young girl screams in a whisper, "Something is eating the bear."

Ani returns her sights to the feasting amidst the bushes and bark. The rippling of scales that cascade upon every bite reveals soft, silty skin under the craggy plates. She hears Tushma's breathing slow before his hand thrusts out to halt her in her steps.

"Rock climber."

The words touch Ani with the grit of a landslide. Her memory unloads the many one-sided conversations he had with her about the abhorrent creatures. Although she never truly believed his preaching, the monster before her was rapidly painting the picture of a fierce opponent.

A wringing of twine drags her focus to Tushma as he draws an arrow, aiming at the rock climber. The man holds his breath to steady himself, and the simple act entices Ani to do the same. She tracks the whirlwind of the arrow's release. A gentle whistle follows the stick of death as it glides, landing in between rising scales.

Without hesitation the creature whips its head to the sky and howls. The atrocious wail leaves Ani in a state of impending fear. A thumping of her heart reminds the young girl of the expectations of a hunt. She raises her spear to be at the ready. Her eye twitches before she snaps a look to Tushma who had already begun his approach. Quickly following him, Ani stalks a good ten strides from the old man in a wider arc to perpetuate surrounding their prey.

The beast jabs its eyes in every direction trying to find the source of its pain. Its long and flat tongue rearing with each hiss it produces. Tushma draws another arrow, but the strain upon his bow is too loud and immediately gains the rock climber's attention. In an act of sheer reflex, Tushma releases the arrow. Before her eyes could blink, Ani witnesses the beast clamp its scales down and deny the arrow.

Ani's ears are jostled as the hissing of the rock climber deepens into a snarl. While passing behind a tree she misses out on seeing the creature for but a moment. As the young girl peeks out the other side, she finds it scurrying away with the bear in its mouth. As Ani crosses to the next tree she watches on as the beast takes its escape upwards and scales the rising cliffside.

Another arrow sounds off, narrowly missing the creature. However, the failed attempt succeeds in forcing the rock climber's mouth open and it drops its meal.

Tushma rushes into the feeble clearing below the looming rockface to let out a deep roar. Ani places a hand upon her brow while tilting her sights up to track the beast's climb. Small shrapnels of stone tumble down, landing harmlessly nearby. As the echo of the old man's cry fades away, Ani reorients herself to the fallen bear.

Well, looks like we still– Where did it go?

"Tushma! The bear is gone."

The old man's jaw tightens on one side. "It wasn't quite dead yet. Good, means we can still get meat."

Ani matches Tushma's gaze as it elongates beyond the clearing into a shaded cave entrance.

"Must have gone in there," she comments.

"Must have," he echoes.

The young girl skips ahead towards the mouth of the cave. The closer she gets, the further the light touches inside. A revealing of stone teeth jutting from each surface sends chills along her skin. A moderate pathway extending deeper appears freshly stained by the bear's blood. Tushma drifts in front of her, blocking her vision with his sweaty back.

"I go first."

"Sure, whatever you say. But I get to do the final kill."

A hoarse grunt comes from the man before he takes his initial step into the dark domain. Crossing the threshold brings an end to the light of day only to reveal a community of glowing mushrooms.

The tops look like butterflies; they're all so colourful and unique.

Her foot bumps into something so she peers down to watch her steps more closely. The faint blue luminescence paints a grim picture for Ani as she scuttles behind the large man.

It was a mother bear… Poor cubs didn't stand a chance.

"What a terrible creature to raid the den of–"

The irritated face of Tushma with a finger over his lips snaps back at her, cutting her thought short. Ani furrows her brow, squirms her mouth, then obliges. Directing her attention to the glowing mushrooms, half as large as she is, she reaches out to touch one only for Tushma to slap it away.

"Poisonous," he utters through his teeth.

She grunts back in even more frustration.

The pair follow the weaving path of bear blood set between the stone teeth for a moment longer before they come to the dying creature. At the sight of Tushma, the bear stands on its back legs, only to bump into the wall behind it. An unnerving crack shims vertically up the wall, the only warning before a slurry of stone tumbles onto the fading animal.

A brief plume of dust assaults the pair. Ani covers her face with her arm. Once everything settles, she looks down at the smothered bear. Without hesitation, the young girl bolts ahead but is halted by the thick arm of Tushma.

He gives a small order, "Wait."

"For what? I think it's actually dead this time."

She tracks his eyes as he checks the remaining walls and ceiling of the cave.

"Do you think it's going to collapse?"

"Not sure."

"How are you going to check?"

"We should leave."

In the wake of the rockslide Ani spots a hole. After squinting, she spies a pristine slab of stone.

"Tushma… what is that behind the bear?"

"I dunno," he quickly remarks.

Ani huffs. "Well, let's go find out."

"Its noth–" the old man's rising angry tone melts away. "What – is – that?"

Chapter 2
The Guardian

Tushma retracts his arm, then skulks towards the lifeless bear laying loosely below the rubble. Carefully, Ani follows the old man, her sights tracking where he looks before approaching behind him. He quietly puts his bow over his head to rest on his torso. She mimics, looking over herself for a place to store the spear, but finds nothing convenient.

Sounds of stone being gently moved alerts Ani that the old man has begun climbing. She quickly joins him, using one hand while holding her long weapon in the other. Soft grunts accompany the pair while clambering up the pile of spewed stones. A subtle shift in the debris forces them to slow their pace. After they carefully take step after step ascending the unstable mound, they stand before the sophisticated tunnel wall at the top.

"This doesn't even seem possible," she comments.

The old man grips Ani's bicep before replying, "It isn't natural. Someone made this."

Only the dim illumination coming from the mushrooms below gives the young girl enough light to see. She frees herself, then swiftly darts towards the black.

"But who?" echoes from Ani as she passes into the tunnel. Her footsteps resound from every surface, forcing an early halt. Dust dangles in the air, crossing through the low light creeping into the tunnel from the cavern fungus. The young girl blinks to try and adjust her sight, which reveals the sheen stone to be travelling in both directions to either side of her. Quickly, she swings an eye behind her. "Which way should we go?"

"Should we really be going in here?"

Ani lays a hand upon the cold stone. Her fingertips can barely feel any imperfections of the wall.

It's like a blade, like steel or something. A purposefully crafted tunnel, walls and all.

"How often do we discover something like this?"

"Never, which is why we're still alive."

Ani shakes her head. While brushing loose hair behind her ear her sights land upon a faint glimmer at the furthest reaches of the left side tunnel. "Fine, this way then."

The young girl braves ahead while Tushma thumps along behind her. Each footstep that Ani takes, sending a faint twang echoing off the perfectly cut walls, is matched by a patriarchal grumble.

Oh, he's not happy about this. Those are the disagreement grunts. But, when we find something to sell off – then buy a new bow or two – he'll be so pleased that we might just come back.

She squints, then widens her eyes to try and gather a better sight of the tunnel's end. A crumbling of stone brings her to an abrupt stop. Behind her, the shuffling of Tushma ceases as well. The cold of the tunnel tugs at the young girl, but the daft silence lacks any suspicion. Ani allows the moment to pass before shifting her foot to recreate the crunching of stone.

"Just us," she emits.

"For now," comes from behind.

Ani returns to her pace, coming towards yet another glimmer in the distance. As she nears, a soft light coming from the walls brings the coming tunnel into better detail. A spattering of green circles an imposing, round door blocking the passage.

"Looks like this is it then," Tushma comments.

The young girl slinks ahead, placing her hand upon the ice-cold frame. She puts effort into pushing upon the door, but it doesn't budge. Ani then gently taps the center with the tip of her spear.

"Hmm," Ani ponders while looking the obstacle over. "Sounds like metal…"

"If you don't treat that right, I'll take it back," the old man comments before lowering his tone to order, "It's time we turned back."

"We can get through this–" a small fart pops from Ani, bringing her thoughts to a swift halt.

She slides a glance to Tushma, watching his face come to an unamused rest while the tiny noise bounces around the hollow tunnel. Ani snorts, but a follow-up grumble of her stomach compels her to stick a finger in her satchel to poke around for her cheese.

While scavenging, she continues, "How about you help me push it open. Do you suppose it's locked?"

"I would lock it," Tushma mutters before arriving at the young girl's side. He places his hands upon the surface, then digs his feet into the floor to provide an honest effort.

Ani does her part, with only one free hand, and nearly falls into the moving door as it relents. She allows a successful chuckle amid her groans. While the pair brings the metal door wide open, she looks down the other side.

That's not a tunnel.

Her eyes wander up, finding a vast and open underground city of the same crafting as the tunnel. From behind, she hears Tushma's muttering.

"This door is too thick. How did it move with such ease? It should weigh more than the cabin, more than... What are they keeping out with such a defence?"

The young girl turns to find the old man still gazing upon the metal door. "Tushma?"

"Yes?" he answers while turning to her. Ani watches as the old man's face shifts between each realization while his eyes scan what lies behind the door. She smirks, then takes his arm.

"I think we found something."

She guides them from the entryway out into a railed plateau. The perfectly etched shapes of the hall's protruding architecture brings a satisfaction to the young girl's mind that she can't quite understand.

Lots of triangles, and – well – that doesn't even seem possible. How can a building hold itself up at that angle? What's keeping it there? This doesn't make sense.

Ani lets go of the old man to bring herself towards the railing, peeking over the edge to satisfy her curiosity. Below is the unyielding depth of the underground city. Countless stone structures line the edges of the space, like teeth in an endless mouth. A lump forms in her throat while looking down, urging her body to back away. She turns to find Tushma still smitten by the world around him. Her eyes find another tunnel to the far left.

"Come on, let's see where this goes," the young girl squeaks out before rushing away. While approaching the new passage she spies a pile of ancient tools leaning in the corner near the open entryway. She stops to examine them.

They look almost like ours, shovels and axes, and yet nothing like I've ever seen before. They don't look that heavy either…

"We're not touching anything until we know this place is long abandoned, do you hear me?" the stark voice of Tushma commands.

After a swift headshake, the young girl bolts up and accidentally hits her spear on the nearby wall. While pinned in place, the dark blade gouges into her right arm. A searing pain shoots through Ani, causing a stifled scream to eject from her mouth. The rattling of her weapon on the solid stone below drowns out all noise around the young girl.

"What happened?" Tushma asks while rushing over to her side.

Ani lowers to one knee, gripping her right forearm firm with her left hand, trying to hold herself together. The old man kneels as well, taking her forearm and slowly rolling her long sleeve up. In the faint light, the fresh wound can hardly be seen.

"It's right next to your scar, nearly hit it."

The young girl looks at her own flesh. Her eyes trace the familiar pattern of skin colliding, not unsimilar to a mountain chain of overgrown muscle. She can feel the firm lump move as Tushma's fingers poke and prod to assess the wound.

"I'll wrap it up, but then we should head back home."

"No," bolts from Ani's mouth. "Look at what we've found… We have to keep going."

Warm air shoots from the old man's nostrils. His jaw tenses while his eyes bounce around. Finally, he silently takes a strip of cloth from his side and wraps the young girl's arm. The tingles and pains of his mending fail to keep Ani's mind at ease.

He probably thinks I'm some kind of idiot, a child. I won't be surprised if he marches right back home, carrying me under his arm...

The old man tucks the end of the cloth under itself to ensure it stays put. He reaches out to take the spear in his hand before standing to his full height. Once overtop of Ani, he extends his free hand in a gesture to help her up.

She takes it in kind. The strength of his grip settles the anxiety brewing within her. Ani looks up at his stoic face, begins to move her lips to speak but he beats her to it.

"Lead on. But I'm carrying Folyash Tartagh this time."

A cold bead of sweat runs down the side of Ani's face. She can feel loose hairs play with the stream until they stick to her. Without giving him the time to reconsider, the young girl charges down the new tunnel. Her mind runs amuck trying to bring back the wonder of this adventure to her.

Wow! I can't believe he actually wants to keep going— Wait, does he actually want to? What's the harm? No one is here... He did say that we haven't confirmed that yet.

Each step she takes upon the flat surface below sends a chilling reminder that she's now in someone else's home.

Who would live underground like this? How would you eat?

They pass through into the next tunnel, then one more beyond that. Finally, the young girl spots a darkened light up ahead. The illumination evolves into a low glow as Ani approaches. A bioluminescence emitting from the network of fungal growth suddenly ignites her mind.

Maybe they ate these!

"Tushma?"

She turns around to look at the old man, who she had only heard following but could now see his grim face. The flexing in his jawline depicted a man very uncomfortable with recent decisions.

"Tushma," Ani continues, "Do you think people who live underground eat mushrooms?"

The stoic expression upon the old man nearly brings the young girl to a giggle.

"What?" she pokes. "Either they do, and won't eat us, or they don't and are likely long dead. Right?"

"Or they figured out some other way," Tushma grumbles.

"As in…" Ani drags out the syllable, luring the old man to respond.

"As in look around. Any group of people – and yes this would take a whole generation – that could construct anything this sophisticated…"

Tushma flails his arms to exaggerate the statement. The following hollow silence allows for an ancient stillness to seep into the pair.

"I suppose you're right," Ani admits.

A harsh breath soothes out the old man. He lingers on the end of his exhale before continuing, "Remember when I first brought you to Barrelwood? And even though they are our neighbours I told you not to trust anyone?"

"Yes," the young girl simply replies.

"Well, I knew them, those people. They have shown me who they are, and I learned from that. But learning isn't easy or painless–"

"So, they will hurt us?" Ani juts in.

"No, no. I'm not saying they will–"

"Then what are you saying?"

Tushma groans. "I'm saying they could, and whatever this is, I'm not certain is worth that risk."

"Ahh, you love me."

"Ani, I'm serious."

"Say it."

"Ani—"

A tumble of stones echoes in the distance. The hairs upon Ani rise in an instant. She rushes to the old man's side, feeling him equally tense.

"Ani, it's time we leave."

In silent agreement, she nudges on Tushma. The pair slink back towards the tunnel they came from. Another echo of stirring stone cries out in front of them. The old man halts, but Ani does not. In her haste she steps ahead, hearing the very localized sounds of chipping wall encircling her. Her eyes strike back at Tushma before stone bursts all around her. A wave of water coats the young girl before the pressures of its flow drag her down to the flat floor. She fights to bring her head above water, but a thunderous breaching of the other wall forces the water through a hole, draining her along with it.

A muffled scream comes from Ani as the water rushes her out of reach. In between the black and wild splashing, she watches Tushma and the tunnel slip away from her. Bits of jagged rocks cut her as she is forced along with the underground river. The moment drags on for what feels like an eternity before the water spits Ani out into a lower pool. The short-lived freedom is quickly wrenched from the young girl as the basin then breaks through into somewhere even lower.

The horrendous fall is brought to a halt by a harsh landing. All the trickling water flees, leaving Ani behind where she fell. Her fear ignites with a scurry into the closest, darkest nook. While succumbing to the black, she takes two rapid breaths before holding to listen amidst the absolute silence.

Where am I?

Trickles of light draw her attention. The girl-sized hole above appears darker than ever while a jagged poolside entrance allows some faint twinkles of the day to cast into the cavern. The natural light provides the young girl with one inherent tool to use in the unforeseen and foreign space. She slowly and quietly scans her surroundings.

Stone and more stone. The only way out is into the pool, or above, that I can see. Who knows what's in that pool, maybe some little-girl-eating fungus…

After her heart slows to merely a violent thump in her chest she crawls through the cave towards the large opening. In a passing glance she eyes a circle of gleaming stones nestled behind a protruding stalagmite.

Those are round, almost perfectly round. I wonder if they're rounder than the hen's eggs at home.

She halts as a swirling of thoughts clutter her mind. The young girl rises into a feral crouch before her hand shoots out to rest upon the stone's side. A subtle warmth cascades her palm.

Yes, yes. I hear your voice. I shouldn't be touching it – but – what's the harm? Is the rock going to hurt me? Though… Why is it not freezing cold?

Just shy of her middle finger the stone bulges and cuts her. She quickly retracts her hand, holding it in the other to soothe the fresh pain. The gleam upon the stone reveals another bulge. Ani blinks a few times while watching the stone push and crack. Tiny chips of granite tumble to the slate floor before the light catches a new substance. A viscous liquid spurts out from under the bulge.

Ani slowly places a hand behind her to begin sliding backwards as the realization envelops her mind.

They aren't just round like eggs…

Two more chips pop from the stone, continually oozing the embryotic liquid. Before the young girl's eyes, a long snake rolls weakly into its new world. A damp, icy blue coats its scales. The blank, unencumbered stare of the infant fills Ani with a mystic delight. Tiny eye movements tell her the creature is processing everything around it.

Should I move? Does it know what to do? The chicks were always fine, but that one calf Tushma hauled out of its mother needed all the help it could get.

A subtle lip quiver, followed by a baring of teeth, presents Ani with her answer. In a fraction of a breath, the creature begins wailing. The unused lungs crack and cough before unleashing an ear-splitting screech.

No. No, no–

A monstrous screech bellows out from the pool.

"No!" Ani belts out as she springs forward. Throwing her hands around the beast's neck, she wrings on the weak structure. She feels her own fresh blood squish along the serpent's scales.

Just like the chickens back home.

The noise within the cavern ceases.

While still holding the limp carcass, Ani becomes overwhelmed by a deep and excruciating pain from within her right forearm. Her eyes quickly snap to find the bandage on her skin exuding a radiant glow, one resembling her scar.

A storm of iridescent nerves flash before her eyes and an overwhelming burning sensation accompanies a blue, spectral stream being drawn into the cloth. Ani widens her sights to see the dead beast having a spectral formation being siphoned from its body.

"What! No! Why!" she screams out.

In a daft fright, she throws the limp serpent away. The remaining apparition crawls up her skin, and into the fleshy domain. Then, the light fades just before the burning ceases. Ani digs her nails into the cloth wrapping, yanking it from her forearm to reveal the scar underneath still appears as it did before, only tarnished by a slice covered in dried blood.

Waves of water splash against either side of the cavern's grand opening. Ani peers over the side of the defensive rock to see the massive head of one of the flying red beasts she had seen by the sea. Its horns, jagged as though something has taken it and bent or twisted them, scrape along the cavern's ceiling. Debris and dust plummet to the wet floor. Ani spots the beast's eyes scan the cavern, landing upon the infant corpse she had thrown only moments ago. The creature's face flares in rage. It widens its gaping mouth, snarls its nose, then releases an ear-splitting screech. The beast spews scorching flames within the cavern, threatening to lick Ani as she crouches behind the stone while closing her eyes tight. A thunderous crack erupts, compelling the young girl to open her eyes once again. Her sights find horizontal bolts of lightning reaching throughout the cave, poking at the furthest walls of the domain. She slams her hands over her ears before squeezing her eyelids shut once more.

The almighty outburst ends, but is then swiftly replaced by two distinct screeches that render Ani's ear covering futile. By feral instinct she rolls to look around the corner to spot a glimpse of the fleeing beasts. To her surprise she also witnesses Tushma crouching beside some kind of device imitating an egg of the beast. Without hesitation the young girl scrambles from behind the stone, rushing to the old man's side.

Tushma's face washes itself of fear while seeing Ani. He wraps one powerful arm around her, then picks the device up. While holding her tight, they dash to the elevated pathway along the outside of the pool's edge towards another tunnel entrance. Once within the darkness, he places the device on the ground before gripping both of Ani's shoulders. His concerned eyes dart between hers while he speaks, "Are you okay?"

Ani looks herself over, providing a quick reminder that her body is covered in scrapes and bruises from being dragged through the water. Thoughts about the sharp pain of her deep slice, and dull muscle ache from the dead beast entering her scar, bring her face into a tense scrunch.

"I still have my satchel..." The young girl comes to the brink of tears. Her eyes swell as she leans in to give the old man a tight hug.

"It looks like we can go back through this way."

The young girl replies with a soft head nod before the pair slip away into the darkness once more.

Chapter 3
The Denizen

"Why?" Ani spits out.

"Why, what?" her caretaker blankly responds.

The young girl takes a reserved breath before unleashing her torrent upon the old man.

"You said that I couldn't ask any questions until we left the mountains. Well! We're outside now, nice fila and fresh air. Give me answers! Where did you go? What was that thing you used? And most importantly," her volume reaches an uncomfortable pitch, "why did my skin glow hot and the spirit of a dead monster crawl inside?"

Tushma stops dead in his tracks. His brow furrows while his eyes remain stagnant. He softly sucks his tooth before drifting his face towards her. The look that Ani expects is one of anger for disobeying him in some way. Or, maybe one of horror from the coming repercussions of the adventure they just endured. Even one of stress under the weight of the many actions taken leading to unforeseen consequences.

His eyes are hollow, sad even.

"Tushma…"

"I knew this was going to happen–" he cuts his words off only to passionately compel himself back in, "I knew this was going to happen and I did nothing! All these years I had hoped that one of the chickens might have filled the void – become your auragonic – but I was sorely wrong. I should have known better, and I am sorry, Ani." The man blinks rapidly a few times. His eyes grow vacant as he begins rubbing his thumb along the rim of the mechanical egg being cradled by his forearm. He forces one quick snort before pressing on, using his spear as a walking stick. Ani watches as he continues his march towards home, but soon his strides shorten until he spins to face her once more. A daft mask of confusion crawls along his face, a variant of her own.

She fills the silence, "Auragonic?"

Tushma's eye twitches upon hearing the word spoken. "Yes, Ani. One of many things that you will need to learn about. Let's get back to the cabin to clean and organize ourselves. There I will tell you everything."

"Tell me now," the words fall from the young girl's mouth.

"I will tell you at the cabin–"

"Why wait? Tell me now."

"You don't understand–"

"You're right, I don't understand! How could I possibly understand? 'Wait until we're out of the mountain', 'Wait until we're at the cabin', soon it's going to be 'Wait until you're older' or, 'Wait until...' whatever the reason. I have a thing inside of me, now!"

"Fine. Let's stand like idiots in the middle of a monster-filled forest babbling loudly. Does that sound smart to you?"

She remains rebelliously silent.

Ani watches as the old man firmly plants the end of his spear into the föld below him. He subtly twists his wrist to slowly dig the polearm's end deeper into the soil. The blade, pointing to the sky, swiftly shifts between bright silver and ominous black. His shirt is gently tousled by the wind, only being held down by the bow string taunt against his torso. The deep blue of his eyes hold firm, matching her grit.

The young girl takes a deep breath, allowing her sights to wander, before continuing, "You know everything?"

A firm and slow head nod comes from Tushma.

"I'm not going to die or explode?"

"I know just about everything there is to know about being a Spirit Anchor."

"...a Spirit Anchor," Ani mumbles to herself.

If he really does know this much, then he would be more panicked already. I'll just have to trust him... like always.

"Okay." The young Ani perks as she skips towards the man. "We'll go home and then you can tell me everything."

The remaining walk home is brisk to avoid nightfall. As the waning heat of the day is choked out by the early year chill, the pair arrive at their dilapidated abode. While the old man remains outside, placing the mechanical egg on a vacant space of one workbench, the young girl enters to unburden herself. She slowly wanders the one room hut, lighting a handful of nearly finished candles. The worn furs lining the beds and chairs remind her she is home. Ani strolls towards her bed, tossing her empty satchel before sitting upon the semi-soft cushioning in a slump. An exhale of relief flows from her as she releases her tired feet from their boots. Her eyes rise, to the handcrafted dresser across from her, and settle on a thick tome with an abundance of dust covering it.

*I don't think Tushma has opened that thing in all my years.
Now I have to wonder what's in there, what's he hiding, what else
don't I know… Well, he did say he would tell me everything. Am I
going to need some kind of paper and ink? Auragonic, Spirit
Anchor… probably need to find a journal for all of this.*

While resting her eyelids for a moment, the young girl
tries to remember every conversation the pair ever had. She
grits her teeth, but her mind fails to serve her and comes to
an exhausted conclusion. Slowly, her eyes reopen. Ani sits in
silence for a moment before beginning to unravel the cloth
wrap of her forearm. She takes special care while removing
the bandage. Once bare, the young girl stares at the scar
she's always had. It speaks no truths to her. Then she
examines the wound she gave herself underground.

Looks nearly healed…

The door to the cabin calmly opens outwards before
Tushma slowly shuffles inside. A powerful quiet assumes
the room while he strides towards one of the hardwood
chairs beside a handmade table. He expels a few forced
grunts while leaning down to remove his boots, then peers
up to the expecting Ani standing and waiting.

"Dragons, those beasts are called dragons," Tushma
breathes out.

"How do you know that?"

He lets out a soft coo before responding, "This is going
to be a far longer conversation if you ask me why I know
things the entire time. You're going to have to set those
insecurities aside while I bring you into an early adulthood
here."

"I don't want that."

"Ha!" The old man shakes his head while staring long
and low. "Neither do I, but we don't get that luxury
anymore."

"Like boys…" Ani concludes.

"…Like boys," Tushma affirms. "I'll start from the beginning. I found you – you know this – and you hail from Ipith, this is what we know. This is what I've told you. After much thought, I had the inkling that you were one of them."

"A Spirit Anchor."

"Yes, and when your wrest," he gestures a weak hand towards the long scar on her forearm, "surfaced it was all but confirmed."

"You told me I cut myself one night while sleeping."

"I've told you many things over the years, to ensure you had a normal childhood."

"And yet here we are."

"'We', indeed. As you might have gathered; you're not the first Anchor that I've dealt with before." Tushma's pause lingers beyond the moment. His eyes drift while his face struggles to hold composure. He makes a grunt similar to that of pain before continuing, "When you killed that infant, you absorbed its spirit and now that resides inside of you."

"Yes, I got that part."

"It's a part of you now. Eventually you'll be able to release it, control it, and – if it comes to it – fight with it."

"How many others are there?"

"I don't know anymore, since spending the better part of a decade out here in the forest with you."

"How many were there, then?"

"Not many last I checked. History has not been kind to your people, and they walled themselves off to protect who was left, in Millown."

"Right, so we're going to Millown!"

"I don't think that's a good idea."'

"Oh, it's just me going?"

"Absolutely not."

"Tushma, I have to go. I can't hide out here and hope for the best. I need to meet them, find out what to do with myself."

"I can help you with that."

"Do you have one?" Ani proudly lifts her scarred arm up to serve her point.

"No," slowly crawls from the old man.

"Then clearly I have to go."

"Ani–"

"Tushma, I trust you – I do – but..." The young girl peeks up to see the old man resting his head within cupped hands. "Who is – or was – hunting Anchors? I don't understand why I'm supposed to be afraid."

Ani watches as Tushma stands up to his full height. He raises a finger to begin a rage-fueled rant, but his silent face compresses. After ducking under the drying herbs hanging from a rafter beam, he approaches his wooden bedside table to begin withdrawing items of interest.

"What are you doing?" Ani questions.

"Gathering my things."

"Are we?..."

"At fila's rise."

The young girl can feel the energy shoot though her as the half-brained idea manifests into reality. "Really!"

After a huff, the old man twists his head to throw an eye in her direction. "I've done my very best to make you into a young woman that can face this world without fear. I'm not going to change that now..."

While he returns to organizing his belongings Ani rushes over to her own bed and pulls out a basket from underneath her hanging sheets. She sifts through the linens to select her finest hunting garments. Each one she finds wafts of old leather and crawls with abrasive, metal studs.

She reaches for her satchel, flipping the cover open. Within the inside are two embroidered letters.

HH

A grin bursts along her face and her hand builds a tension within her until she can't hold it anymore. Ani releases a squeal of excitement slightly louder than she expects.

A gruff voice clobbers the life in the room. "This is not going to be fun. This is not an adventure. There is nothing to be excited about. We are going to meet hardships you've never had the misfortune of facing… and if all goes well, you'll simply be alive by the end."

"Well, that's grim. I've never seen the rest of Goromföld and I think that will be good for me." Her eyes strike out to find Tushma nearing the table's candle, at the ready to extinguish it. "Wait!"

The old man's hand halts at her words.

"You never told me how you survived. Or found me. Or found that thing… what is that thing?"

"Some kind of Nhavyyet contraption." Tushma's eyebrows raise while considering the notion. "It worked, didn't it?"

"Yes. It did quite well. Amazing, in fact. How did you know it would?"

"I…" The old man's words trail off. He lowers his hand, then posts himself in a nearby chair to look at the young girl. "You really want to know?"

Ani's eyes flicker around the room. "I asked, didn't I?"

"I can read their language."

"Why?" she snaps right back.

"Why can I read?"

"Yeah!" Ani prompts before her eyes drift over to the book on the wooden dresser.

A single chuckle shoots out of Tushma. "Alright, I'll give you that one. Haven't needed to read that book in a long time."

"What is it?"

"The words of Ninfaas," the old man quietly answers. "But, it's not in that language. You could read it, I suppose, though I didn't plan on bringing it with us..."

He's leaving things behind? He thinks we're going to come back!

"Yeah, no use... Good night!" Ani spits out before swiftly throwing all of her belongings loosely in her satchel then flipping over to sleep for the night.

"Oh, we're done with questions now... Great."

The word lingers in the old man's mouth. Ani hears him rustle around for a bit longer before the lights around the room go out, one by one.

In the fresh darkness within the cabin, his voice dominates. "Get a strong rest in tonight, journeys such as these rarely allow for it."

Ani lays in her bed, listening to Tushma, waiting until he shuffles under his own covers for the night before piping up, "Tushma?"

"Yes, Ani?"

"You said you waited for me to take the spirit of a chicken... What if you died? Would I have taken your spirit?"

A low growl echoes in the darkness of the cabin. "No. It can't be done. Only animals. Now, good night, Ani."

"Alright," the young girl replies, allowing the silence to fill the space before asking again, "Are you sure?"

The lack of response from Tushma leaves Ani waiting for her mind to cease as thoughts of everything come to pass, and potential futures, keep her from sleep.

"What about dragons? Did you want to talk about them?"

Silence envelopes the cabin.

Well then…

As time in the dark continues for what feels like a lifetime, the young girl finally begins hearing faint whispers coming from Tushma's side of the room.

"The goddess mother protects. Ninfaas… She gives me strength when it is not due. She… when I am weak. Avoiding… Haven and Dak. Find the darkness all around. Those chosen are brought to… …clean and appointed. Where the spirits without bodies go to live. Blessed are those who follow."

It's been so long since I heard him pray… What are we about to do?

Chapter 4
The Archaeologist

Soft winds lap against Fylorn as he sits underneath the tallest tree on the highest bench of the open pit. While resting with his arms wrapped around his knees, he taps his thumbs above his interlocking fingers.

The dust twirling around can stop anytime now. They said they would have it under control, and maybe I haven't been on many sites yet, but I can't see anything.

He casts his gaze out to one visible pile of working men; all short, stocky, and miserable looking. They toil away at the corners of the operation. Each lugs stone from the fresh excavation to a massive metal container. One loads the final piece before smacking the side of the oversized creature strapped to the front. Slowly pulling itself ahead, the beast of burden hauls the load away while slowly disappearing into a swirling dust bowl. The remaining miners shuffle back to work, spouting idle chatter about what they might end up doing after the day's work is finished.

A full race of brothers. I wonder if they ever feel lonely…

His narrow sights move from the hairy men to a muscular beast returning for another haul. Its short head and flat face lacks any struggle in the prevailing dust. Fylorn then notices a clearing. He looks on to see some juvenile play on a distant bench of the site. While he observes the handful of Nhavyyet youths, his thumb tapping slows to a halt. The archaeologist quickly returns to the broad scan of the digging site he had came up here for.

"What did you find!" a rhythmically assertive voice targets Fylorn.

The archaeologist twists his neck to spot a stout Nhavyyet man hustling towards him. Both of the long sleeves of his linen shirt are rolled up as a working man would have them. A loose fitting of his collarless neck to allow his broad shoulders some space – along with a half-buttoned up chest – however, gives the appearance of a soft-handed noble. His short black hair, atop his head as well as reaching from his square and flat chin, remain still in the passing winds. The whites of the man's eyes pale in comparison to the glimmering gold eclipsing his iris.

Mikahram…

"Nothing! Just like I told you," Ram's shouts continue. "You think you're some kind of bird, perching up on high; Y'ain't. You need to be down on the ground, föld in your hands and hair."

"You just want to see me all dirty," Fylorn shoots out with a smirk.

"Don't be starting any rumors," the Nhavyyet says while winking. "You know how adorable our babies would be. My skills and my looks, and your…" Ram waves his hand around quickly in Fylorn's direction.

"You just came up here to bother me, didn't you? What, did you get bored?"

"Ivradamolin says you're being weird and to stop it."

Fylorn remains silent while continuing his scan of the deep pit.

"You know what I gave up for you to be here?" Ram pries.

"Nothing?"

"I mean, yes, but it doesn't mean you can sit here like a dead Edvekrotinyagach."

"A dead what?" Fylorn responds while darting his eyes directly to one of the beasts hauling stone.

"Stop it. I've taught you plenty Bourtaulitanbour, you cheeky bastard."

The archaeologist smiles while chuckling to himself as the Nhavyyet finally takes a seat beside his friend. A moment of quietly gazing out into the fila-bathed pit of dirt and toil is cut short.

"What do you honestly think you're going to find sitting up here?"

"Peace," Fylorn swiftly cracks.

"Really?" rolls out from the Nhavyyet while shooting a crooked eye.

"Ram, you spent almost as much time in Delcrias as I have – some casually say you were born there – and why shouldn't they, it's our home. But... as much time as you've spent among the Hue, you've missed little things. There's something to be found in watching and waiting."

"You think a rock is going to jump out. That doesn't happen here – definitely in The Perfect Wild – but not here."

"Alright, take that bench over there for instance." Fylorn stretches his hand out far to his right, aiming at the carefully cut out section of the dig with rising plateaus. "The way the soil moves around the veins of rock and mineral–"

"My friend..." Ram utters while throwing a soft look.

Fylorn raises his eyebrows in quick realization. "Alright – feel – the soil and stone over there. It worms around that vein, then becomes that one; nothing to be found. Now –

following along that ridge – look how the bumps are in a rhythm, right? Unnatural. There is something there, but I can't figure it out. We all know this is a site – something is here – but it's obviously complicated if you Nhavyyet can't – feel – it out."

The archaeologist awaits a response from his chatty friend, but the coming silence compels him to glance over. He catches Ram gently dragging his hand along the stone shelf they're sitting on.

Every moment or so he jerks his hand; he's finding something.

"Ram?"

"Why didn't you say anything before?"

"I was trying to be polite; you don't walk onto someone's site and tell them how to run it."

"Yes, most people don't, but you have."

Fylorn grunts at the remark. Before having time to shift his sights back to the archaeological expanse, a firm hand grips his shoulder while a thick finger thrusts out into his view.

"There," the Nhavyyet utters.

"Beyond the children?" Fylorn estimates.

"Yes, yes, I'll go get a team now. That's the spot," Ram speaks in a rising tone of excitement until he caps it off by slapping Fylorn harshly behind the shoulder. "You can always surprise me."

"It'd be nice for you to surprise me once in a while," the archaeologist retorts.

Ram lets out a quick chortle as he rises to rush away. While he starts off, he yells from over his shoulder, "If you came out for drinks more often you wouldn't miss those surprises."

Fylorn watches on, as the dust begins clearing and his companion diminishes in the distance.

"Would love to," he quietly comments to himself before rolling back from the ledge. Then begins his long walk along the high bench towards the shelf holding a handful of Nhavyyet children. Fylorn keeps a watchful eye on a distant Ram as he reins the situation under his control so he can delegate men as he pleases. While tending to his own footing, the archaeologist spots the children playing 'keep away' from one of the stouter ones.

"You," he shouts from afar.

The boys take their time but eventually all look at him.

Quickly he waves a hand, gesturing for them to leave, "Get moving, we're going to be working here next."

Slowly, the stout boy shuffles over to his friend holding the ball of desire, then bumps his shoulder before pointing at Fylorn. The three of them begin a small snicker that grows into full-blown laughter at the archaeologist.

I'm funny, am I?

Fylorn drops from the high ledge into the dusty site corner. Without a word he approaches the boys. His Hue stature makes him at least twice as tall as the adolescents.

"Listen up, I know you can't speak yet, but you can listen. Get moving before I throw you."

For a split second he can see the inkling of fear in the stout boy's eyes. After a quick head nod from the three, they bolt away to find a new shelf to terrorize. Fylorn huffs while watching them rush off, then turns to narrow his gaze to the rock wall before him.

Now, where to begin.

The archaeologist assesses the compressed sediment so intently that he fails to hear the excavation crew arrive by his side before Ram yells at him from a short distance.

"Fylorn! Back up!"

He swiftly slides himself backwards, nearly to the steep edge. The marvel of Nhavyyet at work commences before his very eyes. Eight men bring a tunneling device up alongside the wall. They line it up, then one of the men begins manually turning the crankshaft from the back of the machine. Fylorn looks on in wonder as the rock is chewed up by the spinning blades and spit out as discharge. The spewed debris lands paces away from him. As quickly as the pieces land they are shovelled up by other working men.

The entire process is so clean and efficient. I wish I started working with them sooner.

Once the tunneller is finished drilling, the men remove it and set up scaffolding. Within moments Fylorn watches the site become a train of workers chipping away at the rockface, letting the stone drop, and removing it to allow more to fall into its place. The residual plumes of dust from moving föld bring the archaeologist to a cough. Fylorn's mind doesn't have the time to wander away into some abstract thought before the Nhavyyet remove over two arm lengths deep of the wall. With nothing yielded, they continued to toil for hours to come. The archaeologist watches on while the light of day shifts almost a quarter measure in the sky before the men officially rescind to have a well-deserved break. Amid the evacuation, Ram's pacing and unproductive chatter comes to a natural end, which compelled him to walk inside the fresh canyon to investigate for himself.

"Nothing. I felt it; the others agreed with me. How did we miss it?"

Instead of watching his friend stomp around, Fylorn strides into the worksite. He drags his sights along each new wall of layered rock, testing his knowledge of known history to sift out a nugget of truth that might reveal the answer to him.

"Take a feel to check, but I would tell the men not to come back. We're close enough to damage anything we might find," Fylorn loudly informs Ram while continuing his visual investigation.

"Yes, yes. I trust they know," he grumbles in response. Nevertheless, the Nhavyyet returns to the opening of the excavation site to pass on the information to a worker standing nearby. Upon his return Ram hands over one of the pickaxes he holds. The two find suitable points of loose soil, then begin picking away at it.

"What are these made of?" Fylorn loudly inquires. "I feel like I'm barely trying, and the rock is splitting like sand."

"Diamantine," Ram quickly answers. "Most of our tools are made of it. There's nothing sharper."

"Nothing…" the archaeologist ponders. "You think one of these could crack dragonscale?"

"Dragons?!?"

"Yeah!" Fylorn spits out, heavy of breath. "Those flying, bony things."

The Nhavyyet slings a dramatic glare towards his companion. "I know what a dragon is. And, why are you always so concerned about their bones?"

"From what I've heard, they are the strongest; stronger than this… diamantine." The words linger upon the archaeologist's tongue, carrying a distinct cheekiness.

"Dragon's wish," Ram grumbles back. "It'll be a fine day when I see dragon bones best my Nhavyyet skill."

Fylorn chuckles at the thought before pouring himself into the task ahead of him. The following hours of arduous handwork cause the men to be a mess of sweat with dust stuck to them.

Not you. No, no, definitely not you.

"Ah ha!" Fylorn exclaims.

He brushes his hand across the sedimentary soils. The turgid lump displacing the back of his hand reminds the archaeologist of the day's work. Small, subtle pains of a growing infection validate Fylorn's estimate that it will scar, but his mind is elsewhere.

After swiping back and forth numerous times, the encasing below is revealed. An elongated grain of petrified wood is swiftly brought to the surface of the man-sized hole within the freshly chipped hard rock. While Fylorn shifts from a delicate brushing into a firmer cleaning around the edges, he hears his companion approach from behind him.

"I love you, Fylorn, but you and those weak Hue bones aren't getting anywhere. I'm not surprised yous lost the war."

"Yeah, yeah."

Fylorn stands up to step aside for the Nhavyyet bull. His messy hair, and unreliable sleeves, become unfettered as Ram stomps ahead towards the wooden emplacement.

"You think you're so good. It's all luck," the archaeologist comments while looking on.

"Luck doesn't happen this often," Ram returns with a grin before widening his stance. He then shoves one set of thick fingers under the problematic slab covering the find. After placing his other hand upon the protruding rock shelf above he grunts while giving it a good jerk. The stone budges, cracking to form a fault along the wooden edge and beyond into the rockface either way.

"One more should—"

The Nhavyyet's speech gets cut off as his footing slips and the quick rebalancing puts his heavy boot through the wooden piece. Ram tumbles shoulder first down into the elongated chamber. Ancient debris shifts, sending once-settled dust and sand into a plume.

You've got to be kidding me.

"Are you going to tell me that was luck too?"

His companion has a fit of coughing while Fylorn jumps into the hidden chamber. He covers his face with the sleeve of his shirt while casting a critical eye to everything within.

"We need to get Ivradamolin," Ram chokes out.

"Why? I know what I'm doing. He's going to send some bumbling digger down here to touch things."

"This is their site, and they have more to find here than you... Fylorn, is that your family crest?"

The archaeologist whips his head from the side wall he was tracing his finger along to look at the panel of glyphs in front of the Nhavyyet. Slightly deeper inside of the chamber, the angled light fails to reach that far in.

"Ram, I can't see anything over there."

"There's a door – Alokhevryk below – this is exciting. Yeah, across from that is a mural with a ton of symbols. Dunno why that one stood out to me."

"It's because you recognize it," Fylorn pauses for a moment. He grabs the Nhavyyet's shoulder, then gestures for him to break some more wood to let light in. After a few swift punches above, the archaeologist's eyes are astonished at the wall of ancient symbols before him. He tilts his head while looking hard at the side wall once more.

Row after row, and column after column, of drab symbols line the wall. The organization reminds Fylorn of a few of the symbols he learned while at the grand school of Millown.

"I'm betting the Ködiam would kill to get their hands on this."

"You think?" the Nhavyyet sarcastically replies.

With relative ease, the symbol of a metal mask curved in the center and sharp along the edges splashed in orange dye jumps among the rest. The archaeologist kneels down to gather a better look, finding a simple scripture expertly carved beneath it in an ancient tongue.

Ram leans in, bringing his assertive drawl into his friend's ear. "There's no way you read that; it's probably ancient Bourtaolitanbour."

"If I was taught anything…" his words drift off as his mind works away at the scripture.

'The Father, The Father, The Son and The Daughter.'

Fylorn lets out a low moan before needing to hold the wall for support.

"My friend! What happened? What's wrong?"

The archaeologist shakes his head while trying to orient himself once more. Finding the blur of his vision too agonizing, he squeezes his eyes shut to quell the pain.

"Mikahram… Do you remember when we were young, I told you that I heard voices?"

"Yes," Ram responds while wrapping his arm around his friend to ensure he doesn't fall. "You haven't mentioned them in quite some time."

Quietly, the archaeologist nods his head to gather self-composure. "They haven't happened, until just now."

"What did it say?" Ram asks without hesitation.

"The Father, The Father, The Son and The Daughter."

The Nhavyyet draws a long breath of thought before asking, "What does that mean?"

Fylorn understands his companion was speaking to himself. He pats the top of Ram's hand, then shuffles away during the release. Pushing through his new headache, the archaeologist throws his hands up on the broken entrance to drag himself from the hole.

"We should see Ivradamolin," he calls behind him before slinging himself onto the excavated floor of the bench. "I couldn't agree more. Should we stop by the healers first?"

"No, I'll be fine."

"Whatever you say," Ram utters while climbing from the chamber.

After rising, Fylorn joins his friend at the wide bench of the site. They take their time across the site, passing workers standing about in the waning evening light. Along the way back they approach a large pavilion with columns and rows of tents underneath. The archaeologist casts an eye of disinterest at the men being tended to. Various instances of sharp Nhavyyet bone protruding from shins and biceps litter the open medical site.

While mid-stride Fylorn feels the wind be knocked from him as the stout arm of Ram thumps on his chest. Before his hands push the Nhavyyet away, the archaeologist looks on to see a limping worker being carried by another. As he is heaved through the common tracks to the tents, the limping man falters and drops. Instinctually Fylorn lurches forward, but Ram doubles his hold to keep his friend at bay.

"Don't even think about it," Ram exerts out in a firm tone.

A sea of appalled Nhavyyet faces glaring at the Hue. Fylorn swallows hard while watching the injured worker as his companion continues them past, quickly aided by another of their kin. The archaeologist brushes off the imposing feeling while wiping some piled sweat from his brow. He drifts his sights wide to catch a glimpse of his own tent within the site. The diminutive quarters are a poor reflection of the others around it with holes and pieces of broken string flying from it.

While pinching his lips together, Fylorn returns his eyes to his friend. Ram extends his hand to guide the archaeologist ahead. By quickening their pace, the pair bring themselves to the far side of the site.

Elevated above the ground by wooden posts stands the Nhavyyet office of observation. By giving into a subtle hesitation, Fylorn shoulders past Ram and hikes up the short set of stairs to a long porch. He stands facing the door while waiting for his friend to finish his approach. As he hears the last clomping footstep, the archaeologist swings the door open to stride inside.

Clean. Cleaner than any office I've ever been in before. A lean desk… and the man himself. The master of this site, the observer. A Nhavyyet of note by any measure, the man has more of a chin than most, mostly from all the chatter he engages in. Though, hard to complain; he did let me on the site. But that mop of hair and crooked nose… Surely, he thinks he's smarter than he truly is.

Fylorn eyes the two chairs opposite the desk, awaiting the men. The clean air nearly suffocates the archaeologist. He moves ahead to take the seat on the right, while Ram places himself in between to stand with a pronounced posture.

"Word has reached me that our target has finally been found." The old Nhavyyet lowers his long-haired brow while drifting his eyes towards the archaeologist. "Your patience has paid off, son."

"It's all I have, sir," Fylorn quickly responds.

Ivradamolin looks back down at all the papers neatly sorted on his desk. "It fortunately appears the opposite. Many words have reached me, as it were. I've conferred with a few site members, and it appears you are the source of our luck."

"It wasn't luck, sir," Ram interjects. "He fully explained the process to me. Fylorn is a man of skill."

An evidently polite smile crosses the old Nhavyyet's face. "Mikahram, the pride of... someone, I'm sure. It's your skill that fostered bringing the Hue man along on this endeavor–"

"Sir," Fylorn emits, "If I may, I'm not here for praise. I have questions that need to be answered."

The site observer leans back, adjusting in his seat to comfortably rest his thick hands upon his belly. "I see. Then, ask away."

Fylorn clears his throat before continuing, "I did not come to your site with ulterior motives – I would never – but, with that being said, I have found something within the chamber that calls to me."

"I should wish that moving föld and uncovering truths calls to each and every man on my site," Ivradamolin comments.

"Yes," the archaeologist agrees, "but in particular, I– We found a symbol of my heritage within the tomb."

The blank face of the elder Nhavyyet chips away at Fylorn. He allows a breath of time for the man to respond, but no challenge is met.

"It would appear that something of my family's past has a correlation to the past of whomever created, or last resided, in this tomb."

"What is your question, son?"

"I want to know why."

"Look..." An aged sigh crawls from Ivradamolin. "Firstly, we've just uncovered the damned thing. And secondly, we don't have enough evidence that it's related to anyone. The reality is that whatever you found in there is a recurring symbol. Someone in your line of work should know this."

Fylorn's face itches as heat bursts along his skin. He shoots his eyes to his companion, who throws a low set back.

"Sir," Fylorn prompts before bringing his full attention towards the old Nhavyyet, "I wasn't lying when I said the chamber spoke to me. While inside I heard the words written on the wall. 'The father, the father, the son and the daughter' is what it told me."

"You heard this?" Ivradamolin asks, spiking his voice.

The archaeologist nods, while Ram corroborates, "He spoke those words aloud to me the moment it happened, sir."

"I–"

The observer's slow words are stifled as the door to the office opens. A Nhavyyet man of middling age wearing heavy clothes walks into the room, making direct contact with Ivradamolin.

"Sir, we have inspected the site."

After respectfully allowing the new man his attention, the observer returns it to the pair sitting opposite him.

"May I?"

"Of course," Ram responds with haste.

Fylorn silently watches on, opening his mind and ears to everything the new man is about to say.

"Excellent," the new man continues. "And greetings, Hue archaeologist. It's because of you, I hear, that we've made such a grand discovery. Ideally, we shall have the fortune of investigating this site for years to come." After shooting a half-hearted smile to Fylorn he redirects his attention to Ivradamolin. "We've only just begun, and the site has delivered a wealth of knowledge. In the opening of the chamber we are assessing the patterns, symbols, and most importantly the physical architecture of craftsmanship. Most of the findings point to well before our earliest records, which means I've taken the liberty in sending word back to Sierra ta Nhavyyet. All of this is superb news, and what's more, our first section of the symbols has been deciphered to read, 'The father, the father, the son and the daughter'."

The archaeologist can feel his heart jump into his throat. He looks longside enough to see a grin burst onto Ram's face as wide as the room itself. Ivradamolin drops his arm in his chair, smacking his hand upon the desk as it falls.

Amid the gasps of the other three, the new man calls out, "Sir!"

"I'm fine," the observer assures all.

"All is well? Excellent... It's definitively ancient language, but we have the best Nhavyyet men on site to handle such tasks."

"That is not it," the elder Nhavyyet adjusts his jaw while his eyes dart between the men sitting before him. "These two are... unexpectantly honest."

"There isn't a lying bone in my body, sir," Fylorn proudly states.

"Bone is strong as bone, son, and nothing is stronger than Nhavyyet's."

A small burst of laughter comes from each within the space. After it dies down Fylorn's voice rises in, "So, now that you fully believe me, how can you help me?"

The observer's smile diminishes into barely a grin. "I'm afraid all we can do is let you stay on our site, helping out as best you can. Who knows, maybe the voice will speak to you again."

What was once a face of potential upon the archaeologist is now cast aside for a defeated man's scowl.

"Thank you for your help," Fylorn states through his teeth.

He then rises, placing the chair back exactly where it was while avoiding eye contact with Ivradamolin. The archaeologist allows one heated breath to escape him before briskly exiting the office.

Once outside, Fylorn's stride becomes a stomp across the treated wood. His mind rages, barely able to attach itself to any one concept for too long before jumping to the next. He puts his elbows upon the nearby railing while stroking his fingers through his hair.

The distinct wooden sound of a door closing rings out behind the archaeologist, urging his body to form a more appropriate stance. While adjusting his posture, and crunching his face to appear less distraught, the half-sized stature of Ram creeps into the corner of his eye. After leaning upon the railing to mockingly gaze out into the site below, the Nhavyyet speaks aloud to his friend.

"Well, what did you think of that?"

"He's useless."

"That's rude," Ram defends. "It's an ancient tomb, probably. How should he know anything about your family?"

"Do Nhavyyet even have tombs?"

Ram quietly licks his lips in contemplation. Before he can gather a sentence, Fylorn interjects.

"We're going to Delcrias."

The redirected statement sucks the air from the Nhavyyet. He shifts his gaze to his companion. Fylorn meets it, witnessing as the man's golden eyes see right through him.

"Why?" crawls from Ram's mouth. "Don't you want to find out what's in the tomb?"

"I'm sure we will, eventually, but right now I need to go break into the old family home and find a journal that I should have gathered years ago."

The thick eyebrow of the Nhavyyet man raises.

"Don't look at me like that."

A matching grin creeps onto Ram's face, compelling Fylorn to shake his head.

Chapter 5
The Anchor

Drops of morning dew slide off each leaf and onto Ani as she passes. A subtle creaking coming from the large leather bag Tushma has strapped to his back chews away at her mind. The strap of her overstuffed satchel digs into her shoulder with every step deeper into the chilling forest, compounding her misery.

"I don't like mornings," she complains aloud.

"You've said," Tushma blankly responds.

"Then why do we have to leave now? It's our adventure, we don't have to answer to the fila."

"It's best for fishing."

"Fishing?"

"Yes, I'm fishing while you row. You want to eat, don't you?"

"Why are you making me carry all this coin in my satchel if we're just catching our food."

"Do you want to switch bags?" the old man proposes.

Ani remains quiet. She tries to turn her attention to the descending hills towards Lake Barrelwood. The alpine trees thinning out to become a lowland brush gives her a clear view of the deep brown loam creeping to the water's edge. A siege of bright blue herons gently rise from a hidden nest among the reeds. The young girl tracks them until her eyes land on a set of distant islands that pepper the choppy waves.

"Why didn't we live on one of those? It's closer to Barrelwood and has great fishing."

"And no privacy," Tushma grunts back.

"Oh, right, we have all these people trying to find us out here. I forgot," she spits out while throwing a coy look at the man.

"One day you'll understand."

"Sure–" Ani ignores him while flicking her forearm ahead. "You said I can let this thing out?"

"Yes."

"How?"

"By not being a bother."

"I'm being serious!"

"Me too. Do I look like I have one of those scars?"

"It would be more helpful if you did," Ani groans. "What did you call it again?"

"I've heard it called a few things. My favourite was always, a spirit's wrest."

"That's dumb…" She notices Tushma shuffle the pack of supplies on his back. "Right. I get it, but I find it hard to believe you didn't learn how to release it."

"I learned plenty. I've also watched my share of births in my life and still couldn't tell you how a woman pushes the little bastard out."

"Who was letting you watch them give birth?" she lets out with a smirk.

He rolls his eyes, "It's something you feel, is all I can tell you. Reach in and let it out. Some said it was like an itch they needed to scratch."

Ani looks at the edges of her clothing, all wet and tacky.

I sure am itchy.

She closes her eyes.

"Watch where you walk," Tushma blurts out, cutting her concentration.

"Oh, thanks. I'm glad you're here to help me with that."

"Look, it's not long until we're at the boat. You can worry about it there."

"But I want to do it now."

"Fine then, fall. See if I care," the old man says before stomping ahead.

In a passing gaze, the young girl looks off in time to see the reaching peninsula of the lake slip beneath the trees.

We really are close.

The pair follow the well-worn trail winding past ancient trees thicker than Tushma. A dangling of star-shaped leaves tickle Ani. As they breach the treeline, a wave of crisp and harsh morning air blows off the placid water to assault the young woman.

Damn lake! Every time we come here it's so cold and windy.

Tushma's voice booms, "Get used to it, girl."

I look that bad, do I? He's not even looking at me. Is he admiring the lake? His face looks to be in as much discomfort as I feel.

"Boat's seen better days," the old man utters before stomping down the dry dirt path. Ani follows him until they approach the lonely wooden pier. An old, wooden vessel barely large enough to hold Tushma bobs along with the coming tide.

With instinctual memory, the two begin the silent process of loading the boat. First, Tushma tosses in his bag, making the small boat rock. A clunk of metal against the boat reminds Ani of their irregular mechanical object.

Why is he bringing that egg, anyways? We're not going to be finding dragons… Maybe he wants to sell it so we can have coin for food?

Ani stages her satchel while the black-bladed spear is slid in along the length of the vessel. Once everything is in place, she carefully steps in. She steadily moves herself to the front tip of the boat, then tenses herself while allowing the rocking of the vessel to move her body with it.

"Still?" Tushma asks.

In the fledgling light of the morning, Ani peers up to see the old man beaming back at her. She scrunches her nose before retorting, "Standing on solid ground all the time bores me. I like it when the boat jiggles."

"Good, because things are about to feel less like solid ground for us in the coming months." His eyes sharpen on her. "Try and find that itch, now is the time."

A lurch in the boat prompts the young girl to peek behind her. Tushma returns the paddle he had used to push them forwards into the flowing waters. As his rowing finds a rhythm, Ani wiggles to make her seat upon the bench more comfortable. She locks her eyes on the weathered wood below, then closes them.

It can't be that difficult… I'm built for this. This is what I'm made for, this is my destiny. Alright, calm down, Ani. We have a spirit– auragonic. And, it's in its home, a wrest. I'm an Anchor, and… I can do this.

Ani flicks her forearm. Then again, waiting for the spectral beast to emerge. After a third time she lowers her arm.

"Try again," comes from behind her.

"Thanks," the young girl snaps back.

She lifts her forearm up to her nose. Taking her fingernail, Ani begins scratching and scraping at the anomaly on her skin.

"You're just going to make it bleed."

"You're not helping!" she shouts before flinging a glare at the rowing man. "You said, 'It was an itch'."

"I said I didn't know."

The young girl rolls her eyes while turning her head back to the islands ahead. A passing breeze accompanies the obnoxious honking of hidden birds. Ani slows her breathing, trying to ignore the noise while flexing her arm. Nothing happens. In a stewing rage she shakes her forearm about.

"I know that no one else did that," Tushma comments.

"How are you so wise – and – so useless?"

"You ought to hurry up before it's your turn to row."

A consistent lapping of water upon the sides of the boat seeps into the young girl's ears. A chilling spray buffets the wale, coating her shoulder and chin. Ani draws in the aroma of fresh oils from fish in one long inhale.

Is it all me? Do I have to lure it out like a fish, or does it want to come out? It crawled in there in the first place– pretty sure of its own will. A dragon. What would a creature like that want? Its mother? Maybe… Can't go back to that watery hole – well – won't. Creatures near water, of the water…

She abruptly stops, sending her eyes to the water which barely precedes her arm dunking in the frigid liquid. Heat abandons her hand. Quickly she worms her fingers to avoid the restricting sensation. A chill bolts up her arm, landing at her spine. The average feeling steps aside as a jolt plunges down the muscles of her bicep to swirl within her forearm. A cold burning takes over while a numb pain only gives her nerves the warning of her skin taking on a powerful glow; not the full-blown alarm it had back in the grotto.

Involuntarily, her arm shakes but holds firm while the illuminated creature pours from her body into the passing waters. The stream of a blue spirit appears distorted through the glassy surface. Lasting for what could have been a lifetime, the moment finally comes to a close as her wrest flares its blazing nerves, then the glow fades from her skin.

Ani's breathing catches her off guard and she chokes while turning to Tushma. "It worked."

"What worked," the dumbfounded man replies but, before either could carry the conversation forward, their eyes are drawn to the spectacle before them.

A glistening mixture of water with iridescent scales erupts in a mosaic of blue from the lake's surface. Both Ani and Tushma gawk in awe as the dragon youngling uses its inherent nature to masterfully swim around in the aquatic cradle. The boat comes to a slow halt while the rowing ceases. In a flurry of splashing flutters, the majestic creature arcs in and out of the lake.

"Row!" the young girl orders. "Move those oars! Any time now!"

Within the moment, she locks eyes with her auragonic, then quickly loses sight of the spectral beast. She quiets herself to try and listen for the creature. A small splash brings her sights directly to it. The dragon arcs again, this time farther and farther from the pair.

"Tushma?" She waits for a response, but it's met with silence. "Tushma, how far can those things go?"

"To my knowledge, no one has ever lost one."

"That's good. It's getting fairly far out there."

"We were supposed to stop at one of the islands to rest."

Ani watches on helplessly while the dragon swims away, putting a greater distance between the two.

It looks like a glowing speck from here. Does it come back on its own? There's so much I don't know.

"I..." The young girl finds herself at a loss for words. "...I suppose we keep going?"

"Well, it's about time you row."

"That's it? No wise-old-man ideas?"

"Not really. We know where it's going, and it's bound to you."

"Gods, we're going to look so stupid showing up to the rest of the Anchors without our auragonic." Ani carefully shifts her weight while rising to replace Tushma at the oars. As she watches him silently position himself for fishing at the rear of the boat she continues, "You don't care, do you?"

"I care about a lot of things."

The young girl raises her volume, "We just lost the one thing we went on this adventure for!"

As her voice echoes along the surface of the water, Tushma interrupts what he's doing to give her a disappointed glare. "You're going to bother the fish."

Ani's whole face scrunches while she twists to look straight once again. She takes a hold of the oars, then lets out her anger.

"Keep within this side of the lake. If you go too deep those larger waves will flip us."

"Okay," Ani grumbles.

"And there's better fishing in shallow waters."

"I already said, 'Okay'."

Time sets in as the strength to keep her ferocity up fades away. The young girl rows along while the old man catches fish after fish. In the waning light of day, he instructs her to land at a beach on one of the larger islands. They come ashore, dragging the boat onto the sand, then settle in for the night. Tushma stages a fire to roast his aquatic catch. The growing scent of cooking food invigorates Ani as she lays out her linens to sleep upon. Her mind erupts in thoughts.

Oh Gods, where is my dragon? I can't call it... Does it just roam around until it wants to come back to me?

"Is the dragon supposed to just return to me?" Ani softly asks the old man as he checks on the sizzling meat. She awaits an answer but the lull of waves lapping against the shore begins to eat away at her. "Well? Do I get it back or is it going to simply–"

The old man places a plank of food in her hand, bringing her argument to a halt. As Ani swallows her dinner, time slips away from her. A blanket of night coats the beach except for the cooking fire, burning through its remaining wood. Nearing the final moments of fire's light the young girl spots other small illuminations begin to appear. She quickly realizes these glowing green bulbs to be fireflies. A swarm of the insects fly as a unified mist over the beach, showering the sand in light.

Ani looks over to Tushma. Her timing is perfect, as the green reflecting from his smile brings out a youth in the old man that she hadn't seen in a long time. The pair enjoy the bioluminescent wonder, silently hoping it lasts forever. As the last of the fireflies disappears, and the cold dark of the grand lake returns to their lives, both find a comfortable enough nook within the sand to fall asleep.

A chilling morning breeze crawls along Ani's face until she opens her eyes. The light of the early morning fila nearly blinds her. She lifts a hand, only to find a vibrant blue illumination to take its place. The young girl rears her head back at seeing the clear face of an infant dragon nestled upon her chest. After a moment to think, she slowly lowers her hand towards the spectral beast.

In the blink of an eye the auragonic bursts wide awake, then slithers from the young girl. It leaves a small trail in the sand while rushing into the water and away. Ani blinks, trying to process what just happened.

Was that real?

A loud squawk brings her focus to the other side of the beach. Ani watches on as white hawks of the sea fly away into shaded trees beyond. She then shifts her sights to the old man who begins to make groans while combating this morning's non-cooperative joints. The young girl silently rises to prepare the boat for launch. As soon as Tushma's body complies, he joins her.

With little issue they resume rowing across the lake, Ani taking her turn first this time while Tushma trolls for breakfast behind her.

I don't feel as tired today as I did yesterday, I must be getting used to it already.

The light of day fades while a humourless fog rolls over the lake.

"We haven't seen… the dragon, in a while."

"True," Tushma utters with a small nod.

"I should name it."

"Also, true."

A soft wind plays with Ani's hair.

"Any ideas?"

"Nope."

"I'm thinking something elegant, but I'm not sure if it's a girl or not."

"Don't look at me."

"Maybe Ahsi?"

"Ani and Ahsi? Too close."

"Ciryn?"

"Ani."

"Yes, Ciryn and Ani."

"No, there."

"Ani and Ciryn?"

Tushma throws his finger out towards a recess of the fog. Ani twists her head to witness the murky happening of a glowing wyrm being dragged aboard a fishing vessel.

"No!" Ani calls out. She finds no reaction. "That's mine!"

Her voice carrying across the lake's surface is muffled by the man behind her shifting from the rear seat to the rowing position. As the boat rocks with the movement, Ani steadies herself to remain balanced. Her prying eyes helplessly watch her auragonic being stolen away into the unknown.

"Keep your eyes on them as best you can, I'll try and catch up."

Ani grips the wale of their boat while the old man labours. They skim across the open waters into the dense fog until the young girl can see no more than an arm's length away. She can hear Tushma behind her struggling to maintain a pace as the frustration of steadying the course drains him.

Searching within herself to avoid being useless, Ani dips her arm into the evening waters. As the stream passes between her fingers she closes her eyes.

"Come on, come on," she speaks under her breath.

The following moment of rowing and unnatural silence allows the young girl to reach an internal focus. Sharp pricks radiate throughout her forearm but give her no true direction. She opens her eyes to find a massive fish swimming behind her hand, toying with the idea of nibbling on her worm-like fingers. Ani swiftly retracts her hand. After giving a quick peek back at Tushma, and finding the old man growing redder by the second, she returns her gaze ahead in time to witness the fog cascading away.

Ahead sits the city of Barrelwood, nearly ready for the night's rest as spots of lamps begin lighting the wharf's edge. Ani sharpens her eyes while searching for any trace of where the thieving fishermen might be settling in. The flippant waves of the lake can but barely be heard over the violent splashing of Tushma's oars.

"Stop!" Ani calls out the order. "I need to listen."

"Should be able to see it, no?" the exhausted man comments as his rowing subsides.

Her eyes comb the jetty, all along the berth, and under any dim light in efforts of a clue. A faint tickle within her arm draws her eyes to the bollard furthest földic. Within the lapping waters she spots a straggling boat being brought to dock and latched to the wooden post.

"There!" she shouts while thrusting her finger towards their prey.

Tushma doesn't bother to assess the finding himself before he begins to row in the direction he's been ordered. Ani holds her sights on the disembarking men.

They have it— her in a crab pot.

"Stop!" Ani cries out, but feels a boot poke her back before she gets out another word. "What?"

The eyes of Tushma burn into her as his scowl grows. "Don't be an idiot. What did I tell you about your kind; they are not welcome in most places. If you keep yelling like that it's only public hanging you'll be finding."

Ani slowly nods, then turns back to the now empty wharf. Her voice, as hollow as her heart, whispers out, "They're gone. They took her into the city."

"And we'll find it. Don't worry. Barrelwood is as small as a town if you know where to look."

Chapter 6
The Leader

Ani's mind runs wild with images of the many times that she and Tushma had made this exact journey.

The market should be closed now. All those homes, if they bother to keep her overnight. At least three stores that I can remember, but she'll be glowing… and loud.

"Do you think they'll figure out how to shut her up?"

The young girl can see her own reflection in the old man's eyes. Her feeble crying, the quivering pout, and horrid slouch.

"Have I figured out how to shut you up yet?"

Tushma cracks the slightest of grins amid his intensive face. Ani can see him begin to shake as his strength wanes. She wipes away her tears before returning to see their boat closing in on the docks. The pair waste no time as they approach the berth. As soon as the old man ceases rowing, Ani begins preparing all parts of the boat to dock. While the vessel glides into place Tushma ties it off, then heaves the young girl and their supplies up onto the water-logged wood. The dank reeking of today's catch endures along the wharf.

During listening to the arduous process of sore joints pulling the rest of the old man's body up onto the dock, Ani can feel her heart begin to race in anticipation. She tries to settle herself by putting her satchel back on, and holding it close to her body. While supporting himself on one knee in preparation to stand up, Tushma crosses gazes with Ani as she darts her eyes around.

"I told you to relax," he reminds her amid the grunts of rising to his full height. "I told you we would get it back. Now, grab as many things as you can, I don't see us coming back to the boat."

We're on foot the rest of the way, or until we buy hellixes to ride.

Ani leans down and picks up Tushma's spear. She clutches it close while waiting for the old man to collect everything that he can bear. Once piled on like a hauling bear, the young girl follows Tushma as he leads the way. He gives the entire berth along the water's edge a thorough scan before taking his first step along the wooden path. As the pair approach the gangway Ani begins to hear the tired voices of people finishing up a long day's work. Careful not to connect eyes with anyone, she lowers her head but ensures that she follows behind each of the old man's steps.

The worn planks of wood are abruptly replaced by mud-ridden gravel. Droplets of water tap the back of the young girl's head while passing under laundry lines. She peeks up to find the dimming light casting tall shadows against the long houses of the wide street, each having overhanging balconies.

Where is my dragon? It's glowing, shouldn't be this hard to track…

"We lost them," spits out Ani.

"What did you expect, they would be waiting for you?"

"I don't know."

"I do; we're going to the Sunken Wood."

"What is that, a tavern... an inn?"

"Yes."

Tushma strides ahead into the crowd. The young girl watches on as he casually slips within the horde of moving dirty coats. She follows him to the entrance of a humble building pieced together by wood and stone. The old man takes one look behind him before barging in. Ani catches eyes with him, then wastes no time to become his shadow.

The pungent scent of stale ale combats the general waft of fish in the air. Lamps hanging in between unnecessary fish netting line the walls, leaving the counter in the center of the room to be unusually dark. Ani's eyes do little work in adjusting from the dim light of outside to this new dingy establishment. Wandering eyes of patrons peek passed the people leaving through into the reception area. A strong arm swings out in front of Ani. She looks up to see it belongs to Tushma.

"I talk, you listen. Understand?" he utters with a firm jaw.

Ani confirms with a silent nod. He relaxes his arm, then lurches forward toward the inn keeper's post. Bearing an encumbered slouch, Tushma carefully places his fingers along the counter's edge while he leans in to speak with the maid behind the slacked wood.

"One or two?" the maid blurts out at him first.

"Evening, Bilia. Can I speak with your mother?"

The young woman sharpens her gaze. "You don't ask that often."

"Please," the old man asks, echoing his urgent tone.

"Of course," Bilia utters. She empties her hands onto the dark countertop, then shuffles away into the room behind her. In nearly an instant she reappears with a luring hand while calling Tushma back.

The young girl can feel the tension as she watches the old man wander around the counter towards the private quarters. Her eyes are locked on him until he disappears, and even then continues to watch.

What are they saying that I can't be there for? Adults are so weird; do they think that I can't handle it? Or are they keeping secrets from me?

"What's your favourite game to play?"

Ani shifts her gaze to see a girl even younger than herself sitting atop the counter. Her hair, black as night, rests in a braided crown. The girl's smile shines brighter than any lamp in the vestibule. Before Ani has the chance to respond, the girl blurts out, "So sorry, my name is Antella."

"Ani."

"Oh, a very pretty name! Mine is after the woman who built this place."

An air of waiting fills the space while Ani looks around.

"And?" the inn girl's prompts, bearing a tone of growing persistence.

Snapping her eyes back to Antella, Ani finds the beaming smile burning into her.

"Are you," Ani waves a loose gesture behind the bar, "her daughter?"

"No. My family's house burnt down, then Bilia took me in."

Sounds awfully familiar.

"I understand. Tushma took me in."

"You look just like him," Antella quips back.

One of Ani's eyes twitches while she deepens her stare at the inn girl. "No, I don't."

Near instantly, Antella responds, "Sure you do."

"Don't you have something you should be doing?"

"No, no. It's your turn to answer my question."

"I like to play with my pet dragon," Ani sneers at the girl.

Antella scrunches her nose while saying, "You're lying to me!"

"Am not," Ani utters before rolling up her sleeve to show the girl her spirit's wrest.

The bright smile is overcome with a darkness and unease. "You're a bad person."

Ani's smile becomes a sideways frown. While gazing into Antella's eyes the door behind the bar opens and Tushma storms out. Ani snaps her gaze at the fuming man, then gives the inn girl one more look before resuming her place as the old man's shadow.

Once outside, the young girl begins lobbing questions at Tushma. "What happened in there? Why are you angry? Where is my dragon?"

A rough crunching of dry dirt being displaced comes from the old man's boots being thrust into the ground. His head hangs low for but a moment, then he raises it to look up to the fading fila. The darkening orange allows Ani to watch as his eyes dart from side to side.

He's so deep in thought. What happened?

"Tushma–"

The old man cuts her off. His voice is coarser than usual as he explains, "We have to speak with Vheer Bentarm."

"Is that not good?"

"They're not going to let it go without some kind of… deal in place."

"We'll give them what they want."

"Don't say that until you know what it is."

Tushma turns on his heel, then marches off deeper into the city. Ani stands, unsure of herself, then bolts to catch up to him.

"You know where they are?"

"Yes."

Ani deepens her glare upon the side of the old man's head until he catches it with a glance. He doubles back to look at her full on, then purses his lips.

"They're the lords of Barrelwood."

"Then why didn't you call them that?"

"Because I've been around longer than they've been lords, and…"

"And you don't like change?"

Tushma slightly grinds his teeth. "No."

After Ani lets out a dramatic laugh, she opens her eyes to notice the few people out in public have taken to staring at her.

"Are we still keeping ourselves to the shadows?"

"Not much of a point now."

The young girl twists her head around, analyzing the city as they leave a tight street. Time worn cabins once used for hunting, the people had attempted to modernize into family homes, dissipate as they reach the market square. Scaffolding and one crane nearly block off the street to their right. Ani raises her sights up to see a gigantic stone carving of animals centering the square.

A black heron holding a map, and a green wolf. How did they get the stone to reflect those colours?

"What is that?" she asks Tushma.

"That is the embodiment of the Pajiado spitting in the face of the Hue. They would rather have this magically crafted nonsense sitting here instead of paying decent money to have a handcrafted one. Pride, it's a symbol of pride."

"I'm not sure what to think of that," Ani utters in contemplation.

"One day you might." Tushma stops dead in his tracks. Ani watches him scan the market, noticing the oil lanterns begin lighting up around them. "Their hall is over there."

The old man veers towards a grand, wooden structure with intricate sheeting along the bark exterior.

A monument to doing things by hand… I bet I could do better. The crude woodwork along the sides gives the impression that it was made by ancient men… but men weren't here that long ago.

Tushma hops up the three stairs to the large double door entrance. He doesn't bother knocking, simply grabbing the handle and swinging himself in. Ani slips in behind him just before the doors slam back on her. The red paint along the walls appears dark as blood even in the modest lighting. Various body parts of fallen prey are mounted along the ever-extending hallway.

Ani pops ahead to walk beside Tushma, bringing the grand hall into view. A roaring fire illuminates the high second floor above, as well as the intricate centerpiece hanging overtop.

It looks like a metal waterfall, flowing down, almost on the fire. They must have spent all their skill on this.

A muffled conversation begins to touch Ani's ears as the pair leave the hallway of hunters into the lord's domain. Far to their right rests a long table, overflowing with food and surrounded by men and women of wealth. Before either Ani or Tushma have the chance to present themselves, one of the men sitting at the end of the table quickly wipes his young face with an elegant cloth and stands.

"Kindly crossed, Tushma! I was informed you were in our city. What brings you here, my friend."

As Ani listens to the man's drawl voice, she watches his alpine green robes flow down him while stepping ahead towards the two. He flips his hair to one side, revealing tall ears reaching for the top of his head.

"Vyncis," the old man's blunt response nearly deafens Ani while posting directly beside him.

The affluent man coyly chuckles as he tilts his chin. "It must have been some time." He shakes his head while continuing, "Jaemon. You're thinking of my brother... he passed."

"My apologies," Tushma states. "You look just as your father did within this hall."

Jaemon returns a comforting smile to his new guests.

"As I have heard." He swings his head towards the table before speaking, "Do you care to join us? You and..."

The elegant man lingers his arm out towards Ani in expectation that Tushma will finish his sentence. A warm tingle runs through her as Jaemon's fiery eyes stare into her. She turns to the old man, meeting his eyes and watching a flicker of fear within them.

I've seen that before, while hunting.

Ani shifts her sharp glare towards the lord before announcing herself, "My name is Ani."

"I see," the elegant man flippantly states.

As he steps backwards, to return to his seat at the long table, Ani eyes up the others all staring at her. The coupling of deep blue orbs and fiery gazes aimed at her brings an unwelcoming chill to her bones. Their blank expressions are only broken by Tushma placing himself halfway in front of her.

"I appreciate the offer, but I come asking– bearing a request for you."

"Most do," Jaemon responds with a chuckle. "But you have no favor with me, yet. Do you, Tushma? You've

managed to keep to yourself out in the forest; an
accomplishment I'm rather jealous of, mind you."

"I only take what I need," the old man replies.

"And what is it you need?" the lord snaps back.

Tushma holds his breath for nearly a moment while
collecting words for the coming request. Ani bounces her
sights from him, to the lord, then to the audience at the long
table, and back again.

"You have an auragonic, a spirit that belongs to us." As
the final word spills from the old man's mouth, Ani can feel
his thick hand rest upon her shoulder.

Jaemon's face flickers through an arrangement of
emotions before landing on one akin to pleasure. His serpent
lips split open. "My hardworking men and women have
endured much over the years. Yet, my father and his father
have persevered in preventing Anchors from plaguing
Barrelwood. Today I was presented with a 'glowing fish' by
one of these valiant fishermen. A lesser man would have
panicked."

The lord drops his gaze to the platter of food resting
between his clenching hands. He pokes a cutlet of fish,
sniffing it before bringing the morsel up to his mouth. In a
gentle hesitation, he stops short.

"Ring the bell," Jaemon calmly orders, then proceeds to
eat.

Fear spikes through Ani as the shuffling of subordinates
commences. Tushma's hand combats the internal call to
action as the people within the hall enact the order.

"You have passed into our hands," Jaemon's words
break through the chatter. "It is by this divine act that we are
now beholden to the responsibility. You may not like it but
this power we hold over you is out of security, not malice.
One does not retain a city such as this by hiding secrets."

Ani trembles while bearing witness to an iron box being brought from a doorway beyond the table. A young maiden struts out holding the metal ring around the box's top handle. She delivers the container to her lord, placing it beside his dinner plate.

The finger-thick hole in the side of the box is enough for the young girl to catch the sight of her auragonic. The blue glow ebbs and flows as the beast moves around inside of its prison. Jaemon picks up his dinner knife and places it outside of the hole, aiming to thrust it inside.

"Stop!" Ani barks, but the old man reinforces his grip to control her, while delivering a growl of his own.

"Hasn't your guardian explained this to you? The creature can not be killed, how do you kill a thing that doesn't exist?" the lord says while lowering his silver blade.

"Stop toying with it," Tushma demands.

Jaemon tilts his head once again. "I could lock it up indefinitely if I so choose. Keep it below the surface of Föld until Ani here passes away. It's only you keeping it here, girl; within this physical realm. Once you are gone the spirit can move to its next existence."

Ani slowly becomes aware of her locked jaw by the burning of her teeth. A commotion breaks out behind her and Tushma. She turns to find a flood of tired city folk assuming standing room within the hall. Most look towards their lord, while a few curiously lock eyes onto the pair unmoving between the fire and table.

The lord rises to announce his rationale, "I bring the people of Barrelwood here to carry judgement as I hand you a choice."

"I haven't done anything! Why is this happening?" Ani calls out.

"Who is she?" one man interjects.

A woman's voice shouts, "Why are we here?"

"Settle!" Jaemon booms. "The girl is an Anchor. She brings Ardaelius to our doorstep."

Muttering erupts around the room. Ani's eyes drift to a sea of glares targeting her, then rise to Tushma who remains tall and focused upon the lord. Jaemon's recital draws her attention back to him.

"She has brought this into our city, brought the weight of everything that comes with it as well–"

"No," Tushma roars out. "The girl knows not what she does. Being out this far is the creation of those before her, and her actions are only a reflection of ignorance, not malice."

"Yes, which is why she is being given a choice before judgement," Jaemon continues while redirecting his speech to Ani, "You may allow us to end your life on this Föld and free this damned spirit, ceasing the threat upon these people. Or, you can submit to becoming a slave sold to Galiram, donating your value to the well being of Barrelwood."

"What kind of choice is that?" Ani spits out.

"Kill her!"

"Where is the spirit?"

"Sell her off!"

"Sacrifice her to Vihara!"

The compounding shouts burden Ani. She feels the hand of Tushma tense into a squeeze of iron. Looking up, she matches eyes with him. Her lip quivers while words fail to come out. A tear rolls from her eye. The old man slightly lowers his chin, a silent gesture she knows all too well. Ani returns a short nod.

Tushma sends his glare directly at the lord. He broadens his chest by drawing in a large breath, a breath for delivering their decision. "We submit."

Ani blinks rapidly a few times. She twists to face the old man, but he holds his eyes firm upon Jaemon. Turning towards the long table, the young girl watches a sweeping of faces softening. Her shoulders drop, then her head hangs.

The fire behind her blazes, casting shadows in every direction. She watches them dance along the stone slabs of the hall floor, whispers and muttering becoming their music.

As the rattling of armour closes in, the young girl hears Jaemon speak above the rest, "We can't wait overnight. I know it's dangerous, but the longer she sits around the quicker she finds a way out. Grab your best men, we send her now."

A forceful bump taps against Ani's back. Without looking, she takes her expected steps forward.

Chapter 7
The Kin

Bump after bump along the road from Barrelwood digs into Ani. While facing the back of the cage, she rests her chin upon her held knees.

'This is the fastest, cheapest way. You're too young for us to travel alone, that far. Raiders, Arkolox... disease. This is why I came, to make sure that you get there, well defended.'

The drone of wheels upon refined gravel becomes meaningless commotion, as does the continuous passing of trees. Her prison, a simple box of bars looking like a skeleton of the other carts allows the breeze to cut through and tousle her long hair. A trail of fierce guards atop canine mounts lines the road on either side of the caravan. Well reinforced by dull metals and thick lumber, the carts bleed into the darkness ahead and behind her. The muffled thumping of the massive bears hauling each load is barely audible over the howls of the night. Each steadfast face of the burdened creatures has deep red eyes that care not for the world around them.

With a dismissive drift, her eyes land on the cast iron box beside her. The shadow within, of her faintly glowing dragon, brings the young girl a grim reminder of her recent choices. She twists her gaze to the pile of Tushma beside her.

His slow and relaxed breathing while laying on his side gives her the inkling of security amid their capture.

"Tushma?"

The man doesn't respond.

"Are you asleep?"

Tushma lets out a weak groan.

"How can you be asleep right now?"

"It's night. That's when we sleep."

In a huff, the young girl snaps her sights to outside the moving bars. The distant moons being suffocated by dense cloud cover hinders the illumination of the wide trail. An endless black beyond her prison settles into the young girl's mind. While brushing a lock of hair behind her ear she catches a spike of light from within the tiny prison for the auragonic. Ani scoots forward, bringing herself within reach of the finger-sized hole. Lowering her head, she finds two iridescent eyeballs looking back at her. The youngling wiggles each aquatic fin that shoots out backwards, behind its jaw.

Poor thing, I've done this to you.

"I didn't mean to."

The dragon rears its neck; its eyes failing to be shadowed. Ani furrows her brow while a heat washes over her. She moves her hand forward a few times before instinct finally turns a blind eye. The young girl brings her finger up to the hole, stopping just before the cold iron. While blocking her sights, she gently eases her appendage into the dark of the box. A tingle cascades across her. The air around her chills and her bones freeze with anticipation.

After letting out one shaky breath she feels a scaley body rub against her knuckle. The rub becomes an embrace. Ani slowly moves her hand from the box, but finds the dragon playfully grabbed onto her finger with its mouth.

The tension evaporates from her body as more nudges brush against her. As she flips her palm upwards, she looks on to see the auragonic expel a spark of blue. The essence dissolves into a slither of spirit that swims up her fingers. Ani's sights linger on the spirit's return to her wrest. The slight burning taking place under her scar steadily becomes a sensation of joy instead.

A break in the clouds allows for a stream of moonlight to cast upon the convoy. The young girl makes a quick glance around the trail to find they are passing a wide river, then the drone of rushing water envelopes her senses. She spies a breath-taking view as the caravan snakes down the alpine trail. Water flows over the craggy ledges, crashing along a massive figure of a woman. The powerful cut out, standing the full height of the waterfalls, holds out her hands for the river to flow over her shoulders and into the reservoir below.

"That," Tushma's relaxed voice slightly startles Ani, "is Ardaelius."

The young girl looks over her shoulder at the man to find he had flipped over to face her. Only a slit of his eyes appears open.

"That is the goddess?" Ani responds.

"Just a statue; a mountain-tall reminder of whose domain we live in."

"You don't talk about her much," Ani pipes in.

"Don't need to."

Ani watches the glint of moonlight reflect from his eyes as they open. Slowly, they hold onto the statue as the caravan moves. Soon the silence becomes too much for the young girl. "I got the dragon back."

"I know."

"No, it went in my arm again."

"Oh, that's good. Should make things easier when we leave."

"When we leave?" Ani obnoxiously looks around at the securing iron bars. "We're prisoners, Tushma!"

"Is that what you think?"

The young girl kicks at the bar ahead of her causing an imprisoning ring.

"Cease that at once!" a firm voice calls out.

"So very free," Ani utters to herself.

Under the blanket of moonlight, a stout woman bearing a long face rides atop a large canine beast. As she nears the iron bars her eyes stab in.

"Was that you?" Her masculine projection takes the young girl aback. "Keep quiet or I'll open this up and let my hellix have you for a treat."

With remarkable timing, the mounted beast grins. A mouth of pearlescent triangles protruding from blood red gums gleams in the weak light.

"Piss off," the coarse voice of Tushma barks. "If she gets released, they'll put your head on a spike."

The enthrallment evaporates from the woman's face. With a subtle twitch she brings the hellix to a halt.

As the cage passes, Ani snaps her sights to the old man.

"Now, where was I? Oh right, we can leave at any time." She rolls her eyes, returning them to the blissful tumbling of water along the massive statue.

It doesn't look like stone. It's not marble... Seems like a metal almost, but a giant metal statue – out here even – doesn't seem likely.

A glint of blue stands out from the rest. Ani leans forward and grabs the bars with each hand. She tracks the sparkle's movement. It traverses the length of the goddess's robes, then dips below sight, before reappearing among the umber branches of the pines. As the gleam intensifies, Ani whispers over her shoulder, "Tushma."

"What," he replies at full volume.

"Do you see the moving light?"

"Fire?"

"No, water."

"It's probably the moons, Ani."

She extends a finger at the treeline slipping away behind them. The audible arrest of the old man's breath steals her focus, losing sight of the beacon.

"You see it, right? What is that?" she asks.

"Dunno." The quick reply leaves Ani without anything to say, causing a lingering pause until Tushma continues, "What I do know is that anything brave enough to shine at night isn't our friend."

The young girl locks her eyes onto the anomaly once more. Tracking it as it distantly follows in the forest, she feels a tingle spring with her forearm. Her eyes snap to the glowing of her nerves along the spirit's wrest. She allows her hands to relax, and with remarkable ease, the spectral dragon emerges from her iridescent scar. It flows out to coil on top of the young girl's crossed legs. Returning her focus to the distant light, the faint blue hue emanating from the auragonic is nearly too powerful for Ani to spy out into the forest. With some mild twisting, she catches a moment of the glittering apparition hesitate.

My dragon, it sees it. Does it know what it is?

A small mastication from the dragon delivers a rippling sensation along Ani. She peers down to see the serpentile beast wiggle with comfort before rolling onto its back.

Those look like little feet…

"Are you growing?"

"Ani," Tushma interjects, along with an accusing finger towards the abyss. "It's coming closer; put that thing away, you're drawing the light here."

A glance ahead reveals the truth of the old man's warning. Touching the treeline is a dark, rippling glitter of light. Ani snaps her sights back down.

"Okay, go now."

Her straining face and flexing forearm do little to entice the beast back inside.

"This isn't play time." The beast raises its glowing eyes to look into hers. "Another time."

Ani watches as the dragon twists its long neck to look out beyond the trail. A rush of noises returns from the realm of background ambiance. Men spitting out hushes only barely supersede crunches of jagged wheel movements. Piquing interests of caravan riders evolves into warnings and orders. Ani's immediate situation demands her attention as her peripheral vision catches sight of the glowing creature now just outside of the bars. The endlessly flowing liquid encompassing its body never leaves its orbit while compressing into the metal.

A feral growl rumbles from the dragon in her lap. The young girl's eyes strike down to witness a spark of light crack from within its bared teeth before snapping at the immaterial being. In an act nearly breaking Ani's mind, her dragon produces a noise of gurgling suction followed by a hiccup. While Ani hears Tushma's breathing come to a halt behind her the serpentile spirit posted in her lap begins changing. At a nearly blinding rate, its blue hue escalates into a beacon of light rivalling the fila. She closes her eyes while throwing an open hand between her face and the beam. Yips and screams erupt along the caravan as all nearby become alerted to the happening. After reaching a peak, the auragonic's light begins to dissipate, revealing a hulking mount and its irate rider outside the stopped cage.

"Tushma!" the furious woman calls out, "Make her put it back in the box."

Her order quickly sends chills down Ani's back. "Why?"

As the caravaneer holds her stare true on the old man, she barks, "We're changing the deal. We'll not make it to Carcras if she's not to be trusted... as you said."

A burdened grunt rumbles within Tushma's throat. Ani turns to question him with her eyes but is met with a grim face.

That look. It's always that look.

"I'm not going to–" the stern woman cuts her speech short to look down at her hellix. The canine jerks its snout left, then right while drawing in deep sniffs. A distinct energy from the moment produces bumps along Ani's arms. She watches as fire crawls out from the armour of the woman, then her open skin ignites into a controlled flame. The flickers of orange immolate up her face revealing long, pointed ears hidden away. Her eyes drag along the length of the caravan.

She's Pajiado.

Before Ani has time to react, she hears a violent scream followed by a bloody squelch. In daft alarm, her auragonic slips back into its wrest.

Oh, now you come back.

The young girl feels the firm hand of Tushma barely take hold of her shoulder before a wringing of plant-life wraps around the wagon, flipping it on its side. The crash narrowly misses the Pajiado and her mount as it slams into the ground.

Ani connects eyes with the woman just as a jolt of force drags the wagon away into the dark forest. The woman snaps her reins and the hellix gives chase. As a beacon of fire fighting off the night, the Pajiado gains on the wagon.

Splintering wood and scraping metal drown out all other noise. Ani rolls around inside of the bars to avoid being snapped within the gaps or being bludgeoned by the iron box bouncing around. Finally, Tushma wraps his arm around her middle and holds her before throwing them against the sideways roof of the wagon. The lurching weight produces twiney snaps, freeing the wagon while compelling it to flip wheels up, then over onto its other side.

Upon landing, the prison door cracks open and swings freely to smack the inside wall. Ani hangs limply while Tushma carries her through the opening and onto the new plateau among the trees. She scrambles to hold onto her satchel, threatening to slip off and back into the lopsided cage. The cuff of her sleeve snags, and rips from her elbow down, revealing the mountainous scar on her forearm.

Fire leaps from the charging caravaneer, attacking dry foliage in all directions. The starry sky falls on Ani as chaos abounds the area, surrounding the tipped wagon. A wave of heat furnaces the young girl.

"Back to the road!" the Pajiado hollers out.

Shadows evade the coming light as tiny flames stretch beyond their impact. Tushma's grip tightens as he vaults from the height. Amid being jostled about, Ani spies illuminated figures approaching from all directions.

"Go," Tushma orders Ani.

The young girl gathers her balance after being released. Peeking behind her, she finds the old man readying himself. He throws a glance, reinforcing his instruction.

There's that look again.

Ani scrambles to her feet. She bolts to make it beside the caravaneer's hellix. The crumbling of flaming tree limbs, stale breath of the canine, and cold wind biting at her consume the young girl's senses. The Pajiado holds out her hand, but Ani refuses. Instead she pivots, running the way they came into a darkened and destroyed path. The young girl's breath fights against her, but she steadies herself, remembering all the hunts that she and Tushma have been on before.

He'll be fine… he always is.

Avoiding downed bramble, and leaping over gigantic tree roots, she makes her way. A luring glint draws her attention, and in a moment's notice she leans down to scoop up Tushma's spear.

"Come here," ejects from the young girl in between heaving breaths.

She darts through the night, blackened spear in hand, to the trail. As soon as the jarring lights of the caravaneers are in sight she throws a glance behind her, only to find the shadows of looming figures once more. Ahead, the onslaught of fur paws upon the men and women of the caravan deters Ani from joining them. She sprints left to continue the trail on foot as fast as she can.

A sudden thud upon her back nearly knocks the young girl over. Ani's rising sights come to the Pajiado on her beast, galloping back with an outreaching arm. At the moment of connection, a flare of light dominates the trail. The caravaneer tumbles from her mount centering an uncontrolled fire. Her hellix continues for a few paces beyond before being targeted by two tree-sized insects leaping from the shadows. Instinctually, Ani rushes over to help the woman up, but hesitates upon approaching the flames.

"I can't touch you!" she calls out.

After pushing herself up from the ground, the Pajiado snaps a look upon the young girl. "What are you?"

The question catches Ani off guard but remains unanswered as a behemoth of a creature bursts from the left of the trail. With a thick snout and rounded head, the monstrosity looks like a mass of hauling bears sewn together. Nearly as tall as the trees, it hunches in the moons light, covered in meat-laden fur. The young girl watches on as the apex creature shoots a glance at her, then to the Pajiado. It then swiftly snags the two wild beasts assaulting the woman's mount, one in each clawed fist, before rolling across the trail to crash through the opposing trees.

A blue light precedes the familiar feeling of her auragonic releasing itself. The glow draws her attention, bringing her eyes down to see it wrapping its long, slender body around her arm. Ani swings her sights to the flaming woman next to her. Tracking the long gaze of the caravaneer, the young girl only catches glimpses of the carnage in the darkness beyond.

With undersized spite, the dragon spits water at the caravaneer. The cupping-hands worth of liquid produces a grander amount of steam than Ani imagined. Her breathing races, a bead of sweat runs from her temple, and one rebellious strand of hair flips itself in front of her eye.

Upon glancing at the Pajiado, Ani finds her to be deep in thought, spending precious moments unharmed debating every possibility. The flaming woman's bright eyes lock on Ani.

"Do that again," she says through her teeth.

"Are you sure?"

"We aren't far, we can run."

Without warning the Pajiado reaches out her hand and grasps Ani's wrist. The excruciating pain of heat biting at her skin deepens as the flames upon the woman grow larger, brighter, and hotter. Spray after spray from the dragon does nothing to quell the rising energy. A thick smoke grows from each watery spew, surrounding them. Tears roll from Ani's eyes while trying not to breathe in. Her other hand clenches the spear she holds so powerfully that blood threatens to seep out. The pain reaches a limit that the young girl can no longer handle before the Pajiado lets go.

Small sizzling sounds come from Ani's flesh as the woman darts away down the trail. A relieving splash of water jets onto the fresh burn before the young girl joins in the race. As the fading light of the Pajiado leaves Ani she's reminded of the beacon that is her auragonic in the cold darkness of the forest.

"You're too bright!"

The order comes fierce and is quickly understood. Fringes of blue nerves dance along her open arm as the dragon seeps back into its wrest. Now, truly alone, her mind finally talks itself into the truth.

She wasn't helping us. She was making me smell of meat to leave me behind!

A fury builds within the young girl. The growing itch upon her wrist fades away while the passion of bringing the Pajiado to justice envelopes Ani. Only the approaching deluge of Goromföld's predators break through her focus. An inkling of fear deep inside her begins to blossom into full-blown panic as the experienced treading of paws closes in.

Turning a corner of the trail brings her target into sight. The faint glimmer of flames upon the high city wall are nearly indistinguishable from the beacon of light ahead of her.

She's alive.

With increased vigor, Ani charges ahead. Hearing the clicking of mandibles within an arm's distance of her compels the young girl to veer to the other side of the trail. Ahead of her, the flaming Pajiado is tackled by a pair of wild hellix. The flickering light of her skin delivers a full, yet shadowy, display of the woman's demise. Ani stifles her breathing and brings absolute caution to her steps as she quickly treads beyond the feasting. The light behind her guides the young girl as she keeps to the side of the trail while hustling towards the closed gate.

A firm hand triggers a small scream from Ani, but a swift hand covers her mouth.

"Be quiet, girl," crawls from Tushma's mouth as he uses his leverage to situate himself alongside her. Within the shadows of the trail, the old man quickly wraps a loose cloth around her open forearm. His cold eyes lock into hers, then he darts ahead towards Carcras.

A wash of confusion, fear and relief mix in a gruesome battle within her. The only thing she finds herself capable of is continuing her silent run towards the promise of safety ahead. She focuses on the high walls, built of stone and steel, creating a definitive line in the road. Her eyes track the details along the length of battlements perched at the defensive peak that allow for loops and embrasures. Tushma leads them to an outer fortification centralized between the trees that protects the portcullis of the gatehouse.

"Open the gate!" the old man calls out.

The air around Ani changes as the very forest itself turns its attention to the shouting man. Chills dominate her nerves, forcing her burning muscles into a frantic flee. The following moment is a blur for the young girl. Shadows around her bark and hiss. Tree branches are tossed with wild abandon onto and across the dimly lit trail. Her feet operate themselves as her mind ebbs and flows in absolute panic.

Once outside the stone walls Tushma pleads again, "Open the damn gates! Now!"

A handful of steel helmets peek around the battlements making the high walkway of the wall. Drones of orders ring out above the gatehouse.

"It's just the two of us! Please!" the old man hollers.

"Hold on!" the coarse voice of a guardsman calls back.

Ani sets her eyes on Tushma, watching him assess the situation. She turns her view to an endless darkness beyond the wall; a black so absolute that the young girl can't even spot the movement of the trees in the wind. A screech cries out from the unknown, strengthening the spine curling horror. Her eyes dart to the direction of the noise. She moves her free hand from her dangling satchel to double the grip of her spear. A chitter of bones and shell drags her sights back the other way.

"We're surrounded," Ani says through her teeth.

The veined arm of Tushma crosses in front of her. His fist reaches out and relieves her of the blackened weapon, preparing it in his own hands for the coming fight. A crunching of wood sounds off in the distance, then barrels towards the gate. From the darkness bursts a wretched wagon with tree-sized insects wrapping themselves around the weakened walls. Wild hellixes burst from the night to charge the transport. One leaps at the hauling bear, desperate to flee, while two tackle it sidelong into a detrimental flip. Three men crawl from the open hatch, scrambling into the light towards the pair awaiting the gates to open.

A turning of gears and levels churns behind Ani. She keeps a steady eye ahead while her mind counts each click. Tushma steps back, pushing her to do the same.

"They're everywhere!" one man cries out before being dragged away into the pitch black. A jeweled dagger flies from his hands amid the tussle, landing paces from Tushma's foot.

"Reach for it!" the old man hollers at Ani.

Atop the broken wagon emerges a muscular feline of immense size. Bearing violet eyes, it climbs paw by paw revealing three, then six limbs, before finally pulling on the lip of the turned wagon to propel itself forward.

The internal screaming of the young girl is quelled as a barrage of arrows plunge into the beast before her. She turns her head to find an assembly of archer guards above, along with a set of shielded defenders marching out of the opening gates.

"Inside! Now!" the leading guardsmen orders.

Without hesitation the pair bolt from their paralysis towards safety. The sounds of the other two men behind them being crunched and torn to bits digs into Ani's mind as she flees. They break through the line of guards, then stumble through the portcullis and into Carcras.

Chapter 8
The Brat

A late-day fila coats the jumble of worn stones and loose gravel forming the road in a warm orange. The long stretch, extending from the nearby harbour city of Delcrias, rises up through the fields of immature crops being abandoned for well deserved dinners. Soft winds ruffle each row of trees that determines the great divide of the toiled lands. One more shift of the weak breeze wafts the odor of freshly turned soils.

Fylorn paces at the peak of the highway in front of a grand manor meant for those who lord over the fields. His pattern erodes the stone, and with each passing moment the sweat upon the nape of his neck digs at him. While shifting himself to find some comfort amid his wait, his sights cross the manor.

The roof is falling apart, took long enough. I thought they said that they were going to take care of that when they bought it. Father never allowed for such things, of course he also never hugged us, so there's that.

What would Mother think?

Absolutely not. We're not doing this right now. You can come back when you have something nice to say.

Go see what it looks like inside now.

"I'm not going inside until Ram gets here."

"Who are you talking to?"

The coming voice startles Fylorn. Loud stomps flood his ears as soon as he shifts his focus. As he turns, a flush of gratefulness controls his nerves.

"No one, Ram. Just waiting for you. What took so long?"

"You said that there were örum here, so I went to get my good bow and arrows."

Ram adjusts the quiver strapped to his back while sliding the longbow further up his shoulder. The length of the weapon nearly touches the stout man's head and ankles at the same time.

"Your bow?"

An egregious eyeroll comes from the Nhavyyet. "Fine. Our bow. But I did bring my good arrows."

Catching a swift glance of the feathered ends peeking out from the back of Ram brings a pile of questions to the archaeologist's mind.

"Like, arrows with diamantine tips?"

"Why? Are we fighting dragons?" A thick chuckle pours from the stout man. He pries on one of his forearms. The thick rings of leather covering them bear several intricate impressions of Bourtaulitanbour, as well as a crude etching of one of the beasts. "Both you and I know we're not rich enough for that."

Fylorn shakes his head. "Yeah, I guess so. And I said, 'There could be'. Dunno if shooting them is the best solution anyways; those bitterworms are nasty to deal with… I heard that's why it's left abandoned."

"I did think it was weird that a nice place like this was empty."

"The saer I sold it to said he was taking the next manor over as well, planned on bringing all of them – the whole claven – under his vheer. But I was getting the feeling he wasn't going to be spending much time at this manor." Fylorn scans his weather-damaged childhood home as his words soften, "It didn't matter then."

"Does it matter now?"

The archaeologist abruptly strides from the Nhavyyet towards the failing cobblestone wall defending the manor's yard. He lifts his right foot high, then delivers a monumental kick. The stones crumble under the force. Without looking back, Fylorn vaults over the new entrance and into the weed infested yard.

The inside looks worse than the outside.

You know it's here.

He takes a long peek over his shoulder at Ram. His companion of short stature pours himself over the broken stone wall with ease. The Nhavyyet's face conveys no semblance of disgust, instead his brows furrow while his lips are clamped tight.

"You hurt?" Fylorn jabs.

"Are you not? Look at this place, Fylorn!"

"Oh, I see it." The archaeologist eyes the old foyer, the dilapidated tower of children's bedrooms, and the second-floor deck barricaded by rotting wood while drowning in yesterday's rain. "An old reminder that finally looks like the nightmares I would have about it."

Ram steps out into Fylorn's sights. "I thought it was only your father who had the dark nightmares."

The pair approach the front door to the manor. Before reaching out to grasp the handle Fylorn responds, "Not nearly as often as he did, but yes."

After taking a hold of the wrought silver, the young man pulls. The definitive yank yields nothing. He swings his eyes over to Ram.

"Around back it is," Fylorn comments aloud.

"Indeed."

The Nhavyyet matches pace with him as they trail through the natural mess of plant life consuming the property. Thistles poke at the pair, disturbed seeds float off into the air, and fresh scents meander into Fylorn's nose.

The rear yard had always been Iyalla's favourite place to play. I can hear her whining about it now. 'Why hasn't anyone cleaned this up?'. 'How am I supposed to play out here in this mess?'. Unbelievable what she would say.

Using his hands to split the taller weeds nearing the dining room entrance, Fylorn finally breaks through into a clearer patch of yard. Markings of animals having called this place home for a night litters the area.

"Do you think being back will set off more of those nightmares, or visions, or whatever."

Fylorn strikes his vision over to his companion. Ram stands, barely taller than the shifting weeds, picking debris from his linen shirt. The archaeologist quickly cleans his as well. "I hope not."

"Why not? It might tell you what you need to know?"

After a deep exhale Fylorn breathes out, "I don't want to be chasing dreams."

"What are we doing here?" Ram coyly snaps back.

A short groan pops from the archaeologist as he finishes taking the necessary strides to the rear door. He once again reaches out to take a silver handle, then tugs. The latch releases, but the door only moves slightly.

Something is behind it.

"How about you be helpful and use your Nhavyyet strength to open this door?"

"What do you need me for? You kicked that stone wall down."

"I kicked it down all the time as a child, I knew it was weak."

"Alright," Ram utters while stomping towards the stuck entryway.

"And my leg is sore now."

"I said, 'Alright', didn't you hear me?" the Nhavyyet barks back.

"I did," Fylorn grins, "but I enjoy hearing you say it."

"Why do I even agree to do things like this with you?"

"Because you like showing off. So show off, you stump."

The Nhavyyet snaps a crisp glare at Fylorn.

A growing tension is strengthened by the look, but the archaeologist doubles his zeal, "What? Are you not?"

Ram closes his eyes while shaking his head. He then rolls up his sleeves before placing his fist flat against the door. Like a small battering ram, he mocks the attempt a few times.

"What are you waiting for, someone to hold your hand?"

"No," the Nhavyyet grumbles over his shoulder, "I've always wanted to do this, so I'm enjoying it."

"Well, enjoy it faster. If Ardaelius finds us doing this–"

Fylorn's banter is cut short as the clanking of metal meets the cracking thunder of wood being ripped from the door's hinge. He watches Ram create a pile of ruin before him with one well-placed punch. The Nhavyyet leans in to inspect his work as well as the state of the forgotten dwelling. He takes a step forward but then stops to turn and face his companion.

"What is she going to do?" flows from Ram's grin.

A small heat sparks on the back of the archaeologist's neck.

Tell him what she can do, Fylorn.

"No," he simply replies.

The answer stops Ram in his tracks. "No?"

Fylorn shakes his head while retracting his hand from the shattered door frame. "Um, nothing. Bad placement... What do you see inside?"

Without listening, Fylorn carefully places himself within the threshold, taking in the view as the Nhavyyet had just done.

The floors are warped and cracked. The paint is peeling. That portion is sectioned off, condemned. I thought it looked bad from the outside.

"Fylorn–" Ram begins but is swiftly cut off by the man himself.

"I know, I can see."

"No, I was asking where you wanted to start."

After a powerful breath out Fylorn closes his eyes, then answers, "I'm... I'm sorry."

"I just don't know where we're looking, really. Is there a shelf, or desk?"

"I'm wondering where they kept the log."

"My friend, there's plenty of logs out in the wilds."

"A log is a journal. A record of my family history; where my vheer came from."

"Log?"

"Oh, yeah, Mother sailed. She used to call everything we wrote down 'A log'."

"I know she sailed; I remember..."

"You can say it."

Ram remains silent.

"Alright, let's start in the cellar."

"The cellar? Doesn't that kind of stuff get stored in bedrooms, or the study?"

"The only thing Father kept in his study was broken emotions."

Ram twists his head while replying, "Say no more. Let's go."

Each man takes great care with their steps to avoid the jutting boards of the damaged floor. Fylorn spies the remnants of animal droppings from long ago. He flicks an eye at Ram, who returns an affirming glare. The pair pass though the dining room into the grand hall of the estate.

The many open doors allow a substantial amount of light to enter, leaving nothing to the imagination at the state of the hall. Sizable paintings depicting Fylorn's line of ascent ward in place, one after another left untouched by the decay common to the rest of the manor.

"It's so weird, it's colder in here than the dining room. I'm freezing, Fylorn."

"I hadn't noticed," the archaeologist spits out while scowling at a portrait of a middle-aged man wearing brilliantly orange robes.

Great-grandfather Fronyne, as uninviting as ever. You know, I wondered if it would warm your heart to know that you now get to glare upon some other delinquent children roaming these halls. Now I know that Ardaelius was a far more cruel mistress when she spawned me. And now you hang alone waiting for eternity in silence, just as you always wanted.

"Fylorn?"

The assertive voice of the Nhavyyet clears up the fog within Fylorn's mind. He rapidly blinks before turning to look upon his companion. While putting on a forced smile, he spins to cut across the empty hall. As the moment catches him, he stops to look around.

"Ram? Are some things missing?"

"It's not your house, my friend."

With exaggerated force Fylorn juts out a thumb to the paintings still hanging excessively upon the wall behind him. One single laugh bursts from the Nhavyyet.

"Okay, fine." Ram looks around at the state of the great hall. "Iyalla's screaming seems to be missing, but I might be deaf."

After a playful eyeroll the archaeologist spreads his hands wide in a blatant gesture. "The table. The massive table of petrified wood."

"Oh my, your mother said she was taking that to her grave with her. I thought you got rid of it after…"

"After they died aboard The Azephyre's Grace? No. I thought about it but…" Fylorn's gaze tracks Ram's to the opposing wall. His nose quivers.

That pale green stain still crisply plays the backdrop to the grandest painting of all. Even in this light my hair still looks darker than it should, idiot painter. I'm still angry he never fixed my face. It looks like my nose is twice as big as it should be. What am I, a bird?

The archaeologist's voice wavers as he continues his rant, "That's just a boy I used to know."

"Stop it!" Ram demands. "You might have… feelings, but I was there. Your parents, you and Iyalla. That's a happy family. Look how sharp your father looks!"

Fylorn silently fixates his gaze on the family portrait. His focus keeps the other three fuzzy within his peripheral vision. Iyalla's long, dark black hair pinned up just like their mother's. Her sharp chin and sharper eyes, a mirror of their father's.

Mother said the truth, and she meant it. Vihara judged them while coming to see you, and then judged me in being the last of the Vheer Dagus — a burden you never had to bear — and look where we are now…

"Fine," Ram's thick voice chokes off. "We don't have to talk about it."

The Nhavyyet's words fall on empty ears as Fylorn pushes into a firm stride from the great hall and onto the kitchen. Steady clods coming from behind him affirm that Ram follows in toe. Fylorn approaches the extra-wide entryway, places his hand upon the darkened trim, and leans inward to inspect the scene.

The stairwell is caved in. Damn it!

"We can't go this way," Fylorn calls out in a low tone.

"I can see that."

A chilling silence wraps around the companions until Ram finally breaks it.

"So, are we stomping through the floor?"

I don't really want to go through the floor.

"Everything is about tunneling with you Nhavyyet."

"Shut up! How often do I talk about that."

"Next time you do, I'll let you know. Now let me think."

As Fylorn ponders the issue, Ram dares to step into the kitchen. Soft padding turns into horrendous crunching as rotting wood buckles under the Nhavyyet's wide feet.

"What was that servant's name? She used to bake for your family. I swear I think about that smell all of the time. She did something to those rolls; I know she did. Nothing should taste that savoury. Eventually I forgave it, accounting for the rich ingredients laying around, but that recipe. Good gods, what I wouldn't give to know the ins and outs of it."

"The conservatory," the archaeologist burst out.

Ram twists around to look at Fylorn.

"The conservatory," he continues, "that's where we grew the food. And, there's another passage to the cellar from there."

"Oh, was it not used often?"

"Basically, only for the servants. Mother felt they needed their own."

"So out and around?"

Fylorn shakes his head. "We'll cut through the servants' quarters, over there."

He points to another door in the far corner of the kitchen. Without another word, Ram makes his way towards the entry. While the pair approach the door together the Nhavyyet quickly opens it. The wood swings hard against the wall holding it, causing a loud disturbance. Fylorn catches sight of some field mice scurrying away amid the ruckus. His sights rise to see a sombre shade set upon the space.

"Sad state of this room too," Ram comments.

"Not rotten enough," Fylorn retorts.

The Nhavyyet snaps a disturbed look upon his companion. Fylorn returns a grim face.

"Erza was a twat," the archaeologist utters.

"The stewart?"

"Yeah."

"Aren't they all?" the Nhavyyet replies, drawing out his words.

Fylorn doesn't waste another moment lurking in the room. He hustles past the dilapidated beds and shelves lined with dust and mold. As he grips the handle to the opposing door, the one he knows leads to the conservatory, he pauses. The tacky grim upon the cast iron knob forces his face to squirm. He quickly wipes his hand off on the pant under his robes, then begrudgingly twists upon the metal while forcing the door open.

Light pours into the dank space. An overabundance of green and yellow life fills his view. Fylorn can feel Ram lean against his shoulder while trying to peek around him.

"How does the garden look better without people taking care of it," comes from the Nhavyyet.

It looks worse than ever. Practically eaten through by whatever has been calling this home.

"Its only weeds left. You want to eat weeds?" Fylorn replies.

Ram barges past his companion, out into the thriving space. He walks over broken pots only to step upon a fallen shovel. The snapping of its rotting handle forces an involuntary eye twitch in the archaeologist.

"There's plenty here. I remember when you would come steal snowcorns and Iyalla would be so angry, good times!"

The Nhavyyet breaks into a chuckle so contagious that Fylorn lets laughter overtake him. After he gathers his breath, the archaeologist allows a more melancholic scan of the misused garden to seep into him.

"You know, we were in the middle of removing half of this stock. Father had caught wind of the giantberries; he sourced one of the traders from Driftwood to bring us seeds. He was going to turn this whole back area into a little operation, maybe even the fields beyond…"

A cold wind nips at the back of Fylorn's neck. His speech dribbles away as he shifts his sights towards the furthest reaches of the conservatory. The broken windows, stained with age, blurred the image behind them. A pocket of fur glides along the razor-sharp edges of glass, toeing towards the open doorway.

"Ram…" the archaeologist whispers while lifting a finger to point for his companion.

The Nhavyyet's understanding is silent and swift. Before the hellix fully reveals itself, Ram has his bow drawn at the ready. The beast stops mid walk to glare upon the pair. Its deep blue eyes flick between either man as a snap of

a taut string sends a swift arrow directly into one. The hellix
lets out a dying yelp while keeling over, becoming a limp
pile of fur.

"Ram!" Fylorn spits out. "We didn't know if it was
going to attack us."

After a contemplative breath, the Nhavyyet replies, "It
was blind to what it was doing. It's just an animal... they're
all like that."

Fylorn's elongated gaze upon his companion flicks to
the weathered door behind. He silently passes Ram while
stomping towards it, then lifts his leg to forcefully kick the
rotting wood inwards.

"I didn't realize you cared that much."

The blatant comment coming from behind the
archaeologist stops him in his tracks. He swings an eye to
the side, spotting a long-abandoned torch that hadn't been
used. He reaches out to grab it, then strikes the nearby flint
to light it before returning to the doorway.

"We need to hurry," Fylorn orders in a low tone.

A grunt shoots from Ram as he catches up to his
companion descending the tight cellar stairway. The steep
decline forces the archaeologist to use his spare hand,
carefully bracing against the cold stone walls. With the
reaching light of the torch, the pair spot an open doorway at
the bottom, and the cellar floor beyond that. When he
reaches the bottom, Fylorn stops to look around while Ram
swaggers past him into the room. He watches on as the
Nhavyyet does a small lap within the cellar.

*Robbed, completely stripped clean. All of the cabinets and
shelves are still here, covered in thick mold–*

It matters not.

The damp air sticks to the archaeologist as he finally
steps ahead to approach the brick counter centering the

room. He peers inside, eyeing for anything that might be lurking. The blackened hole reeks of musty linens. Within, he finds a pile of rags that has completely succumb to blue and fuzzy gunk. He reaches his hand in, giving the slightest hesitation when the mass undulates, then pulls on the handle of a drawer. A creaking of shifting wood within the wall beyond brings a startling gurgle from Ram. Fylorn looks up to find a settling of dust expanding from the door.

"This has been here the whole time?" the Nhavyyet blurts out.

"For family only," the archaeologist peers over at the stuck entryway. "Though, Father never let me in here."

"Was he hiding something in here?"

"Mhmm." Fylorn grumbles as he approaches the notched locks holding the steel in place. He goes to lift the middling one, stopping halfway.

"If it's too tight, I can do that." Ram offers from behind.

"No, it's not stuck; it's a sequence."

Fylorn proceeds to lift the other two latches, the bottom a quarter of the way before cranking the top one fully open. A plume of stale air ejects from the lip of the frame as the archaeologist brings the door wide open. The dark crypt inside holds a danker smell than even the cellar. Turning to Ram, he gives the Nhavyyet a quirky grin before bringing his torchlight into the secret chamber. A chill runs along the nape of Fylorn's neck as he passes the threshold. He drags his eyes along each wall before making his next step.

Directly ahead of him is another door, this one bearing a glowing inscription on it. Embedded groves about the size of the archaeologist's hand form a refined mask of wavy lines near the center that sharpen around the edges. The slight orange glowing from the symbol does little to brighten the space while creating a persistent hum.

"The father, the father, the son and the daughter," slowly comes from Fylorn.

The door ever so slightly brightens before revealing a hidden handle within the dark of its adjacent wall. Carefully, the archaeologist reaches out and pulls upon it. With a reinforced thud the entryway ahead of him clicks, then swings open. Without saying a word, Ram places a hand upon his companion's shoulder. Fylorn pats the hand in assurance, then strides ahead. The chamber within rests in a dark calm of absolute quiet.

Just the way I imagined it. Nothing special, and yet guarded like the king's treasure...

"Is it a normal looking journal?" Ram asks in a hushed tone. Fylorn steps aside to allow the Nhavyyet a full look inside the diminutive library of empty shelves. The pair make a quick scan before meeting eyes. "Can't imagine I know what I'm looking for. Here, give me the torch and I'll be your light."

After a short nod, Fylorn hands over the torch, then begins scouring. He goes over each shelf meticulously, finding less and less the further back he goes.

"You know, I expected you guys to have piles of gold, or maybe priceless art down here," Ram jokes.

"Father, and Mother, lost it all on bad deals."

"Really? I thought your family was doing so well before they passed."

"All a show, one big gamble..." Fylorn's fading words are met by a clicking of his tongue as he darts ahead to a low shelf. He withdraws a leatherbound tome with an extending strip from its cover being used as an enclosing wrap.

"Looks like a log," the Nhavyyet jokes.

The archaeologist raises his hand to present the bound book for his companion. He then uses his knee to stand back up. Surrounded in a heavy silence, Fylorn looks to Ram who keeps a solemn set of eyes on the tome. After clearing his throat, he uses a shaky hand to untie the leather knot and unveils the pages within.

Ram's voice spikes with anticipation, "What does it say?"

"Patience." The sole word from the archaeologist fails to break his concentration while reading.

The Dagus… We… are a vheer heavy with debt. After a deal made with… a god of trickery, the vheer Dagus was denied what we were owed. We will take what is due.

Fylorn shakes his head in a fury. He clamps the book shut then lays a glare upon his companion.

"What?" spurs from the Nhavyyet.

While raising the book in his hand as a tool of his rant the archaeologist spits out, "Mutterings of a madman. That's what they hid from me all of these years."

"It can't be worthless…"

In a wide reach Fylorn spreads his arms and makes half a spin. "It's all that's left. Everything of value was taken. All of it lost."

An uncomfortable squirm edges onto the Nhavyyet's face. While lowering his book, and his tone, Fylorn asks his companion, "What are you thinking?"

A long, exhausted breath crawls from Ram. He pinches his lips, circles his jaw, then finally speaks. "Iyalla–"

"Nope," Fylorn stunts the man's thought. "I will not go crawling to her. It says the Gods owe us, then we shall go speak with the Gods."

"My friend…"

The drawn-out word of the Nhavyyet only fuels the archaeologist's temper as he barks out, "We're going to Mashar Pelim."

Chapter 9
The Ancestor

A lone man stands inside the complex walls, eyeing Ani and Tushma. His long and worn coat is barely visible in the deep night. The flood of others rushing to attend to their duties leaves the man's glare resting upon the two. Some faint light crosses his hideous face before he speaks aloud.

"You folks are lucky, go find somewhere to stay for the night– And it better not be on the street!"

The watchman's crooked teeth settle back into slimy gums as he passes by the pair. Arduous grinding from the massive gates being locked tight behind them muffles Tushma's stomps ahead.

"Where are you going?" Ani demands.

"To an inn."

"I thought we were travelling?" the young girl asks the shrinking back of the man.

Ambling footsteps flutter out into the night around Ani. She chases after the old man, keeping up to his ever-adjusting pace. They rush by a grand stockyard of wood before passing a row of shops with smoke rising from their chimneys. Above each door she spots a matting of bramble and weeds.

After catching her breath she spits out, "Do you just do whatever people tell you?"

Tushma glares back. "Look, we're tired and hungry; we're going to an inn."

"You know, I don't remember saying either of those things."

An exaggerated puff of air leaves the old man. "You barely slept and, if I'm being honest, were bloody well embarrassing back there."

"Me!?!"

"Feeble," Tushma enunciates.

"Are you serious?"

"Absolutely, we need to find that inn."

"No! Feeble? ...helpless! You had us carried away in binds. You made that decision, not me."

"You decided to agree."

"I trust you, you old fart. And speaking of trust, what about you back there?"

"What about me?"

"You can become a bear or something."

"What bear? I was off the trail fighting beasts trying to protect you."

"That giant bear, it looked at me– You looked at me."

"If I was a giant bear, I think you would know by now. Don't you?"

"Yes, exactly! That's why I'm asking."

"Well, stop asking silly questions. Maybe shake your head a bit if you're seeing bears."

The young girl huffs, throwing her sights anywhere but at the stubborn old man. Whimperings of torchlight within the street give Ani little to see within the murky blackness. While the pair passes more of the strange stone and clay homes within Carcras, her eyes catch sight of a familiar piece of artwork.

That heron and wolf statue again, though much smaller. And this time a bit different with the wolf holding the map in its mouth.

Swiftly, the young girl's feet guide her towards the artistic wonder.

"Where are you going?" Tushma barks.

"Who's asking stupid questions now?" she quips back before settling into an introspective mutter, "Feeble… So, he thinks I'm feeble now."

"We need to get you a weapon, train you with it for combat – not hunting – and figure out how you can use that dragon better."

"It spit on that Pajiado."

"Spit lightning?"

"No, water."

"Weird."

Ani allows moments to carry forward while she stands amidst the intersection of shaded streets. She prods her eyes between the map and the blackness around her to find anything of interest.

The old man's shifting boot upon loose gravel builds into a dry voice, "You're also injured, did you notice that yet?"

"It's making me stronger while I figure out where we're going next, seeing as you won't tell me things."

"We're finding a ship in the morning to sail around the coast."

"Things like why everyone out here is fighting."

"It'll be safe and fast."

"Like, are the birds and dogs… friends? Brothers? At war?"

"They need each other," Tushma softly replies.

"Sounds familiar, except all the fighting and war."

"I kept you on the other side of this, where no one would expect to find an Anchor."

She looks him dead in the eyes. "Are Anchors bad?"

"It's complicated, but we do need to keep your wrest under a sleeve for the time being."

Her eyes return to the etching on the old stone. She drags her sights along the details of the city.

Graveyard, a mine, and there's a grand hunting hall.

"How old is this place?" she mutters to herself.

"Old enough. You remember I used to live here; I'll tell you whatever you want to know when we settle in."

Above the intricate outline of the city, she finds a trail drawn away from the sea towards the hills beyond. Along the road are more plots of distant cities, only named and not detailed.

The frustrated tone of Tushma spills out, "We can't travel at night, Ani."

"Filaash, to... Wellias, it looks like."

"No, absolutely not."

"Tushma, I'm not running from something, I'm running towards it. That Pajiado woman back there could have killed me on the spot but didn't–"

"It's not that; the city is gone. During the civil war it was... destroyed."

"Oh, great, more you haven't told me."

"Ani, I've told you everything you've needed to know. I haven't told you about the assassins of Galiram, or the Wöllralt tribes along The Mouth of Ardaelius either."

"I'm not angry, I'm just asking you to tell me. Now."

"I'm trying..."

The old man's words are cut short by an alarmed utterance. Ani twists to find a small hound covered in a greyish fur rubbing against Tushma's heel. It weaves between his feet before widening its yellow eyes upon the young girl. Ani falls into the innocence of the hellix pup while its tongue darts around amid panting.

"You want to go filaash?" the old man slowly asks.

"We practically lived by the sea. I haven't been to," she calmly gestures at the map, "all of these places. How else am I supposed to grow up?"

"It's going to be longer and more importantly—"

A squeak bursts from Ani, halting Tushma's words. She quickly keeps the conversation alive, "Expensive, I know."

"Dangerous."

"Perfect."

The young girl proceeds ahead with a hop to her step. Her eyes wander around once more while keeping a pace just slow enough for the old man to take the lead. He cuts across two intersecting streets until he ducks into an alleyway. Bright lights fill the thin space, leading them to a perfect wooden door covered in bright orange paint.

It looks like stone is pouring from either side of the door…

Ani reaches out her hand to touch the fascinating craft, but Tushma slaps her hand away. He brings himself close to the door, lifting up his clenched hand to chest height, pressuring himself to knock. Time drags on, until Ani reminds herself to breathe. Then, a firm rap resounds from the wood and the air stills in anticipation.

"Who is—"

The irate words are cut off as the door creaks open. A blackness within is traded for a shambling frame of an old woman in a tattered, green smock. Her dull eyes recede into an oval face. The wrinkly and spotted skin of her scowl is swiftly flipped into mild delight.

"Master Tushma."

"Yever."

"You're looking older than ever."

"Yes, Ma'am."

"What are you doing out this way?"

Ani catches the old man's eyes drift towards her, then Yever follows.

"I see," the old woman utters. Her flat and wedged nose quivers while looking Ani up and down. "Well, come in."

Tushma strikes another look at the young girl, ordering her to do as the woman asked. "I'll stay out here."

"No, you won't," Yever barks from within.

"Please, I don't want to go alone," Ani pleads.

A soft glaze crosses the old man's eyes. He silently puts his hand upon the back of her shoulder, then follows her inside. The elegance of outside is swept away by the clean and simple domicile of the old woman. Odors of ancient wood and powerful salts steal her attention. She scans the bleak furniture and cold kitchen bringing her brow into a furrow.

What was she doing before we arrived? She responded too soon to be asleep…

Ani allows her thoughts to slip out, "You don't keep a lot of things, do you?" She glances at Tushma. "I think we have more at the cabin."

"I don't like clutter," Yever comments before taking a seat on the edge of a wicker stool. "Come, sit here facing out."

The young girl raises up her blackened wrist, allowing her loose sleeve to slide down. "But my injury is here–" Ani snaps a startled peek back at the rustling of Tushma settling into a corner chair.

"I know, come sit," the old woman answers, her voice dropping to be smooth and coddling. "I'm guessing the old grump failed to mention that I used to help him keep the other young Anchors healthy and spry."

She knows what I am!

Ani's voice creeps in, "His mentioning skills have been poor, especially as of late."

Yever's chuckle nearly drowns out the aged groan coming from Tushma.

"Yes," she continues, "He's always been this way; a man of action and few words." The old woman lifts both of Ani's arms amid her recital. "I remember, well– I remember many things, but he rarely ever led us down the wrong path."

Ani casts a soft look at Tushma only to find the old man locking a sour eye on Yever.

"He won't admit it, but he cares more than most." The old woman pushes on Ani's back, then on either of the girl's sides. "I've told him for years, 'It's not bad luck if you bring it upon yourself'." Yever lets out a reminiscent sigh before cutting her breath short and dropping her tone. "It's not a curse, thank Vihara, but it will require atonement."

"What?" Ani blurts out.

"Your wrist; the mark is an impression. You're to be judged."

Ani shuffles from her spot to face the old woman.

"Don't look at me that way, girl. I'll gather the necessary herbs and have them ready in a poultice for you by morning." The young girl motions to speak but is quickly cut off as Yever continues, "The skin will heal, but, you are being called to action. You will need to rescue someone who is worthy."

"Worthy of what?" Ani spits out as fast as she can.

"Do I look like a seer to you?" Yever retorts.

A deep chuckle rolls from Tushma, reminding Ani he's still here.

"Yes?" the young girl says while shaking her head.

"Have you taught her nothing?" Yever releases with a bound of jovial laughter.

"You should try, sometime," Tushma replies.

Ani looks down at her fresh wound. As she examines the charred flesh, wondering why it doesn't ache as much as it appears to, she feels a movement from under her other sleeve. A gentle blue hue shines out from below the cloth wrapping before the spectral serpent itself slithers out and onto the dusty floor.

One frantic gasp from Yever startles both the young girl and her auragonic.

"Get that thing under control!" Yever cries out. "A dragon! A dragon, Tushma?"

"Yes–" the old man tries to explain.

"Why? How!?"

The old man stammers, trying to find the best approach to explaining the situation while Ani reaches down to pick up the baby dragon. After wrapping itself around her hand, the magical beast locks eyes with the young girl. The gleam in the creature's eye touches her mind. She begins to speak but her nose quivers.

You sweet little thing… Once we find the others, then I won't have to hide you.

"It chose me, and I'm failing it…" falls from the young girl's mouth.

The soft tapping of Tushma's leg ceases. Ani can hear the heavy breathing of the old woman round out. The young girl raises her eyeline to see Yever shaking her head.

"Alright, girl. Gather yourself. I'll do what I can about the burn mark." Her sights drift behind Ani, towards the corner of the room. "You two need to go get all the rest you can. I'll find you in the morning."

Ani looks back down at the dragon. She allows a small smile to creep onto her face. A surging of her scar is the only warning the young girl receives before the spirit precedes back into its wrest.

"Alright," grumbles Tushma. "Let's be off then."

His usual shuffling echoes as he reaches the door. Ani checks with a peek to confirm, then gets up to join him.

"Thank you," the old man says before leaving Yever's home.

"Yes," Ani squeaks in after him, "Thank you."

"Tomorrow," the old woman comments before shutting the door behind them.

Tushma wastes no time, returning to the street ahead.

"Tushma?" she calls ahead.

"What?" he responds, coming to a slow halt.

"What about dragons? Could you tell me more about them?"

The old man turns to the Ani. "No."

"I feel like I barely know anything about them and now I have one… Why not?"

"I don't like them."

"Okay, but I have to learn about them, don't I?"

Ani watches on as Tushma's face contorts under the pressure of her logic. He finally mutters, "Alright. We'll find you a dragon expert, or something."

Gravel crunches under the old man's boot as he shifts his weight to dart right. The young girl follows him, street after street, while gazing around. Lights dancing in the faint black of night fight to brighten the center of the city. A reflective obelisk, standing cold and alone, piques her interest.

Terribly hard to see in the darkness, thankfully they keep it well lit. It's made of the same stone – metal? – as that statue.

"What is that black thing, over there?" Ani asks the old man while nodding to the city center.

His reply is sharp and humourless, "The House of Ardaelius."

A house? It's as thin as a tower! I wonder who comes out to pray at night… Tushma prays just before bed most nights.

"You haven't spoken with… Nifis?... In a couple nights," seeps out of the young girl.

"Ninfaas doesn't speak back." His crisp tone warms before he comments, "I've not had as good a time with the Goddess of Chaos as others have. One of the joys of living in Carcras was the cooler heads. The differing Gods meant I could… well, I speak with her when I need to."

"How come you've never made me do it?"

Tushma chuckles while a grin pinches the corner of his mouth.

"My mother was devout. I am not." He stops in his tracks to swiftly turn, then places his hands on each of the young girl's shoulders. His eyes settle into hers. A flickering of flame plays in the reflection of his iris. "You will make up your own mind one day."

The old man stands to his full height, taking advantage of the moment to allow a powerful stretch. His eyes cut across, luring Ani's to follow suit. She spots a bustling front door to a wide wooden structure. Light forcing its way through every open window or thin curtain creates an array of silhouettes on both floors of the establishment. The young girl takes a step forward, but is blocked by the back of Tushma's forearm.

"Not there," he grunts.

She looks up at him, enticing him to elaborate.

"It looks inviting, but it's a mess." His finger angles towards the dim door two down from the lively tavern. "We're going there."

"Why there?" slips from Ani's mouth.

Tushma casts an aged look with a cocked eyebrow at her, then stomps away towards the dim door. The young girl follows quickly, in time to be beside him as his knuckles rap against the black wood.

"Yes?" a hoarse voice calls from the other side.

"It's me," the old man whispers through the door.

"No, it isn't, I'm in here."

"How can I be in there when I'm out here, still?"

"Right," the voice inside admits.

The blackened door creaks open to allow a flood of light to cast out of the entryway. Spying through a crack between Tushma's elbow and hip, Ani finds sets of fine tables and chairs affront a lengthy bar covered in elegant bottles filled by colorful liquid.

"Tushma?" the coarse voice asks.

Ani looks at the man standing guard behind the open door. His grey mustache is longer than the tufts of hair that circle his balding head. The large nose, resting below scrunched eyebrows, gives the young girl mixed feelings.

Is he supposed to be scary or funny?

"It is," Tushma blankly responds. "I figured you would be long gone by now."

"Gone where?" the guard touts. "When's the last time you've seen me leave this place?"

"There was a womanly man this one time—"

The guard's hoarse voice climbs to a shout, "Get in and shut up!"

Tushma chuckles while entering the tavern. As Ani follows him in, she smells the reek of something old and bitter. Her eyes wander to the guard who flares his eyes back at her.

"Should I ask who she is?" he barks.

"I–" Ani begins speaking but the firm tone of Tushma shoots across the room, stilling all within.

"I'd rather you didn't."

Amidst the settling of the dust, Ani watches the guard sniff hard through one nostril before closing the door and returning to a worn stool beside the entry.

A square hand catches the young girl's shoulder, bringing her deeper into the tavern. Ani allows the pull to guide her towards a far-off table. While passing by the menagerie of patrons, she finds less than half of them interested in the pair's affairs. The swath of men and women being Hue are outshined by a handful of Pajiado and even less Vidicai.

Wow, I don't even recognize some of these people. That one has scales– And that one is green with tusks from its… his?… mouth.

Tushma sits her down, then picks a seat of his own with its back to the far wall. He carefully leans his spear to rest within reach before leaning forward on the table. His fingers interlock while he softly allows a puff of air to leave him. After a grim scan of the establishment, he turns to look at the young girl.

"Are you hungry yet?"

"I could eat," she swiftly replies.

Before Ani could take a second look around the room, a maiden arrives at their table. Her long black hair rides high in a sophisticated braid resembling intertwining snakes.

"Kindly crossed. It's getting late but I think I can convince the roaster to make one more meal tonight. Anything on your minds?"

"How did you get your hair like that?" Ani blurts out.

The servant's delicate eyes beam a smile at the young girl. "You know what, I'll tell you after you help me get you fed."

Ani feels a heat grow along her cheeks.

"We would be gracious if you brought what is hot and ready," Tushma responds. "Many thanks."

"And to drink? Perhaps an ale?"

The old man looks over to the young girl, then returns a squirming of his eyebrows. "Water will be fine."

He then waggles two fingers to draw the servant in. As her ear approaches him, he covers his mouth while passing words to her. She pinches her lips in a smile, then shuffles away.

While sitting under the weight of residual silence, Ani's bored eyes start to wander. Her gaze lands upon a peculiar gentleman being the only loud enough to be heard above the casual chatter. Holding a tall hat in one hand while sloshing a half-filled drink in the other, he cackles along with his audience. His boasting is embellished by hand gestures and silly tongues from his scarred face.

"And that is how I met the woman who told me she could lure animals out and kill them. Of course, I went on to have many children with her– I wonder if any of them also became Takers? You know, if I could remember it, I would tell you all the story she used to recant. There's a prophecy among the Takers, of one who can steal the very spirit of a man. One of great power, that even they themselves keep at bay. Can you imagine? Dirty spirit takers, coming from me, out there stealing people's wealth and… spirits… Oh, excuse me."

The man drops his hat while stepping up onto the top of his table. After gathering his balance, he dips two fingers into his drink, then marks a long line across and a wide line down his open chest. The young girl nearly chuckles at the sloppy antics.

"Kazdim to Gire, Sight to Stomach. I have faith Sephro will relieve the famine. Gorge yourselves in his name!" His trailing finger is guided by the bar maiden bringing steaming plates to Tushma and Ani's table. "They also dine with Sephro."

His yammering fades into the background as the woman delivers their hot meals. She places everything out for each, then slides a mug of ale towards the old man.

"Ardaelic Sting, first one is free."

Tushma returns a thankful nod before the pair dive into the food.

Oh wow, everyone keeps telling me this is going to be tough, but this is some of the best food I've tasted in forever.

The young girl busies herself with eating while her ears pick up the splintering lecture of the drunken man.

"...Speaking of family, who here doesn't know about my great, great grandfather? I'm sure I've told this before, but for anyone new here, here we go!" He takes another massive swig of his drink before continuing, "Gatrus, the man who built the church here in Carcras. Of luck and the sea, words I live by. A shrine to Sephro, made by a Created no less. Not by your mother, no, no, by the Gods themselves. Sent on a visionary mission with the God-Prince Avco until damn sea-pigs attacked them and Avco's life was ended. Poor Gatrus found meaning here, and spread it to all. Leading a new life, and spread it to all."

With one weak knee, the man buckles, slipping and falling in a thump to the ground. A mild round applause circles the room.

Ani begins to laugh, but instead belches aloud. After a quick blush, she emits a devious little laugh while grinning at the old man, then returns to her feast. The pair continue eating until Ani nearly explodes. After pushing their plates ahead, the maiden arrives.

"Fine dining, as expected," Tushma comments in-between his final bites. He receives a pleasant smile back from the woman before continuing, "Alright, Ani. Pay the woman."

A flush of heat cascades across the young girl's face. "Me? What do you mean... Oh, right."

She reaches down into her satchel to poke around for the heavy coins.

"How much should I give her?"

"Why are you talking to me? This is part of growing up, you have to deal with her."

"Alright," Ani slinks out before raising her eyes to the maiden. "How much for the food?"

"We came here to sleep, didn't we?"

The young girl strikes a fierce glare at Tushma.

"Come to the bar, we'll sort it out there," comes from the serving woman.

She takes the soiled dishes and glides away. The pair follow, sorting out the coin and acquiring a room, then retire to bed for the night. Ani finds her mind racing.

"That guy talked about a prophecy, and taking human spirits."

"He doesn't know what he's talking about. Had a few too many drinks. No human spirits, understand?"

"He also called us Takers, not Anchors."

"A slur, don't worry about it."

"Why does everyone think Spirit Anchors are bad people?"

"People are scared of what they don't know, and some are twice as scared of what they do know. You aren't going to change that. Worry about yourself."

A firm ruffle echoes around the thin walls of the room as the old man rolls over.

While quietly curled up in her bed, the young girl closes her eyes and whispers to herself, "Good night."

Chapter 10
The Bloomer

Aches and pains tear at Ani. As she wakes up in a sweat, she is surprised by the spectral blue of her dragon sitting upon her stomach. Resting its two front legs out, it posts itself to look down at her.

Two legs?

"What happened to you?" she utters with a dry, morning mouth.

The creature twists its head, then two undersized, bony wings arc up from behind its back.

"Growing into a real dragon, are you?"

A quick spin of the dragon brings it into a roll atop her. Once satisfied, it lies down on her chest with its tail wrapped up along its side to nearly touch its mouth.

How does a spirit grow?

"Bah!" Ani lets out in frustration. "Just another thing Tushma either doesn't know, or won't tell me."

Her eyes wander until they rest on the dragon's round, scaley face. The four horns sprouting from the crown of its head give Ani pause.

They aren't straight like fangs, but snapping and twisting like tiny bolts of lightning... Lightning? Why did Tushma mention lightning?

Ani sits up, sending the dragon into a soft tumble onto the wool blanket beside her. A sluggish rise drags out her standing to get dressed. The faint discomfort of her arm draws her eyes to the burn mark of her forearm. Not letting it bother her, she throws on her torn shirt. Then she finds the belt around her waist pinches her sides.

How much did I eat last night? Should have put some cheese in my...

She looks around the room to find her satchel isn't where she left it. After looking under the bed, and behind the bedside table, she gives up. She casts a gaze to the dragon perching on the bedpost.

"Come on, we have to go."

The serpentile eyes stare at her with the dullness of an animal. Ani holds out her arm, aligning the wrest to the creature. It retains its stare while its essence evaporates, wisping into the young girl's arm.

While attending to the growing rage burning behind her eyes, she leaves the room and marches down the hallway. Subtle tones of music and chatter rise as she reaches the stairs. Her hand strongly grips the railing while her eyes scan the tavern floor below. A midday feasting roars as bar maidens hustle between tables overflowing with patrons fighting for elbow room.

Hue, Vidicai, Nhavyyet, Pajiado... He's got grey skin, never seen anything like that before. And a giant man? I thought Tushma was tall– Tushma! Where is he?

Ani hops the final steps. She strides over to the bar and places her elbow comfortably upon the wood.

"Where's Tushma?"

The barkeep gives the question a quick glance before shrugging it away.

"Where's Yever?" Ani calls out with increased volume.

A snarl forms on the barkeep's face before he bares his yellowing teeth. The young girl's cheeks heat up, then she drifts her eyes across the room once more. The menagerie of working men, aging soldiers, and overweight merchants gives her nothing to work with.

She pushes away from the bar, slips between the boisterous crowd, and finds herself out on the street. A high fila pours light on the city of Carcras, revealing hidden treasures the young girl couldn't see in the dim night.

Look at that! We had a well at the cabin, but the spring of water coming from this one is beautiful. And those massive stone walls wrapping around until they touch a... barracks? Garrison? I don't know. Look, a bridge over the river– thank the Gods we didn't have to cross that last night. Could you imagine?

A hellix pup scampers from around the corner of the tavern. It darts directly to Ani, shoving its cold snout into the back of her knee.

"Could you imagine?" Ani growls playfully while bending down to scratch along the pup's back. "Where did you come from? Do they just let you littles free around here?"

The hellix closes its eyes to enjoy being pet, then opens to longingly stare at the young girl.

"Tushma never let us have one of you. I always told him we could use you to hunt, but–"

A yap springs from the pup.

"Something about being a distraction."

It barks again, then runs in a circle before coming a pace ahead of Ani to yap once more.

"What's the matter–"

Five cold fingers wrap around her shoulder, bringing her speech to a halt while sending chills along her spine.

"Ani," the cool voice of Yever seeps into the young girl's ear. "Ani?"

While turning to face the old woman, Ani witnesses a whole display of emotions cascade along her.

"Come with me," Yever forcefully instructs while taking the girl's hand.

She leads the two beyond the street, passing a shop trading both food goods and smithed wares, then to the old woman's door.

"What is going on?" Ani squeaks out as the pain of having her wrist wretched upon nearly brings her to tears. "Where is Tushma?"

"Don't worry about the old man," the old woman spits out. "Inside, now!"

Yever cracks open her door, then shoves Ani inside.

"Are you mad?" the young girl shouts. "Tushma will come find me, you can't just steal me away!"

"I hope he does, he needs to see this," the old woman comments absent mindedly while placing Ani down in the same spot as last time.

Ani feels Yever sit down, then shuffle until the exact position from yesterday is recreated. The young girl stares blankly at the empty seat across the room, while hearing the old woman make growingly inquisitive noises.

"Are you going to tell me what this is about?"

"Look at your forearms."

The young girl does as she is told, finding sprouts of hair from before had flourished overnight.

Yever's creaking voice breaks through Ani's thoughts, "Now feel your chest."

"What!?!" Ani exasperates.

"You have grown, girl– well, no. You're a woman now."

A knock comes at the door. Yever rises to go attend to it. The sounds of her footsteps fade into a muffle as Ani looks to her legs.

More hair… What happened to me?

Ani curls her arms around the foreign legs, drooping her head into her lap. Tushma's voice crashes through her mind.

"What? I've been looking for her, we need to– Ani?"

The young girl raises her eyes to witness the old man silently assess her.

"Overnight." Yever's voice dominates the space. "I knew as soon as I saw her. I took her measurements yesterday."

After her glare becomes something more inquisitive, the old woman passes Tushma to go to a neat shelf on the other side of the room.

"What is happening to me?" Ani quietly asks, verging on tears.

"I…" the old man runs out of breath while searching for words.

"I'm going to tell you," Yever interjects.

The soft padding of her worn shoes muffles the old woman's glide back towards her seat. With a tattered book in hand, she cracks open the cover, then uses her bony finger to flip through the tome. Crispy pages bending after years of neglect is all to be heard within the room.

Yever clears her throat before continuing, "I have seen this before. Ani, release your auragonic."

For a moment, the old woman's instructions remain unacted upon while the pair are stilled in a daze.

"Hurry up," Yever gently urges.

The young woman surrenders to the words. She lowers her arm, allowing the spectral dragon to wisp from its wrest.

Upon its release, the beast lands with solid feet and expands its wings for all to see.

"Yever," slips from Tushma's open mouth.

"Yes. Yes it has," the old woman replies.

"She hasn't been sleeping well," he continues.

"No wonder," she concludes.

"Did I do this?" Ani loudly asks.

A deep sigh rushes from Tushma.

Yever places a hand upon the young woman's shoulder. "You, as an Anchor... Typically, with practise, Anchors are able to manipulate their auragonic. This– we've not seen a dragon before, and it seems to be growing rapidly, which is aging you just as quickly. It's feeding off of you, Ani."

Tushma's grumble becomes coherent, "You'll burn twice as bright for half as long."

Ani's eyes wander.

We don't have as much time until we find the others, or time with them at least. What else don't we know?

"Where were you? Where is my satchel?"

The old man puts on a soft smile. "I spent the morning arranging two hellix mounts for our journey. Your satchel is already packed on one; I figured it should know your scent. But... we should sail, save us time–"

Her eyes twist to Yever while standing up. With a locked-in stare, she speaks aloud, "Go prepare the hellixes to leave. Yever, teach me everything I need to know about being a woman. Please."

With no hesitation, the old man rises. He strolls over to Yever, giving her a soft smile, then walks out of her home. Ani watches as the old woman shifts from pride to exhaustion the moment that Tushma leaves. Her aged sights fall back to the young girl.

"Ani... there isn't much for me to pass on."

"But–"

A dark sadness consumes Yever's eyes. She shuffles ahead, placing her bony hands upon the young woman's shoulders. Silently, her lips curl as her face reddens.

"You will learn everything you need to know, with time."

"I don't have time…"

"All the more reason to go out there."

Ani sighs. Yever slowly returns to the shelf across the room. As the young woman turns to leave, she hears a groan echo out.

"Don't forget this."

Quickly, Ani snaps her sights to find Yever holding out a dried leather sack. "The poultice."

"Thank you," crawls from the young woman's mouth as she crosses the room. She gives the old woman a tight hug, takes the leather sack, then promptly leaves as her eyes begin to swell. Her grip of the poultice tightens while she returns to the street. It doesn't take much effort to spot Tushma, posted ahead with both hellix, ready for their journey. Within a few moments, she approaches, mounts the brown beast, and then they venture from the town.

"There has to be a better beast to ride," Ani comments out loud while adjusting the way her saddle digs into her.

The young woman tightens her grip whilst deep in a struggle to retain a balance. She tenses her feet in the stirrups of her saddle before looking over to Tushma, perfectly mounted upon his hound. The old man holds his right arm out at a crisp angle while gripping the reins. His eyes drift towards the young woman.

"Are you going to help?" she calls out to the silent man. "How are you doing this so easily?"

He laughs, then points to his arm. Ani holds her arm up in an earnest effort.

"What did Yever tell you, after I left?" Tushma softly inquires.

"Lots of things about being a woman. Why, are you interested in being a woman?" Ani cracks back.

The old man throws a bashful grin at her. "No, I was wondering if she mentioned anything about your burn mark. Did she give you that poultice she promised?"

Ani lifts her left arm to showcase the red wound. "Sure did. It feels warm though, it might be infected."

"It's probably just you; we've been riding directly under the fila for far too long; even I'm sweating."

"Right," the young woman mutters before her forearm muscles combat the rising sensations of the spirit's wrest. A dim glow precedes the auragonic's flowing exit. The dragon floats for a moment before slithering onto the hackle of the hound below it. While the hellix adjusts, as though sparks are jolting through it, the spectral beast curls into the thick fur upon the mount's back. The hellix buckles, shifting Ani harder than before.

"Just relax," Tushma coaches.

"Oh, I'm so glad I get your help while out seeing this world, because it's definitely me that's the problem." She locks her glare at the back of the hound's furry head. "I'm trying!"

As the beasts find a natural cohesion, Ani realigns herself into a more proper posture.

"Is this better?" she asks the old man.

"Nope," he quickly barks back.

"By all the Gods. Any advice, please."

"You need to follow step one first, then we'll work on improvements."

Relax? Right, of course. As the new owner of a beast never tamed before I should just relax. What great advice! When I have children, I'll give them the exact same words of warning...

A soft question rolls from Ani like a distant echo, "What were my parents like?"

"I haven't the faintest idea."

"Were they good people? Were they Anchors?"

"Alright, new rule: while spending most of the day travelling you can ask one question. Once per day, just one."

"When did you realize your life was meaningless?"

A harsh exhale flows from Tushma. "You already asked your question for the day. Try again tomorrow."

"How many days is this going to take?"

"Too many."

"So should I prepare ten... twelve questions?"

"You should be preparing to be silent for most of the time."

"That's no fun." She pauses for a moment, the dry padding of the hounds' paws eroding stones screams at her. "Does my dragon need to eat?"

Tushma remains silent while Ani gasps aloud.

"Will there be dragon-sized poop? Oh my, what shall I do? Will I have to let it out occasionally? Will it poop inside of me??"

"I said no more questions," Tushma grumbles out.

"I wasn't asking you; I was just thinking aloud."

The drawn-out sigh from the old man brings a grin to the young woman's face.

"Look." He throws a flippant hand ahead. "Up there will be Wellias. If you can keep quiet until then, I'll allow another question."

"Oh! Deal," Ani squeals out.

The following time of hollow riding brings her idle hand to be occupied by playing with the dragon still nestled upon her hellix's back.

I really need to name you. Averna? Scalia? Something-ia? Gendreg? No… that's a boy's name! Are you a boy? Doesn't matter, if I was to give you a boy's name it would be Tushma, just to bother him.

Ani chuckles to herself. Her drifting eyes catch sight of the creeping death around her. The vibrant greens and yellows of the trees fade into browns and deep reds as they near Wellias. Clumps of bushes and weeds stand between the decaying wood, dried and petrified all their own.

What happened here?

A low groan from her hellix entices Ani to cast her sights ahead. The chips of uneven stone underneath slowly evolves into an abandoned street. Fractured walls looking like half-made fencing line the edges of the flat space between rising hills. A chittering hum draws the young woman's attention to the higher balconies of the ruins. Massive lengths of rehabilitative plant-life encase every reaching structure still strong enough to stand. Amidst the cracks are small movements and scurrying creatures.

Ani's hellix halts autonomously. The abrupt stop stirs the dragon's rest, toppling it over the side. Without hesitation, the spectral beast swiftly expands its wings to find a reasonable glide towards a landing. As its fledgling feet touch the ground, the dragon hops with delight. After a quick scuttle back and forth it scours for a ledge to leap from and glide again.

Tushma slides into the young woman's view, casting a disgruntled gaze before groaning.

"What?" Ani asks bluntly.

"It's been so long since I've seen this place…"

A row of mushroom tops bob as they march in single file in the distance. The overgrown foliage clinging to them dances along to the movements.

"Looks as if it's someone else's home now," the young woman comments.

"You know, occasionally I think of something a dear friend once told me: 'Sometimes one man's disaster is another man's miracle'."

"Uh huh," Ani utters before clicking her heel to move her hellix forward, then shouts over her shoulder, "You had friends?"

In a grand bellow Tushma shouts, "Stop!"

"Why?" the young woman questions while doing as instructed. "We said we were going through here to Mashar Pelim, right?"

The old man points a finger to a rotting corpse of a man, leaning against a wall as the plant-life around him slowly harvests the flesh from his bones.

"I don't think it's a smart idea."

"Or, ah – you know – we could do as we say we're going to do…" In a flash the dragon returns to Ani, slowing her speech. "…just a thought."

"Or–" A quick snap of the dragon's eyes to the old man brings him to a premature silence. Tushma cocks his head. The spectral beast's locked-on gaze draws an uncanny smile across his face. "Or, ah."

The serpent's tail flows into a small waggle while drifting closer to Tushma.

"Ani, I think it thinks its name is Ora."

"Ora?" the young woman spits out, only for the dragon to spin on its heels while bringing its direct attention to her. "Ora…"

With a quick slink, the auragonic approaches, then gently climbs up to the warm patch of fur it had been resting in before. Ani extends a hand, slowly stroking the neck of the creature while uttering, "Ora."

The passing of a cloud allows for a clearer look at the crystalline paintings that are the creature's eyes. A soft rumbling from within reassures the young woman, bringing her chest aflutter.

"Ora it is," Tushma comments aloud. "Now, let's venture down that road there, and avoid this mess."

After a firm whistle and yip, the old man brings his hellix to his right, steering it to a twisted path veering away from Wellias. Ani gives the broken and lost city ahead of her one more look before guiding her own hellix along behind Tushma.

Chapter 11
The Desecrator

The young woman catches her hair from blowing in the harsh wind rolling over the wide fields ahead. She then peers out into the long rows of grass. Her sights drift to the old man riding a few paces ahead of her before lowering to Ora. The dragon rests, nestled up on the back of the hellix they ride. One eye of the serpent opens to look at the young woman.

"Good morning," Ani coos to her auragonic. "How are you? Fine, as always. You missed it, Tushma calls this one Dead Man's Road, which is silly because we haven't found one dead man yet. But we did pass a few groups of travellers, all of which were very much alive. Though, none of them knew about dragons. The old fart kept saying that was a good thing, only after he scolded me for talking to them in the first place. He still thinks that we need to be a secret, but I keep telling him that no one knows us out here…"

She watches the spectral dragon close its eye and fall back asleep. The gentle rising and falling of its chest prompts a deep warmth within her.

"You rest; I'll keep my eyes open for danger."

The following days of riding are filled by silence and fuelled by the tension of each shadow housing a new and unstoppable threat, but the attack never comes. Visions of the caravan to Carcras keep Ani on edge. One night, while camping on a high ridge, she bursts awake. Her arms wrap around Ora. Feeling the dragon's limbs, longer than her own now, brings a warped sense of security to the young woman. Her eyes immediately snap to the waning fire across from her, illuminating the closed face of Tushma. He sits, holding his knees, dangerously close to the flickering heat.

"Are you okay?" she utters out towards the still man.

With as little effort as possible, he replies, "I could ask you the same."

Ani feels the chill of her own perspiration dig into her. Her eyes linger on the bright light in between the two. She chews on the inside of her cheek before confessing, "I've had different days... still wondering if they were better, or simply... different."

A low grumble rolls out of the old man.

"Are you praying?" she asks him.

"No," he softly answers. "Thinking."

"Thinking? About what?"

"Praying."

The young woman lets out a half-chuckling snort. "Then pray, what's holding you back?"

Tushma sighs before finally opening his eyes, locking a grim gaze onto her. "There is one thing that remains consistent between the hills and the plains; they love their goddess... they love her to death."

"What is that supposed to mean?"

"It means that even after everything that has happened... people are going to be happy with being unhappy."

The Desecrator | 137

"This is what you think about at night?" Ani jokes. "It's no wonder you can't sleep."

"You're right. Get some sleep for the both of us." Tushma says before lying down on his side and rolling away from the fire.

In the morning Ani wakes to Ora leaping from a reaching ledge above. The dragon glides down to a rock, bringing the young woman's gaze squarely out to the stretching valley below their cliffside camp. A magnificent array of structures reaching for the sky dominate the horizon. Even at this distance, many valleys away, she can see the towers peaking out from the gargantuan walls of sheer metal glimmering in the morning light.

Ani can't help but crack a smile looking upon the wondrous feat of mankind. A crunching of sticks coming from behind draws her attention. She swings her face to witness Tushma marching around his hellix, only steps from the treeline. The old man adjusts the mount's saddle on one side, then tilts the worn leather pouch filled with goods on the other. She stares at him for some time before he finally breaks.

"You've seen me do this before."

"I've seen you do many things before, but a bad example is still teaching me something, isn't it?"

He slows his hands while tending to a loose strap. "Am I supposed to feel good about that?"

"Just think about it," Ani toys with him, then cocks her head before blurting out, "What do you think we'll see in the big city?"

"Nothing," Tushma bluntly replies.

"Nothing! What do you mean? There will be plenty of things going on in a place like that."

"I'm sure there will be, but we aren't going there."

Ani's shoulders sink. "Why not? I want to see things, remember?"

The old man assures all of the joinings are taut before furrowing his brow and staring at the young woman.

"It's out of the way, and also I didn't spend the last nine years avoiding the Legion just to bring you to their doorstep. We ride for Tombra."

"Tombra?"

"That's what I said. 'The scum of Goromföld'. You want to see what the world is really like, let's start from the worst, that way it can only get better."

"Or," Ani interjects, having her eye unconsciously drawn to her leaping dragon, "we would just go to Mashar Pelim and read about the scummy place."

"Read?" The old man releases a howl of laughter. "There's no time to stop and read. What kind of journey do you think we're on here?"

"I was hoping for a fun one."

"Yeah." Tushma is overcome by a deep sigh. "Me too."

The old man finishes packing his mount while Ani gathers her things. Before long, the pair are back on the road. Quickly the silence consumes the young woman.

"What kind of person was my mother?"

"You've asked this before; I didn't know her."

"Yes, but you know a lot of people and never told me."

"What is that supposed to mean?"

"It means you knew I was an Anchor, and you saved other children like me, a bunch from what Yever says. You probably knew my mother."

"It's not as though I haven't thought of it before, but… Unfortunately, it doesn't mean anything, Ani. Maybe I knew a girl once that slightly resembles you. That doesn't have any impact on who you are."

"It could help me figure out who I'm supposed to be," the young woman argues.

"You keep that up and you'll be sitting with me all night by the fire, unable to sleep. Do you want that?"

"Not really..." Ani's voice trails off.

She waits for Tushma to reply, but one never comes. After winding trails and weaving roads, the pair arrive outside a lousy set of wooden gates. A sole man with grey skin and ratty hair stands outside the muddy entrance.

His eyes crawl to Tushma before spitting out, "No hellix are permitted inside. They must stay in the stables."

Ani watches as a bit of spit lingers on his lip while standing his ground between them and the open gates. Without a word, Tushma dismounts, then brings the lead towards the man.

"You'll have to pay as well." His words peck at the young woman's ears, making her eye involuntarily twitch.

Ani follows suit, swiftly grabbing her satchel of valuables before handing the hound off. Tushma drops two coins into the man's cupping fingers. A stench runs from his grey mouth as he grins to the pair, then slinks away with the mounts.

Without hesitation, the old man charges ahead towards the city's entrance. Ani keeps alongside him, feeling the wet soil grip on every step she takes. The attending guard to their right barely shifts from his post while his eyes track the coming travellers.

Are they not worried about raiders simply walking in?

The light of day does little to brighten the weathered grey wood of the grim streets ahead of Ani. A waft of stale alcohol and urine assaults her nose as she scans the many dilapidated homes and taverns. The murky brown under the lazy commotion of people bleeds across the land to the chipped stone of some older walls keeping the grime inside Tombra.

Her eyes snap beside her to Tushma as she breathes out, "This place?"

She spots the growing of a smirk upon his face. He raises his eyebrows towards her, blinking slowly before replying.

"I thought you saw the good in everything?"

"I can see it, sure. It's harder to smell it though."

Tushma cackles before sauntering ahead.

"Where are you going?" Ani bursts out.

Holding his head high, the old man continues forward while shouting over his shoulder, "I'm in the mood for some music."

"Some music?" the young woman mutters under her breath before clomping forwards through the mud. Arriving at his side provides her with a fresh sight upon the expired city.

Carts rolling in the distance, heaped with… some kind of meats… Nope, none of my business. And everyone has torn clothes, everyone? Are there no skilled seamers? Maybe one of these taverns should close down to become a tailor… Why is that man leaning against that wall moaning?

"Gods above! Tushma, can we just be thoroughfare? I don't feel like we're going to find any fun here."

"Gods, you say? We could visit the House of Ardaelius if you want to profess your faith. Or – bear with me – we could go get some tasty drinks and listen to a bit of sweet drumming. How does that sound?"

"It sounds like we don't have time for reading," Ani barks back. "Or like we could be on our way to Millown by now!"

"Look, little girl. This is my adventure as much as yours and I haven't been in a lavatory like this in nearly an age. Humor me, please."

One firm heel brings the young woman's steps to a halt. She snorts while casting a gaze around. It lands upon a strung-up pile of men and women on their knees awaiting a master's decision.

"This is humorous to you?" Ani ejects with a scathing finger point.

The old man ignores her while bringing himself to the patio of a tavern. The young woman slowly lowers her arm. He raises a finger to the sky while throwing a raised brow at Ani. Soft tones of string instruments breeze into the young woman's ear. She watches as Tushma glides over to the open window of the tavern to peek inside. A flood of emotions dance across the old man's face. His checks grow red before turning back to her and abandoning the porch.

"Not for the eyes of the young, I'm afraid. What about…"

Ani watches as the old man's sights crawl towards the heinous activity she had been pointing to. A nearly imperceptible quiver stirs along his mouth. While looking into his distant eyes she approaches to take his hand. Ani gathers the set of limp fingers, shaking them until Tushma registers himself.

He looks down at her, a soft red growing around his eyes. "You know what, I think we should stop by the church and give some folks a prayer."

His grip tightens as he turns on his heel, bringing her along with him. The pair march past gatherings of drunken farming men and homeless women. They turn a dark corner under a pavilion that opens to a widening street. Ani's sights are consumed by the House of Ardaelius. The tall, black obelisk gleams while surrounded by bone ladders covered in vine trusses. A small gathering of people in tattered robes and dresses are assembled in the open hall, standing before one refined man shouting while reading from a book.

"And I read from The Will of Ardaelius: She is absolute. There is nothing after. This is what I was told, not by her hallowed sound but by lesser men. I have found more, in her. She has shown me the first steps of foundation on this journey to building a better world for her. Not sorrow. Not waning. She gives me solid, inescapable resilience. Her whispers are not tantalizing; they are truth. And I the better. We the better."

A cold wind passes through the open hall, touching Ani and sending a chill through her. She reaches her hand out to find Tushma, only for him to arrive first for the warm clasp. She blinks a few times, her face contorting in thought.

"You don't talk about Ardaelius often, at least not before we left."

"There's a bad history with her and Anchors that I didn't want to scare you with."

"Scare me? We're already on our way to go meet the rest of the Anchors and you think it's still appropriate to protect me from scary stories?"

A rising in the volumes within the open space overshadow Tushma's voice. Ani looks over to find the leading man has placed his book down to impartially speak to the assembly. His teeth shine in an unhealthy white, so divine it nearly consumes Ani's entire mind.

"We don't have much time until the carts will be coming to gather the dead, please prepare those who have passed for their proper burial."

He removes himself from the stoop he stands upon. The grey skin of his bald head avoids shadows while cutting

through the heap of people. As he passes Ani he abruptly
stops, drifting his eyes towards her. The muttering crowd
continues on their way as he angles his chin to speak at her.

"Are you to be delivered to the carts as well?"

"No," the young woman softly utters.

Tushma steps ahead, then speaks to the man, "We are
simply here to pray for some people we know who are in a
tough spot right now."

The Ardaelic man purses his lips. "Our Goddess has no
place for the antics of hatred or mercy. They both stand in
the face of progress and nature. Perhaps you should find a
better use of your time."

"We didn't mean to offend," Ani spits out.

"All are welcome within the home of Our Goddess," the
man recites with a pleasant smile. "There are those who
dream and those who see, both find clarity of vision while in
her home. The windows of The House are open and
welcoming. Worship is not expected, nor is it demanded, it
will be received willingly."

*I don't think he needs the book; it feels like he knows it all by
heart.*

"Thank you for your words, Master Saent," Tushma
says heavily, with a thickness in his throat.

"I am no saent, merely a disciple."

With that, the man nods his head to walk down the
blackened stairs back to the street. Ani casts a perturbed
glance at the old man, still red in the face.

"I don't think this is the right place to pray," he utters.

"Did you notice that he mentioned I smell of death, as
Yever did?"

Tushma's face flickers while trying to remember the
instance from only moments ago. "Perhaps we have to take
this…"

"My atonement?"

"Yes – that – more seriously."

"Well," the young woman lingers on the word. "If we're being serious, then maybe we should actually do something about those slaves out there."

The old man's face switches from a flicker to a twitch.

"That's not a 'No'."

"No, it wasn't," seeps from Tushma as he sets his gaze long outside the House of Ardaelius into the street.

Chapter 12
The Loner

A soft rain creeps in, relatively quiet to Fylorn's mind. An itch on the back of his neck, growing during the damp journey, begins to gnaw at his focus. His resolute eyes avoid the cart ride's passing view, instead settling into the firm grip he has on the hilt of the silver sword resting within his lap. Careless chattering of the six other sell-swords ebbs and flows from the archaeologist's ears but fails to rip his attention from the fuller of his blade. Small engravings of Nhavyyet scripture line the metal valley, markers of who and where the piece was made.

It would be hard not to respect the pride and professionalism of the Nhavyyet. They take so much care with everything they do, something the Hue have not found the wisdom in… quite yet. A shame, really. If we had that same semblance of order, we could accomplish things the world would be in awe of. I mean – sure – we've spread far and wide, owning most of the lands of Föld, but we still depend on others. Dak, the Nhavyyet and Höllron built Mashar Pelim. The city should have been a beacon of Hue architecture, but instead it stands as a reminder that we are dependent.

"Should we set up an Ardaelic wedding? I wish a woman would look at me like you're eyeing up that sword, my friend."

Fylorn elongates his blink before raising his sights up to Ram. The Nhavyyet's face is swollen by a devious grin. A quick scan of the others aboard the paid ride shifts to the back of the cart where he inspects the loose pile of items hidden underneath of a thick oxen-skin.

I wonder if whatever is under there is still dry...

"No," falls from the archaeologist's mouth.

"No? Well, you've been too quiet this trip. What's on your mind?"

An involuntary twitch on Fylorn's cheek pulls on his upper lip. The build up of liquid on his nose finally brings him to the brink of madness, compelling him to furiously rub it dry.

"The Hue."

"Oh, yes, quite remarkable they've made it as far as they have," Ram quickly replies.

A half-hearted scoff comes from the man across from Fylorn. The archaeologist drags his eyes across the row opposite him.

A weak old man, barely strong enough to call himself a sell-sword. I pray we don't find a fight solely to avoid being within range of his swing. And the slave master; the man who paid Ram and I for 'our services'. Those brown robes have more holes and frays than the worst burlap I've ever seen. And beside him is his prisoner... of peculiar skin. It makes me think of winter pines. Not quite white, not quite green, but somewhere in between.

"The Nhavyyet have gone nowhere but to Vralara," slips from the archaeologist's mouth while eyeing the dishevelled prisoner adjusting his hunch. The fresh misting of rain gathers within the harsh creases of the foreign man's lowered face.

"We didn't have to," shoots from Ram.

Fylorn's face squirms in friendly disbelief. "What is that supposed to mean?"

"The Nhavyyet, the Höllron, the Vagenkar..." Ram loosely gestures to the man of marble skin. "What do we all have in common?"

In an honest attempt to consider the notion, Fylorn groans while staring off.

We all need things?

His short companion doesn't skip a beat, "It's never made sense to me. All this time I've spent amongst you and there's never enough. Now – mind you – the Nhavyyet have done their share of expanding, but it's because we were optimizing the Imperadomanhavyyet."

"We?" Fylorn cuts in.

"My friend," Ram spits out while throwing a dismissive hand at the archaeologist. "Just because I'm a földwalker doesn't mean I'm not one of them. It's still 'We'."

"Ram, you practically grew up in Delcrias. What is to be gained by drawing that line?"

The Nhavyyet throws another hand. "You wouldn't get it. You lost everything; I chose to move."

A grim voice crawls from the man of marble skin, "Why did you?"

Both Fylorn and Ram twist their heads to face the newest member of the conversation.

"What?" the Nhavyyet barks back.

"If you still love your people, then why leave?" the slave responds.

The archaeologist drifts his sights to the man's handler.

Swiftly the slave master connects eyes with him, then clears his throat. "I don't mind. It's hard to keep him quiet."

"See," Ram's words rush from him, "the man chose to be like this."

Fylorn shifts his weight to better face the man of marble skin before speaking to him. "I don't like talking to people without knowing their name."

A pair of yellow eyes rise from the wooden cart floor to inspect the archaeologist. He wiggles his lower jaw slightly, allowing the two larger teeth protruding from the corners of his mouth fresh space before stretching his cheeks wide with a smile.

"Aal-Ivus," the slave grumbles to Fylorn, then darts his eyes to Ram to directly answer him, "I did not."

"You simply didn't fight hard enough," Ram quips.

"The only person I would choose to be a slave to is Ardaelius," the chained man explains while widening his frame in an upper body stretch.

"Is she really a person, though?" the archaeologist questions.

Aal-Ivus snaps a grin back to Fylorn, "It matters not; I was born for her."

"How does that work?" Ram asks.

Fylorn squints at the man of marble skin. "Is she... Are you...?"

After a quick chuckle Aal-Ivus spills, "No. It is far less than that."

"Is it some Vagenkar belief, then?" Ram juts in.

Aal-Ivus strikes out a fearless glare at the Nhavyyet. "Hal-Vagenkar, never seen a full-breed myself– Or were you confusing the two?"

"I read," bolts from Ram's mouth. "What's the distinction if only one exists?"

"History, brother. It's always about history," Aal-Ivus explains.

"So, half a Vagenkar. What's your other half?" the Nhavyyet deviously inquires.

A low chuckle comes from the slave before returning his gaze to the sopping floor once again.

"Let me guess, Hue?" Ram bumps Fylorn on the shoulder before raising his tone, "It's always Hue. All the half-breeds are. Now there is power, and some history for you, my friend."

Fylorn can feel his skin itch as the Hal-Vagenkar recites out across the cart, "Power comes through the strength of belief. There is no honour, no mercy, and no need for preservation. There is no shame in it, brother. You are as you are, as she wills."

"Her will has little bearing on me," Ram spits out between his teeth before breaking out into laughter.

The man of marble skin doesn't join in, instead moving his gaze along the horizon until landing square on Fylorn. Slowly and deeply, the archaeologist scratches his growing itch. His eyes fish in a circle, not truly seeing, until he clears his throat to present a point.

"When belief is killed, culture rests in the corpse of that old power. Power is not strength, strength wavers. Power is keeping chaos at bay. Lords and kings manifest chaos and keep it at bay to retain leadership, or are you blind to this?"

Aal-Ivus puts on a huge grin, nearing a fierce scowl.

"The man isn't blind, Fylorn." Ram injects before shifting his gaze to the Hal-Vagenkar. "What he's trying to say is—"

"I heard him," Aal-Ivus cuts him off. "And I understood every word. I know exactly what he means, and so does he, my friend."

The slave master rests a hand upon his property's shoulder. Placing a bit of pressure triggers the man to rescind all passion. His breath flattens as his eyes avert to anywhere but on another being.

"It is good that he has such strong beliefs about Ardaelius," the master professes. "Especially coming all this way to a land in her name."

"How did you get a hold of him?" Ram asks.

A rumbling occurs in the distance. Fylorn twists his head away from the ongoing conversation towards the potential alarm. The hauling bears bunch and huff aloud in the middling distance. Ram stands up to find a better view. Fylorn returns his eyes to the cart's members. He witnesses Aal-Ivus nudge his owner, then gain approval to rise as well. The reaching height of the Hal-Vagenkar far exceeds the Nhavyyet.

"A raiding party," Aal-Ivus projects.

"You have to be kidding me," moans Ram. "Fylorn, I told you we shouldn't have come this way."

The archaeologist's eyes rest upon the sword in his lap.

To think, I had dared to hope. Now, I must acknowledge this call to action— Heed, heed is the word.

"Still yourself, Ram. We agreed to defend the master," Fylorn blindly lifts his sword to gesture it horizontally towards the slave master across from them, "and defend him, we will."

After standing, Fylorn casts a gaze upon the green-skinned prisoner aside him. The wagon comes to a stop as each of the travellers ahead halts in the way. Aal-Ivus reaches out, holding a docile fist to support the archaeologist from falling backwards amid the abrupt force. Fylorn swings his eyes to match with the Hal-Vagenkar's, and is met by a reassuring wink.

Returning his sights ahead, he spots a hulking figure emerge from the crest of the forward hill. A beast among men, the man's feral shouts towards the others sets him as the leader of the group. The long, tied up hair on his head is beset by stains of blood to bring an amber tint to the natural black. His thick moustache dangles low, bouncing upon a ragged sheepskin shirt. Fylorn gazes on as he orders the gang of men to assault particular sections of the convoy. Each raider, bearing thick padding and choppy haircuts, quickly divides before rushing off in an organized fashion.

From behind, Fylorn hears the bursting of drums. He tilts his eye to find Aal-Ivus amid the now exposed clutter of items in the back of the cart with the protective oxen sheet shuffled to the side. He sits mounting a set of the leather-skin instruments, beating them with his bare hands.

Immediately a tingle overcomes him. He feels his blood slamming through his veins, and his focus narrowing in. Streaks of fur, moving at blinding speeds, quickly steal the archaeologist's attention. He tracks the movement, finding an encircling of hellixes.

He's herding us like stock.

"They're herding us!" Fylorn addresses the cart, but a wretched howl drowns out his words. Tracking the noise, he finds the bears of burden stomping and thumping. The hellixes follow up with a vicious snap at the oversized beasts which brings life back to them. Paws and growls intertwine before the bears begin to flee. The cart's shafts are splintered in the scuffle, shifting the cart and forcing Fylorn off balance.

The wolf and the bear.

Not right now!

The archaeologist's sights swing sideways as he topples off the cart, landing with a thud upon the muddy ground. Barely missing his face, the silver sword smacks beside him,

thrumming upon the embedded stone of the road. His
vertical view brings a new perspective to the ongoings along
the length of the convoy. Each cart ahead of him has two or
more raiders yanking well dressed men and women away.
The handling of each is brutal and unforgiving.

Look at the sheer beauty of strength versus madness.

I told you; this isn't the time.

*Oh, young one. There is no such thing as the wrong time,
only those unprepared for it.*

Fylorn groans while pushing himself up from the mud.
His right hand is nearly squashed as a wide boot lands
directly next to it. Tracking his eyes up, he finds Ram to be
placing himself between the approaching beasts and the
archaeologist himself.

"My friend, gather your sword!" the Nhavyyet calls out.

Without hesitation Fylorn does as instructed, stretching
to grasp the handle, then standing as tall as he can. The
display of combat ahead of him, of raiders kicking helpless
travellers and chunks of fur being ripped from animal
combat, ignites the adrenaline within. Beads of sweat begin
running from the archaeologist's forehead. His eyes try to
assess the situation, while he doubles his grip on the sword.

Ram strikes first, landing a massive pummel to an
approaching raider. The crack of bones alerts a nearby hellix,
which begins to circle around the pair. A dank smell of wet
fur fills Fylorn's nose.

It's not that close.

As he turns his head, he catches the final blink of
another hellix pouncing at him. The creature clamps its jaw
onto Fylorn's side, sinking teeth into his back and stomach.
In a force unlike anything the archaeologist had felt before,
his entire body is lifted and limply taken away. The hellix
holds a firm grip, increasing the already agonizing rips and

tears upon Fylorn's body. A blurred field of red corn races past him, occasionally pelting the back of his helpless head.

He tightens his own jaw, then begins pounding his fists upon the beast's snout. Strike after strike does nothing until a well-placed arrow lodges itself into the nose of the hellix, narrowly avoiding Fylorn's flesh. As the creature slows its pace, a second arrow swiftly enters the hellix, breaching its neck and spraying blood upon the crops beyond. The fading life of the beast brings a release to its hold of the archaeologist, and both beings flop onto the wet mud below.

Before catching his breath, Fylorn locks eyes with the hulking figure soaked in blood and rain. An unkind grin underneath his soiled moustache broadens the man's thick face. The archaeologist attempts to bring himself onto his feet, but keels over at the movement of his torn abdomen muscles. As he flinches, a familiar arm wraps itself underneath for support. The powerful shoulders of Ram hoist Fylorn's failing body enough to reconnect eyes with the master of raiders. He watches as the hulking man barges through his own men, even backhanding a hellix which draws a yelp from the poor creature, as he approaches.

"We can take him, Fylorn. Where is your sword?" the Nhavyyet says through his teeth.

One does not need the help of weapons when facing their own doom.

This isn't my doom. This is one large man outside of laws and without order. A man who…

"Ram, hit me."

Fylorn can feel the jarring of the Nhavyyet at the queer request. "Why? Get a weapon, we will–"

"Mikhiram!" the archaeologist cries out before conserving his energy by speaking softly, "Hit. Me."

After one short snort Fylorn feels the impact of a firm Nhavyyet fist upon the side of his skull. The fading and blurring field of combat quickly becomes black and white while the archaeologist's vision slows.

Fylorn blinks rapidly to see glistening brown fill his entire sight. He moves to drag a hand but can only draw a moan from within himself. From an outside force, his body is flipped. His view is then filled by open skies of grey before the leading raider's smug face enters, looking down upon the archaeologist. The hulking man asks a question, but his voice is too deep to understand the words.

"What?" Fylorn slowly counters, shaking his head while pinching his eyelids shut. Upon reopening, a coating of unclean breath bathes him.

"What's your name?"

From the mixture of disgust and distress emerges a groan unlike the ones of pain he had previously been allowing. Afterwards, he manages to reply, "Fylorn."

A blood curdling laugh assaults the archaeologist. His half open eyes find an extended hand hovering above him. In confusion, Fylorn puffs a breath in return.

"Come on," the deep voice consoles. "We haven't got all day."

Reluctantly, the archaeologist lifts his arm. A coarse hand, feeling nearly of gravel, snatches and brings Fylorn's body upwards twice as fast as expected.

"Kill the weak, rob the rich!"

As swiftly as he had been raised, the head of the hulking man slams into Fylorn's forehead.

A deep voice's hum draws the archaeologist back into consciousness. His eyes flutter while he tries to move. The locking of his limbs sends a panic to his mind, and his eyes burst open. In the following moment, he struggles with the taut bind keeping him in place within the corner of the moving cart. His eyes dart to the deep voice. A beaming smile comes from the hulking man.

He shifts in his seat near the cart's opening, placing a hand upon his thigh. "You have a perfect skull, you know that?"

"Not really something someone wants to hear while waking up," a rhythmical Nhavyyet voice replies.

Fylorn shifts his eyes to find Ram pinned down, equally secure as he is, between Aal-Ivus and one other sell-sword.

"Shut up," the hulking man barks back. "If I have to tell either of you again, I won't bother selling you and simply bask in the pleasures of your blood."

"Ugh, that didn't sound great either," crawls from Aal-Ivus's bruised lips.

The master of raiders nearly stands, placing his hand upon the highest bar of the carts metal containment. As he leans down towards the chirping pair, Fylorn emits, "Please, spare them. They've always been like this."

Bloodshot eyes within the hulking man's head snap towards the archaeologist. He relaxes his arm, then returns to his more comfortable post.

"You travel with them?" he mutters.

Fylorn gives one slow nod, revealing the extent of his cranial injuries as every part of his neck flares while performing the simple task. His winces do not go unnoticed.

"I like you," the hulking man continues. "Most other men are unfit for my fields of battle."

"Thank you?"

"You remind me of a dragon I once fought. Tough bastards – to say the least – but this one enjoyed it. Me and my brothers always wanted to claim a dragon, use its bones to make a sword... or something. We finally found one, tiny little fire-breather too – we were careful about those lightning ones – and it played with us for a while. I would smash its head, then Korvyn would swing his massive sword at its legs. Ardaelius only knows what that big idiot, Hirvain, was doing back there... We played until I got bored and then snapped its neck, quickly picked the thing clean of its scales and sold them for ten silver a piece."

The man broadens his chest while sucking in a long breath. He lets it out, flapping his lips and puffing his moustache, before setting his gaze far. In a jolt, he rises, grasps the metal bar above, then swings onto the ground while the cart is still moving.

Once a moment passes, and the hulking man doesn't return, Ram utters, "I don't believe he killed a dragon."

"Really?" Aal-Ivus quips. "I'm surprised he admitted there were others, and he didn't strangle it naked and alone."

The pair share a small chuckle before both swinging their eyes towards Fylorn. Even with a hanging head, he can see them silently asking him if he's okay.

"I'll be fine."

"I didn't think you could take a blow like that," the Hal-Vagenkar admits.

"What are they doing with us?" the archaeologist wonders aloud.

"Selling us off," Ram quickly answers.

Fylorn holds his breath, then quietly asks, "What happened after I went down?"

"Not a lot," Aal-Ivus begins. "He gathered all of the rich folk, had them gutted for his own amusement, then tied everyone up and continued the convoy along like his own. Threw us in here, said 'We were special'."

"I think he was close to changing his mind before you woke up," the Nhavyyet adds.

"Oh well," sadly falls from Fylorn's sore mouth.

It's not like I lost much, just that–

"Where is my book," he strains out. The panic in his eyes startles the two across from him, and they shake their heads while shrugging their shoulders in unison.

Oh, Gods, no. That's it, that was it.

There will be more to come.

"Shut up!" Fylorn barks.

Ram's brows flicker while Aal-Ivus rears his head.

"Are you sure you're alright?" the Nhavyyet harshly demands.

"...I don't know," the archaeologist admits.

The tumbling and crooked wheels shift their soft treading on mud into a coarse grinding upon gravel. Fylorn raises his head to spot the tall stone walls of a city they are being carted towards.

"Do either of you know this place?" Aal-Ivus mutters.

"Tombra," Ram answers, also keeping his tone low.

Tombra: the scummy swamp of Malaron, perfect...

Fylorn watches on as the gates are swung outwards to allow for the coming wagons. A set of crooked men stand sentry atop the wall, looking down upon the wealth of slaves being brought in. The rancid smell of unwashed streets lingers in the crude portal as an unwelcome warning to visitors. The archaeologist snorts to push the stink away, but to no avail as it swiftly returns with his next breath.

"What do they produce here?" Aal-Ivus quips in disgust.

An oversized hand grasps the ledge of the cart, pulling the hulking man back aboard. He swings into his seat once more. Ram winks before sliding into a hushed rant, "That's the smell of an entire population lacking satisfaction. The men, the women– Gods forbid any children live here…"

The Nhavyyet shutters, luring the attention of the raider.

"Better get used to that, little man. Where you're going – well – it might not be as pleasant as this… You know how to punch stone, right?" A bellowing laugh cracks from the oversized man.

A soft snarl erupts onto Ram's face, but he quickly forces it away. His eyes snap to Fylorn's. The meeting sends an entire conversation of thoughts between the two long-time friends. In his peripheral, the archaeologist catches the Hal-Vagenkar assessing the two.

"It's just one step further towards our goals, you see," Aal-Ivus spits out in rehearsed comfort.

The convoy of carts is guided along the main street of Tombra. Passing by a slew of taverns, inn, and darkened shops brings the hairs on Fylorn's neck into a raised panic. Groupings of sickened people standing in a unified slouch stifle their chatter before moving aside. The unkind respect of disturbed eyes brings the archaeologist's sights back to the floor of the rolling cart. Whispers and heinous muttering assaults his ears before the wooden vessel turns onto another street, one less crowded, then finally onto a third.

This stretch of worn gravel is filled side to side by armoured soldiers. Each stand posted with a spear as their flapping capes display a black and emboldened symbol of a dormant dragon. The tarnished silver of their metal cuirass is barely brighter than their grey skin.

Those… are not the king's men.

"The Ardaelic Legion," Ram spits out.

Another bout of laughter comes from the hulking man. "Who did you think was going to take your sorry lot?"

The outburst harkens the coming soldiers' attention. They calmly conclude the conversation at hand to come attend to carts. Quickly, the hulking man shuffles from his seat. His leap from the cart forces the wooden vessel to shift. He lands with a stone splash upon impact. After shaking his head into a commercial grin, he shoves one hand into his side pocket while using the other to lean upon the wagon. The man then taps twice with his leaning hand before announcing himself for the coming crowd of soldiers.

"Another fresh batch! You better believe our last agreement is still in order." He pushes himself from the lean into a saunter towards his business partners. "And after the next pile of meat, we will renegotiate."

While trying to witness the interaction, Fylorn pinches his hip while bringing himself into a slant upon the wood behind him. The leading Legion man bears a striking nose, akin to the arrows his companions carry upon their backs. His dented helmet presents all the confirmation the archaeologist needs to affirm his worst fears.

"I don't know if we're getting out of this one, Ram," he slips from the corner of his mouth.

"I can't see," the Nhavyyet complains.

A reaching neck from Aal-Ivus confirms sight of the man before coming to a silent agreement with Fylorn. He inquisitively hums while spying on the affair. Turning his head, the archaeologist does the same.

"…quite. We'll always be along the border of the plains. I can't tell you where, but trust that we have forts at the ready," the soldier confesses.

"Aye," the hulking man agrees with a soft nod.

The Legion man wanders his eyes along the length of the stolen convoy. He sucks his teeth before inquiring, "Are any of them Spirit Takers?"

Fylorn watches the back of the raider's head shake. "There might be… are you paying extra for them?"

A sharp grin crawls onto the soldier's face. "The most."

The crisp words hit the archaeologist's ears just before the man's eyes lock onto his. Fylorn returns to hanging his head, then realigns his sights to across from him within the wagon. Ram's face becomes a softer white as every second passes. The Hal-Vagenkar adjusts his jaw, moving the enlarged tusks in a circular motion.

"Alright," the Legion man calls out. "Chain them up!"

A distant screech steals everyone's attention. Fylorn twists his head to spot a vibrant blue dragon with wisps trailing from it as it soars towards the convoy. As quickly as it had appeared, it arcs away up the street beyond. The rallying of shouts from Legion men deafens the archaeologist. They quickly set on in a march towards the spirit, leaving a meager few behind at the carts. Aal-Ivus rises to look out once again, and Fylorn spots a glint of hope in his eyes.

A young woman's hand wraps along the edge of the cart, pulling up a head of dark hair and set of puffy, tired eyes.

Chapter 13
The Redeemer

Ani pulls herself into the slave cart. She stills for a moment to look at each of the tied-up men. Her sights land on a Hue man with black hair, blue eyes, and blood seeping through his linen shirt.

"Are you going to live?" she asks him.

"He'll survive," the Nhavyyet across from him blurts out. "What are you doing?"

Her eyes snap to the stout man. His short black hair and flat chin paints him in a portrait of anger, something his jovial voice betrays.

"I'm here to save you," the young woman answers.

"Why?" comes from the green-skinned man beside the Nhavyyet.

"How about we save you first?" booms from Tushma, climbing up behind Ani. "Then we can ask why later."

After a round of nods, from everyone but the bleeding young man, Ani and Tushma make quick work of untying the group. A grizzled Hue, reaching his final years, immediately charges past everyone to leap from the cart and run away. With unprecedented force, a massive sword cleaves the man, producing a crunching of bones and small gurgling from the escapee's now bloody mouth. The wielder of the sword pushes through the frail man to present himself. A mountain of enormous stature, he removes his soiled blade from the limp man's flesh before directing his attention to the remaining slaves being set free.

"Everyone! On me!" he calls aloud.

A rush of warm blood sets Ani into a quicker pace while she locks eyes with Tushma. She returns her widened sights to the massive man, bearing witness as he takes a step forward but stops. He grins at her, baring his yellow teeth, then drops his sword to fling his right hand out. The bare-skinned hand of the man connects with the throat of Ora.

The dragon flaps its wings while clawing at its captor's iron grip. Ani goes to move ahead but the stiff arm of Tushma juts out in time to halt her.

"We need to move!" he orders.

While a wave of recently released slaves pours out of the cart's opening, Ani's sights linger on Ora and the hulking man. Before her eyes, the smile upon his face is splashed by an electrical charge from the dragon's mouth. A cry of distress accompanies a tightening of his hand. Ora swings her face to Ani. The young woman, still standing on the very edge of the raised platform that is the stationed cart, watches her auragonic evaporate into a blue wisp. With excessive speed, she feels the spectral mist trailing into her arm's scar. The blackened face of the hulking man twists to see the wonder before him, then leans to grab his sword.

Uh oh!

After leaping from the height, while holding tight onto her satchel, Ani flees from the cart as fast as she can. Ahead of her is a long, straight street that broadens as she makes it further. Climbing higher and higher onto ascending plateaus, the rising city has little to hide. Each amassing crowd of farmers and merchants stands still while looking at her, then stares beyond. Ani never glances behind herself to check on the burnt man as she desperately searches for Tushma. After the third intersecting street, she hears a whistle and blindly dives towards it. The young woman lands in a pile of straw adjacent to the street, and the harsh cobbled stone below shreds her elbow, instantly drawing blood.

A second whistle draws her attention. She scans around to find the Nhavyyet lurking in the crack between two wooden buildings. Crawling on her belly from the straw, Ani passes behind a grey barrel sitting aloof in front of the home to her right, before scampering into a sideways shim between the structures. She pops out into a dank alley where Tushma, stands with most of the saved slaves. Her eyes trail along each before landing on the old man.

"Now what?"

"What do you mean, 'Now what?'. This was your plan." Tushma firmly replies.

"You're the adult here, make a decision!" she barks back.

"According to Yever, you're a woman now," the tone of the old man rising until he spots the sea of glaring eyes upon him. "...so, I guess you can make decisions too!"

A rallying cry fills the streets and echoes into the alleyway. After the chattering of men from all directions ceases, the deep voice of one calls above the rest. "A bounty for the Taker, as much silver as you can carry, plus one coin. The rest are regular price. Find them!"

"We have to move," the green-skinned man orders.

"Who put you in charge?" the Nhavyyet combats.

"Certainly, the old man and the girl aren't leading us against an army."

"Who said it's an army out there?" Tushma comments.

The pair look at him with tired scowls. Ani tilts her head to spy the young, bleeding man leaning against the wall.

"What about him?" she asks. "Someone will have to help him."

"Sure will," the Nhavyyet quickly retorts before returning to his argument with the other men. "Look, we don't have one of those Takers with us, they'll be looking for them. Sure – if they find us – they may want to take us again, but we can talk our way out of it."

"Maybe send them on some wild chase after the Takers?" the green-skinned man adds.

"Yes! See, Aal-Ivus has ideas. What else do you..." the Nhavyyet continues but his voice becomes ambient noise as Ani brings her full attention to the bleeding man. She saunters over, then crouches to bring her face to his level.

"My name is Ani. Are you sure you're not dying?"

The man holds back a laugh. He raises his deep blue eyes to gaze into hers. "Kindly crossed, Ani."

"That's not an answer."

She bunches her lips before extending her arm to move his. While inspecting the wounds along his ribs, she catches his eyes locked upon her forearm, and her scar. Ani swiftly retracts her arm while covering it with her sleeve.

"What happened to you?" she asks.

His eyes dart back and forth before replying, "Hellix got me."

"Ooh, what did you do to deserve that?"

The man's eyebrows worm while beginning to speak, but he doesn't make a sound. He leans his head back against the wooden planks behind him, twisting his face to look towards the small argument brewing just beyond.

"You don't have to tell me. But, I should probably know where you're going so that we can bring you there."

"You know you're bleeding too. Why don't you just leave us and make your own escape?"

"I didn't save you just to leave you helpless, that would be silly."

"I mean, saving us is silly to begin with."

Ani beams a wide smile at the injured man. "You never told me your name!"

"I've already told someone my name today."

"Great, so you know how to do it." Her glare burns into him while he tries to ignore her.

"Fylorn."

"That's a great name, Fylorn. Now, where are you going?"

"Galiram."

"Galiram!" bursts from the Nhavyyet across the alley.

"Keep your voice down," Aal-Ivus ejects.

"No one is coming this way yet."

"How do you know?"

"I can feel them all walking."

"What?"

"Fylorn, you said we were going to Mashar Pelim. Now we're going to Galiram?"

"Yes," comes from the injured man next to Ani.

The young woman turns to see the Nhavyyet man fuming with rage.

"Now we're going to Galiram? We could have avoided all of this if you had listened to me in the first place."

"Well, I don't have anything now."

"Oh, you don't have some stupid book you hate so now you think it's finally time to go to your sister… to look feeble? Why don't we stay? We could loot until we can afford continuing on. That sounds smarter to me!" In a huff, the Nhavyyet man storms to the far end of the alleyway. Ani turns to watch Fylorn's eyes follow his companion for the length of his walk.

"Ram has a temper."

"He's always like this?"

Fylorn grins, but holds a laugh back. "He'd do anything for me, and I keep making it more difficult." His eyes trail off as his mouth shifts from speaking into a hesitant squirm.

Ani darts her eyes around, checking every possible exit from the grim alleyway.

I can't imagine there are many of them. And we could go up... no, if more come then we'll be stuck between them. If we knew where they were–

"Ram," she calls out to the Nhavyyet man. A quick twist of his head shows off his astonishment of her saying his name. "You said you can feel them, what do you mean?"

"I..." he starts, but his eyes jump to each member of the group before confidently continuing, "The Nhavyyet can feel through the ground. I sense every little tremor through the föld I touch. Right now, there are fifteen men marching past us up the street, in a pack, none the wiser."

"Excellent," the young woman squeaks, before quickly growing red with shame, and lowering her voice to a whisper. "Can you guide us through?"

"Through to where?" he quickly replies.

"Yes," the green-skinned man adds. "Where, indeed."

Ani eyes the long-toothed man as the Nhavyyet continues, "Aal-Ivus, where will you be heading?"

His face squirms before shifting his lips around his elongated, bottom teeth. "Can't really go anywhere without being noticed, but ideally, I wish to be in Mashar Pelim– in the grand church there. I can be a welcomed traveller at the Manse, for a time."

"So, filaash. Anyone else going that way?" Ram asks the group.

"Millown," Tushma prompts while eyeing Ani.

"My lord, so every direction it seems." Ram holds onto the word while rapping his finger upon his own lips. "We need to follow and avoid the guards in a circle while sending each off. Does that sound do-able?"

Ani witnesses a sea of head nods, all except Fylorn. She turns and kneels to speak directly to him. "Are you not able?"

"Not a disagreement, just didn't feel like adding one more to the pile."

"I see," she says, then ejects a hand out for him to take. "Come on, I'll help you out."

Fylorn takes a hold of her hand, then pulls himself back to his feet. Once balanced, he immediately places his hand on his wound.

"Is it still bleeding?"

He pulls a reddened palm from himself. "Appears that way."

"We can't drag you around the city while like this." Ani brings her voice out towards the group, "Who here knows medicine? We need to stop this bleeding."

Ram's eyes light up. "You're still bleeding? How haven't you bled out yet?"

"Unclear," Fylorn plainly replies.

Tushma rushes over to take the injured man's other side, then looks at Ani. "I'll see what I can do, you go start the hunt with Ram."

Ani sends back a quick smirk before skipping away to the Nhavyyet's side. The short man only nods at her before posting himself at the closest alley between buildings. She follows him at his heels while he lurks out, bringing himself to the brink of the street corner. He leans out, twisting his head both ways to ensure that the street is clear.

"We don't have long, we need to move right," he calls out in a whisper behind him while waving a hand.

Silently, Ani keeps in his tracks, occasionally looking behind to check that the rest of the group is following. She catches a glimpse of Tushma walking Fylorn along. With the confidence that the old man was taking care of him, she doubles her pace to come alongside Ram.

This burn mark is going to get me into even more trouble if I don't figure out what I'm to do with it. At least I'm saving people, right?

"Has he always been like that?"

"Who?" the Nhavyyet asks.

"Fylorn?" One soft chuckle comes from Ram as his eyes dart back and forth counting the men and women on the street. "Yes."

"Is he worth saving?"

The Nhavyyet strikes a look at her. A subtle squirm of his mouth and tilt of his head tells the young woman everything, "What about you?"

"What about me?" creeps from the young woman's lips.

"You're a peculiar one. Came from nowhere, like some hero, to free us. Then, want to get to know us... who are you, little woman?"

I'm an Anchor. I'm a young girl who's now a woman. I'm an orphan. I'm a failure. I'm everything I've never wanted to be, and yet so close to have the one thing I've always needed.

"I... I don't know yet. Pretty sure I'm a monster."

"You look fairly normal to me. What do you have hiding behind those tired eyes?"

Ani twists her face away to poke below her eyelids. She utters while turned, "That big soldier saw me, he'll spot me before any of you."

"Unlikely. A Nhavyyet and a Hal-Vagenkar? You're about as normal as it gets!" Ram allows a hearty chuckle to burst from him. "Besides, they're looking for one of those Spirit Takers. Could you imagine? I'd rather be torn apart by a dragon."

"What do you know about dragons?" the young woman snaps back.

"You'd be surprised," the Nhavyyet swiftly replies.

"What, are you some kind of expert on them?"

"No," Ram answers while holding back laughter. "But I read. And, would love to see a dead one... one day."

Have I got the perfect opportunity for you...

"Why?" Ani breathes out.

"Their power is unmatched."

"What do they eat?"

The Nhavyyet tilts his head while looking at the young woman. "Why the interest?"

"I'm thinking about raising one as a pet."

One loud bout of laughter forces its way from Ram. "You really are crazy."

Ani glares at him until he explains himself.

"There be two basic things to know about dragons. One is they are guardians of magic, tools for The Gods to reign power over us lesser beings. And two, no one has ever seen a baby dragon, let alone got to raise it."

"What if someone could?"

Ram lowers himself to place a flat hand upon the ground beneath him. "Then they better pray that it doesn't eat them alive."

The young woman allows a breath of silence while the Nhavyyet peers around the corner to ensure that his senses are on point. As he steps ahead onto the dusty street, Ani clears her throat before asking, "Have you always looked down upon the Anchors?"

"Anchors?"

"Takers, whatever..." the young woman mumbles.

"I don't look up to many." His eyes lock into hers before a wide smile creeps onto his face. "In that sense. There aren't many, let alone an entire den, of people I've found to be so substantial they are above being scrutinized."

Ani's blank face brings a genuine sparkle to Ram's eye.

"You should talk to more of us Nhavyyet, could learn a thing or two."

"I'm talking to one right now, aren't I?"

An unexpected chuckle comes from behind. Ani twists her neck to find Fylorn holding his side, trying not to continue the laugh. Her sights return to the displeased Nhavyyet.

Ram lengthens his gaze down the street, eyeing up a grand pavilion of stalls below a wide staircase, before uttering, "Should be a good spot ahead to get Aal-Ivus out. Barely anyone walking up on those higher plateaus. Now, what to do..."

The dry voice of Fylorn cuts in, "We'll split up in case we need to cause a few distractions and confuse them. You go at the soldier head on. Tushma will worry about carrying me to the next street. Ani, do you mind going with Aal-Ivus so that it seems more casual? Have a normal conversation, but remember to still try your best to keep out of sight."

A responsive grunt comes from behind. Ani doesn't bother turning to check, knowing full well that it's the green-skinned man. The group charges ahead until they come to the wide berth of merchants peddling wares. Wooden crafts and poor-quality provisions line the ramshackle carts. One patrol of five soldiers is set in the center of the market square, stationed and at the ready.

The Nhavyyet casually walks out, passing a burlap covered stall. He goes to pluck a cob of red corn from the lopsided pile but makes a dramatic act of changing his mind. After silently having a standoff with the stall owner, he flippantly waves at the man. Ram then swiftly strikes out his golden eyes at the group.

"He's telling us to go," Fylorn grumbles out.

While supporting the young man, Tushma steps ahead to catch up with Ram. The young woman feels a gentle touch on her lower back, turning to find Aal-Ivus using the top of his hand to nudge her ahead.

"You're a very nice criminal," Ani jokes.

"Not a criminal, youngling," the Hal-Vagenkar quickly responds. "Just a lost spirit."

"Who isn't?" falls from the young woman's mouth.

The pair walks ahead. She checks one side of the pavilion while Aal-Ivus scans the other.

"Quite a wise statement coming from someone early in their years," the Hal-Vagenkar comments. "I did find it unusual for such a young girl to be travelling around."

"More unusual than a green-skinned giant to be flapping about in Goromföld?" she snaps back.

"Witty."

"Yeah, I guess you are only barely bigger than Tushma…"

As her voice trails off, she hears a rising of volume from across the pavilion. Ram stands, engaging in conversation with a Legion soldier, waving his hands wildly.

"That way! I saw one of the Takers running off vastern!"

A flurry of citizens twist to look to the general direction of the Nhavyyet's accusation. Without hesitation, the Legion soldier rallies his men to charge off down the street.

You have to be kidding me!

Out of the corner of Ani's eye she watches Aal-Ivus come alongside a set of docile stalls. She turns to find the set of grand stairs aligned up beyond the shadowy crack between. He squints, looking long at the other men, then tracks the moving soldiers before shifting his eyes to Ani.

"I would say that I'd miss you, but I doubt we'll see each other again."

"Yeah, goodbye to you too!"

The Hal-Vagenkar gives a smirk before disappearing between the stalls. Her eyes linger on the small hill of roots and breads displayed ahead of her. A deep burn inside of her reminds the young woman of how long the day has been. She looks down to find her fingers playing along the lip of her satchel's flap, toying with a fraying thread. The lump through her sleeve, her spirit's wrest, draws her full attention. A surge of heat cascades from her heart to the length of her body. She slings a glare at the men lurking at the other side of the pavilion, awaiting her.

Chapter 14
The Taker

Ani makes powerful, purpose-fueled stomps through the marketing square until she comes face to face with Ram.

"There was no reason to do that!" she hollers at him.

The trio widen their eyes while absorbing the words she speaks.

"What are you talking about?" flies from the Nhavyyet.

"You could have used any excuse, but you chose to use a wild Taker! Literally anything else. What have they ever done to you? Those soldiers weren't even curious…"

"Why are you being so defensive? Who cares?" Ram questions.

"I care," Ani defends. "We aren't going to use an entire group of people as bait, vilify people we don't even know!"

"Everyone hates them, what's the harm?" interjects Fylorn.

"That's exactly what the Legion is doing here! Are we just like the Legion! I'll answer that for you, No! We will do things on our own terms and be better than them."

"She's right," crawls from Tushma.

The Nhavyyet projects a fierce glare at the old man. His jaw squirms but no words escape his mouth.

"We managed to get Aal-Ivus out, we can keep going," Fylorn suggests. "And if we can, without exploiting Takers, I guess."

"You guess?" Ani spits out.

"Ani." A thick drawl comes from Tushma. His low-set eyes speak for him.

"I can feel the next patrol passing opposite us now, we need to leave," Ram states.

A round of soft head nods precedes the Nhavyyet scurrying to the nearby nook, then back into the street. Ani watches as the man checks either way before slinging a loose hand to gesture the rest to come. She bolts ahead to find to her left clear, and to her right thin enough for them to pass through.

The group dutifully follows behind Ram as he guides them beyond this street and the next. They come to a set of stairs completely covered in Legion men. Their hollers thicken the air of the walkway. Disgruntled eyes strike out at anyone who will make contact. Tushma stands as a barrier between the stairs and Ani while they form a line to enter the closest alley. Once out of sight, the group sprints to the connecting street, only to find it densely packed.

"Are you going first?" Ani asks the Nhavyyet.

"I'll stay behind, make sure that we aren't sending more out into danger."

Tushma nods before placing his wide hand on the short man's shoulder. He gets an approving nod, then shuffles into the street. Ani gazes on as the man disappears before her eyes. The idea of being alone nearly brings her to tears, if only for the moment.

"Ani," comes from Ram.

"Remember what we were talking about earlier," the young woman mumbles out.

Fylorn grunts before complaining, "Look, this isn't really the time—"

The Nhavyyet swiftly raises a hand to his companion, stopping his speech in its tracks. A substantial beam of light crossed over the man's face to bring his golden eyes to life. They bring his scowl into a sharper depiction.

"You're going to be fine, Ani." His words set off a warmth in the young woman, one she hadn't felt before. A heavy hand lands on her back. While being guided out into the street, Ani hears Ram's joyous voice whisper out, "Go catch up with Tushma."

A fusion of body odors and high-pitched shouting making the cramped space unbearable. She scans the river of bodies trying to spot the distinctive old man but finds he had done his task well and became one with the crowd.

"Tushma," she yells in a hushed tone.

The man is nowhere to be found. Ani slinks ahead, narrowly avoiding being knocked over by the bustling crowd forming. She looks around until she finds a fallen-over barrel. Squirming between farmers and merchants, she makes her way over, then clambers onto the makeshift stool.

Bringing her sights slightly above the masses sends a chill down her spine. Ahead of her is a herding of citizens in a fearsome line in direct opposition to a standing force of Legion soldiers. All of whom are brandishing shields to keep the public at bay. Each silver monster holds the line, and brings the street to a horrible close.

Every hair on her arms stands up. She can feel her breathing grow rapidly. A thick hand clamps onto her forearm and drags her back down to the solid mud of the street. She sends panicked eyes to her captor, only to find an accusatory glare coming from Tushma.

"What are you doing?"

"I'm looking for you!" she squeaks in response.

"Have I taught you nothing? Are you predator or prey?"

Ani remains silent while furrowing her brow at him. An irregular coo coming from her left compels her to turn her head. She spots Ram aiding Fylorn through the crowd. They come up alongside her, putting the injured Hue shoulder to shoulder with her.

"We need to move," Ram breathes out. "I can't tell who is who in this size of a crowd."

"I couldn't agree more," Tushma spits out between his teeth while holding his glare on the young woman.

Moving as one, the group squeezes through the thickening crowd. A rising of shouts creates a pitch too loud for Ani to handle, forcing her to wince.

I have to keep my thoughts in order, or else I'll lose my mind and sprint away like some prey…

"What do you think is happening on the other side?" the young woman asks Fylorn.

He simply responds, "Could be anything."

"I saw the Legion holding up the road. What are we going to do when we get there."

"Get through."

"You don't sound like you care."

The young man's deep blue eyes strike at her, forcing a weight onto her unlike anything the shrieks of the mob ever could. "People don't hold me back."

Ani silently nods. She casts her sights ahead as they near the frontline of the conflict. In between the swinging arms and flailing scythes, she watches the soldier make a step forward. The glint of prepared spears shifts the flow of her blood. Quick solutions burst from the young woman.

"They're moving at us. Do we turn back? There has to be an alley–"

"Hold," Ram orders.

Tushma and Fylorn do as such, the resolve in their eyes is founded by the tight grip of their fists. Ani brings her full attention to the soldiers ahead. As they progress each step forward, the crowd around the young woman tightens.

Above Ani comes a wisp of spectral blue. She rapidly checks her arm but finds nothing. A wide berth of citizens opens, giving her a full view of the auragonic beast ahead of her.

A söcartya!

The vivid creature stands tall and lean, a proud defence against the astonished soldiers. Its predatory snout, striped fur, and hollow eyes make a ferocious display before it rears and bellows in its naturally wild laughter.

Two adamant soldiers lunge out, swiftly grasping onto a young man in soiled pants and a ragged shirt. The auragonic lashes out, clamping onto one Legion man's vambrace, drawing a scream of alarm from the soldier.

A thick hand grips Ani's shoulder. The gentle pull from it cut off her line of sight to the spectral beast, leaving only the screams of men to bloom her imagination. Sharp sounds of metal meeting cloth and flesh ignites the crowd into a panic. A wave of resistance surges forward, and the young woman moves with it. The power of the crowd swells and washes Ani along. She passes over the corpse of the young and ragged man, now housing a severed spearhead within his unarmoured chest.

The mass spreads into the street beyond, slowly thinning as they come to the following intersection. Dust swirls in the hollow plateau beyond. Ani twists her head to find any of the men, and quickly finds Fylorn leaning against the nearby dirty, stone wall. As the young woman arrives next to the injured man, so too does Ram and Tushma.

"Are you still bleeding?" Ani asks with a shake in her voice.

"They found their Taker," Fylorn utters in response.

"Yes, so let's get out of here while everything is settling down," Ram commands.

Ani looks to find Tushma's powerful blue eyes locked onto her. The whites of his eyes grow red as he holds the stare.

"I'm still here," she says.

The old man leans in to give the young woman a bear hug. He then keeps his arm around her while guiding them behind the other two who were already moving through the crowd. Robes and elbows splash upon the group as they slip between the flowing mass of people. Once they near the set of stairs, leading to a lower plateau, pockets of freedom begin giving them the space to move faster.

Even Fylorn is putting in the effort. I can't believe he's even moving at all; a wound like that should be keeping him on the ground. ...He never said why he's going. It's none of my business, but I do wonder what a man like that is up to. He has the clothes of a labourer, but the way he carries himself – the words he chooses to say – are something more. This, this is the kind of person I'm meant to save for Vihara, right? Or am I thinking about it completely wrong...

High in the sky, the fila had moved further to Ani's right, threatening to bring the day to a close. The edge of the taupe plateau slowly begins revealing the next street below as Ani approaches. A battered staircase at the peak lures her, but as she nears, the blackened face of a man brings her feet to a halt.

That soldier from the cart!

"The big man is back," Fylorn utters over his shoulder to the rest of the party.

"What is he doing?" Ram questions.

"Guiding his men to—"

The thick finger of the man shoots out directly at Ani. She takes a step back, believing herself to be fully shrouded by the robed citizens ahead of her.

"There!" the hulking man shouts. "Everyone to the stairs!"

After the bellow of the leading man, Ani has barely two breaths before a hail of arrows thump into the world around her. She looks aside to find Fylorn under Tushma's arm as they follow Ram laterally to a nearby alleyway. Men and women cry out in panic as the soldiers and raiders surge towards each other to try to apprehend the party first.

Ani's eyes widen while shrieks turn into blood filled gargles, and bodies fall to the dusty ground. One man, having an arrow pierced into his cheek, falls like a sack of grains and leaves one dead eye open to stare at the young woman. She hears a familiar groan ahead, and whipping her sights to the haven alley, Ani watches in time to see Tushma hold his right shoulder over the impact of an arrow while unintentionally dropping Fylorn.

Quickly pushing between two chaotic people, the young woman rushes ahead to her companions. As she reaches Tushma, Ram throws Fylorn over his shoulder before the party bring themselves past a putrid building reeking of rotting food.

Once inside of the alley, Tushma leans against a wooden wall to look at his fresh wound. The old man winces while his fingers gingerly explore the open fringes of the impact site. Ani hears Fylorn groan, then turns to see Ram putting him down to sit on the ground.

"What do we do now?" slips from her lips.

The three men all turn to her, then take the moment to sling weary glances at each other. Each bleak face builds upon the next as the party comes to a grim conclusion.

"Someone find me a bow and arrows," suggests Ram.

"We don't have much time," Fylorn says through his clamped jaw.

Ani swings her sights back to Tushma to find him holding the small knife he uses for hunting to try and dig around the arrowhead. His distorted face compels the young woman to look away.

I've done this. This is all my fault because I wanted to be some kind of hero, and now… and now everyone around me is paying that price.

She brings her hands up in front of her face. The grime from weeks of ranging along the old roads and through the wild forests brings her mind into a bitter rage.

I am an Anchor. I'm not some animal to be hunted, and I'm certainly not some trophy to be hung up. I will not allow this to be my fate!

The young woman's face hardens. She brings her glare around to face the Nhavyyet tending to his friend. Her fist balls and her eyes dart to the scar on her forearm.

"You need to get through that gate, and I'm going to make that happen."

Ram tilts his head.

Tushma sputters out, "What are you talking about, Ani?"

After a growling huff, Ani bolts from the safe alley back into the street. The citizens of Tombra finish scattering to find haven from the aggressive soldiers, giving her a clear path ahead. She targets the stairway and the growing mass of raiders preparing a full-scale invasion of the plateau. The young woman raises her arm high, then flexes to expel Ora from its wrest.

Every man and woman in the clearing stops to gawk at the event as a flying, spectral dragon manifests out from the young woman's arm. Ani locks eyes with the hulking man pushing himself through the crowd of mystified men.

"Ora, attack!" she orders.

The dragon rolls in the air, then flings a spectacular breath of electrical energy towards the pile of raiders. Ani sprints ahead, then leaps from the clear ledge, across the steep drop. As one foot lands on the stairs beyond, the other misses, throwing her into a tumble. Each crude hit of the roll down to the base of the descent hurts more than she's felt in a long while. Once on the solid ground below, she scrambles into a clamber ahead that becomes a frantic scamper away. Ani twists her neck to find Ora finishing her breath attack before running off the open edge into a glide below.

Such a vibrant blue emanates from the dragon's spread wings in such a grace the young woman nearly forgets what she's doing. As the feet of the spectral beast hit the ground, causing a plume of dust, it nudges its Anchor in between its wing and shoulder. A harsh burn assaults Ani's lungs as she charges ahead. The stale air of Tombra nearly chokes her. Each step she takes sends a jolt up her leg. She reaches out, grabbing a hold of an angular spike, then takes a leap.

Together, the dragon swings the young woman onto its back, and she gathers a hold. Nerves cascade across her body as the moment submerges her mind in a welcome euphoria. Every movement of the spectral beast courses through Ani. She gives one glance over her shoulder to spot the company of rotten men giving chase to catch her. A slight twang of pride washes over her as she sees that her plan was working.

At the intersection of streets, beyond a pile of carts, Ani's grip tightens as she watches Ora come to a head with a crowd of farming men moving their stock. She cries out, but the dragon hops overhead of the awe-stricken people. A waggle of its tail for balance disturbs the young woman, and she rolls off, plummeting onto a cart of red corn before landing in a mucky midsection of street.

Ani scrambles to her feet, trying to weave between the gathering, but it brings her pace to just shy of still. The young woman swiftly checks behind her to spot Ram walking a stumbling Fylorn in the far distance, towards the földic gate.

I did it!

The delight is short lived as the Legion men fill her view. Using her smaller stature, she manages to squeak through the farming men to the other side of the street. A brief moment of gulping down every breath she can gives her time to scan vastern.

I could make it, but where is Tushma?

Within moments, the farming men clear and she has a direct line of sight on the raiders as they come to the intersection. Her feet instantly begin moving her along the street, but her ears let her know it isn't enough. A whoosh of Ora returning causes a frantic shriek of grown men behind her. She peeks behind herself to check the situation, only to find a pack of free hounds leading a charge beyond the defending dragon.

The young woman swings her tired eyes ahead, bringing them to a fearsome sight. Bursting from a rickety shack on the ledge high alongside her, comes the same bear creature from the wilds outside Carcras. With a distinct rage, it dives from the height to land near Ani. The ground shakes as the beast makes contact. She falls to her scraped knees, sending familiar pains coursing through her. Lifting herself with her hands, the young woman bears witness to Ora swooping overhead the astonished raiders, twisting into a wisp and plunging itself into the bright wrest on her forearm.

Such a force knocks Ani over, but the bear's powerful grip snags her, throwing the young woman onto its back before storming to the end of the street. Amidst shouts and banging, the feral creature's deep voice grumbles out, "Hold on!"

The unnatural bass of the beast's words sends twangs of unease through Ani. She scrunches her face while the crescendo of wood being broken to bits blasts off around her. Her grip on two tufts of fur reaches a maximum, compelling her to open her eyes for what comes next. Ahead of her lies an endless expanse of rolling moors. A tranquil wind grazes her long hair before the distinct ruckus of the Legion on veteran hounds rips the delight of freedom from her.

Ani swings her shoulder around to face the taupe city hurtling away from her. The sight of Legion men slowly becomes a blur as nothing can stop the bear creature's supernatural race away from Tombra.

Chapter 15
The Tamer

Tushma's big foot kicks over the remnants of last night's fire. He groans, clenching his fist before bringing a delicate hand up to his shoulder where the wound from Tombra lingers. A sharp red circles the defiant puncture.

"We can take a longer break, Tushma. You could use the rest."

"We don't have that luxury."

To his credit, we've been just narrowly missing those huge forts they have placed near the roads.

The young woman tightens the drawstring of a mangled sack while staring at the ignorant man. She strides past the white embers to gather her drying shirt. "They haven't found us yet; we're nearly out of the forest."

"Uh huh," the old man utters.

"Tushma, we'll get you another spear. It's not that big of a deal–"

"You think I don't know that?" he barks, his tone rising.

Ani snaps right back, "Don't talk to me like that!"

A symphony of feral howling erupts in the distance. The young woman's eyes widen before finding Tushma.

Hellixes!

In a hush, he orders, "Run."

Ani's eyes dart to her satchel lying half-prepared upon the mossy rock.

"Run, damn it!" the old man doubles his volume.

Driving her heels into the loom below her, Ani sprints from where she stands. She aims herself towards the földic direction they have been travelling. Before the young woman can even make three steps, a band of Legion soldiers riding hellix mounts cross her trajectory. The sight of their silver armour emblazoned by the shadow of a dormant dragon immediately freezes her thoughts. Her legs ache while bringing her body to an immediate stop.

"Tushma!" she cries out.

One animalistic growl dominates the acoustics of the hollow trees around them. Ani glances over her shoulder to witness Tushma's skin peeling off. The hideous transformation from man to beast stills the air, letting a sharp chill creep in with the wind. His oversized hands commence shredding the loose covering to allow the immense, fur-covered creature out. As the old man's face elongates and his hips shift to facilitate the growing mass, Ani darts sideways to begin gaining some ground from the affair.

Behind the young woman, an orchestra of crunching bones and bloody screams sounds off. She takes a tailing check behind to secure her escape. The rapacious battle between the beast that is Tushma and the veteran hellixes brings Ani no joy to see. Swinging her sights back ahead alerts her to the coming tree. The young woman takes the brunt of the ancient wood to the shoulder, spinning to land on her knees. Without looking anywhere, she rises and tries to move forward once more.

Clanking of metal and shattering of bones grows nearer as her hobble slowly speeds into a run. Four arrows slam into the tree to the right-side ahead of her. The power behind the sticks of death is so grand the impact knocks the trunk backwards, creaking as the very limits of the wood are tested.

Days of avoiding roads and camps, only for those relentless Legion riders to always find us. It's like being in their house and they know every nook and shadow.

Suddenly a firm grip takes a hold of her shirt collar and lifts her up. Before Ani knows it, she's tossed onto the back of the massive bear creature. The increased gallop of Tushma in his wild form brings the world around the young woman into a blur. One of his huge paws pushes a leaning tree out of his way, but the jarring action leaves Ani unbalanced. The young woman is nearly tossed off of his back. A complementary sidelong tackle to the ribs of Tushma by a mounted hellix throws her into the air. The blade of the Legion soldier's spear grazes Ani's cheek. Her limp body rolls in the air, landing with a back crunching thump into a bramble of vibrant green growth. Without thought, she rises and begins sprinting to the perpetual bear creature.

Her breaths fail to catch up to her. Ani chokes, then stumbles. She watches as Tushma continues charging steadily ahead, in complete ignorance of her. A quick peek over her shoulder affirms the worst; other riders are making ground on them.

I can't keep going like this.

After a swift return to bolting between trees, she throws out her arm. Using only her mind, she calls upon Ora. The magnificent creature emerges from the illuminated scar on her forearm, extending each limb into a gallop forward. Ani watches hopefully as the spectral beast manages to match pace with her. Before the moment is over, Ora fully lengthens its wings, only narrowly missing the enclosing trees.

"Lower your wing!" Ani calls out to the dragon.

Without hesitation the beast obliges. Rendering her last bit of energy, Ani leaps atop the grown serpent, grasping on to any firm surface that will allow it. Finally, she holds a wisping spike in each hand before screaming, "We need to–"

Ora forces its wings down, bursting ahead into a glide, and nearly throwing Ani off. Before she can catch her breath amid the air screaming past her, the dragon rises even higher above the canopy of the forest. Rolling hills appear within the bright daylight in all directions. Ani doubles her grip, then leans over the side of the slim serpent body to scan the treetops below.

No! Tushma, where is he?

"We have to turn back!" she orders, her throat aching in pain whilst trying to reach volumes that surpass the winds cutting at her.

The beast makes no efforts to listen, nor to act accordingly. As a youngling's first time at flight, Ora soars. It twists and dives. Ani can feel a pleased humming coming from its mouth as it travels along its body.

"We have to turn back!" she calls aloud once more.

She notices the dragon tilt away from the forest they had come from, instead shifting its view to a distant city. Ani leans over to spy around the beast's long neck, finding the pile of Hue structures to be centered by a tower and surrounded in seemingly endless fields. The young woman turns her head back to the forest slipping away. She reaffirms her grip before attempting to manually yank the beast back towards the trees.

"Please, we can't leave. I need my satchel. And Tushma would come for us– He has come back for us!"

Ora tilts once again, revealing a commotion happening in the fields near the city. Massive war machines being marched by a formidable army.

They look familiar… The sleeping dragon! That's the Legion! What are they doing out here starting a war? Wait a moment.

Ani uses her entire bodyweight to swing the dragon, turning it around as Tushma had taught her to do on the hellix. Ora resists being guided, continuing a steady course towards the combat ahead.

Fine. Let's think rationally then. Tushma can handle himself, we were heading this way anyways, and if anything were to happen to him then he would be coming to a nearby city to rest up, right? Right. Right?

Her eyes drift down to the burn mark upon her forearm.

Right… What did that woman say again? I have to save someone to be worthy? Do I want to be worthy?

The young woman's eyes crawl to behind her once more. She feels a burning sensation trickle down her spine. Her face scrunches. A tear is ripped from her cheek and thrown away into the winds. The city ahead of her grows nearer. Sounds of a gruesome raid feel closer. She digs her fingers in tight around the bone handles upon Ora's back.

What's the harm?

Droplets of fledgling clouds mist the young woman on Ora's back as it weaves high and low. Her aching fingers continue their fierce grip as the majestic creature soars before plummeting into a dive. Squinting just enough to be able to see, Ani's heart lurches as the ground rapidly approaches. The dragon swiftly flips into a spiral, nearly tossing the young woman off.

"Don't throw me!" bursts from Ani.

The rhythmic humming from within the glowing beast slowly calms the young woman's nerves. Ora levels out for them to glide just above the jagged stones below. The lands ahead open wide into vast rows of nurtured grain and roots. She tilts her head to observe the vastern fields better, learning everything she can about the invading army as they approach.

Those small people aren't that small at all, they're giants!

She witnesses two beings, twice as tall as any man she has ever seen, toss massive boulders at the diminishing walls of the city. The pelting of stone upon stone delivers a splitting crack echoing out into the fields. A jarring twist of Ora brings the pair gliding long-side the event. The humming ceases as the dragon tightens its flight to bring them around to the other side of the city.

Ani is quickly brought to face the extending river and distant shore of a sea she's never seen before. The cutting winds leave her face chilled as Ora rises to match the height of the city's dominant tower. After circling, the young woman finally hears a thunderous chanting from far below. On further inspection she spots a wave of fleeing soldiers, running from her and the dragon.

Ora rapidly descents towards the burning fields being ravaged by the invaders, revealing them to be Legion units arriving. Once coming from the földic fields, Ani spots them preparing to shift from a general assault to direct combat with the flying beast. Her grip is challenged as Ora tilts right to avoid an incoming boulder. She loses one hand, nearly dangling along the dragon's side but kicks twice to find purchase on a now horizontal spike. The tilt reverts back to being level, throwing the young woman into a slide along the scaley back. Her dedicated hand swings her back into a familiar mount on Ora.

"Hold steady or warn me!" she calls out to the beast.

A wave of muscle shifting the scales lets Ani know that her words are finally heard. She tightens the push of her feet on wayward spikes, then raises her eyeline enough to witness the coming battlefield. A spattering of guarded soldiers stands awaiting the dragon's next action. With a subtle hum, a throbbing builds along the dragon's neck before releasing an onslaught of arcing electricity towards the Legion warriors.

Sparks hotter than any forge Ani had ever come across bounce along the neck of the rapidly moving serpent. Smoky, hot fumes encase the young woman, forcing her eyes closed. Eruptions of grounded energy nearly deafen her, but the firm grip of her hands retain their hold. Tears breach her clasping eyelids, flying off aimlessly behind her. The final touches of heat pass her forehead, enticing her to open her eyes.

Her heart leaps out of her chest at the image of a small mountain hurtling through the air at her. A forced pull drags Ani from the trajectory, leaving her to helplessly watch on as the mound of stone pummels into the city's wall. The splashing of chipped stone in all directions causes another bout of agonizing screams to chorus across the fields. As fast as they move from their path, Ora brings them back on their approach. With the power of a god, the dragon opens its wings to bring itself to an early halt. The braking of speed allows the beast to comfortably snag one of the siege towers with its rear claws.

In a stupendous heave, Ani feels Ora lurch upwards while holding onto the machine of war. A whirlwind of arrows being fired upon them narrowly miss the young woman, bouncing from the dense spectral scales all around her.

"What are you doing? Drop it!" Ani orders her auragonic.

The dragon flaps its wings in a fierce rage. It climbs steadily up into the lowest reaching clouds.

"Drop it!" the young woman calls out again.

A crunching of claws being removed from the wooden siege tower brings Ani some relief, but the following screams of men still inside forces a different feeling to streak through her. She yanks upon the spikes she holds, this time averting the grand serpent to turn back down towards the falling machine of war. Ora sets off into a streamlined dive behind the machine. While racing, the air burns Ani's face as they leave the wet clouds. Soon the pair's speed outmatches the falling tower, and they find themselves buffeted by powerful winds.

What can I do? We can't stop it... Or hold it, without killing me. Are they even good men? Are they worth saving?

Ani's eyelids flicker while Ora takes course. The dragon brings them under the falling device, flicks her tail, then darts ahead. Twisting her head, the young woman watches helplessly as the war machine smashes into the ground like an egg into a frying pan. Bits of metal and wood explode out, pelting the field with debris.

While returning her eyes ahead, Ani spots a blazing farm field beyond the grand walls defending the city. She narrows her gaze to find a small family attempting to hold their own against a battalion of the invaders. With unbridled gusto she yanks the spikes towards the farm. Ora tilts as she is instructed, bringing their elevation into an easing trajectory.

One older man, the father. Five – no! – six young children, most barely able to hold their axes... Where is the mother?

Scanning the burning fields surrounding the family garners no answers for Ani. She braces her face as Ora brings them in low for a landing. The impact of the dragon's feet upon the soft soils spits out collateral debris towards the humble farmhouse beyond. A warped wisp of Ora's spectral blue shifts and flows before returning to its body.

The young woman shakes her head before sliding off, glancing towards the family while absorbing the full experience of standing upon solid ground. After slinging an authoritative glance to Ora, she charges towards the farming father.

"Are you alright?" she shouts ahead of herself, settling into a confident tone. "I saw the Legion approaching."

"We can't find mother…" one small voice calls out.

Neither can I.

"It's okay–"

"Is it?" the father shrieks. "What is that thing you're riding?"

Ani quickly snaps her head back at Ora, half expecting to see a nightmarish beast befitting the wilds. Standing with its chest puffed and chin high, the dragon never looked more majestic. The young woman squints at the infant serpent that she had been caring for, finding it no longer existed. She has now become the guardian of a divine monster.

"It's called a dragon!" Ani proclaims before returning her sights to the family in time to spot the filed battalion crossing through the smoke and breaching the closest field. "Get inside or run to the city!"

The frozen clumping of people do no such thing. She bolts ahead, snatching the bow from the eldest boy's hands before shoving them out of the way. With one quick draw she nocks an arrow, then sends it into a leading soldier.

"I said move!" Ani bellows to the people.

Clouds of static touch the nape of her neck while Ora saunters over top of her. She can feel the energy course through her auragonic just before it releases a slew of lightning upon the invaders. Ani stands angled with the bow in hand as she watches the men fall. The moment comes to a screeching halt when the dragon rears back while reaching the end of its breath. A unanimous roar of the Legion doubling their efforts precedes the flood of men charging over their charred comrades to continue the battle at hand. A chill flushes the nerves along the young woman's body. She goes to turn when another screech is heard, an avian one.

Angling her sights, Ani witnesses a blue cloud gliding across the skies above. The cloud tilts to reveal itself to be a spectral bird bearing a rider. Blue hues reflect from the creature as it dives into the battlefield ahead of the young woman. In an instant she sees the spirit impale a soldier with its beak, then rip it crudely in half before soaring away.

A hellix bearing a Legion soldier atop its back bolts from a gathering of men towards the young woman and the hesitating family. She charges sideways into the group to corral them towards the farmhouse. The mass rushes off, but the youngest girl trips. Ani leans down to scoop her up while running, bringing the girl with her as they flee to safety.

As they reach the fringes of the simple door to their home, Ani ushers them inside before turning back to face the coming threat. Her eyes track to Ora, preparing another breath attack, but land on a rogue man sprinting through the field.

He's not Legion.

The long, dark hair of the man flows behind him as he sprints towards the coming hellix and rider. Flawlessly he flings a dagger ahead of himself. Ani watches as the grin of the Legion man fades, blood spilling from the fresh hole within his side. As agile as any beast of the wilds, the dark-haired assailant leaps to tackle the man from his mount. In a flash, the hellix halts, spinning to face its attacker. The dark-haired man flips from rolling, with the now dead legion man, in time to catch the pouncing hound. Holding the beast in his left hand, the man inserts a dagger held within his right into his prey's neck. While the life is drained from the hellix, Ani witness's blue wisps flow out of the carcass and swirl around the man's hand before seeping into him.

A line of Legion men enters her sights, keeping her blind to the events beyond. She flutters her eyes as the approaching soldiers become an immediate threat. The smell of day's long war reeks from the well-armoured men. Each step they take forwards stirs up dust from the dry soils below. Ani flings her sights towards Ora, hoping the dragon is aware of the pending danger. A clawed paw extends in a crushing sweep across the outer line of Legion men. Some bother to look, while others keep their focus on the young woman. As Ani slowly backs away to give herself some room, a few men trip, sliding away into the field beyond. Then more stumble and yelp, until finally the closest soldiers are halted before the young woman. Thick, reaching vines both green and slimy wrap themselves around the Legion men. The undeniable hue emanating from the plant-like appendages pulses before bringing the men to the ground, then swiftly drags them away.

The view of the battlefield opens wide for the young woman. She gazes on in awe while an oversized amphibian creature with a highly mineralized exoskeleton stomps across through the remaining soldiers. A bright aquamarine hue that radiates from the beast is intercut by shoots of steam being released between the ridges of its carapaces. The oversized chelae on its two large front limbs snap and pinch at the fleeing men. Ani tilts her head while trying to process it hopping on thick, back legs while two more medium limbs reach out on surfaces to aid versatility.

Smoke fumes the skyline in all directions. She looks in a full circle at the destruction around her. Her eyes land upon the deep oranges glowing. The remnants of fires, now fragile and turning into a crumbling ash.

"Kindly crossed."

Alongside the soft and effeminate words touching her ears, a firm yet almost familiar hand lands on her shoulder. Being completely ripped from the moment, Ani jerks her head and shoulder away to find a hearty woman rearing her hands in response.

"I apologize; I didn't mean to startle you."

The young woman's face crinkles while rescinding to emotions. She looks on at the hearty woman, forcing a smile.

"Not at all," Ani cracks out before clearing her throat to continue, "Are the family– Is your family fine?"

"My family?" the hearty woman questions with a rise of her cheeks. Her tone drops into a smooth drawl, "Not sure who you're speaking of, we only saw you and your dragon out here, lovely."

Ora!

Ani wildly searches the battlefront, trying to find her auragonic.

"Settle," the hearty woman coos while taking a soft hold of Ani's wrist. "It went back to its home, trust me."

After an involuntary eye twitch the young woman blurts out, "Who are you?"

A twinkle cuts across the hearty woman's eye as she responds, "Call me Zeela."

"Alright, Zeela. What happened?" Ani begins thrusting her hands out in varying directions while spouting off, "Who were the other people here? Were they Anchors? Are you the farmer's wife? Where were you? Why are the Legion attack– Is!?! Why is the Legion attacking?"

The limp arms of the young woman bring her hands into a sad clap upon her sides. Her tired eyes begin to sink to the ravaged soils below but are quickly drawn to the bright green vines twisting themselves around the hearty woman's leg. The plant creature lingers before plunging through her dirty green pants. As the vibrant hue dissipates, Ani drags her eyes up to find a wide and welcoming smile emanating from the Anchor standing before her. Zeela then wraps an arm around the young woman, cautious at first in a subtle request, then tight and warm.

"Yes, well, out here we are called Tamers. Which brings me to my question…" The hearty woman curls her short black hair back behind her ear while swinging around to look Ani in the eye. "Where did you come from, lovely?"

Zeela's eyes snap from the young woman to out behind her. Ani turns to find three others approaching the pair. The man with long, dark hair rides atop his newly received hellix spirit alongside a shorter woman with sharp eyes and rosy cheeks. She chatters with the older looking man on her other side. He bears a lanky frame, and makes no effort in hiding his tall ears protruding from his shaggy, grey hair. Behind him waddles the oversized amphibian beast.

"What's her name?" the short one calls out.

The hearty woman grins. "You know, I haven't asked yet."

"Ani," the young woman pipes in.

"Ani?" the long-haired man confirms. "How did you get an Ardaelius-damned dragon for an auragonic?"

Auragonic... So Tushma did know some things. Tushma... I can only imagine what happened to him. I have to go back, but... Just me? I can't even control my spirit yet... my auragonic.

"It's a long story." As Ani's words end, the four look at her awaiting the young woman to continue. She drifts her sights from one to the next until cracking a small grin. "I can tell you all about it if you bring me to Millown."

Chapter 16
The Inheritor

The stacks of wooden and clay homes atop one another always remind me of the ant colonies I would study as a child. On the mainland it makes sense, only together are we strong enough to survive the nights, but out here on the Vastern Isles… it doesn't seem necessary.

"I know you aren't fond of this many people, Fylorn," Ram pipes in. "I mean, Galiram is starting to feel as busy as Oldston."

"When have you been to Oldston?"

"I read."

Fylorn gives one long chuckle.

"You might not be as interested in the world, worrying about being the next great archaeologist and all, but some of us like to think that one day we'll get to go see it."

The archaeologist locks his eyes onto the massive dome structure ahead. He can see two of the three large archway doors he knows it to have. Most of the plaza surrounding the monument is filled by pods of people gossiping or trading.

"I hope so too," Fylorn utters.

He spots a grand gathering outside of the nearest doorway. Gracefully, he slips between robes of silk and velvet to find a suitable vantage point. At first, he spies the

head of a tall Wöllralt woman, dressed in pointed robes of
blue and black, then her companions appear between a
break in the crowd. An older Hue man among them strides
ahead to grasp at the forearm of a working woman passing
by. Fylorn approaches in time to hear his words.

"Kindly crossed, m'lady. My name is Shulath. If you
have the moment, I am distraught. I have searched this great
city and have yet to find a House of Ardaelius. I love
Ardaelius, and I believe you should as well. And Ardaelius
loves death – loves it – so, I say we build a church for her
right here in Galiram. The church will need sacrifices of
course, but I expect that can be taken care of." The woman
fights to get away from the man, then storms away while
clutching her forearm. Shulath proceeds to scan the crowd
around him before continuing his plea. "There are many
people in Galiram; few more important than Ardaelius. No?
Well, I propose this then. For everyday there isn't a church, I
will be performing the sacrifices regardless. I do hope you
change your mind. Bloody streets are a nuisance to citizens.
Oh well."

Fylorn feels a hand grace his shoulder, a familiar
Nhavyyet hand. "What have you found here, my friend?"

"It appears to be some Ardaelic cultists."

"Cultists? All the way down here? Curious..." Ram's
eyes wander off to a pair of slender women entering the
archway.

"Faith spreads."

"Yes, shall we spread ourselves into The Hex now?"

The archaeologist cracks a grin at his companion. As he
strides around the clumping people, he hears a new uproar
emerge, coming towards the group.

*Animalistic shrieks and growls, though they definitely sound
like men and women.*

Fylorn cocks his head to find a band of women breaching through the crowd. Each are covered in sky blue paint across their faces and shoulders, while the remainder of their body carries loose wrappings of the same colour.

The Blue Sisters, I'm surprised it took them this long to arrive.

The leading sister among them, having a fully shaved head bearing ornate earrings of silver arrows, comes within steps of Shulath.

"You heathens shall leave at once!"

Her shrill voice cuts the idle chatter of the plaza. Even Ram returns his attention to the religious affair. Fylorn's eyes dart between the two disciples of faith.

Shulath strikes a grin, revealing his sheer white, but crooked teeth. "Vihara believes herself to be all-powerful, and yet, is not within the cycle of life and death."

The remainder of the cultists line up beside the man. Fylorn spots Hue men and women, the Wöllralt, and a dark haired Vidicai among them.

Even an Ostit stands for Ardaelius; I hadn't dared to imagine someone among the Pajiado would rally against Vihara, but these are the times we are in.

Better times are coming.

"Did you see that half-breed?" Ram whispers.

Fylorn throws a look over his shoulder, then slowly nods in confirmation to his companion. Returning his gaze ahead he finds the Blue Sisters assembling to establish an intimidating presence.

"This Ardaelic brotherhood is not welcome in Galiram. There is no House, and there shall never be, understand this," the leading sister proclaims.

The cultists remain still.

"Are they not scared?" Ram injects. "They are outnumbered more than twice, and that's before the people of Galiram get involved."

"I don't know much about Ardaelic beliefs. But, from what I've heard, they fear nothing; for life means they can act for their goddess and death is also in service to her."

A heavy breathing crawls out from the Nhavyyet. His hand lands on Fylorn once more. "Let's get going. Isn't your sister waiting for you?"

She has no idea that I'm coming. I would have had to send word, and Ram has been with me the entire...

"Yes, let's move along."

The pair shuffle between the wavering citizens in front of The Hex's grand entryway. As they approach, the crowd thins out until a team of guards stands at a defensible point. Fylorn can feel the energy exuding from Ram fall away while leaving the plaza, but rise once more at the sight of the metal plated men. The archaeologist adjusts into a strong posture and slides into a stride of ease. A hint of delicate music touches his ears from within the dome.

Ahead of reaching the guards, Fylorn announces himself, "Kindly crossed, men. My name is Fylorn Dagus and I am here to see Iyalla, wife to Rahnarn of Vheer Graveford."

Deep blue eyes within each silver helm lock onto Fylorn. None of the men move, but before the moment has passed, one speaks out in a gravelly voice, "Iyalla's brother? She hasn't spoken of a brother, prove it."

A sweat builds up as the base of the archaeologist's neck. His eyes wander while trying to produce the best way of explaining his relation to Iyalla.

I could explain how she looks, but anyone could do that. Maybe explain something from our childhood, but how could some guard verify such a piece of information?

The enthusiastic voice of Ram chimes in, "She has red leaf tea every night precisely between filafall and midnight. The same red tea that her and her mother would have before she passed."

A sea of blue targets Ram. Fylorn can feel his companion flinch at the stiff judgement upon him.

"I fail to believe that you," the guard stops to look the Nhavyyet up and down, "are the brother to the Lady Iyalla."

"He grew up with us, as a brother," Fylorn explains. "In some ways she probably knows him better than I."

A snort shoots from the guard before one another among the line up speaks, "I have not heard her speak of her mother before, however I do know that she takes a tea in her room – in private – every night. And… the man does seem to look akin to her."

Various helms among the guard turn to look upon their peer. No words are spoken as all slowly return to their statuesque post.

The guard continues, "If what you say is true, then I will allow you in, under the condition that I will first consult with the lady to find the truth. Inside you will have to wait under watchful eyes."

Reflexively, Fylorn replies with a silent nod. The guard breaks from his post, stepping back to allow the pair through. As they follow the walking silver armour, Fylorn casts a look behind them to spot the hole being compensated for as the guards realign. The rising of delicate music draws his attention forward once more while his view is filled by stone pillars larger than two sailing ships.

Such a structure could not be made by the Hue. Someone paid for the Pajiado to make this. Gods, I feel like every time I come back here I notice something new about the place– though it's not fresh additions, but rather my sight has changed.

You should appreciate having a more powerful perspective.

"How long has it been since you were last here, Fylorn?" Ram asks.

"Quite a while, I believe just after I sold the manor off."

"Oh, to come tell Iyalla?"

"I may have left that bit out."

The Nhavyyet releases a deep laughter that echoes around the reaching heights of the hallway. A strict glance comes from the guard that quells the joy on sight. Choking pathways ahead of them brings the short walk to an end as they are treated to the vast arena inside. The rising circle of benches for seating around the sporting dome end just below the balcony of which the guard has brought them to.

Fylorn moves to lean on the railing, allowing himself a full view of the event within. Bathing in hot fila light is a stone-floored theater of combat. Multiple voices of guards exchanging words trickle in from the corner of the balcony, but the archaeologist remains focused on the arena.

I'm out in the open, simply watching the event. I can't imagine they'll think I'm up to anything. Besides, I have nothing to hide.

We only have things to discover.

"Ram?" Fylorn calls. He quickly shifts his glance to catch his companion slide up to the railing beside him. "Quite the show they have today."

His gaze falls back to the combat taking place down within the arena center. A hexagonal arrangement of walls creates a dynamic field of battle for the fighters. Within the borders are a host of medium to neck high walls set in an almost floral pattern to keep the event tense amidst the hunt.

Barbaric? On one hand, yes, having man hunt down man is quite uncivilized. But, on the other bloody hand is history telling us that real barbarians simply fought in open fields beating each other to death. No games, no entertainment. So, which is worse?

"You think that hulking raider would do well in here?"

"I try not to think about him," Fylorn quickly responds.

"Oh, come on. You took that punch like a true warrior."

"And I'll do it again," the archaeologist jokes with a half-hearted chuckle.

"Have you heard of any Butchers coming from The Hex lately? I feel like it's been a while since I've heard of a real animal in here."

Fylorn sharpens his eyes on the combatants circling within the pitch. One in particular catches his attention, a Hue man. His stark white robes dangle to touch the stone ground as he crouches behind a chin-high wall. With expert precision he jabs his dagger held hand around the corner to open another man's throat. A weak scream precedes a gurgle of crimson spilling.

"Did you see that!" Ram shouts while slapping Fylorn on the shoulder.

"I did," Fylorn calmly confirms. "The man didn't even get blood on his robes."

The Nhavyyet flicks his chin ahead before toting, "Yeah, those white robes, do you know what that means?"

"Not really?"

"He's an assassin."

Unconsciously, the archaeologist flips his hands while shaking his head in a mildly confused response.

"I read," Ram cracks out.

Fylorn rolls his eyes before fixating his view on the event once more. He spots a swift blur. Tracking it brings his sights a young girl leaping over one of the hip-high walls without touching it. Her light brown, sleeveless coat plumes while airborne. The hood upon it flies back, revealing hair whiter than the assassin's robes.

White hair for someone so young? And those ears...

She's Pajiado.

Her agile stride brings her towards a one-on-one fight of strength going on between a Vidicai and a Hal-Vagenkar over a nasty looking polearm already dripping blood from it. She slides under the pair, then rolls out of sight. Fylorn scans every angle he can. Finally, he finds her approaching the white assassin. As she slows her run into a hunter's stalk, Fylorn notices the robed man playing with her. After lobbing a stone to distract her, he slips around to a wall alongside her, waiting to strike. Even at this distance, Fylorn can see the young girl twitch her index finger.

The firm hand of Ram slaps the archaeologist's shoulder once again. "My friend, the assassin has her! How did she even get in this fight? How did he? This is wild!"

Fylorn feels a grin about to naturally creep onto his face from the infectious joy, but the young girl's hesitant step steals the entirety of his attention. He holds his breath as she swishes her foot in front of her, seemingly moving debris or loose soils. Then her hands snake out to make a twisting of fingers upon her chest before she falls backwards and disappears. A thunderous roar nearly shakes the foundation of The Hex. Fylorn closes one eye while verging on covering his ears. His open eye locks on to the assassin to find even he is startled, snapping his head up and around at the booming excitement.

As the archaeologist opens both eyes, he witnesses the young girl re-appear behind the assassin. An anomalous blurring of the space around her warps Fylorn's mind. She reaches her hand out and pulls the man back in before disappearing once more. The air stills within the arena. Even the music quells as the moment lingers. With a pitiful thump, the body of the assassin falls limp upon the centerfold stone slab. A steady stream of blood pours from the decapitated gape. Then, less than a breath later, the young girl reveals herself from around a wall while holding the man's head high for all to see. The overwhelming sounds of cheering along with Ram's tight squeeze nearly break Fylorn. Holding a stoic posture with one hand covering an ear supports him through the ordeal. Though, even as he withstands the experience, he still carries a wide smile to look at Ram's matching expression.

His turned gaze catches sight of a waving hand from the guard at the deep end of the balcony. Fylorn heeds the beckon, and upon arriving next to the guard, the cheering ceases.

"Your sister has asked for me to bring you to her," the guard shouts. "Just you."

Fylorn casts a glance at Ram, still enjoying the remaining combat within the arena. The armoured gauntlet of the guard touches Fylorn's shoulder.

"He can stay. She said she remembers him, and is providing him with suitable comforts," the guard assures the archaeologist, before pulling upon him.

As he leaves the balcony, Fylorn watches a platter of meats and cheeses be brought towards the Nhavyyet. Once inside of the long, darkened hallway the noise returns to the subtle instrumental from before.

"He'll ask where I went," Fylorn says.

The guard remains silent while escorting the archaeologist through a set of doors, past an office of financial accounting, and then to a stairwell of Pajiado crafted stone.

Remarkable work. Living around this all the time must make one numb to it.

"What did she say about me?"

The silent silver helm snaps over his shoulder before ascending the stairs. His heavy armour resounds up the spiral steps. Fylorn bunches his lips before following. At the top the guard awaits him.

"She seemed confused, but excited," the silver helm utters before elevating his volume, "Go to that door across from the sailing ship painting. She'll be inside."

Fylorn sets his sights down the bright passage. Only the floor on this level is made of the same exquisite stone as below, whereas fine timber planks comprise the well-decorated walls. Pits of flame centering the floor deliver a comfortable heat as well as the adequate lighting. He gives a quick nod while looking ahead before moving past the flickering wisps until reaching the grand painting.

From the floor to the ceiling, quite a mural. Tens of well laboured ships...

He lets out a huff before turning to the metal reinforced door from the guard's instruction. Out of habit he knocks thrice upon the door. The cold steel against his knuckles calls on an ancient memory from when he lived at the manor.

"Fylorn?" the elegant tones of his sister's voice call out from within. "Come in."

Fylorn pulls upon the iron lever and lets himself through the door. Inside, a bath of warm light covers an elongated table with two sets of dinner steaming at the ready. At one end, nearing the far window, sits Iyalla. The dark brown grace of her extensive dress reaches well beyond the table's width. Her long hair absorbs any light touching it while maintained in a tightly pinned up bun. A cheery smile thins her sharp chin.

"Time has left you be, I see," Fylorn enunciates.

She allows one soft purr of laughter before rising from her seat. "Please," she emits while extending her hand to the other end of the table prepared for dining.

After the archaeologist closes the door behind him, he slides over to the masterfully crafted wooden chair blooming with cushion. He eyes the carefully founded hearth, hosting a modest flame, set on his side of the room. Taking his seat puts his sights directly down the length of the table to Iyalla.

Her sapphire eyes blink twice before she speaks, "I didn't expect you. Hasn't the dig site been keeping you busy?"

Fylorn feels the twang of a crooked smile pull on his face while dropping his eyes to the feast below his mouth. A slow hand reaches for the glistening fork waiting for him. "I did not expect to be coming this way for some time, but – as usual – life brings me on its strange journey."

"As usual, indeed," Iyalla replies.

He raises his sights to match his sister's. "I– How have you been?"

Iyalla's smile weakens while her eyes drop slightly then return to his, baring her passionate resolve. "Better, and better again. Life has been more kind to me than time. Rahnarn has done everything in his power to keep me comfortable–"

"Good!" Fylorn blurts out.

"Yes, quite… good." Iyalla shifts in her seat, then gathers her fork to begin eating. Before the moment of silence draws too long, she asks, "What is it you want to say?"

The fork in Fylorn's hand drops as his grip loosens, making a hideous screech upon hitting the porcelain plate. A slight quiver pulls on his cheek. His burning eyes rise once again to find his sister's indifferent gaze.

"What makes you think I have something to say?"

"Is it money?"

"Do not try to get a rise out of me, Iyalla."

"Did the coin from the manor finally fade away?"

Fylorn swallows hard.

"I see," she concludes. "Well, is it finally time for you to come under the vheer of Graveford? No need to marry, we haven't the traditions as other vheers. Though, we may host a celebration."

"Iyalla…" Fylorn weakly interjects.

"Yes," she quickly responds, then stills for him to have her full attention.

"I have already answered this before."

"Life may have changed your answer."

"It hasn't"

"Fylorn, you are all that remains of what was our Vheer."

"And?"

"And why are you holding on to it? Furthermore, why have you come all this way – abandoning whatever it was that you were toiling over – to simply see your long-forgotten sister?"

"Can I not come visit you now?"

"There is nothing within my life that will ever hinder you coming to spend time with me. Absolutely nothing."

Iyalla firmly returns to her dinner. Fylorn pinches his lips together before gently placing his utensil upon the immaculate wood of the table. He carries a breath into the next moment before bolstering his sensibility.

"I wish for you to speak truthfully to me," he states. "When you were passed off as some piece of meat, I lost my sister and Vheer Dagus 'Gained' an asset. I sold the manor so that I could make something of myself, Iyalla. That place will always be our home, regardless of whoever lives within it."

"No one does, since you left. It sits empty."

"How do you know?"

"I asked my darling husband to purchase it."

The air rests so thick and still that only the flickering of the hearth behind Fylorn threatens to cut it. His nose raises into a snarl while words begin knocking at the door of his mouth. One carefully released breath retrains his tongue enough to allow one quick statement.

"It will always be the house of Dagus."

"As of right now, it is a hollow reminder," Iyalla strikes back.

"I…" Fylorn's face furrows.

"Perhaps we should go attend the event?" the elegant woman's sharp eyes wander along the spread of food placed before her. "My appetite has been playing children's games with me as of late."

"No." The archaeologist finally composes himself to construct a sentence to his liking, "I didn't come here from the dig site. I have found news which I elected to come share with you."

Her chin raises while her eyes perk up to match her brother's.

Fylorn continues, "I found the symbol of Vheer Dagus within Nhavyyet ruins; somewhere it shouldn't be."

Iyalla's breathing slows while she digests the words.

"I may not have always been the most studious of young men, but this is no apology. I find myself coming to ask for your mind. I come here from the manor, Iyalla. I was just there, at that poor dilapidating home of ours. I found one of the old tomes that Father would hide from us with secret words. Do you remember the whispers he would make in the cellar?"

"Yes," Iyalla immediately, but absent-mindedly, responds.

"I found them. Those ruins told me what to say, and then went inside. I opened those papers covered in our blood's name to find that it is not just I who is owed, Iyalla. Our whole bloodline, each and every one of us is bearing the weight of a debt left unpaid. Do you hear me?"

"Fylorn, this is my family now and you should—"

The archaeologist's tone rises to heights and depths, "My name is Fylorn Dagus, and I will reclaim our family's honour."

As the final word leaves him, Fylorn finds himself heaving on each breath while standing from his seat resting a bright red fist next to his displaced fork. Both sibling's eyes cut to the door as a silver powerhouse forces himself into the room. The reinforced steel upon the wood rings out across the wall from the energetic swing.

"My lady," bursts from the guard.

Iyalla bolts up from her seat to raise a hand towards the defending man. "Please, it was nothing more than heated debate. Please."

The man's shoulders drop while his hand relaxes from its sword hilt post. Cold sweat builds on the nape of Fylorn's neck as the silver helm turns to him.

"Would you like me to stand guard within the room, my lady?"

"No," Iyalla orders while subtly shaking her head. "I am fine– We are fine."

"As you wish," the man states, then removes himself from the room.

An aggressive click of the shutting door resets the room from its high emotions back to a weak fluttering of eyes and tapping of fingers. Fylorn finally speaks, "I am sorry."

He watches a faint smile cross his sister's face before she utters, "Rahnarn ensures I am quite comforted."

"I see…" the young man reaches within his mind to find the words that will take him from this moment into one of more fitting, but none come.

"I… wasn't aware the manor was in such a state."

"Yes, well… neither was I."

She hums before intrigue envelopes her voice, "You said we are owed something? What is it?"

"I don't know," Fylorn explains. The growing disinterest in Iyalla's eyes spark the words within him. "The papers, I lost them on the way here. I wished for you to see them. They spoke of the Gods owing us. Someone, some Dagus, made a deal with them. It was unclear who made the deal with which god, what the deal was, or even when."

"I can't see it being our parents."

"Me either." Fylorn taps his thumbs upon the table, then twists his head. "You don't remember anything? Nothing Father told to you, even in tales before bed? Maybe Mother said something in passing?"

Iyalla draws in a deep breath while her nose wanders, then explodes, "No, no, but I do remember them talking about going to see the seer."

"The seer?"

"Yes, the seer of Úlcida, just on the other Vastern Isle. Those hill people, the Pajiado. Plenty of people go see them to speak with their seer about Vihara."

"Vihara..."

"I mean, we have plenty of faith around Galiram, but if I was to ask anyone about the Gods, it would be the seer."

"If you were?"

She tilts her head, pursing her lips. "Fylorn... I can't."

A wave of heat covers the archaeologist; not from the hearth, but from within. His thumb tapping returns, but slow and powerful.

"Listen. I will make sure it's done. Pay for your travels to the seer, and supply you with whatever you need. I want to know what this is about. I'll do it from my own pocket too, I have coin all my own from some witty investments – you would have loved to see how those Nhavyyet – ...I'm getting off topic–"

The bright sapphire eyes of the elegant woman cast a gaze at Fylorn that brings him out of the moment. She brings him right back to being the boy who would take her favourite stuffed bear, just to return the lost comfort, so he could feel her gratitude for being a big brother.

His slow head nod turns into humble words, "Passage to the seer would be lovely, thank you."

She beams a bright smile towards him, then says, "You know, you don't have to leave right away. You and Ram can stay for days, a week even! I'll be glad to host you."

"I mustn't grow too accustomed to this life," he chuckles. "How about we talk about all of this..." Fylorn waves his hands about while grinning.

"Ask me anything, what do you want to know?"

The siblings gossip back and forth about for the following hours while finishing the meal. After detailing

where he and Ram can stay, Fylorn leaves for the night only
to find the Nhavyyet passed out amidst a pile of empty wine
and ale bottles on the balcony. He beckons a guard to assist,
and they bring him back to their humble room for the night.
As time wears on, the archaeologist lies awake, ruminating
about the seer to the sounds of Ram snoring.

Chapter 17
The Successor

A brisk morning fog dampens Fylorn's face as the small sailing vessel docks along a stone pier. The clean stone of Pajiado crafting displays the algae-green tinge of its age. Once down the quarterdeck ramp, Fylorn and Ram watch as the boat's captain putters around doing routine work. The pair reflexively scan around themselves to only find white and grey in all directions. Soon, they surrender and follow the instructions that Iyalla had given them to simply stick to the one trail up into the hills. The unwavering fog keeps the men from knowing how far they have gone, or where the water was in any given direction. The march retains a crisp morning silence until Ram eventually finds something to talk about.

"You think your sister sent us away so that she would never have to see us again?"

Fylorn shakes his head before breaking into a small chuckle.

"I'm serious!" The Nhavyyet leans into the joke while laughing along. "If I were her, and I know us, I would have sent us to some backwater island with 'The Legendary Four-armed Rat Demon' just to see what would happen."

"This is why people don't come to you for help."

"Well, that was uncalled for. I happen to be highly requested among… people."

"Uh huh."

The wind shifts, thinning the fog, and reveals the rising emerald hills of the island. Nestled up within the highest peaks is a village of expanding rings. Fylorn extends his arm to find it to be about the size of his hand from where the pair stand.

"Not much further," he announces.

"What makes you say that?" Ram asks.

"I just checked."

"I can see it's right there, what does your hand measurement mean?"

"Look, I know you and your underground senses can probably tell me how many people are up in the village, so just let me."

Ram grins. "It's twelve."

Fylorn rolls his eyes, then marches ahead.

"What?" Ram shouts ahead. "You know I can't walk as fast as you, get back here."

"The twelve villagers and I will wait for you when I get there."

"My friend!"

The pair make the remainder of the climb up the growing incline of the trail. As they approach the outlying steps of the village Fylorn spots two majestic carvings of dragons posted on either side of the open gate.

"Dragons… That's a good sign," Ram considers aloud.

"My question is why do they have a gate if it's always open, or do they know we're coming?"

"They probably saw us from afar."

Fylorn turns to his companion. "In this fog?"

The Nhavyyet stops in his tracks, then raises his hand to point. Fylorn twists his head back to see a spattering of figures standing along rising ledges looking down on the two men.

Six– no eleven… oh, more. Lots more than twelve. All wearing sleeveless coats of leather, some have fish-scale armour pieces, at least I think it's from fish. Red hair, long noses, and pointed ears.

"Pajiado…" Fylorn utters.

"I think they heard us coming," Ram quietly remarks.

Fylorn back hands the Nhavyyet upon the shoulder before speaking aloud for the villagers to hear. "My name is Fylorn. I've come here to speak with the seer, your seer."

"I think they know who you're talking about."

"Then one of them should respond, no?"

A clapping noise echoes from beyond, drawing Fylorn's sights to the massive central staircase that runs up through the numerous plateaus beyond.

Each ring of the village carries a set of Pajiado-crafted structures, not unlike those made in Galiram.

His eyes catch fields of taraxacum growing in the distance before landing on the source of the noise. One sole Pajiado loudly walks down the steps towards him while all the others remain stoic. This one man in particular, holding a spear in one hand while extending a flat hand with the other, glares upon Fylorn. His fiery and angular eyes speak a thousand words while he strides forwards.

"Kindly crossed, my name is Fylorn–"

"Master Fylorn," the Pajiado man's voice strikes out, "What brings you here?"

"Uh," the archaeologist's mouth fumbles until it finds words, "I have come to see the seer."

The Pajiado's face remains firm. His long nose, angled brow, and long ears form an arrow. "What business do you have with her?"

"I have come to ask what she knows about Vihara, about the Gods, and my family history."

A small rain begins to spit upon the village. All of the stoic men and women shift their eyes above, then towards the central man. Fylorn feels the chilling liquid grace the back of his head, but continues to lock his eyes ahead. The Pajiado man lowers the base of his polearm to place the end on the mud ground below. He closes his eyes, then drops the weapon upon the ground.

"You are to be judged, Vihara calls for it."

"Just what we're looking for," Ram mutters before walking ahead.

A sudden flexing of each villager urges Fylorn to respond, "He is to come with me! Where I go, he goes."

"So it shall be!" a musically effeminate voice reaches out from the highest ring of the village. The elder Pajiado stands with a mangled cane of driftwood. Her sleeveless coat, bearing harsh protrusions along every edge, covers dignified sapphire robes. "You – too – have come to be judged, have you not?"

"No, thank you," Ram calls out.

"One does not travel this far to stand aside and watch," the seer professes before turning to disappear behind the staircase peak.

The pair shares a glance at each other before Fylorn steps ahead. Rain falls upon him as he takes another. Every Pajiado continues to cast their glare as he proceeds towards the staircase. He can hear the heavy steps of Ram behind him, assuring him that he isn't being held behind.

They reach the central Pajiado who stands aside, but locks eyes with Fylorn as he passes to utter, "May she be fair."

A swift nod comes from Fylorn before gliding ahead to the stairs. He holds on to the pristine railing while beginning his climb. The rain is complemented by winds while they ascend, spraying the archaeologist in his eyes. Steadily, the pair pass one plateau after another. Each section has a set of solid, one-piece structures being used by a handful of villagers. Pajiado young and old gaze at the men as they journey up the steps. Upon reaching the peak, Fylorn is buffeted by rain but holds a hand over his brow. Ahead of him, his eyes are consumed by a grand edifice. But, he squints in time to find the seer slipping through the hanging fur of the palace.

This temple is unlike anything I've ever seen before. A wide and flat triangular base with a rising hall of an inverted triangle. The tallest part of the hall seems to be open too, peculiar.

For Vihara.

"You know – I'll give it to them – they do make nice, big things. But, none of it has any character. A Nhavyyet hall – especially the ones in Mashar Pelim – I could stare at them for days, maybe weeks. This thing," Ram throws a limp hand at the palace, "After a couple breaths, I've seen everything it has to offer."

"Everything has value."

"Yes, like I said, it's nice and big."

"Are you going to be talking about this through the whole thing?"

"No, no. Just your part."

Fylorn cracks a grin. "Oh, so you're to be judged now?"

The Nhavyyet puts up defensive hands. "Woah, no one is coming anywhere near me with judgements."

A wide smile opens the archaeologist's face as he examines his companion, sopping from the growing storm. He then makes the final steps to the small set of stairs leading into the palace. After leaping up to the hanging fur of the entryway, he peeks back to find Ram ogling a bulbous quartz mounted on the railing post.

"I thought you said it was boring?" Fylorn calls out.

"This wasn't made by them," the Nhavyyet replies.

"Hurry up."

Ram bares his teeth, but complies and finishes his journey up the staircase. Fylorn holds the fur up for his stubby companion, then spins himself inside. A blue light covering the entire hall takes the archaeologist aback. He gathers his senses to justify the sight before him.

Stained glass, reflective even in a storm it seems.

For some, there is always a storm.

Three of the mystic woman's kin stand posted in the rear of the hall. Each, of varying sizes and shape, wear the tradition sleeveless coat tinged by a light blue dye atop robes of a blue as dark and deep as the sea. The set of Pajiado, with their heads and faces covered by their coat's hood, give Fylorn a disturbing chill; a contrast to the warm room. His eyes adjust to the shifting light inside as the seer lights a candle in each of the stationed members hands. They then spread around the room, assuming a corner of the triangle and casting an equal glow amid the space.

"Come closer," the mystic woman beckons the pair.

Fylorn steps ahead. The muffled clapping of his feet upon the perfectly level floor barely comes louder than his intrigued grunts as the muscles in his body all become more comfortable. Mild groans from Ram behind him fade into a hum as the archaeologist approaches the seer. Her elegant, fiery eyes dig into him as though she reads his mind and learns of every memory housed within.

"Why have you come?" she enunciates.

The deep scowl of the woman digs into Fylorn. His brow quivers while searching for the proper response.

"He comes to question you," the Nhavyyet calls out behind him.

"He may be the one to inquire," the mystic woman orders.

"What is your name?" the archaeologist finally asks.

"I am Bleari, seer of Vihara, and elder of Úlcida." Her following silence forces the skin along Fylorn to rise with bumps.

"Well, Bleari of Úlcida, I have need for an answer, one I'm hoping you can provide."

"Ask me the question!" the mystic woman demands.

"Tell me what Vheer Dagus is owed," Fylorn shouts in response.

Bleari takes a step forward, then another. She raises her hand and places it upon the archaeologist's chest. He feels a force flowing through it before the white heat exploding from her hand consumes his very being. Fylorn allows one yelp to exit his mouth, prompting Ram to step forward.

In a unified shuffle, the three wardens of the palace match the Nhavyyet's pace, bringing him to a halt.

"Still!" Fylorn ejects between heavy breaths.

His voice rings out in the hollow space. Bleari places more pressure against his chest causing the archaeologist to take two more steps before being bathed in light. The seer snaps her fingers. In a flash, a swift wind precedes a harsh rain pouring in the open center of the hall. Flooding water rushes across the space, spreading out in every direction. As the flood pools along the floor, a splashing of wind and water drench everyone within, and brings a compounding chill to the once comfortable palace.

Powerful words flow from the mystic woman, "Let the sapphires of storm say their peace. I hold you accountable for your actions; the many upon the föld you walk. Waters yet to come find solace alongside the lightning of her judgement. Vihara will not strike twice. Once that which has been said, has left her lips, your journey is set. Find those waves and winds on the broad roads your eyes are set upon. See the quiet fires blaze from afar. Rest your head against the speaking stones. Bring only half the handful you need, and twice the spirit!"

The seer falls forward on to the floor. Her long, woven hair dangles to rest upon the cold stone beneath. With eyes wide open she begins to speak, but a crunching thunder deafens the hall. Fylorn watches as her chest heaves, gasping for a breath. His eyes never wander, his focus remains on the weathered woman as rain continues spitting at him. His jaw clenches in anticipation.

Bleari draws in a mighty breath before unleashing it across the floor below her face. The powerful winds splash along stone, forcing all present to hold out their hands in futile defence. The rains are blown away, being finalized with the bright light overhead settling into the dusky storm of before.

A soft ringing lingers in Fylorn's ear. He can feel his hand shaking, but instead of looking at it he gazes around to find the hall dry. The winds from the woman had rid the space of any invading waters. He slowly runs his hands through his hair.

Not even sweat…

His crawling eyes meet the seer's once again. Her fiery pupils hook on, drawing him in. He takes one step forward.

His mind ignites in a blaze of rebellion. The autonomous next step compels his eyes to widen. A musical chorus of pelting rain upon windows consumes him. After one final step, he leans his ear towards the woman's mouth.

"The father, the father, the son and the daughter," drips into his consciousness from her lips.

Fylorn's head begins shaking. He falls to one knee before the mystical woman. His shoulders slack behind him, throwing his head backwards. The lids of his eyes slam shut while the wisdom of the seer's words take him over.

"Of the many sons that come from the one. A baneful brute, clad in blade and ability. The trade made by blood of the shade. Summoned by the divine to remain aside from time. The dagger is to be a god; you are owed reverence."

A seizing befalls the archaeologist. The shouts of Ram break through his trance. Splitting open his tense jaw allows Fylorn's quick words to be pressed out. "What. God."

The voice of Bleari seeps into him once more, turning all around him to shades of black and blue.

"I. See. Ayagog. Dagus."

As the mystical woman's mouth comes to a close, so does the energy of the room. Fylorn is released, plummeting to the floor. His skin soaks in the stone, feeding his body a warmth it desperately requires. The black around him thins into greys. Shadows become silhouettes. Winds become voices. He digs his soft elbow into the hard floor to raise his torso.

Ram rushes over, picking his companion up. The archaeologist utters a muffled decline, but it is faint and unheard. Once on his feet again, he lifts his chin until his falling eyes can look upon the seer. To his surprise, she is in an equal state to him.

A concerned woman's voice breeches through. "Your past has... made an impact on my mother."

Fylorn snaps his eyes to find a younger rendition of Bleari standing beside her. Few things differ between the two women, aside from age and the younger having stark white hair.

That's... She's the one from The Hex.

"You..." Fylorn lets out while flexing his abdomen trying to regain comfort.

"You don't know me, I assure you," the young Pajiado spits out while eyeing over her mother. "You two, bring her to her bed, she needs to rest."

A pair of coat-wearing Pajiado slide into the sides of the seer, attempting to gently lift her. The old woman refuses.

"No, I am not done. I still have to discuss–" Bleari's speech is cut short as she sucks in a breath to alleviate an ache.

"Speak it quick, Mother," the crisp voice of the young Pajiado orders. "I may be back, but that doesn't mean I'll be taking your place."

A shade of forlorn etches into the seer's face. She gives a short nod before emitting, "I saw a village to the filaash, one of Wöllralt. They know everything."

The two Pajiado walk Bleari from the hall, leaving the young woman with Fylorn and Ram. As the echoing sounds of her mother's departure fill the space, she continues a grim stare upon the visitors. The archaeologist reciprocates, studying the Pajiado with an effort to gleam any information about the woman.

Worn coat, but her hair is cared for. Perfect shoes, but the blackness under her eyes means she doesn't sleep, or well in any case. She's tired... but of what?

Fylorn opens his mouth, but Ram beats him to it.

"We came here to see the seer, we appreciate what she's done – but if you don't mind – we'd like to stay until she is satisfied with telling us everything."

"We do mind," the young woman bluntly replies.

"What's your name?" comes from Fylorn.

Her eyes, a deep roaring fire, strike at him. A flinch of her nose precedes her answer, "Elijou."

"Kindly crossed, Elijou." Ram steps back into the conversation. "I believe–"

Elijou strikes her words at Ram, "She has given you what you came for, I believe."

With the arm that he's currently using to post himself up, Fylorn double taps Ram. "It is okay, my friend. I believe we should leave."

The heat radiating from Ram is clearly felt. After releasing one huff, the Nhavyyet pivots with his companion, then proceeds to leave. Before they reach the door, Fylorn finds the strength to continue on his own two feet. He takes the moment to settle himself, while throwing a glance over his shoulder to check that the Pajiado still lurks in defence of the palace.

"You spoke of not staying, correct?"

Elijou replies with a menacing sigh.

"I could use someone with your talents on my journey." Fylorn presses.

A reply so crisp it threatens to crack the very stone around them booms from the Pajiado woman, "No."

"Are you sure you want her coming with us?" Ram argues in a whisper.

The archaeologist steps ahead of him, a pace from the open door, and stairs below. He leans over to place his hand upon his Nhavyyet companion, who silently obliges in helping him through the fur-lined exit. While descending the first step Fylorn replies, "It matters not."

Ram grumbles in agreement. As the pair reach the first plateau Fylorn halts to cast a look far into the waters on his right.

"Thoughts?" the Nhavyyet questions.

"I've never heard of Ayagog before. I don't think he was a relative in my parent's time."

"Some ancient bastard made a deal with the Gods. That doesn't bode well."

"And I'm wondering; if my family doesn't have record of him – especially missing those books – then who would?"

The pair look at each other for a long moment before coming to a simultaneous conclusion.

"The Ködiam," they say in unison.

Fylorn releases a small chuckle while matching the Nhavyyet's grin. He makes a large stretch before attempting the next set of stairs. As his toe touches the lowest field of Úlcida, he doesn't look back. The archaeologist marches down the final steps, passing the dragon statues, and considers the long journey ahead of him.

Chapter 18
The Victim

Engrossed by the aging Pajiado walking alongside Ani, the long road ahead is completely ignored.

"That was Ipith?" she exclaims. "You know, I've heard about the place all my life, I kind of... expected more."

"Like what?" he asks with a kinked neck.

"I don't know..." she waves her hand around while searching for an answer. Her sights finally register the fields filled by red corn on one side and blissful farming oxen on the other. "I don't know."

She quickly looks at him, smirks, then chuckles quietly before shifting her gaze to his arms. The loose clothing wrapping the man from neck to ankle avoids his arms entirely. Furthermore, his open bicep flaunts a vertical scar identical to Ani's. As her eyes linger on the spot, his words break the silence.

"Yes, they all look the same. A unified symbol of who we are."

"We..." Ani holds on to the word for as long as her breath will allow.

The man's fiery eyes see right into Ani. She relaxes her shoulders before throwing a finger at the amphibian behemoth waddling beside him.

"Is it always out?"

"Mostly," he replies with a soft laugh. "But he's kind of slow, so sometimes I have to take him back when we're in a hurry."

"Isn't it a spirit... weightless?"

The aging man's eyebrows flex while he nods at the notion. "For someone who has an auragonic such as yours, it would appear to be, yes. But, I've developed him over the years – something you'll come to learn – and now he's something much more."

Raising a finger his own, he points to the beast. "See those middling legs, they weren't always there." His finger trails back towards his own heart. "I've spent some of myself to grow him into something wondrous."

"You've traded some of yourself?" Ani utters. Her eyes drift down to her own scar before commenting, "I've only been alive for ten years. I'm in the body of a woman now... I guess, because I've done the same thing."

A groan crawls from the man, not one of envy or sorrow, but of simple understanding. She looks back up to him, finding small nods with a tight jaw.

In a perky tone she comments, "It's okay, I've grown used to it."

The response of a smile widening the aging man's face is contagious, bringing a light to Ani's heart.

"As we all have," he professes, then raises his volume, "As we all have, haven't we, Nevdall?"

Walking alongside Zeela, nearly fitting into her shadow, the petite woman gently tousles her long, black hair while casting a sharp eye behind her at the pair

"Don't know what you're talking about, Akaifi," Nevdall squeaks out. "I found my gorgeous My'To'Tang just as she is, and I'm going to live forever!"

Each twang of joy thrumming from the petite woman strikes Ani. The heat washing across her fights a touch of chill to bring a complex mixture within Ani. She feels a firm hold upon her shoulder. In a natural reaction she twists to look, finding Akaifi's aged and veiny hand. The young woman smiles faintly, to reciprocate the understanding, then redirects her energy ahead.

"My'To'Tang?" Ani barks. "I've never heard of that before."

"Birds, you know?" Nevdall tilts her eyes to gander at the majestic flight of her auragonic as it nearly slips into the clouds above. "They travel and I happened to be in the right place when this beauty came from Teremföld."

"That's far," the reply comes blissfully from Ani before her tone drops into one more serious. "So; a Hellix, My'To'Tang, Crab creature–"

"Gibby," Akaifi interjects, before casting a long gaze towards his own auragonic. "The Nhavyyet have a long, silly name for them, but that's what I call him."

Ani can't help but smile as she joins the gazing, then shifts her view back to Zeela. "And you have that plant thing, right?"

"Indeed I do, lovely."

"...do you keep it inside a lot?" the young woman asks with a trailing tone.

The hearty woman chuckles before casting a beaming grin at Ani. "He thinks Gibby falls behind; a plant is painfully slow."

Laughter bounds from the three Tamers, showering the young woman in a warmth she's never felt before. Her eyes track to the long-haired man by his lonesome, riding his spectral mount at the head of the group. Ani's eyes sharpen while looking towards the beast, feeling flickering remnants of sorrow and frustration.

"What about him?" she blurts out, quelling the joy around her.

"What about him?" Nevdall snaps back. "With or without us, Olokk travels his own road."

Ani tilts her head while keeping her sights set on the dark man.

"Do you understand?" the petite woman asks.

"I think so," the young woman softly replies.

"It shouldn't be much longer," Olokk's coarse voice cries out from the middling distance ahead. "Or we could rest for the night."

A crippling tension grips the muscles along Ani's back compelling her to quickly press. "At an inn?"

"Of course, lovely," Zeela quietly answers.

After an involuntary eye twitch, she spins to face the hearty woman. "It's not safe outside at night. The… monsters will get us."

The quirky twinkle in Zeela's eyes fade as she considers the words of the young woman. She brings her pace to meet Ani, then carefully rolls her words out. "You never really answered me. Whereabouts did you come from? Were you a… slave, or abused?"

Immediately the young woman shakes her head. "No, nothing like that. But, when Tushma and I were travelling this way, we had to travel at night."

"Who's Tushma?" Nevdall inquires.

"He's my… father. We came from just beyond Barrelwood, made it to Tombra and then the Legion chased us. I lost him and Ora flew us away to Ipith. He'll be fine, nothing can kill him."

"Damn Legion," Akaifi spits out, the grim taste of the words leaving his face in a scowl. "Feeding on the pus of corruption like maggots."

"Yeah," Ani mutters. "I didn't know any better; Tushma had kept me safe all these years. But they found out I was an Anchor and, well… I found out."

Zeela wraps her arm around the young woman. "That's why we do what we do, lovely. We fight for people like those farmers back there. And once we make it to Millown, you'll train to do the very same thing. It'll feel good to help when you know exactly what the Legion has done – And! – we'll find some time to find your father, okay?"

Ani's bottom lip begins to quiver. The pressures behind her eyes keep any words from properly slipping out, leaving a dribbling mess behind. She swiftly wipes the pooling tears before throwing on a happier face. "Okay."

After a moment, a little burp fights its way out of the young woman. Her face goes red before she spits out an explanation.

"Sorry, I haven't eaten in a while and that happens." Ani's eyes trail down to her side, and a wave of regret washes over her at the lack of her satchel. "Normally I carry extra to eat…"

A small coo comes from Zeela before she whispers, "Don't worry, lovely. There's more than enough back home. We'll have you full in no time." The hearty woman then delivers a curt smile back, before offering a hand to hold. Ani scoops it up, gently swinging it as they walk.

As nightfall consumes the road of twists and dips through endless fields, the company finds their pace quickening enough until they reach the stone walls of Millown. Almost as one grand castle itself, the imposing curtain crosses from one shore to the other, enclosing the rising city.

With ease, the guards allow them into the city, and the young woman follows the Tamers through the dark streets. Olokk guides the way, still casually riding upon his spectral hound. A few paces behind him are Akaifi and Nevdall, both avidly engaging in discourse on the topic of why roads weave and bend. Trailing the pair is Gibby, waddling the best he can to keep up. Just barely ahead of Ani is Zeela, walking with her head low and one hand nestled into her hanging pouch. The melodic tap upon sophisticated pathways washes away her unease, allowing her mind to soak in her surroundings.

The same salty air from the grotto, and Carcras... We arrived there at night too, but I can see so much more out here, as if being by the sea makes the nights brighter.

She gazes at the twin moons, hanging in the sky. Then her sights drop to the complex outline of streets and alleys that make Millown. Countless archways, for shielding heads, connect the walls of the tight alleyways. Paved stone in intricate divisions set the houses in a precise arrangement. The timber framing, nearly reminiscent of Barrelwood, is marked in prismatic colours and structure the homes to be spired and gangly. Each public square they passed through has beautifully laid slabs of stone cut in triangular patterns.

They approach a brilliance of architecture in the form of a monumental tower with a turret clock, surrounded by wide, rising stairs that are consummated by flawless statues. A flush of awe trickles along Ani as she stops to gawk in amazement. The young woman's fixation is superseded as her sights register the harbour beyond.

It's unlike anything I've ever seen before. The other cities, any of them, none are even close. That pier goes on for... ever. So many boats; sailing boats, tugging boats– pretty sure someone lives on that one!

A grin encapsulates Ani. The gentle hand of Zeela comes to wrap around the young woman's shoulder, coaxing her to keep moving. Their long walk up the gradual incline, passing through the remainder of Millown, brings her to the pinnacle of the city. Before her stands the grand symbol of the capitol's strength

The castle of the king.

Lingering with tired eyes but a fascinated mind, Ani is carefully bumped.

"It's late," Akaifi grumbles, then takes a hold of her shoulder to guide her in through the massive portcullis. "We have all the time in the world, tomorrow."

Inside, the grass of bailey appears clean in the crisp night. One final, but gentle, rise builds the clearing towards a decorated hall. It stands proud between two aging towers so tall they nearly reach the moons. A warm yellow light is cast from the open doorway, and within the illumination is a barely visible shape.

Ani brings her hands up to wring her tired eyes before making a second look at the creature. With its head low, and stance wide, a spectral hellix posts itself. Wisps of glowing red spirit emanate from the beast creating an obscurity in the faint light.

Echoing from the distance comes a powerful growl. The hairs on Ani stand at attention as she snaps her head back and forth to see what the others' reactions are. Olokk veers towards the side of the yard while the remaining Tamers continue ahead.

"Where's he going?" the young woman quietly asks.

"To let that hellix free. The only true joy he finds is in taming," Nevdall casually responds.

Let it free?

A pile of questions barrels out of the young woman, "Letting it free? What do you mean? How do you do that?"

The groan of a low chuckle crawls from Akaifi before he comments, "Don't worry about it, Ani. You're never going to get rid of a dragon auragonic."

As they approach the doors to the grand hall, Ani turns to see the old Pajiado give a small wink before the vibrant wisp of Gibby circles from the ground. It trails up into the spirit's wrest on the side of his bicep.

Ahead of them, the red hellix sits on its hind as a shadow crosses into the gleaming doorway. Ani focuses her sights as a woman breaches the light to stand beside the hound. The cool evening breeze moves her wrappings to blur the lines between the burnt orange of her robes and the torchlight.

Long black hair, tall posture, very... very beautiful.

The striking woman shifts her gaze from along the other Tamers to land on Ani. A shiver from unknown depths of the young woman's mind twangs at the sharp features focusing on her.

"And who might you be?" The stiff words of the striking woman combat the bright smile on her face.

"Ani," peeps out of the young woman.

"Escrah here was so excited, he must have sensed someone new was coming home," trickles from the woman's sharp mouth while her eyes linger on her new guest.

Zeela places a comforting hand upon the shaking shoulder of Ani while breathing out, "This is Shyvesh. She's the grand tamer; the master of our order."

Shyvesh delivers a curt head nod to confirm, before asking, "Ani, I have this feeling you have an auragonic. Am I correct?"

Ani peers down to her arm, then rolls up her sleeve to reveal the small mountain sitting on her forearm. The steady flow of breathing is the only thing to move on the grand tamer's body.

"If you don't mind..." falls from Shyvesh's mouth.

The young woman furrows her brow, before feeling the reassuring squeeze of Zeela's hand. Ani exhales, then closes her eyes for a moment to search for a worming feeling. Once the muscles of her arm begin to engage, she opens to watch as the familiar wisp of iridescent blue emerges from her spirit's wrest. The spectral flow splashes out ahead of her to converge and become the dominating visage of an adult dragon.

Shyvesh loses her composure for the slightest of moments as her face expands. The flare is short-lived. A feral rumble comes from the red hellix beside her. Her hand reaches out to grip the fur of its hackle before using a sole thumb to stroke a calmness into the creature.

Ora tilts its head, then swings its sights around to Ani. In the moonlight, the eyes of the beast are all-consuming jewels of light. The dragon lowers itself into a curl below the young woman, with its chin nestling upon the top of her worn shoe.

As Ani blinks a few times amid gazing at her auragonic, she finally remembers where she is. She cracks a chuckle while looking ahead to lock eyes with Shyvesh.

"Impressive." The word is isolated while the striking woman casts her sights to the blackened sky dotted by bright stars. "If you so choose, you may become one of us. Meet me tomorrow, and be our company in the meantime."

A genuine smile crawls onto Shyvesh's face before she turns back into the grand hall behind her. As she saunters away, the red hellix dissipates into a fluid wisp back towards the door.

The moment stretches as Ani looks on. The corners of her vision become fuzzy until a cough brings her attention behind her. Akaifi makes a swift glance to one of the reaching spires of the castle before pressing the joints of his left hand while striding away.

"Good night," the old Pajiado says over his shoulder.

Ani watches him go inside, before spinning around to find Nevdall missing, and only Zeela remaining. She stands a few paces away, with all of her weight on one leg while the other is lifted so her toes are barely touching.

"Come with me, lovely."

The hearty woman ushers Ani into a distant tower within the curtain wall. Through each rising window, the young woman spies more and more of the glistening waters waving in the endless dark.

Zeela promptly stops outside of a smaller door. Turning on her heels, she lines herself up with Ani. "This one will be for you."

A warmth rolls along the young woman, and before she knows it, she has her arms raising out for a hug. "I can't thank you enough. This has been more than I ever could have expected to find."

"You are among family now. Enjoy it." The hearty woman waits for Ani to open the door, then quietly departs for the night.

Inside is a basic space filled by one candle's trying light. She assesses her new home.

A simple bed suitable for one sleeper, a desk with a chair, and a... worn, old trunk. I wonder what's left behind in it.

She walks over to the end of the bed, flipping the trunk open. The inside is even more empty than the room itself.

"Hmm," crawls from the young woman's mouth.

Her eyes track to the sole window of the room, lacking any glass to repel the tower's high winds. A crisp night's air reaches in, bringing a burst of energy the young woman hadn't expected. One loud clunk comes from the falling lid as Ani abandons the storage container. She slowly rises, then strides to the wide opening. Placing one foot out to test the support, she places herself on the edge of the open window. After a few fleeting moments, she casts her gaze down to find the rear of the castle blooming into a wide and vibrant courtyard leading to the sea. Her sights glide to the very edge of the garden space before losing herself while looking out into the black unknown.

A family... My family? It's weird, I don't think I ever imagined finding a family out here, but... what did I expect? I came looking for others like me– the only others like me. Of course they would bring me in with open arms.

Ani feels the usual burn of her muscles as Ora releases itself from her arm, emerging in a wisp while spreading both wings. The spectral dragon flies off before relaxing into a glide away from the tower and over the lip of the cliffside. A vibrant blue hue emanates from the auragonic, quickly becoming a dominating beacon of the night. The dragon makes a wide circle coming back above Ani, then enjoys its freedom within the bright night. She spots ships sailing along in the night.

Where are they going? I think they probably should be at port right now.

Beyond the edges of land, a deep night's sea glints. The flickers of white moonlight gain her fixation, and she becomes mystified by the gentle lapping of water.

I made it, Tushma. I'm looking at the sea.

Chapter 19
The Tribute

A hearty breakfast – basically two by any measure of what I've been eating lately – then a walk through the halls of this monster of a castle. No end, literally haven't found the same corridor twice. But, empty. A few servants here and there– Actually, I think that lord in Barrelwood had more or a court than this king… Right, I should probably go meet him – but – first I need to go talk with Zeela again.

Paintings decorate one side while decorative cloths paint the other. Ani flows through the passages of the rich estate until she turns a corner to enter a vast hall with trims of silver and blue. The dim torchlight is greatly overcast by the wealth of fila pouring in the tall windows along the space. Rows upon rows of pews fill the center of the hall, while a library of literary possessions litter the walls. A lone woman stands at the far side of the room. At the sound of Ani's footsteps the woman turns, revealing herself to be Shyvesh.

"How was your morning?" the grand tamer calls across the hall.

"I didn't expect you to be in here," the young woman blurts out.

Shyvesh gives a small chuckle. "No one ever does. Were you avoiding me?"

A chill runs down Ani's spine at the question. "Um, no. I just…"

As words fail her, the grand tamer fills them in. "It's alright. Anyone who's come to stay here spends the first day trying to find every room. And, no one expects me to be in here because – unfortunately – there's no one to teach right now."

Ani takes a second scan of the hall to piece the new information together.

Desks, chairs, books… pretty sure that's some kind of board to write on.

"Zeela mentioned I'm to be trained."

"Yes, training. But it's equally important to be taught our history, and our ways."

"Are you going to teach me your… our history?"

A pleasant smile crosses the grand tamer's face. "I'll tell you anything you want to know."

The thudding in Ani's chest catches her off guard.

Anything? Everything? I'll truly get to find out who I am?

"You start, and I'll tell you when to stop!" flies from Ani before falling into a joyous laughter.

"Alright. Well, this is our teaching hall. Over the years we have had many pupils; the Tamers you have already met are some. The recent years have been lacking, but I'll admit, it has been a pleasant reprieve."

"I think you've already told me that," Ani spits out jokingly.

Shyvesh raises an eyebrow, then continues, "Perhaps it would be easier to find out what you already know, and build from there…"

Ani holds her chin while her mind tirelessly scrambles to collect everything she knows. "Anchors absorb the spirit of a creature they fell. Takers are what the Legion calls those with an auragonic. And… Tamers are what the trained version of us are?"

"Not bad, who taught you all of that?"

"My father, Tushma."

"I see. He must be quite old to still call us Anchors."

"He was– is an old man. Also, stubborn; he didn't trust coming all this way…"

"Our reputation has… shifted over the years. Something I should explain to you." Shyvesh strides over to pull down a wide map off a shelf. Her orange robes flow with a glimmering grace. "Filaash to The Plains has always been disputed, but, for many years it was our people – The Anchors – who reigned terror on these choppy-water shores. Right here," the grand tamer's finger traces a chunk of land beyond the seashore of Millown, "The Peninsula of Spirits, is where the first Anchors come from. It's unclear why, or how many, but they settled and began raiding the coastal cities of Goromföld."

"Oh," slips from Ani's mouth.

"Not unlike the Wöllralt of today," Shyvesh continues from over her shoulder as she begins perusing the nearby shelf of tomes. "Now, I'm telling you all of this so that my next question makes more sense. How much do you know about Ardaelius?"

"Um, Tushma–"

"Ani! Shyvesh?" a wildly effeminate voice calls out behind the young woman, enticing her to swing around.

In the doorway, she spots Zeela in a set of pale blue robes that allow her shoulders and ribs to breathe. The hearty woman marches into the teaching hall, then leans her hand upon the back of a pew. Within the moment of silence, heavy of breath, she manages to spit out, "For some reason, I didn't expect to find either of you in here."

"See," Shyvesh utters.

"Wow," the hearty woman continues after swiftly gathering herself, "you two look a lot alike in the light."

Ani tilts her head at the grand tamer while inspecting every measure of the woman again, this time with a more critical eye.

"A lot of young women look like me," Shyvesh quickly responds before redirecting her attention back to Ani. "You said 'Is' and then 'Was'. What happened to you father?"

"He... Uh, I left him behind while he was captured by the Legion."

A slow sigh is released from the grand tamer before she comments, "If the Legion took him, and he's still alive, then he's at their prison in Mashar Pelim."

The room goes silent.

Zeela clears her throat before standing up from her lean. "Well now, we can't have our newest rank without the proper garb. Shall we bring her to the tailor?"

"Is that why you came to find us?" Shyvesh sternly asks.

"Yes," the hearty woman quickly answers. "They just arrived."

"Proper garb?" Ani pipes in, trying to keep her voice high and lively.

"Every Tamer gets adequate attire, Ani. You'll be no exception. That means we'll have to get you measured. Are you okay with that?"

The genuine look in Shyvesh's eyes makes the young woman turn into a puddle of herself. She quietly replies, "Yes."

"Good," bounds from Zeela. "Then let's get a move on. You can ask more questions, or whatever it is you were doing in here, along the way."

The grand tamer delivers a powerful head nod towards Ani before gently placing a hand upon her lower back. The trio move from the teaching hall into the elegant corridors outside. Shyvesh steers them up towards a small set of stairs, and within moments Ani begins exploding with questions.

"What makes people so scared of us? What is our purpose? Do spirits get damaged? Would they need to be healed? Can I commune with spirits? Can auragonics learn magic? What happens if an Anchor physically loses their spirit's wrest? ...Like what if my arm gets chopped off!"

Ani's intense breathing gets quelled by Zeela's big hand landing on her shoulder. "Now there's a lot of questions." The hearty woman looks up to Shyvesh. "In fact, I don't think I know the answer to half of them. Would you mind?"

Shyvesh allows herself a small chuckle before she dives into answering, "Spirit Tamers are the guardians of The Plains. We are, by all accounts, good people. Over the years there have been different methods of using one's auragonic. Some Tamers simply house the spirit, others find a way to commune, and some of our best can grow and change the creature. Primarily we bring the spirit into a physical form, but that does have its own limitations, so I have yet to see one use magic on its own."

"You'd have to be a Pajiado, no?" comes from Akaifi as he veers from a nearby corridor to join in the walk.

"Spirits of men don't count," pipes in Ani. "That's what Tushma told me."

A crisp silence overtakes the conversation. The young woman glances around in wonder of if she misspoke.

Finally, Shyvesh speaks up, "Being born with a vertical scar on your body is a sign of being able to harness spirits. When a person was found to have such power, they were hunted and recruited. Children with an empty spirit wrest would be brought forth to the grand tamer to acquire their spirit. Traditionally, they would have been brought in with open arms, but rogue Tamers were being found." Her voice slows to a crawl. "We have to be careful about our people, Ani. It has been said that a being born of perfect spirit, being born of two Tamers with the same auragonic, could be catastrophic. This child of prophecy, we believe, could strip any being of their spirit, including men. The Peninsula of Spirits, that I told you of before, is the place Tamers would go to find their appointed auragonic, but… Times are different now."

"Quite different," echoes along the hall.

Ani twists her head to find Olokk strolling up to meet the gathering.

"Where is Nevdall?" he continues.

"Why do you ask?" Zeela snickers.

"She would love to see the new girl getting fitted. Give her all kinds of tips and… Say, how big did your mother get to be?" Olokk tilts his head while eyeing up the young woman.

"Maybe she takes after her father. How large was Tushma?" Shyvesh asks.

"He's more of a… father in spirit. I don't know who my real parents are."

Zeela holds back, only to blurt out, "Well then, you could be her mother, Shyvesh!"

A fierce glare emanates from the grand tamer. "I raised all of my children."

"You do look strikingly like her, Ani. It is interesting..."
Olokk spits out towards the young woman.

"You never said you had a child," slowly crawls from
Akaifi.

As the Tamers' walk along the glimmering corridor
stalls amid argument, a chill overtakes Ani. She turns her
sights to gaze down a blackened hallway that leads far into a
chamber. Sitting at the penultimate center, undeniably
visible, rests a king on his throne. A small shiver dominates
her body as, at the breathtaking distance, he lifts his hand
and beckons.

"Ani." The voice of Shyvesh assaults the young
woman's ears as reality pours back into her consciousness.
"That is King Malaron. He would like to see us now."

"What about the tailor?" comes from Ani in a whisper.

The young woman's eyes stay fixated on the dark hall
while she hears the grand tamer bark orders.

"You two, go speak with the tailor, send my apologies.
Zeela, it's time."

"If they ask, I want pockets–" The skin of Ani's lower
back that the warm hand had graced earlier was now
haunted by the cold, firm hold that Shyvesh takes this time.
As she guides the young woman down the dusky walkway,
she continues, "If you'll follow me – I understand it's a lot to
take in – but we must meet the king. It will all make sense,
but there are still some things I believe you'll need to know
ahead of time."

"Why does the king need to meet me?"

"To be a Tamer is to be one of his royal guards."

The young woman's eyes glaze over and her feet come
to a stand still.

"We're not making you a soldier, Ani. Perhaps, in a
sense, but ultimately you will be a hero to the people."

Hero to the people? I've seen how the people treat Anchors—Tamers, whatever.

"How far is the king's reach?"

Shyvesh's pace comes to a complete stop. The moment thickens until she turns to face Ani directly.

In the silence, the young woman continues, "As in, how far do Tamers need to travel? I was found in Ipith, but would a Tamer need to go as far as Tombra? Or Carcras?"

"No," the grand tamer sharply answers. "No, sometimes Delcrias, sometimes Ipith, but never that far. As it has been, we barely leave Millown, aside from coming to the aid of those under attack by the Wöllralt."

A stark silence envelopes Ani.

"Do you understand?"

"I don't know."

The thumb of the grand tamer slowly rubs where she holds. "I'll be here with you the entire time."

"Okay." After the simple reply, the pair move on.

Thousands of pale stone blocks comprise the grand throne room ahead. The stark thudding of steps upon a sheen floor echoes throughout. Ani examines each wall, taking note of the hanging blue banners bearing symbols of a hollow eye. Passing into the hall coats her in a quiet chill. Still, atop a black marble pedestal, rests the king upon his decadent throne. The glowing orange from the encircling torchlight bathes every edge of the space, bringing a lingering life to the hallow hall. With one leg resting long, and his opposite fist holding his tilted head, the king barely shifts his gaze while the company enters his domain. Covering his face is a mask designed by masters of art and craft; an intricate depiction portraying a woman's face. Only the eyes of the covering are open, but within is the darkest black Ani has ever seen.

The face from the Fall's statue… and the house of… That's the face of Ardaelius.

"King Malaron," Zeela addresses her lord. "Here is the young woman carrying the spirit of a dragon we found near Ipith."

A heavy voicelessness coming from the king imposes a crushing weight on Ani. The emboldened blue of the dangling robes covering the still lord disregard the low light of his hall. His slow, methodical head turn from Zeela to her and back brings the vast room in on the young woman. She resists buckling under the pressure, using every measure of strength she has to retain her composure. Finally, the king's gravelly voice ejects across the room at the young woman.

"Do you hear the voices?"

A terrible pain stiffens Ani to a point of which she can't move her jaw.

The hanging silence is broken by King Malaron. "No, of course not. I have been told that you are not a disciple of our lady and savior, Ardaelius."

"I do not," the young woman finally manages to answer.

"Do not fret, relax. You are among family now, and this family only tips our cup to one goddess. She who speaks to us. There is no greater suffocation than the silence of Ardaelius. Her words are our eyes, her voice pumps our blood—" Malaron cuts off his own words to curtly nod towards Zeela.

Ani quickly snaps her sights to her side, watching as the hearty woman shuffles away to attend to the silent instructions.

The words of the king grip her focus, pulling it back towards him and only him. "She is all, the end to every means. Those who fight it will only submit sad and disgraced, but she will still see them. One day they will realize it, she has always been theirs, and them hers. Her cold embrace will give you all the warmth you need to move forward, for her."

In a rhythmic order, the king's pale fingers drum before flipping into a beckon for the young woman. Ani eyes the vast throne room, anticipating some grand summoning on his behalf. All within the space stand tall and stoic, stone guardians to the will of their king. She brings her sights back to the black seat, then the dark master sitting on it. Her feet begin to move. Step by step, her compelled motion brings the young woman's whole mind into a state of panic. She flares her widened eyes at the man in time to find his hand held up flat, and her feet cease moving.

"That was not mystics, little girl." The words crawling from lips behind a mask sink into Ani. "With the right whistle, men become sheep. I insist that all under my care understand this. Each and every Tamer who lives within my realm has power over this duty. It is intrusted. It is a sacred oath."

A heavy door is dragged open at the far side of the throne room. The unbothered lord continues, "Ardaelius often prompts men to make choices, as she does not care about the outcome, but revels in the chaos. Ardaelius knows the righteous, but the wicked, those who love violence, she loves them with a passion."

Ani's eyes finally find the courage to trail to her left. She finds a grim-faced Zeela catering a podium on wheels towards the throne. The gangly vines of tortured wood the rolling table is composed of climbs for the sky. Each petrified branch spreads out to create an adequate surface for a sole object to reside.

A book… The book! The same as the man in Tombra held while reciting about Ardaelius–

The young woman's thoughts are choked out by the dry drawl of the king as he raises his volume. "In Ardaelic belief, Haven is a place where devout followers of Ardealius go to live with Our Goddess – the woman herself – for their endless days beyond life." A sharp grinding cracks out into the hollow hall as King Malaron's fingers squeeze upon the cuff of his throne's arm. "Dak is believed to be a place where she sends all who oppose her to suffer."

Followers… Does he? I think they want me to worship Ardaelius. Should I tell them no? Ask them for time to think about it? If they care they'll give it to me. But, these people, are they my family– Tushma… He would know what to do.

A swelling behind Ani's eyes forms. She begins fidgeting her fingers upon her side to quell the feelings being imposed upon her. Her chin quivers before a squeak crawls from the young woman's mouth, leaving the hall still and waiting.

If I can't make my own choices, then I am just the child that Tushma always saw me as– Always… the man was a father right up until the end– No! Absolutely not. The man isn't dead. Tushma is family, my family, and I will find him. I will be the woman he always wanted me to be, the one who can make her own decisions.

"Um," she manages to utter. "I–"

"Ani." The king lowers his head, angling the mask, and softens his tone. "You are scared, but there is no reason to be. Death is not something to be feared, nor avoided, nor longed for. The only one who craves death is the one who can't have it, and I know exactly where death rests."

The creaking of wheels dies away as Zeela brings the podium to a halt. Ani watches on, feeling the sweat build in the cracks of her back as the hearty woman lifts a grand tome from the mangled, wooden surface. Bound by leathers and metals that reflect entire spectrums of blue and black, the tattered volume is carefully transferred to the dormant lord upon the throne. Zeela retreats from the space between Ani and King Malaron, leaving the masked man to linger his blackened gaze upon the young woman.

"Filled with pure scripture from the hands of Our Goddess herself. The Source Dominium, called as such for it is a charge of her ownership over you; as she is now your lord."

King Malaron drags his fingers across the cover to open the tome. "My mind is not what it used to be, and with you not having read this before – I take from the look you gave the volume – it will be best if you repeat after me."

"Repeat after you?" the young woman asks aloud.

"Perfect," the king lingers on the word. "To take a vow to Ardaelius, one must recite her tenets. Are you ready?"

Never before in the young woman's life had she felt such an indescribable weight blanketing her. Her shoulders slump while struggling to stand tall. The back of her eyes grow tired over her internal struggle. She looks to her right, catching the stare of Shyvesh. The grand tamer's dignified tension gives Ani strength. She returns her eyes to the dark king.

"Begin," she orders.

"Thou shalt hold Ardaelius above all else."

"Thou shalt hold Ardaelius above all else," Ani echoes.

"Thou shalt spread the means to an end."

"Thou shalt spread the means to an end," Ani echoes.

"Thou shalt entice and mold the weak."

"Thou shalt entice and mold the weak," Ani echoes.

"Remember the sacrifice, and bathe in its blessings."

"Remember the sacrifice, and bathe in its blessings," Ani echoes.

"Do not honour thy followers: be twisted, be corrupt."

"Do not honour thy followers: be twisted, be corrupt," Ani echoes.

"Thou shalt not falter from the path," King Malaron erupts.

"Thou shalt not falter from the path," Ani matches, her face scrunching as the tainted words are bellowed from her mouth.

"Thou shalt not cheat Haven."

"Thou shalt not cheat Haven."

"Thou shalt know patience before force."

"Thou shalt know patience before force."

"Thou shalt hold the inherit."

"Thou shalt hold the inherit."

"Thou shalt forsake the tribute," the king recites.

The young woman allows the powerful words to ring around the grand hall and come into a grim silence before finally uttering, "Thou shalt forsake the tribute."

A stark chill runs along Ani's body. She darts her eyes around, questioning if everyone around her feels the same, but the stoic rendering of the Tamers is unchanged. Her sights drop to the black stone floor below her. The young woman listens to her own breathing while her mind assumes control.

Do I feel different? Have I made a huge mistake and ruined everything— wasted every effort that Tushma and I made just to become a puppet for this false king? Is Ardaelius my lord now and he truly means nothing... Or am I the fool for listening to these myths and tales?

"We are not done yet, child."

Ani raises her eyes to look through her brow at the masked man.

"She needs you to speak the vow before you are truly hers."

The young woman crushes her eyes closed while slowly nodding her head. Her shaking jaw asks, "What is the worst that can happen?"

A supernatural suspicion leads Ani to feel King Malaron grinning behind the divine mask. "We hear her words and see her path; we carry out the charge entrusted. The seventh is near. Now is to fear. For my haven cometh. Do not deny this. I shan't save you. An arranged night tis. She will arrive, Ardaelius."

Dry tingles dance in the back of Ani's throat. She clears it with a cough before quickly repeating the speech before she forgets it. "We hear her words and see her path; we carry out the charge entrusted. The seventh is near. Now is to fear. For my haven cometh. Do not deny this. I shan't save you. An arranged night tis. She will arrive, Ardaelius."

"May she trust her followers to breathe death and chaos into the lands of Föld," comes from the right side of the hall. Ani recognises the voice but can't wrap her mind around the words. She twists her heavy head to find Shyvesh finishing her statement before laying half-lidded eyes upon the young woman.

"Am I free to leave?" crawls from Ani.

Shyvesh silently gestures towards King Malaron.

"Do you hear her words?"

I can hear the dust settling. I can hear the pulse of my own heart. If I strain, I could probably hear the marching of ants on the floor. But, no god speaks to me on this day.

Ani's lip quivers. "Yes."

"Then go listen to her."

The young woman swallows hard before turning on her heels and briskly walking from the grand hall. Only Akaifi breaks the statuesque line of Tamers by walking his eyes along with her as she passes. Each step forward echoes louder and louder as she enters the corridor outside. With one final look, she turns around to spot Shyvesh striding up to King Malaron's side and leaning in to hear his words.

Probably telling her that I'm a liar— a miscreant. That I'm not worthy of being a disciple of Ardaelius, or even a Tamer…

A long sigh flows from Ani as she holds back tears.

"Ora? Care to have a relaxing flight?"

Her eyes watch as a reflexive blue glow hums from underneath her sleeve. Without another thought she dashes through the stuffy walkways, one after another until she finally breaches the shade umbrageous grove of the castle and into the fila's light. A bath of warmth and positivity elevates the young woman's spirits as she leans her head back to close her eyes and basks in it.

Ani barely notices Ora letting itself free before the spectral snout nudges her elbow. She quickly mounts the beast, gripping the usual spikes on its back. The rush of air washes away the flustered heat that had been building underneath of her as the pair rises. Once the climb levels out, she casts an introspective eye out across the water crashing on the shore. With little effort, she spies a distant treeline reaching from the dominating mountain line beyond.

The peninsula. What a story… I can't believe that the auragonic and Ardaelius have been connected this whole time. It really makes me wonder; does it even matter how I feel about being made to take the vow? I mean, if the two things have always been one, then what does it matter. The goddess of death… does she control death? Gain power from the dead? Can she send someone she doesn't want back from death to life? Can turn those alive, dead? So many questions, but—

Ora makes a plunging dive that forces Ani to double her hold and focus to stay on.

"Hey! Does that bother you?"

The beast snorts in response.

"Yeah, well… I am what I am. I don't know if I would call myself 'Ardaelic' just yet. I am an Anchor, and that will always be, but… Above all else, the only thing I truly have is you." The young woman presses out a heated breath. "Well, maybe I have to figure out what any of that really means."

A beam of light crosses over Ora, making the spectral dragon nearly transparent.

"Oh, no. Let's circle back."

One drawn out rumble comes from the spectral dragon's neck before it tilts in an arc back towards the castle.

"This is really simple, actually. An Anchor is what I am, and the others are my family, so that is the vow I take. I don't care about what anything else means, this is where I belong, and these are the people I will watch over."

Ani feels a cold wind touch her back as Ora glides far above the splashing waters of the sea.

Chapter 20
The Commander

"Two bundles of bread, three whole barrels of mead, and I told him, 'Bring me more!' Can you believe that?"

Fylorn tilts his head to move his ear from the unsavoury boasting of Ram. The Nhavyyet had spent most of their time waiting while loudly recanting the prior evening, a night of fine dining and elegant conversations.

A hollow affair. Though, I'll never quite figure out how to properly thank Iyalla for her hospitality… Not at this rate anyways.

All will bend in thanks for what you are about to accomplish.

His eyes drift towards a towering row of statues. The set of sculpted fighters, strategists, and those gifted by mystics stand atop a great hall having pillars circle it.

The Hall of Prominent Honour… It doesn't even look like there's any more room for new heroes up there. An era solidified, untouchable.

He drops his vision to just below the dominating shadow of a great hero to find the Ardaelic cultists from outside The Hex in a semi-circle. Standing in their pointed robes of blue and black, they cast shifting stares and avoiding glares. The hidden gathering rattles the archaeologist's mind.

That older man is still with them. I suppose he lives to serve his goddess another day. And the Wöllralt, not as tall and proud as she was before– Wöllralt tribe to the filaash… A tribe that I don't believe would bother with a faith in Ardaelius. How curious.

Go ask them.

Why? I'm going to Millown, to find our oldest records. How would I not find the answers I'm looking for there?

"Are you even listening?" The gravel in Ram's voice nearly startles Fylorn.

"Yes," he blankly responds to the Nhavyyet, not moving his sights from the shaded trio. "See, those cultists are waiting for something."

"And?"

The tonal shift within one word eats away at the archaeologist. He finally brings his face to meet his companion's. "I'm going over to talk to them."

A short groan crawls from the Nhavyyet. "My friend…"

Fylorn propels himself forward. All sounds fade from his ears while he marches towards the cultists, mind racing to connect the appropriate words. He slips between passersby, avoiding eye contact as he mutters simple apologies. His feet bring him within steps of the darkened leader.

What is his name…

Shulath.

"Shulath?"

A sharp grin snaps onto the man's face. "Indeed, it is."

The Wöllralt behind him delivers a nudge before whispering in his ear. A flow of small movements along Shulath's face paint an intricate picture for the archaeologist.

"Anything of interest?" Fylorn interjects.

"Doryen is reminding me that my efforts haven't been in vain. Some are remembering me."

An eyebrow twitching on the Wöllralt's face draws the archaeologist's attention. He shifts his view to fully examine the enlarged woman before him.

"I have, but find myself here to speak with Doryen." Fylorn extends his hand towards the Wöllralt. "If I may."

Shulath's eyes widen before settling into a more comfortable scan to nearby crowds. Doryen steps ahead to present herself.

"What do you wish to know?"

The deep voice of the large woman takes Fylorn aback. He quickly resets himself while pinching his lips. "Tell me of the village to the filaash."

"Not much to tell, why?"

"The seer told me to go looking for the Gods there."

A flash of interest glimmers in the Wöllralt's eye. "It won't be any god you have heard of. And besides, they aren't true. Any other being asking for worship will only play with you. Ardaelius is the only divine to love you in return."

"The goddess of death and chaos loves you?" shoots from Fylorn's mouth.

"At what precipice of love for her people does Our Goddess bend to the whim of misery? Allowing her children to succumb to the sickness, the disease... The longest wait is a prelude to her, a test of your willingness. It is a choice with no other answer than action. It calls to you. It calls for her."

Ramble. Unintelligent rabble.

A long exhale seeps from the archaeologist while his lips waver in finding a selection of words. His eyes soften while coming to a suitable conclusion. "Does Ardaelius owe her people anything?"

The thick chuckle exploding from Doryen nearly covers Fylorn in spit. She holds her stomach while casting a low glance to her companions. On return to the archaeologist, she tightens her slouch and grins.

"If a people greatly owed is what you seek, then there is no better source other than the village of my people."

Quickly, a soft warmth creeps onto the nape of Fylorn's neck. He delivers a polite head nod before departing the trio. The entirety of his approach to Ram is met by the Nhavyyet's solemn despair. A cold air precedes Ram's words.

"Learn anything?"

"The Wöllralt have a god we don't know about."

"And you think it might be the one to have made this deal?"

Fylorn shrugs. He looks up to find the fila sitting around half-day. After conferring with the Nhavyyet, the pair leave their station to walk through the bustling streets of Galiram. The sacks burdened over the archaeologist's shoulder, holding valuables for the many days to come, swiftly works up a sweat on his back. The crowds grow thicker as they near the port. A grand display of the city's fleet, brimming in the finest sails and sailors, litter each dock. Fylorn spots the vessel that Iyalla had described they would be boarding.

Vibrant, silver plating lines the trim along each intersecting board of the ship's hull. A grand mast, bearing more sails than the archaeologist cares to count, restrains a wild flapping in the steady winds.

"Fylorn, that one?" Ram asks while ejecting a thick finger towards the figurehead of a dragon proudly displayed below the vessel's bowsprit.

"I believe so," he replies. "Seems Iyalla has a sense of humour after all."

"Why? I love dragons. I'll be glad to board a ship warded by such powerful creatures. I mean, in spirit of course. Gods forbid we actually end up seeing one while sailing, that would only end in…"

The Nhavyyet's words trail off as his eyes avert from Fylorn to pick over the many features of their paid transport.

Fate is fate…

A cool breeze holds his hands while passing him. He takes a deep breath of the salty air; an air he never cared for and certainly brought no ease to him now.

"Oh, come on," a musically effeminate voice yells aloud. "I said, 'No'."

Fylorn swings his body towards the familiar cantor. Coming down the nearby plank towards him, a thunder of clogs brings someone dressed in a sleeveless coat of brown leather. Her set of fiery eyes hiding behind strands of long white hair extinguish the chill on the archaeologist's skin.

"And you meant it," Fylorn comments. "What are you doing here?"

"I'm being paid to accompany… whoever shows up for this ship." Elijou peeks over the archaeologist's shoulder. "Maybe it's him?"

It seems my sister's latest joke has no end.

"He's with me." Fylorn pokes over his shoulder as a smile begins to grow across his face.

Ram barges forward to stand beside his companion, then moans, "You've met me; I was at Úlcida!"

The Pajiado girl shrugs it off. "Forgettable face."

A thick Nhavyyet finger points ahead while its owner grumbles, "Look here, friend. I might be the only one of my kind you've ever met. And I'll swallow comments about being short, or calling me stupid, but I will not idly stand by and be forgotten."

Fylorn rests his hand on the short man's shoulder. "No worries, my friend. I will not be forgetting this."

The archaeologist's lengthy chuckle evolves into a stroll ahead, smiling at the Pajiado girl as he passes. Her smell, of damp morning flowers, eats away at his thoughts. By the time he reaches the end of the plankway, standing before the sailing ship preparing to depart, he entirely forgets what he is doing. Sharply turning around, he throws eyes at the two still standing idly as they were.

"Well, let's go then."

"I'm still not sure it's you," Elijou counters.

"It's him," Ram grumbles before making his way towards the ship.

"Did you pay for me?" she questions.

"Nope," Fylorn promptly replies.

"And you don't care who did?"

"Oh, all the coin I have rests on the bet that it was Iyalla, my sister."

"Isn't it her coin," the Nhavyyet remarks from afar.

Elijou saunters past the archaeologist, splashing her scent upon him once more. Her vibrant eyes look him over before turning to gracefully step aboard the quarterdeck ramp. From over her shoulder she calls, "That would be the name I recall. She mentioned needing a slayer of assassins to watch over some weakling."

Fylorn smirks while watching Ram scurry up behind her to board the ship as well. He makes one final look back to the bustling docks behind him.

The Great City of Galiram, may you treat Iyalla better than I have.

The archaeologist grasps both railings while bringing himself onto the vessel. Once on the deck, he nearly crashes into two separate sailors while finding his bearings. Swiftly, he spots Ram engaging with a man almost as stout as he is.

The grand hat and crisp red of his coat bring a sense of precedence to him.

Must be the captain.

Narrowly avoiding another sailor, Fylorn stumbles over to the stairs leading up to the raised deck with the wheel.

Leaning beside a closed door, Ram throws an eyeball at his companion while amid his words. "See, I expected a water dragon, being a sailing ship and all. But a wind dragon! Now that brings some character to her– Fylorn, doesn't that bring some character to her?"

"Every ship I've ever seen has a figurehead."

The Nhavyyet blows some air while flicking a hand. "Don't listen to him. Bright boy, but has no sense when it comes to being distinguished."

"That's because I like substance," the archaeologist quips in return.

A rumbling laugh expels from the captain. While holding one hand atop his protruding gut he whips the other out for a handshake.

"Kindly crossed, Master Fylorn. Call me Captain Forberst."

"Kindly crossed, Captain Forberst."

"Anyways," Ram brings himself back into the conversation, "My friend here is an archaeologist. Have you ever come across dragons underwater? Or perhaps bones washed up in your travels?"

"My contact mentioned him being an academic."

Fylorn bounces his eye between the two as the Nhavyyet glares in response to the remark. "And, has aspirations to find the remains of ancient dragons one day."

The captain returns his attention to the archaeologist. A subtle squeeze from his bottom lip brings a groan of consideration onto the sailing man's face. "We won't be seeing dragons this far out, but I'll keep you safe if we do."

His glib reply compels a twitch in Fylorn's one eye. The archaeologist tightens his jaw before countering, "You'd be surprised."

"And I will," Captain Forberst snaps back before swinging a hand out to clear a way between the companions so he may climb up to the wheel.

Ram strikes a glare at Fylorn while words spill from his mouth, "Why do you have to be like that?"

"I don't think he actually likes dragons."

"And?"

"And I'm not having half a conversation."

His lingering eyes are met by a scowl from Ram. "Fine, go have an intellectual deliberation with the pretty girl of substance."

The Nhavyyet man flippantly waves while turning to follow the captain up to the wheel. Fylorn looks to the bow of the sailing ship to find Elijou resting upon the railing. Her legs dangle over the edge as she gazes out into the open sea ahead. The archaeologist makes his way, passing busy sailors, to come alongside her. A damp feeling seeps into him as he presses his folded arms on the same railing.

"You might fall, sitting like that."

Her white hair floats up, then sticks to her forehead. She wipes it away before looking down to him. "I'll be fine."

"Been taking care of yourself for a while now, I imagine."

"A very accurate imagination you have."

Fylorn chuckles, then sets his gaze as far as he can out into the waves. "Do you think being tough helps you survive?"

"What do you know about being tough?" Elijou releases a small chuckle. "Your sister sent me to watch over you."

Wind brings the brine of the open sea to touch Fylorn's face. He allows the moment to pass. Waves succumbing to larger waves hold his attention until he feels Elijou adjust how she sits. A fraying string from her leather coat touches his arm, but he pretends not to care.

"Do you have a sister?"

"Yes, and a brother; twin idiots. I believe you met the latter as you entered Úlcida. After– ...he's a bastion now, defender of the village."

"You seem fairly versatile; you could be a village's bastion."

Elijou breaks out into laughter. She throws Fylorn a look before exhaling the fit away. "Do you use words like 'Versatile' often?"

"As often as you avoid the question."

"I don't avoid questions; I avoid answering them."

"Why?"

"Why not?" the Pajiado girl snaps back.

"Wow." Fylorn rolls his eyes. Bringing them back to Elijou, he finds her stare to be longer and deeper at sea. "I haven't been on a sailing ship, not this size anyways, for a very long time. When I was younger my parents died while sailing to Galiram, on the exact opposite course we're taking right now."

"I never knew my father," she blankly responds.

"In some ways I would have preferred that to losing him. And in other ways… I've always been the father in my family."

Elijou turns to face him, investigating each one of Fylorn's eyes for a silent moment, then says, "So she cares about you?"

"I wasn't sure." He playfully nudges the Pajiado girl's shoulder. He watches as they drop, and her face softens. "Alright, that was one from me, now your turn. Why did you call yourself an 'Assassin slayer'?"

"I never agreed to this," she blurts out while rearing her head back. After licking her lips and delivering a half-hearted stare she returns her eyes to the sea. "The Veil's Hand, have you ever heard of them?"

"Nope."

"And you never will, unless you read about them."

"Nah, that's Ram's job."

The Pajiado girl furrows her brow, then continues, "I was finished being... beholden to people. And they killed the only man I ever knew to be a father."

"Without hesitation, I would do the same."

"No. What I did was different. It wasn't revenge, it wasn't a good deed to defend the people of Galiram, or Úlcida. I was practising."

"Well, whatever your goals are, you don't have to reveal them– not to me anyways. But what I saw in The Hex was masterful, and am glad to have you aboard with us... Speaking of which, how long are you being paid up to? Millown? Until I die?"

"Millown."

"I see."

"Fylorn!" a rhythmically assertive voice calls out.

The archaeologist turns his head to find his Nhavyyet companion hailing him from the raised deck while holding the wheel. Fylorn waves to confirm he understands, then slowly turns back to the Pajiado girl. Her dangling legs knock upon the weathered wooden boards behind her heels.

What do I say?

Does she even want to talk?

"I should get moving; he has a temper, I find. Do you want to come with?"

"I come and go as I please, you'll be wise to remember that," Elijou comments. The whimsical notes of her voice give Fylorn everything he needs to push from the railing and make haste towards Ram.

Moving along the deck, the archaeologist swiftly weaves between the sailing men this time. He ambles up the steps to the raised platform. Before he approaches the wheel, his Nhavyyet companion boasts from afar.

"The captain says he knows about the Wöllralt village!"

Fylorn stops in his steps. He flickers his sights between the beaming Ram and the drained mug of Captain Forberst.

"How did you pry that from him?" the archaeologist quips.

One sole laugh bursts from the captain before sliding to the wheel and relieving the short man of any duties. "He did, indeed. Not the plan, of course, as our course is set for Millown. But I have had the occasional fortune of enough coin to bring my lady out that way. The waters are not kind up towards The Mouth."

"I see," Fylorn remarks. "And how long is this course expected to take?"

"Hard to say," Captain Forberst tilts his head in exaggeration while toying with the calculation.

Ram nearly snaps his neck twisting it so fast as he brings his own report. "Five days."

The archaeologist squints and smiles at the grotesque snarl that emerges on the captain's face.

"About that…" Captain Forberst chews on the words before quickly announcing to the crew, "Draw the plank, we leave at once."

The sailing men spring into action while the captain returns his focus squarely on Fylorn. "I suggest you get used to it."

Captain Forberst widens his snarl into a grin, then swings his neck over to begin barking orders at the men below. Ram rests a hand on his companion's shoulder, but Fylorn shrugs it off to begin his descent back to the deck. Along his way he lets out a mumble to himself.

"Oh, I will."

Bring me the one I require.
There is no one to bring to you.
I am your master, and you shall do as I ask, or else.
I never agreed to this. There is nothing to be gained for me.
You are correct, there is only loss in your future.

Fylorn awakens, still as stone but sweating profusely. He slows his rapid breathing, bringing himself from the panicked state. The blackness surrounding him is complemented by the harsh lapping of waves against the outside hull. While sitting up in the bed, he notices the wet stain left behind from the nightmare.

I thought I was done with those. They're getting worse the closer I get to finding the truth. That seems like a good sign, but it might take more. Much more than I have to offer… I need some air.

He leans to stand up. After loosely dressing himself, Fylorn finds his way to the ship's deck. The pale light shining from the moons is shaded by the mighty mast. He listens to the steady rhythm of waves while bringing himself against the port side railing. The slow passing land keeps his eyes busy while his mind wanders once more.

I never thought I would find myself on a ship like this again. Not by my own will, at any rate. And, I find myself sailing above the same waters that took you both. Took... it's not as if the two of you were around a lot. It makes sense that we had servants, but also... Iyalla was lucky to have someone other than me trying to take care of her.

Fylorn puffs air while waggling a frustrated face.

All of these years and I thought she was the one hurting, thinking it would be up to me to make something of our vheer as though she never existed... I can't even handle my own problems, let alone lead a new family into greatness. Those damn nightmares Father gave me are going to plague me to an early death, and Ardaelius knows if any son of mine will be subjected to the same thing. The family is ruined and I'm out here risking my life to bring it back from the dead... because a book told me so.

"Fylorn?"

The delicate tones of a Pajiado woman carry through the night to the archaeologist's ears. He turns his head to spot Elijou leaning on the center mast of the sailing ship.

"That's me," he coyly replies before returning his sights to the trailing landmass.

"Also can't sleep?"

"Yeah, and if you want to talk, come over here. I'm not talking behind myself the entire time."

"Ooh," her tone shifts into its usual jesting. "Very tired, I see. Has the darkness started slipping in?"

"More than you know."

The Pajiado woman skips across the deck, adorned in a sapphire blue robe. Coming to stand next to Fylorn, she leans backwards against the railing while grinning at him. The moonlight brings a faint life to the sunken black beneath her eyes. "Tell me all about it."

Even in this starry night, Fylorn can still see the shine in the fiery eyes of Elijou. "No."

"No? That's it? I came all the way over here for nothing?"

"If you want to talk, then talk." He exhales a quick snort while shifting his gaze far ahead of the ship. "And hurry up, it looks like Millown isn't very far."

The archaeologist swiftly snaps his sights around to the captain. His murky face hides much of his expression, but Fylorn could still recognize the man was tired while diligently holding the wheel through the long night.

He returns his eyes to meet Elijou's.

"I heard you and Ram discussing that village."

"You heard that, did you?"

She rolls her eyes.

Fylorn continues, "Alright. Yes, we did, but..."

"You're going to Millown."

"It seems to be where my road is leading."

"Really? Because the seer told you about the village, so isn't that where you should be going?"

"I don't know where the village is, or what to tell them..." Fylorn grips the wooden railing, clenching his teeth until they hurt. "I don't know anything, alright. I keep telling myself that I know what I'm supposed to be doing, but every choice I make leads me to failure."

"Every choice you make? Going to Millown isn't a choice; that's letting life make choices for you. You, you silly little man, want to go to the Wöllralt. You want that, don't you?"

"I wanted space, and that's what I got."

A cold wind graces the archaeologist. He tenses the muscles of his arms, pushing them further into the wood they rest upon. The sizable moment comes to a neck-braking halt when he feels the pads of soft fingers daintily land on his balled fist.

"I've had space."

After closing his eyes, Fylorn allows a long breath to escape him. A warm breath that he knows splashes across the Pajiado woman's hand, but she doesn't move. From the corner of his mouth he answers, "Your mother believes I'll find my answer there?"

Her hand quickly retracts before Elijou's chipper voice raises to nearly a shout, "Perfect, then go tell the captain we're going there."

Fylorn tilts his head before speaking to the Pajiado woman. Her stare is long and deep, not unlike the starry night above.

"You're only coming with us to Millown."

"Until Millown... So, whenever we get there."

Her words fuel the archaeologist. With his bolstered energy, he pushes from the railing and marches up to the raised deck of the wheel. He looks back once, finding Elijou remaining in the chilling breeze, gazing out at the slow-moving land. Fylorn itches his scalp while climbing the steps to the raised deck in grand leaps. As he arrives, the dim outline of the captain is brought into a haunting and gloomy portrait.

"Captain?"

A drowsy mumble comes from the sailing man. His hands shift the wheel ever-so-slightly.

"Captain Forberst?"

"Uh. Um... Yes, son. What do you need?"

"Are you fit to sail?"

"As fit as any man ever has been."

With a twisting of his head, Fylorn looks ahead before returning to the glossy eyes of the sailing man.

"How can you see anything?"

Captain Forberst releases a chuckle that swiftly alters into a tired moan. "Nothing? Go. Stare into the night's cold black eyes, see what you find."

Fylorn can feel his eyes already growing dry and tired from the nocturnal affair. He casts a glance ahead once more, putting on a proper show for the fading captain. After a few moments, the archaeologist begins to turn back but stops short. He blinks, trying to sharpen his vision as best he can.

No. No! Really? That blue, is that her dragon? That girl's spirit! How did she make it to Millown? Good for her– Good for her… We're almost near, and Millown is nice, but–

"Captain Forberst! Look portside! It's a dragon!"

After hollering as loud as he can, the archaeologist gathers his breath while looking back to the captain. The faint light that he had seen in the wavering night flashes powerfully in the reflection of the man's eyes. A mighty, blue serpent spreading its wings is clearly visible. Fylorn's face falls as the spike of victory rushing through him rapidly melts away into panic. The frozen man before him doesn't sail away, or slow his vessel, but simply does nothing in the fright.

Captain Forberst's chattering teeth evolve into words, "They, they, they're, they're, not supposed, supposed to be out here!"

The sailing man burst into action. He leans over, blowing into a stationed horn. Immediately Fylorn can feel the ship shake as every man aboard springs to life. The rumbling of movement seeps into his bones. His eyes wander back to find Elijou grinning wildly at him before bolting away. All around him the energy rises as sailing men make haste to bring the vessel to maximum speed.

"Captain!" Fylorn hollers at the man standing directly next to him. "Where are we to go if Millown is under siege?" Captain Forberst's brows sharpen as the years of experience settle the aging man's nerves. "We'll have to bring her out to sea and turn back for–"

"No," the archaeologist abruptly cuts the captain off. "We can't leave them helpless. Why don't we…" His mind rattles for a rational way to convince the man of what he wants. "Why don't we go to that village and get the Wöllralt to aid Millown!"

A powerful flexing of Captain Forberst's jaw precedes flared nostrils and feral eyes. "Those beasts will never aid the Hue, not after what we did to them."

"We?" Fylorn gathers the rising pitch of his voice to retain civility. "Imagine, Captain, jumping at the chance to kill dragons once more. Those giants would do anything for another chance at… that."

The captain forcefully snaps his head away. Fylorn can hear him muttering something to himself in private before bringing his head back up, raising his chin high, and lining his sights straight ahead. He lets out a rallying cry, before leaning over to blow on the mounted horn once more. As every sailing man aboard turns their full attention to their captain, Fylorn can feel a chill run down his spine. The air rests flat for the few breaths before Captain Forberst speaks.

"We are no cowards! We shall not abandon those in need! We sail for the Wöllralt village!"

Even the pale light of the moons couldn't deter the wash of grim faces. Taking turns, the crew all make a quiet look to the dragon beyond, then silently focus on the task at hand. Fylorn remains by the captain's side while the harsh waves and crippling winds make the deck of the ship unbearable. Within the shadows, a rummaging of work can be heard as the sailing ship is tied off to set course for The Mouth of Ardaelius.

Chapter 21
The Father

The long night holds its own against the coming morning as fog rolls in, keeping a damp blanket around the vessel. Tried and true sailing brings the ship from the claws of uncertainty and into the fresh dawn of the following day.

A sight befitting a voyaging king, the golden shine upon the glistening water of the gigantic bay lifts Fylorn's spirits. He witnesses in awe as the captain brings his lady in along the frigid coastline, aiming towards an oversized wharf ahead. The many daunting ships tied off to the algae-ridden planks brings a tightness to the archaeologist's chest. He shifts his sights from the fleet back to the shoreline. Stretches of alpine forest ebb and flow atop the land.

Curious, so many trees are broken and pushed aside.

Fylorn spots a breach of the wild growth. His eyes narrow to the wonder, but it reveals an underwhelming space beyond. The wide field running uphill from the waters has a scattering of stone huts, all surrounding one grand structure. Centering the string of homes is a steady rising of massive, flat stones forming a staircase suitable for the giant beings. The archaeologist spots a few Wöllralt puttering around within the main encircling of huts, but the nearest one catches his eye.

The lone female near the water tends to a line of hanging fish set above the largest barrels Fylorn has ever seen. While turning to eye the coming vessel, she displays a placid face painted in blacks.

Not a scowl. Not eyes of fear for coming danger. Simply a clear lack of excitement.

Remember how you looked upon those ants.

A shaking hand grasps Fylorn's shoulder. The chin of Captain Forberst slides into his right-side view. "Dunno if they'll be as friendly as last time, son. My dealings with them are few and far between, for good reason. It likely goes without saying, but I'm a skeptic of a man, so here goes. They are stronger than us, even the younglings. We do as they ask, speak when spoken to, and please think before you open your maw, son."

"I'll do my best," the archaeologist softly replies.

The unnerving crunch from the tip of the sailing ship brings the vessel to a halt. Fylorn casts his view behind, to empty waters along the silted delta. His sights return to find the crew of the ship are all stoic, awaiting any orders that would keep them from leaving the sea. Captain Forberst passes him, making long strides down the stairs to the main deck before scanning the line of standing sailors.

"At ease, men. Only I and our guests will be going into the village. No need to bring more attention than needed."

A handful of relieving sighs roll through the sailors. Fylorn quickly joins the captain, finding both Ram and Elijou at the ramp awaiting him to disembark. Every footstep rattles the boards as they make their way down the weathered quarterdeck. A distinct shift to silence as their weight bears no stress to the plankway's wood clings to the archaeologist's mind. He turns his attention to the bollards that line the wharf.

Each the size of boulders. Each hosting mooring lines as thick as oxen.

"You've lived in a village before, right?" Ram says to Elijou. "Why don't you talk to them first and use that charm of yours."

The Pajiado woman, head shrouded by her hood, doesn't even scoff while coming to the end of the plankway. Fylorn casts a disapproving glare at the Nhavyyet as the pair follow the captain. The captain hustles, trying to make it off the wharf as quickly as possible. while descending to the cold riverbed below. To his left, the archaeologist takes one more look at the fish-handling Wöllralt. She gives him a quick flick of her eyes while carrying on with her duties. Returning his sights ahead informs Fylorn that a team of Wöllralt had assembled at the stoop of the first wide, stone step. While awaiting the giants to make some form of declaration a low but effeminate voice calls out from behind.

"Welcome."

The party spins to find the woman from the shore stepping towards them.

"Thank you," Captain Forberst quickly replies with a bow.

After everyone takes a look at each other, the rest of the group bows as well.

"I've seen you before," the Wöllralt woman booms at the captain before scanning the remaining people before her. "A Hue, a Nhavyyet, and a Pajiado... What brings so many differing people to my hohrt?"

Hohrt?

Their word for tribe.

"We come asking for your help," Captain Forberst begins but is quickly cut off by the woman.

"We have nothing to offer your kind. Be gone."

Without a second thought, the captain moves ahead, walking back towards the river. After a few paces he turns back to see the rest of the party remaining still. "What are you waiting for? Them to bring you by force?"

Fylorn drifts his eyes to either side of him. Glares from both Ram and Elijou burn into him, awaiting him to make the decision. The archaeologist lifts his chin before setting his eyes on the Wöllralt woman ahead of him.

"What do they call you? I do not wish to have such an important conversation with a stranger."

The heart inside of the archaeologist's chest beats so hard it nearly brings him to tears. Eyeing the stoic face ahead of him unconsciously brings his breath to a short, quiet pace.

"I am the mossteev. I carry the burdens of bone and blood. It is through my wisdom that my people do not perish from poor family lines." She draws a gulp of air, swelling her chest. "It is also my place to pick who may seek our council."

"I seek it," Fylorn promptly responds.

"For what reason?"

"The story is long, and I shall not waste either of our breaths. I come seeking guidance from your god."

"What do you know of him?"

"Nothing yet."

"And you seek him, why?"

Tell them who you are!

"My name is Fylorn Dagus, and I–"

A wave of gasps burst from the Wöllralt around him at the utterance of his name. The mossteev shoots glares at her people until only the drone of hushed words can be heard. Her eyes dig into Fylorn before words cross her lips.

"I shall bring you to our lrotirölt." As a smile slowly trickles onto the archaeologist's face her words boom loud out for all to hear, "You, and only you. The rest must return to your ship."

Fylorn feels a hand grace his shoulder before Ram speaks, "It'll be fine. We'll wait for you."

He shifts his sights to Elijou who silently nods in agreement. Fylorn returns a nod of approval, then his companions bring themselves from his side to journey with the captain back to the ship.

While standing tall, the archaeologist waits for the mossteev to escort him into the village. They cut through the line of Wöllralt men guarding the first stone plateau. Each step the woman makes brings an uncomfortable shake to Fylorn's bones. Once standing alongside them, the massive height of the giants finally sinks in as they tower over him. Moving ahead, the scents of purple arctic flowers and juicy spit-roast meat begin to play with his nose. She leads him up into a crest of stone huts surrounding a roaring fire.

Sitting on boulders circling the cooking meat are three Wöllralt. Two men both appear much younger than the oldest man. All of them wear bear skin cloaks and fur hoods. A scowl ejects from the young men at the sight of the archaeologist, but the older man's mouth quivers while holding back a smile.

The mossteev speaks to him in their native tongue, so fast and fluently that Fylorn can but barely grasp at a few words.

Woön... Nito... Eöin... Heltörs, and lrotirölt again.

Once the woman finishes her speech to the older man, she gestures for the two young men to come with her. They bring their haunches of meat with them while strolling away, leaving only the lrotirölt and Fylorn near the fire. The pair sit in silence for a while. Slurping sounds of the Wöllralt eating echoes around the hollow place. Crisp winds flow down the open land, delivering a new chill to the archaeologist.

"Cold?" the lrotirölt comments at the first shiver of Fylorn.

The archaeologist clears his dry throat before responding, "I haven't been this far filaash before."

"Not many have. Not kind for your kind."

"Is that why the village is up here?"

A long chew of gristle proceeds the old man's answer, "No."

Fylorn waits in the silence thinking of many questions he could blurt out to keep the conversation going, but holds his tongue.

"No," the lrotirölt continues, "We once lived filaash The Perfect Wild. This feels like home to us."

"Why didn't you go back?"

"Some questions are left unanswered." The old Wöllralt coughs before spitting out a hunk of half chewed meat. "She tells me that you come seeking our god. Have your own gods failed you?"

"I wouldn't reach to say I am a man of any god. But, those who do follow have told me my answer lies with your people, here in this village."

"This hohrt."

The archaeologist's tongue slips, letting a quick question out, "What is a hohrt?"

A small smile crosses the lrotirölt's face, exposing his large teeth that have bits of meat squeezed between them. He exudes a breath of the hot dinner. "I didn't expect one of the Hue to carry such an interest in my people."

Fylorn grins in return. "I've never felt myself to truly be a part of the Hue. They seek more, and more, and bigger, and stronger. Yet, don't seek you. It hasn't made a lick of sense to me."

"We didn't allow it." The old man's hands raise to spread wide in a gesture across the hohrt. "And this is what we got. The final hohrt. The only remaining tribe of Wöllralt. The last of our people."

A hearty chuckle falls from Fylorn. He watches as the lrotirölt shifts between confusion, shame, and bitterness. "No, my giant friend. I laugh because I am the last of my family, and it is the exact reason I come to you."

The enlarged eyebrow of the lrotirölt strikes up. "We are not friends. The Wöllralt have not had friends, only those who wish to use us. I care not for the words of why you come here. Greed and power are it, the only sense of Hue worth I have ever found in all my years. You step onto my ground, asking it to be ours."

A grand frown compresses Fylorn's face. He takes precious breaths before uttering, "You look at the steps I have taken, but alone they make no sense. They follow one after another, so you must look at the composition of my path to see the way I walk. Only then will it make sense."

Three cracks of bone upon the stone below come as the meat slips from the lrotirölt's hand. He stands, casting a chilling shade over Fylorn. With absolute silence, he walks off towards the stone steps. Each booming step of the lrotirölt strikes out on his journey to the gigantic stone structure at the precipice of the stairs. The archaeologist swiftly rises to follow him. As he glides up the wide and flat stone, the aged Wöllralt turns and gently places his wide hand on Fylorn's chest, bringing his stride to a strict halt.

"Only those of our hohrt are permitted inside."

"I need to know. About your god, about your history."

"Then you will need to prove yourself worthy."

Fylorn looks over his shoulder at the tiny ship floating at the wharf. He returns his sharp eyes to the aged Wöllralt.

"What do I need to do?"

The lrotirölt grinds his teeth while raising his sights to the village. A mighty wind pelts the man's face, throwing his long hair about while ideas steal him from this world.

Finally, the aged Wöllralt eyes snap to Fylorn. "The Hue, those who call you kin but you deny them, they are greedy. They chose to hold us down by means of food. They enslaved us without chains, using threats of starvation. We cannot live together without killing one another." The lrotirölt raises his oversized hand flat to guide Fylorn's focus to the fields nestled behind the horht. Out in the mulched patches are the differing growths of massive berries and nuts. "This is the truth. We kidnap the Pajiado and bury them to grow our fields. Without their blood, we die. Do you understand?"

Fylorn's deep breathing fuels his words, "What do I need to do?"

Without hesitation, the elder Wöllralt lowers his head, bringing him face to face before speaking, "The one we call Full Giant. He was taken during our last struggle. Tongues have brought word that he is being imprisoned in Mashar Pelim… Bring him home and you may call it your own."

Mashar Pelim… No, not that prison. A prison I've only heard whispers of, but whispers they needed to be. A horrendous nightmare I wouldn't wish for anyone.

The eyes of the archaeologist glaze over. His nose snarls while his breathing slows.

"It will be done."

Chapter 22
The Daughter

Energy surges through Ani as she wakes with a gasp. Now sitting up, she shifts her head while drawing in deep breaths. At the end of her bed is a dark silhouette.

"Ahh!" she screams while shuffling up the sheets towards her pillow.

As she adjusts her sights to the dim light of space, she slowly realizes the figure is a mannequin suited in a set of intricately made leathers in precisely her size. Her eyes dart around, reaffirming the young woman of where she is.

The room— My room. Red curtains... awfully black for this time of day. And that looks to be the armour they had me sized for. Not quite what I was expecting... and why did they bring it in overnight? Strange...

While letting her eyes linger on the Tamer's armour, the white of a closed letter draws her attention. Sitting at a casual angle upon the nearby desk, Ani flicks her sights between each until a thought impedes her morning.

Ora's always out in the morning...

She scans the space carefully to find a lack of the spectral dragon. Donning a concerned face, the young woman lifts her forearm up to her eyes, nearly touching her iris with the scar.

"Are you in there?" she whispers to it, her lips playing with the ridge upon her skin. "Look; it's just us now, no other friends. We're going to get used to having such a large family... which means we need to enjoy the little time we get alone."

Ani feels her eyes begin to swell as the distinct lack of wisps deliver a silent message.

"Ora, please. If I've done something, I am sorry. I know we've had some hard conversations lately– damn it, I don't even know if you understand what I'm saying. You've never made anything clear. You remind me of..."

Quivering lips halt anymore words from leaving Ani. A swift swallow is followed by the return of the mannequin to her sights. The dark corners give her little to admire. She slowly shakes her head before rolling out of the bed. The chilled floor below her feet brings a tingling sensation that lifts her mood. She releases a wide yawn while stumbling towards the nearby window. After a deep sigh, she takes the dangling velvet and slides it along to reveal a morning so early that the fila has only cracked streaks of light across the vast sea beyond.

"Oh," she utters. "It's so early."

She twists back to look inside, reminding herself of the letter on the table. After a relaxing stretch, she saunters over and picks up the folded paper.

Just 'Ani' on the front, again. I really hope it's good news this time.

The flaps of the paper release with ease, revealing the short note within.

'...There has been no sign of Tushma.' That's barely news at all.

Her fingers restrain from crumpling the letter while she flippantly tosses it back onto the desk. She tilts her head to closer examine the leather armour being displayed just within her reach. Ani takes a lateral step to bring her sights headlong to the piece.

Sturdy, woven, no fraying. It could be nice to have while riding Ora... Although, I'm pretty damn certain that I asked for more pockets. I could really use that satchel again—

She wiggles her lips while trying to keep her composure. Her eyes slowly descend to her spirit's wrest once again. The light of the morning casts a long shadow across her forearm as it graces the ridges of her scar. Ani brings herself back to the window, then holds her arm out into the open air.

"Go fly, if you don't want to be here!"

The shout sends a tingle along her skin. She draws in one sniff as the wrest remains dormant. Her sights trail down the warm light touching craggy stone bricks until finding a woman striding between open walkways towards the distant garden. The blue accents lining her flowing dress tickle the young woman's mind.

Shyvesh?

Before giving it another thought, Ani swiftly returns to the mannequin and slips into her new armour. Every edge caresses her body instead of digging or stabbing like her other clothes have been as of late. After having it completely on, she gazes down at herself.

This body I'm in now... Maybe one day I'll be as comfortable in it as these garbs make me look.

She shakes her head to expel all thoughts, then quickly bolts to find the spiral staircase which leads out into the courtyard. Walkway after walkway brings her nearer to the gardens. Once at the same position she had spotted Shyvesh, the young woman follows the natural winding of the path.

She wanders up and into the decadent gardens overlooking the salty cliffs.

Wide lengths of hedge, and plumes of various flowers, decorate the regal space. A clear line brings Ani towards the middle of the gardens, where a square yard made of stone and retaining walls provides an adequate place for rest and thought. Poured into one of the numerous metal chairs is Shyvesh casting a gaze towards the morning fila.

What do I say? Am I interrupting her? I bet she's already angry; who wakes up this early in the morning to watch the fila rise?

"Come sit," the grand tamer calls out.

The muscles along Ani squeeze on her bones at the beckon. She spends a moment loosening herself before striding into sight of Shyvesh's turning head.

"Don't be shy," she squawks at the young woman. "For Ardaelius's sake, you are one of us now. Come act like it and watch the horizon with me."

Ani silently does as she is told. The deep-set compulsion to do exactly as the grand tamer orders sets off a cold sweat along her back. After resting in the seat beside Shyvesh, Ani locks her eyes ahead before letting words slip from her.

"Do you come watch the fila often?"

"Sanctuary, no. I only come out here this early when I have things on my mind that need to be thought through before I begin my day."

"Thoughts such as…" Ani prompts the grand tamer to continue.

Shyvesh delivers a one small laugh before holding her fist out long and angular. Ani looks on as a familiar spirit's wrest sits on the equal but opposite side of the grand tamer's forearm as hers does. A wisp of red surges from the glowing scar, creating the image of a spectral hellix. Its front paws land upon the cold morning stone ahead of the pair before its shape is completed. Once full and magnificent, the creature twists its face at the young woman before lying down at its tamer's feet.

"Ani, I think you should let your dragon out for a while as well."

The clawing metal of the chair assumes a powerful forefront in the young woman's focus. She lifts her arms to free herself of the discomfort. With raised arms, her eyes are drawn to the scar upon her. While forcing a look away, her drifting sights land on the curious eyes of Shyvesh. A softening of the elegant woman's face brings a subtle warmth to Ani.

"You know," Shyvesh begins with a rising tone, "when I was your age, Escrah here used to find some silly joy in disobeying me. Her actions spoke words that I hadn't quite understood yet, and to this day I still find her being difficult... even at the best of times."

Ani's eyes line back up with the scar on her forearm. She aimlessly investigates every detail of the deformation she bears while listening to the grand tamer continue.

"One of the first things I tell new Tamers is to remember that you aren't just carrying a thing inside of you; it used to be a being. It thinks, it wants, it has a will all its own. Ironically, it's not meant to be tamed."

The hushing coo in Shyvesh's voice draws Ani's sights back. The elegant woman rests her hand upon the spectral hound, gently digging her fingers along the head and neck of the creature.

A small sigh releases from Ani before she feels the usual rush along her arm. Suddenly, a surging glow emboldens the nerves along her forearm as Ora pours itself from the wrest. The dragon emanates blue more powerfully than before as it emerges from Ani. Using its serpentile length, Ora wraps around the young woman's arm for only a moment before being too large to be supported. Landing on all four clawed feet, the dragon stretches its wings, entirely blocking the expanse ahead of Ani.

"Oh my," Shyvesh utters.

Ora's chest pumps with powerful breaths as it scans the garden around. Ani watches in hesitant wonder as the dragon steps ahead, snaking its long neck to approach the curled hellix only a few paces away. The young woman moves to stand but quickly an open hand is thrown by the grand tamer to halt her.

"No," Shyvesh slowly orders. "Let them."

She twitches while eyeing the elegant woman, then Escrah, and finally her own auragonic as all three play a small game of introductions with each other.

"It warms my spirit to see one of the dragons finally join us," the grand tamer comments while rising from her seat. She toes beyond her resting hound, making each stride half as long as it could be. The effort gathers the attention of the scaled beast. Ora angles her head around to aim at Shyvesh. The grand tamer holds still, keeping her hands low while only moving her chin and eyes. "Such a creature is not for the weak of heart. How did a woman such as yourself come across it."

Ani stands, bringing herself to the edge of the spectral wing of Ora. She extends her left hand to grace the boney spikes angling from the appendage while keeping herself facing the grand tamer.

"I came across it as it was born, then took its life."

One deep hum precedes Shyvesh's words, "You grew the auragonic... no easy feat."

"Yes, but it aged me. Now, I'm an eleven-year-old woman."

A chill and stillness blankets the air for a moment. Ani's hand upon Ora curls and falls slack to her side, then the dragon shifts its highest wing to allow for the fledgling light of day to cast upon Shyvesh. The illumination brings her face into grand view, a grim scowl.

Ani flexes her cheek as a growing itch builds on her own face. After clearing her voice, she continues, "Akaifi, he said that he had to stop enhancing Gibby or it would kill him. And I've heard some other stories… Is Ora going to drain my life until I die?"

"I, um… I don't know." The elegant woman's face becomes covered in shade as she turns it away from the angled light.

"Shyvesh?" the young woman asks.

"No, I'll be fine. I–" the grand tamer cuts off her own words with a forced exhale and shaking head. She retreats from the dragon, bringing herself to the opposite side of Escrah and setting her sights far down the földic coastline. "I was lying before. Some are old enough to know, but respectfully hold silence on the affair regarding the daughter I once had."

Ani abandons all other thoughts and feelings to set her full attention on the confessing woman, only to interject within the grand tamer's rambling, "What happened to her?"

"…The tales spun surrounding a person of perfect spirit," the tamer continues. "Well… they are highly held beliefs around here. It might sound like child's play, but we do not mingle with others carrying the same auragonic. And being the grand tamer, holding a hellix, means that another cannot."

The elegant woman's hand reaches out to touch the magnificent beast once again. Ora drops its head and neck to worm in for a scratch. Subtle quivers ripple around Shyvesh's face while allowing the moment to overtake her.

No one else has a dragon, which means I'll never have to avoid anyone. We can have whatever family we want. Go and find Tushma, bring him here or… Ora and I can grow old together… Until…

"I…" Ani fumbles for words. "How long ago?"

Shyvesh's eyes sharpen while her frown deepens. "About eleven years ago."

A complex splash of emotions washes over Ani. The morning fila brightens the elegant woman's soft nose and sharp chin while darkening her hair and blue eyes. Every measure of the young woman's focus is centered upon the grand tamer standing before her. Ani finally drops her face, bringing the charred mark upon her left arm into the forefront of her sights. She looks at it for some time, running her eyes up and down.

"Shyvesh?" Ani asks aloud.

"Look, we can figure this out–"

"I want to go home," falls from the young woman's mouth. As the grand tamer opens her mouth to speak, Ani beats her to it. "I know, I'm not ungrateful– I'm so grateful for everything the Tamers have done for me… It's just, I know where home is now, and I need to be there."

"This is not a prison."

"Okay," slowly falls from the young woman's mouth.

Shyvesh scoots across the open space to Ani's side. She reaches out and lifts the young woman's charred hand before settling a deep gaze into her eyes. "Take some time. Think about things. But remember, that dragon's home is here now."

All Ani can bring herself to do is give a short head nod. She feels the grand tamer's hands squeeze around hers before letting them go. The tiles beneath her feet are all she can see while the wisping sounds of Escrah returning to Shyvesh haunts her ears. One beam from the fila crosses into her vision, making a disturbance enough that jars Ani from her trance and brings her face back up. The garden, now a glowing yellow, rests cold and empty aside from the young woman and her dragon.

"Ora…"

The echoed word is all the order needed for the dragon to dissolve from its spectral form and wisp back towards Ani's forearm. She gazes out into the Mouth of Ardaelius once more before storming away. Each footstep she makes away from the gardens brings her closer to the castle, but further from any resolution.

What does that mean? Is she my mother? What happened to me that I was raised by Tushma out in the wilds? Where is my father? Wait, wait, wait! Did she give me up? Or did the king already try to kill me? Ugh, what am I doing?!? She's not. Why would she be? I'm just some dumb kid who came looking for the wrong thing.

Ani releases her built up fury by kicking a nearby stone. As it rolls along the tiled path ahead of her, she looks down at the ridges of her spirit's wrest.

"Now it's just me and you. And you… are killing me."

She frowns at herself.

"Do you even want to be in there? If I sent you free like Olokk would you be happy?"

The young woman stops in her tracks. Her gaze wanders from the lengthy path ahead towards the doorway leading all the way to the dining hall. Amid the back curtain of the castle to her left is a small entrance dug into the wall.

A tarnished, silver doorknob is the only distinguishable piece from within the blackened shadow.

Where does that lead?

A girlish curiosity compels her, and she darts ahead into the blanketed shade. She reaches to the knob and turns it. A prevailing creak erupts from the aged joints of the hinges. The room inside is damp, but beams of glistening light coming through high windows present the pluming dust within the air. Ani covers her mouth with her sleeve as she walks into the space. The clear path ahead leads her eyes to another doorway. Piles of chairs upon tables, covered in thick layers of cobwebs and grime border the walls. She scans both sides of the room, watching as the light reveals how old the chairs truly are.

Aged, and warped. I can't imagine they've been used for years. Years upon years, really.

Her eyes fall on a large faded brown sheet covering a tall and round object beneath. She toes towards the sheet, slipping a finger into a crease before yanking on it to unveil what lies beneath.

The tired eyes of a woman stare back at Ani in the perfect reflection of an elegant mirror. Her breath stills as her eyes can't take themselves from the creature she's looking at.

My eyes have never been so sunken in… My face is so blotchy, and – oh my – when's the last time I had someone properly fix my hair, it's disgusting.

She lifts her finger to poke at her face, but stops just shy of her skin as her eyes widen to view the dancing of blue wisps along her shoulders. The mirror can barely contain the entire image of Ora expanding behind the young woman. Before her very eyes, an aged face shifts from horror to disdain.

"How much bigger are you going to get?" she spits out while eyeing the dragon in the reflection. "How much bigger are you willing to get before you kill me?"

A jeweled iris of Ora's matches Ani in the mirror. The silent disapproval of the question brings a fire to the young woman's skin.

"No, of course it isn't your fault. It's my fault that I killed you. It's my fault that I absorbed you. It's my fault that I don't know what I'm doing with you! It's all my fault!"

Ani looks on as tears begin rolling down her face. She goes to wipe them but spies Ora staring at her in the reflection once again. A heat crawls along her face while her eyebrows furrow.

"If I figure out how to stop growing you, would you be happy?"

The stoic eyes of the dragon hold as stone while watching the young woman's face contort with each wave of emotions befalling her. Her eyes snap to the spectral beast, to detail every scale and spike along the dragon's length. She longs for her sights to creep to the animated snout of the beast, only for it to lean its head closer.

"Are you not happy you get to actually live?"

A soft plume of air from Ora's snort bathes Ani's back. The young woman slouches, letting her arms hang limply as her stare finally moves from the mirror to be idle while her mind takes over.

"You're just a dumb animal that used to be alive…"

Ani feels the pressure of her muscles as Ora puts itself back into her forearm. She lifts her arm to look at it head-on, then slowly turns back to the mirror. The young woman lifts her face, bringing the charred mark upon her left arm into the forefront of her sights. She looks at it, up and down, for time beyond the moment.

"You don't have any answers. And I've only taken care of you the best I can. I lived years without, it'll take some getting used–" the young woman throws her hand aside. A rage consumes her voice. "Is this what being a Tamer is? I thought I would come out here and become something… something I could be proud of. I expected to find a home!"

Her shriek echoes around the dusty room. She slowly breathes in the diminishing noise until she is left in the silence of her thoughts.

The door further in the room swings open. From behind the damp wood, in peeks the head of Shyvesh. Her face clearly at the ready to scream at some insolent child for their inappropriate behaviour melts away at the sight of Ani. The sudden change leaves her only about to coo while fully opening the door to come inside.

"I…" Ani bursts into tears. "I don't think I'm the kind of person that can handle this anymore. I'm not a hero. I don't know what I'm doing, and, and, neither does anyone. I'm not afraid of dying, I came all this way and made it with barely a scratch, but now what? I'm not going to just sit here and wait for Ora to take my life. What do I do? …Before I burn myself out."

The pleading eyes of the young woman impale Shyvesh, forcing her to swallow deeply to control herself before speaking. "There is a way. Olokk does it all of the time. Below the castle is a place, a pool of spirits, that we can draw the dragon from you. Then we can get you a… simpler auragonic."

Ani wipes a tear away while consuming the information. "If you are my mother… would you let me do it?"

"I will be with you every step of the way, Ani."

Soon the young woman realizes she's biting hard on her lip. She releases her teeth, tasting the iron of her blood. Ani turns to look at the floating dust of the space once more, and before her is a stagnant room. The quivering of her bottom lip reminds the young woman of her split flesh. One tear rolls from her eye.

"Take me to the pool, please."

Chapter 23
The Embrace

I still can't believe that at no point during the journey from the camp, passing through the repairing Ipith, or walking most of the long highways to Masher Pelim did Elijou complain about not arriving to Millown. We didn't take many breaks, and we barely talked – which is odd for Ram – but I think that's the way she likes it. I mean, I'm not one to complain. If she wants to help me with my problems... How in the Dak am I going to repay her for this? Well, I suppose I'll put her on the list with Ram and Iyalla.

"Do you think the Legion will recognize us?" Ram ponders aloud.

The light of the day nearly blinds Fylorn before he moves his stiff neck. He blinks until he registers that they're arriving at a set of monumental gates. While standing amid a line trailing out along the wide road leading to the plains behind him, he broadens his sights to the hills ahead. The grand city, holding the ground between, dwells as a triumph to architecture. Monumental towers of stone, reach towards the sky.

Those aren't watch towers... people live in there. And that, those unbelievable spires of Ardaelic Ardent, must be the Manse.

A beacon of all she is.

"Fylorn?" the Nhavyyet's assertive voice cuts through once again.

"Not likely," the archaeologist concludes. "Though, I wonder if Aal-Ivus ever made it…"

"I sure hope so, I miss that ugly mug."

"Aal-Ivus?" Elijou questions.

Fylorn twists his sights to the Pajiado woman. The common men and women shuffling about behind her, with their grey skin and tired faces, paint an exact counter to her. The brilliance coming off the single lock of white hair dangling from her hood draws his focus. His wandering eyes then find the strength in her strutting legs is too much and he shakes his head. Looking back at his Nhavyyet companion, he catches a grin crack onto the short man's face.

"Stubborn fool. A Hal-Vagenkar…" Ram's words trail off as the Pajiado woman's eyes fail to register their meaning. "…Right, I forgot you can't remember anyone's face." Elijou's eyes roll as Ram continues, "Big, green, ugly people."

"You already said 'Ugly'," the Pajiado retorts.

Ram chuckles to himself. "You'll understand if we see him, it's his best quality."

"Enough," crawls from Fylorn while eyeing either side of the massive portcullis within the sheen walls. Thrice the size of any other city walls within Goromföld, the structure looms overhead of the three. The archaeologist toes ahead to the man-sized doors being guarded by well-armoured sentinels.

"Do they allow Pajiado this far filaash?" Ram utters.

"Why don't you worry about yourself," Elijou barks behind her. "Maybe they eat silly, half-men here."

"Doubt it…" the Nhavyyet mumbles to himself. "Bones would hurt."

Fylorn strikes a glare behind him, quieting the chatty pair. He returns his sights ahead, keeping himself along a steady pace to the checkpoint. Once they arrive within sight of the guards, the archaeologist puts on an indentured face to portray a common simpleness. The steady line brings the party to armoured men who thoroughly eye each of them, up one side and down the other.

"Business?" one sentinel asks aloud, his dark eyes locked onto Elijou.

"Pilgrimage," Fylorn pipes in. "They are with me; we have come for the Manse of Ardaelius."

The guard's eyes linger on the Pajiado woman while following up, "A disciple, is she?"

Hot breaths from the sentinel splash across Fylorn. He checks over his shoulder, finding Elijou delivering a curt head nod to confirm, then quickly brings his face back to the armoured man. The guard's holding stare weakens, scanning the line behind them, before shifting his jaw.

"You get into trouble, and I'll find you."

One thick hand moves behind Fylorn, nearly pushing him through the city's entryway. The archaeologist wastes no time, shuffling through the portcullis and striding ahead along the perfectly filed stone bricks making the wide street. Within a few paces, he sees the other two lining up beside him.

"See, look what shutting up gets you," Fylorn remarks, not bothering to watch the reaction as he views the grand display of architecture ahead of him. The rising towers of Nhavyyet mastery draw his eyes along from height to gut wrenching height with sturdy bridges connecting the peaks of each.

An absolutely astounding work of architecture. I really, truly, should have begun working with them earlier– Though, I wouldn't have found that tomb... probably.

The very tip of destiny's claw-ridden reach rarely avoids its target.

I appreciate that, even when I'm not asking, you always have something marvellously wise, yet barely understandable, to say. And, as someone who demands that I listen, you are as deaf as ever.

A step ahead brings the archaeologist from his mental debate and back into the reality around him. Far up the street to his left reveals a wonder of elements. He pivots where he stands to charge towards the visual mystery.

"Where are you going?" Ram inquires.

"I want to see what this is," he quickly answers.

"Shouldn't we be…" the Nhavyyet's bearded face squirms from the mental acrobatics. "Actually. Elijou still hasn't explained her plan to us."

The archaeologist continues ahead while keeping half an ear on his companion's conversation as his eyes sprawl across the abundance of wealth the street carries. From men and women in the highest fashion he has ever seen to a miniature hanging garden every few paces, the pristine walkway ahead makes the rest of Goromföld seem barren in comparison.

"Alright, Elijou. So how exactly are we going to do this? Fylorn and I have come up with plenty of decent ideas and you keep telling us we're trying too hard."

The Pajiado woman winks before saying, "It'll be easy, don't worry about it."

"No," the Nhavyyet comes right back. "I will be worrying about it. A lot, in fact. Do you know what kind of prison this is?"

"Never been there, hence why we're walking right in."

Ram picks his jaw from the floor. "Let me help you out. It's Nhavyyet designed and Wöllralt made. It's a dagger into the black abyss of the Underföld, a place no one returns from."

"Why are we walking in if you can disappear amid the air and be anywhere you like?" asks Fylorn.

Elijou's eyes trail over to him. "It's not as simple as that."

"We saw you do it in the arena," totes Ram.

Holding a firm glare on the archaeologist, the Pajiado woman continues, "I need to visualize the place to bring myself there. At the arena I was treated to seeing it all from above ahead of time, so using my mystics to jump around wasn't an issue."

"Can't we just appear ahead of where you can see a few times until we're in there?" Fylorn questions.

"Also no," she snaps at the archaeologist. "Don't you know about Pajiado mystics?"

"He doesn't read," the Nhavyyet juts in. Both Elijou and Fylorn roll their eyes at the comment. Ram continues, "It's in your blood, right?"

"It uses our blood; I can only use it so much or so often before needing a break."

The archaeologist feels his face go white as he ponders the revelation.

If she uses too much, it could literally kill her. So, we can't be wasting it... or taking unnecessary risks.

"These jumps," Fylorn begins but halts himself to gather his words. "...We saw you take the assassin with you and release him on high."

"Yes, I can take others with me – but – I've never taken more than one before."

"Sounds like we should have tried this out on the way up here," Ram spits out.

The Nhavyyet receives a grim glare from Elijou, only broken by Fylorn's words.

"Add it to the list of things we should have done to stop us from being here in the first place."

Ram grumbles while the Pajiado upturns her nose to look at the imposing structures around them.

A bath of flowing waters gently pours from reaching heights to come down as a transparent curtain along one side of the street. The other side holds the domain of the smiths, hosting grand fires fueling massive forges large enough to build entire caravans inside of.

"Why do we even care about other places?" crawls from the Nhavyyet's mouth. "Seems like we should just live here and enjoy the rest of our lives."

"I'm sure someone like you – would – enjoy a place like this," Elijou murmurs.

"What? Afraid you'll fall while teleporting around like an idiot."

"I'd rather be 'like an idiot' than actually be as dead in the head as you are!" the Pajiado shouts in return.

After a few turning glances from the public, Fylorn halts his step and takes hold of each of his companion's shoulders.

"Look. We can't make a huge commotion around here or…" A wash of connecting ideas floods his brain. "Or we'll get sent to prison."

His eyes slowly shift to Elijou who stands with a huge beam on her face.

"You have to be kidding me," Ram complains. "That couldn't have been your plan."

"Well," the Pajiado holds out a hand to the archaeologist, "Him and I were smart enough to think of it. How does that make your puny brain feel?"

A powerful crimson flushes the Nhavyyet's face. Before the short-tempered man begins unloading his rage, Fylorn interjects, "Fastest way to be imprisoned is theft and murder–"

"And you couldn't murder a fly," Ram spits out through clenched teeth.

"Right. So, I guess we should go to the closest market and stir up trouble."

The archaeologist shakes his head while hearing the stupidest words he's ever spoken leave his mouth.

"Could be fun!" Elijou pipes in, bursting with excitement. She then skips away and promptly stops at the first person she bumps into to start a conversation.

Fylorn throws a tired look at Ram, then hears the stout man utter, "What happens when they split us up in the prison?"

"It's honestly not the worst idea, admit it."

"I'm not admitting anything. In fact, I want it to be written down in all of the records that I directly opposed this idea."

"Duly noted," the archaeologist slowly replies before marching ahead to meet up with the Pajiado.

Before he comes within a few paces of the woman, she barks out, "They told me where the market is. Try to keep up!"

As the Pajiado bolts away into the crowd, Fylorn feels the dense shoulder of Ram brush by while he starts after her. The archaeologist swiftly follows suit and joins the race. In a quick hunt, the pair find Elijou only a few streets away, standing on a raised slab of stone looking down into a bustling plaza below. As they approach the beaming woman, Fylorn scans the crowd to comfort himself that they'll be able to have city guards spot their petty theft. Ram unleashes a hearty laugh before shaking his head, then tilts his sights while charging off immediately and is absorbed into the crowd. Making great progress, the Nhavyyet swims towards the further end of the plaza until he halts. The man looks down each extending walkway before raising a hand to point far to his left.

"Have you two ever been here before?" Elijou calmly asks the archaeologist.

Fylorn allows one small chuckle before explaining, "You'd be surprised how little I've travelled for how much I know. Or, how much Ram will claim to know. Keep up."

The archaeologist places a quick hand on the Pajiado woman's shoulder before striding ahead. He veers to the outer edges of the commotion, avoiding the major groups of stalls and their patrons, until he spots the Nhavyyet once again. Walking up behind the man covered in a grand shadow, Fylorn analyzes as Ram stares longingly at one of the dominating towers of the city.

"Think you could do better?" the archaeologist asks.

"No, I just…"

"Miss it?" Fylorn finishes the fleeting sentence.

"Yeah." Ram pinches his lips before looking over his companion's shoulder. "I don't think stealing bread is going to cut it, they'll just chop a hand off or something."

"You read that somewhere?"

The Nhavyyet puffs air at his companion before taking a wide glance around. Fylorn tracks the scan to find a nearby leather stall having three guards lingering alongside it.

"I think we could use some extra straps, don't you?"

"Straps?" the soft voice of Elijou cuts in. "What are you boys doing while I'm not around?"

A unified eye roll from the pair precedes Fylorn ordering, "Alright. Are we just going to go up and pick a fight, or steal and flee?"

"Flee? I thought we were trying to get captured?" the Nhavyyet counters.

The archaeologist turns to face the stout man. "Yes, flee. You literally just said they would start chopping off limbs. Believe it or not, I don't want that."

"And you think I do?"

"I have–"

A hard wallop of leathers slams into Fylorn's chest. Within the briefest of moments, he watches the blur of Elijou leave the evidence in his instinctual clutches and zip away. Then, the darkened eyes of silver-plated guards lock onto him. A heat builds in his chest as the weight of the situation sets itself into him. He flicks a look to Ram, only to find him already slipping through gathering people.

"You!" one guard hollers out.

The accusation is all the archaeologist needs to trigger his legs. He immediately drops the leathers and scrambles away. Using his hands to reach out and balance himself at tight turns, Fylorn manages to catch up to his Nhavyyet companion with ease.

"Where did she go?" Ram breathes out.

"She was right here," Fylorn answers while swinging his wild eyes behind him. "I didn't think I would have to start watching where she goes now."

A high-pitched holler calls out, drawing the men's attention. They look up to find Elijou nearly two streets away, leaning against an imposing statue at an intersection of the walkway they flee down.

"Hurry up!"

The pair look at each other before cracking a small grin. Ram bolts ahead, sneaking his way through the overdressed crowd, using his short stature to his advantage. Fylorn reassures that his bow is sitting tight on his shoulder before he darts in between two flowing gatherings of people. Without checking on his companion, the archaeologist weaves and bobs, almost causing an alarm amongst the idle men and women of the street. The bumping of his strung bow against the back of his head forces his hand to grab a hold and keep the weapon tight to his body. Out of the corner of his eye he spots a blur but swiftly has to refocus ahead as he nearly tumbles into an elegant pair of aristocrats strolling while conversing.

"Sorry!" he calls out, promptly receiving a deathly glare from the couple.

Fylorn doubles his speed. He conserves his breath while analyzing the intersection ahead in search of Elijou. Standing with her arms crossed, the Pajiado glares at him. She pulls on the tip of her hood, then throws eyes far to her right. The archaeologist tracks her sights to find a gathering of guards hollering at a pile of ragged men.

Uh oh.

His boots dig into the stone below him while trying his best to slow his pace. Frantically, he scans around for Ram, only to find him cutting between a moving sect of Ardaelic disciples before strolling up next to Elijou. Fylorn nearly chokes from his laughter as she bats his open arms away while informing the stout man of present dangers. The Nhavyyet's smug grin melts away before he quickly spots his long-time friend.

After adjusting his robes and raising his chin, Fylorn steps out from a crowd to meet his companions. Ram stands watch, eyeing the extending intersection for coming guards while the archaeologist denies the Pajiado woman's opening mouth with his own scolding. "Are you serious?"

"What?"

"No plan, or anything?"

"What do you mean, 'Or anything'? We planned on causing problems, having a little fun, and eventually getting caught."

"I don't remember agreeing to 'Having fun'."

"You never do," comments the Nhavyyet.

The archaeologist's eyes dig into Elijou's. Finding nothing but rebellion, he averts to the astounding towers of solid Ardaelic Ardent dominating the end of the street behind them.

I guess we at least found the Manse.

Making the hills beyond appear dull and plain, the Manse boldly casts extending shadows from its four primary obelisks. Each spire reflects beams of the bright day's light, causing Fylorn to mildly squint. He lowers his sights, nearly losing focus as the offset pillars making the walls of the church throw off his depth perception. Lowering his gaze further targets the crowds surrounding the rising steps to the Manse; a different breed of peoples.

Mostly Hue, a handful of Vidicai. Lots of dark robes, not unlike the cultist back in Galiram… I suppose I should be calling these people cultists as well? Or maybe they're all simply disciples. Honestly, it matters not. What I should be doing is finding myself a robe so that I can slip inside unnoticed.

They will accept you with open arms.

"This idea was stupid," he slowly mouths out. "We need a plan."

"Like sneaking in?" Ram offers. "Maybe we could disguise ourselves and pray to Ardaelius that we aren't found."

"No."

"Right, because you have a better plan," the Pajiado jokes.

"Also no."

"Well, if you don't then we're sticking with mine."

"I don't want to be a prisoner, again," stumbles out of Fylorn's mouth.

A spattering of fierce words from Elijou batter the side of the archaeologist's head. "Are you deaf, or stupid?"

"Both," the Nhavyyet promptly answers for his friend.

"This is dangerous," Fylorn defends. "Why are we standing around in the open– I could spot you two from a city away! We should be somewhere smart, thinking about our next move. What we should be doing is investigating the prison so we can…"

The archaeologist's words trail off as his eyes connect with the surging walls of armoured guards coming down each street. Each set has their sights locked on the Elijou and Ram. The Nhavyyet turns from his companion's rant to witness the gathering for himself.

"They weren't lying about finding us…" falls from Ram.

No one man leads the charge as the wave of sentinels approach and become one interwoven army. Every nerve in Fylorn's skin buzzes, each hair rises.

"Surrender!"

The booming order clears the air around the intersection. Citizens flee to avoid the situation happening before them. All eyes within the street turn to the three standing in direct opposition to their city's defence.

"Surrender, now!"

Each step the archaeologist takes backwards is followed by Ram and Elijou, and challenged by guards taking two forwards. Fylorn's eyes flair before the words bolt from his mouth. "We will not be taken in; we have come to seek refuge at the Manse!"

The wall of silver comes to a distinct halt. None within the line defy the order. As a united front to the three, they stand assuring the city will not have criminals re-enter its streets. The archaeologist quickens his stride away, bringing him to the first grand step of the monument to Ardaelius.

Each step is twice as deep as it needs to be. Probably some symbol of faith to her… I'm sure there's so much I don't know about Ardaelius, and now I'm walking into her most prominent church. Anyone else who comes here would be splitting open like an oversized sack of apples, glee pouring from their face as they can't believe they're here… Believe me, I also can't believe I'm here.

We need to go inside.

I agree.

With a bolstered sense of urgency, Fylorn whips his head around in search of Ram and Elijou. They share a gaze before slowly joining each other. He pinches his lips, then gives one firm nod before moving ahead, careful not to disturb the huddling pairs of disciples discussing religious matters. Without waiting for the groans of the public to amount to words, the archaeologist leads his companions up the stairs towards the tall and thin doors of the Manse. At rest in a half measure open, Fylorn strides through with ease.

Once inside, the archaeologist is met by the grandest mural he has ever seen in his entire lifetime. Stretching from one side of the divine space to the other is a wall of perfectly depicted variations of the goddess herself. Etches of her

bearing masks of blue with robes of orange ebb and flow
around the ceiling. As Fylorn drags his eyes from left to right
they land on an embodiment of Ardaelius in robes of blue
with a faded eruption of orange transcending from her face.

The goddess of chaos hiding who she is, typical...

Ahead of him, a mass of devotees surrounds a tall and
thin man draped in robes of rusted orange amid the sea of
black. The archaeologist throws a look over his shoulder at
the pair trailing behind him.

"You two need to stay with me," Fylorn ejects in a hush
behind him.

"Why?" the Pajiado counters.

"Because! That's why!" the archaeologist halts in his
steps to turn towards the other. "Why do you think?"

Ram takes one more step, then extends a hand to rest
upon Fylorn's shoulder, "My friend..."

The archaeologist matches with a firm hold of his
companion's shoulder. "I know, I'm getting worked up.
Just... We need to figure this out, then we'll be on our way–"

A growing symphony of footsteps coming for the three
brings Fylorn's thought to a standstill. He perks up his ears
and twists his head in time to see the grey face of the man
draped in orange casting a lingering look at him. Before he
can turn to his companions, the archaeologist stands witness
to the pious man strut across floors of grim black towards
him. The flow of followers gravitating the robed man brings
the interior of the Manse directly to Fylorn within a single
breath.

"Kindly crossed," ejects from the pious man. "Have you
come to speak with our lord and saviour, Ardaelius herself?"

Those forming his following ebb and flow into a rigid
semicircle nearly encompassing the three. Fylorn flings a
quick look over his shoulder once again to confirm that his

companions still stand with him, then releases a warm breath of relief to find himself not alone.

"I speak with you, young man. Not those in your charge."

"Are you some kind of idiot?" bursts from one of the grey-skinned man's closest disciples.

The unexpected roar erupts along the fringes of the Manse before muffled words call out. Shuffling robes covering panicked feet bring hushed mouths to the pious man's ear. He glares upon the messenger before swinging his dark sights back at the three before him.

"We do not hold secrets in this house. Speak it aloud."

A weaselly voice begins, "These three have been found to be thieves. Now they come to seek refuge in our home."

"Have they now?"

"We stole nothing," Ram defends from behind Fylorn.

"Our Goddess, she is not the fickle temptress that many make her out to be." His thin lips play with his words. "She has no mercy for such things. Take them to the Endless Prison."

"Iby edvekrotinyagach!"

"Ram!" Fylorn orders.

"Iby sheshtash!"

"Ram!"

"Or'nada Alokhevryk plunayad bya, Syagrukhymi!!"

"Mikahram!!" the archaeologist shouts.

The stout man holds his breath. His bright red face shakes in pure emotional exertion. Fylorn's extended arm holds firm in fostering the civility of Ram. Across from the three, standing nearly a head above the archaeologist, one of the disciples pulls his hood back to reveal the man inside. A green and tusked smile provides Fylorn with a wave of relief.

Aal-Ivus…

"My saent. These peddlers aren't worth your time. Return to your work. I shall bring the prisoners to their cells, as Ardaelius wills."

A daft silence entrenches Fylorn. The silence around him is a vacuum. Nod after nod from the robed men ahead of him precede a firm grip on his forearm. In alarm the archaeologist snaps his head to look upon his assailant, only for a burlap sack to cover his face.

Chapter 24
The Parting

The soft echoing of footsteps resonates all along the massive tunnel leading from the castle's foundational floor into a cavern. Each is a reminder of Ani's choice, and sends a burning along her body. Nearly twice as wide as Ora, the perfectly etched steps descend into a sheen chamber dwarfing the passage leading to it.

It feels like I'm in a whole new world down here.

"How is this place so big under the castle?" Ani asks the silent Shyvesh guiding her.

"It was a natural formation that previous kings paid the Pajiado to enhance. It goes under the seafloor well into the Föld."

All of the dampness around the young woman unmasks itself as the information seeps into her.

"You're not saying that all that water could spill in here, right?" Ani softly inquires.

A sole laugh from Shyvesh travels around the hollow chamber.

"You are quite safe down here," she comments before striking out a finger towards the constructed fountain centering the space. "There is the pool. Do not fall in."

"Obviously," Ani remarks.

"Things need to be said for a reason..." the grand tamer emits.

The pair glide from the stairs into the wide-open center. Ani squints upwards to find the tiny hole above that allows light to pour down to the space. After she feels content with the finding, the young woman watches Shyvesh approach a ring of white stone. The grand tamer leans over the rim of the pool to inspect the wonder.

"How does it work?" Ani asks from afar.

Shyvesh casts a glance before instructing, "Come take a look."

Ani toes forward. On her approach she can see the swirling of spectral blues, greys, and even greens seeping out the top of the basin. Along the edges of the white stone she spots delicate markings that depict a variety of people beside creatures.

"Are those ancient Anchors?" the young woman asks.

"Tamers," the grand tamer answers in a dropping tone. "You'll have to stop referring to us at that, Anchors are meant to reach the bottom."

The young woman purses her lips before leaning at a distance towards the white stone rim to match Shyvesh. Her eyes inspect the murky solution frothing inside.

Appears entirely uninviting.

"I don't have to go in there, do I?"

"No, no," the grand tamer replies. "You call upon your auragonic and it will do the rest. Like I said, Olokk does this often, it's safe."

"Have you given up your auragonic before? Does it hurt?"

Shyvesh's face squirms before shooting a playful eye towards Ani. She rests her hip on the pool's elevated rim, then recites, "Our Goddess, she gives us strength when it is due. She elevates my deformations into abilities when I am weak. Those who are empty, and those who are hunted, will avoid the call of Haven and Dak. We find the darkness all around us, where those chosen are brought forth with open arms. Cataclysm is born clean and appointed, where the spirits without bodies come and go. Blessed are those who follow our way."

Reflexively, Ani asks, "What does that mean?"

"It is something my mother used to tell me when I was young. It's part of an old story that she would put us to bed with."

"Tushma only put me to bed with grunts and the occasional, 'Good Night'."

"I don't figure he was a Tamer, though."

"He surely wasn't."

"It's different to be raised by those we are like."

"Is it better?"

Shyvesh slowly shakes her head before softly responding, "No. Just different."

Ani's gaze lengthens until the wisping liquids beyond are well outside of her thoughts. "In some ways, I wish that I hadn't wasted all this time to find you. Maybe being around Tamers when I was young would have kept me from making so many mistakes."

"Ani, then you wouldn't have your dragon…"

Moving slowly, Ani approaches the pool before her. A mild tingle akin to static ripples along her skin the closer she is. Within a few steps from the pool's rim, she feels a crippling agony writhe throughout her body. At first, her jerking face catches a glimpse of Shyvesh in sheer astonishment, then her flexing arms raise to reveal an emerging scar forming on her left arm. Lightning bolts of blue nerves gleam through the young woman's skin. In a mirror to her first, a second spirit's wrest presents itself.

Amid the cries of intense pain, a swirling of spirits grows within the pool. Shyvesh bolts from the edge before a surging of illumination paints the distant reaches of the chamber in a bath of ambient blues. Ani's eyes fail to have the strength to follow the grand tamer, instead locking ahead at the rupturing stream.

Birthing from the glow comes a nightmarish creature of scale and steel. With legs as thick as oxen, but an agile and triangular torso leading to powerful arms, the monster is displayed from the other spirits hurtling around. The grey essence peels itself from the stream to assemble into a solid form. Elongated blades harnessed to each of its dangling arms extend, reaching a harrowing distance. More metal strikes out from its knees and shoulders, until finally a wreath of daggers rises from its crown.

Shyvesh utters a single word that dominates the young woman's ears, "Gykeng."

A violent shriek booms from the creature's scaley lips before ebbing and flowing into a thick wisp that strikes out at Ani.

"No!" the grand tamer cries out.

The young woman is blown backwards by the tremendous force imposed upon her. While on the brink of passing out, her tilted head looks on as Shyvesh's face of awe is now a dark scowl.

Ani blinks rapidly to retain consciousness. The waning glow of spectral hues bouncing around the room fill her eyeline. She rolls onto her side, placing a supportive arm underneath to lift herself up. While swinging her head to search for Shyvesh, an unmatched ripping of pain assumes her senses. Ani falls onto her back, witnessing a swirling mix of blue and grey as both her auragonics release themselves in unison. The divine cries of Ora are challenged by the feral screeches of the new beast.

Lifting her head up, the young woman is presented with a grim display of Shyvesh standing at the ready with her auragonic, Escrah, defensively raising its hackles. Ani is barely allowed to draw a breath before the spectral creatures explosively charge as each other. She raises herself into a backwards crouch to scoot herself away from the combat.

Escrah dives under Ora, narrowly avoiding the bladed beast, then uses its experience to breach towards Ani herself. Before Ani can close her eyes, her dragon swoops past, snatching the spectral hound in its dangling claws, and sailing to the other side of the room. With one powerful leap, the gykeng attaches itself onto the hind of the hellix, being carried away as well.

The air around Ani is too thick to breathe. Her chest convulses while trying to get to her feet. The grand tamer lurks before her, keeping a cornered eye on the carnage happening to her auragonic.

"Ani! Put them back in the pool!"

Flexing her forearms forwards accomplishes nothing. "I can't!"

"You must!" Shyvesh shouts while approaching the fallen, young woman.

"I've already told you, I don't know what I'm doing!"

"If you can't," a darkness envelopes the elegant woman's face, "then I will have to."

The grand tamer stomps forward.

"What are you doing?" Ani whimpers.

"We were all so afraid, afraid that we would be our own undoing. That the end times were upon us and the lands would be ripped in half," Shyvesh's pitch reaches screeching heights, "Now look at us! It's you, and I have to put you down like a dog… my own daughter."

Her pace builds into a run towards Ani. All the young woman does to prepare is raise one hand above her in hopes to defend against the coming assault. She can feel more tears crawl from her eyes.

He was right…

Between her held out fingers, Ani witnesses Escrah and the bladed beast be thrown into a tumble between the grand tamer and the pool's edge. As the footsteps of Shyvesh clomp into range, a powerful jaw clamps onto the top half of her. With an animalistic tug, Ora splits the elegant woman in two.

The remaining corpse falls lifelessly to the floor below.

Ani spies a distant movement. Set within the shrinking stream of spirits is the gykeng, shaking its gnarled head at dissipating red wisps. The visage of Ora landing to her right, then twisting to proudly look on at its Tamer is all the young woman sees before eyes blur and she loses control of her neck.

Chapter 25
The Extent

The slow and agonizing opening of Ani's eyes is accelerated upon catching sight of murky blue wisps around her. She wildly throws her head around as she flips her body while scrambling to her feet. Every direction she looks is only an obscure and endlessly glowing hue.

I thought I was underwater!

She gathers her breath while trying to focus on anything. The flow makes her eyes play games with her until she spies a broken structure in the distance. After shuffling a foot forward to ensure herself that the world she stands upon is solid, Ani dares a full stride ahead. The transparent support below her feet brings an immense unease to the young woman. She stalls, making a second inspection of the structure ahead of her.

Everything looks like a cloud, or some kind of spirit.

Ani drags her sights in a full circle to acclimate herself. When she faces the floating structure ahead, she takes one more step.

…What's the worst that could happen?

Step after step brings her closer. Soon she realizes the ring of stone and mortar walls is actually above her. She raises her foot to find it be well secured on yet another support her eyes cannot grasp. A deep breath flows from her before ascending the hidden steps with a trusting pace. The climb takes but moments before she places her hand upon the closest brick of the stone wall. Cold seeps into the skin of her hand, reminding her of the world she was accustomed to.

How did I get here?

She brings herself around the stone wall until she finds an opening. Walking through guides her into an open courtyard with spectral grass, then a balcony overlooking an endless flow of glowing blue. Her brows furrow at the expanse no different than the illogical fields of spirit she had just walked here on.

"What does this mean?" she calls aloud. The corner of her mouth pulls wide while unnaturally winching after making such an open declaration in a place so uncertain. Her eyes wander around in a full circle once more, hoping for anything else that resembles a reality she could connect with. Three quarters of the way around sets her sights on a lone figure centering the courtyard she had come from. She calls out, "Who are you?"

The figure twists their head to face the young woman who made the call. From this distance Ani can't make out any recognizable features of the person. Before she makes a definitive choice, the figure glides towards her. The closed robes of glowing orange make no effort to break open for moving legs, creating a warped image approaching the young woman.

Ani pats her own body, attempting to find anything to strip from herself and use as a weapon against the coming invader, but nothing cooperates. She huffs while raising her fists in anticipation of a fight. To her puzzlement, the figure passes her and brings themselves to the very edge of the balcony so they may look out into the abyss. Swiftly shaking herself of any confusion, Ani gathers her courage and joins the figure.

After setting herself next to the figure, the young woman dares to look at the mysterious being sharing her presence. The plain brown hood, concealing much of the being's face, only allows their nose and chin to be revealed.

Not much to go off, but a man's wide jaw.

"Kindly crossed?" Ani asks.

"Indeed," the hollow voice of the mysterious man replies.

"Am I supposed to be talking to you?"

"In a sense." While extending a long arm to point towards the distance ahead he continues, "Though I suggest you watch, and listen."

Ani turns her face back towards the flowing wisps of glowing blue to see the image of a forest emerging from the hollow space. Alpine trees foreign to her dot the horizon, while bringing back feelings from days long gone. The lingering tufts of snow settling upon the sturdy branches slowly melt as a raging fire creeps into the picture ahead of the young woman. Sweeping her vision, a devastating forest fire assaults the innocent woods. The mysterious man's extended finger flicks to broaden the visage, revealing an entire peninsula burning.

"Am I supposed to know what this means?"

"I believe someone has told you about The Peninsula of Spirits, have they not?"

Peninsula…

"Oh! Yes… someone did."

"What you are seeing is the end of this place."

Ani allows for a moment of silence while watching the destruction. Her eyes linger while processing a hollow feeling within. She loses focus before turning her head back to the mysterious man.

"What does it mean?"

"It is not for me to say, but as the world works, when one thing ends, the next begins. There will be those who fight to keep the old, while others will give up everything to grasp at the new. One thing remains true of both; as the inevitable occurs, neither will be satisfied."

"But you've shown me this. Are you asking me to make sure it never happens?"

The mysterious man flicks his finger once again. Ani swiftly turns to watch as the bright flames grow fierce before dividing to allow for a sole figure to walk between. The young woman tilts her head as the image shifts into a manifestation of a man in a mask.

"That's the king!" she hollers out into the abyss. "He burns it down!"

Ani swings her sights back to the mysterious man, only to find him gone. An underlying chill crawls up the young woman's spine as the wisping spirits around her cease their flow. The stilling of the plane plays tricks on her eyes. She whips her sights back out into the fiery abyss to find the king disappeared. Now, a young image of Ani stands amidst the flames. The girl extends, growing to become a mirror of herself, then Shyvesh.

"No," Ani utters.

The portrait of Shyvesh standing behind a young Ani is warped to have another figure appear beside the grand tamer. As she holds hands with the new figure, the young Ani evaporates while the pair walk away into the distance.

A bright eruption nearly blinds Ani. She blinks again and again until registering the flames of the distant visage are creeping towards her. While turning to the passage she came from, her sights land on a growing fire from it as well. An enclosing circle shrinks the world around her, nearly setting her ablaze.

A screech cries out from above. The young woman throws her head back, looking directly up. To her wonder, a shimmering silhouette of a blue serpent writhes in the mists overhead. The glimmering fails to blind her as it approaches. Just before the flames lick at Ani's feet, the spirit wraps itself around her, lifting her from the circling blaze.

"Ani," A dull voice whispers in her ear.

She opens her eyes to a wash of water passing over her. Splashing around, she feels around for something solid enough to push on. Bursting above the water, she gasps for air. Her eyes immediately fall on Ora, perched over her with its long neck arcing down to bring its head near to hers.

Ani reaches out, suddenly feeling the cold air combating the heat desperate to cling to her wet arm. The tips of her fingers graze the nose of the dragon. A tingle runs from both shoulders, compelling her other hand to raise and grasp the creature's snout. Once both hands grasp Ora, a brilliant scintillance cascades from within her finger, and before her very eyes she watches the dragon's limbs elongate and its body crest with uncanny growth. Her eyes return to Ora's, finding a calm love revealing itself from within the jewels. The juvenile creature she had been caring for now towers before her with a commanding respect. After the moment runs dry, Ani feels water embrace her knees, and the sounds of clawing grace her ears. She snaps her head around to find the bladed lizard attacking a corner of the immense hall.

"What is it doing?" she cries out.

Trailing her eyes along, she can see the corridor that her and Shyvesh entered from is now caved in. She returns her sights to Ora.

"What happened?"

The majestic beast twists its head to aim towards the corner of the room that the gykeng chips away at. Ani jumps to her feet, fueled by the rising water levels. She rushes over to the corner to find an impact hole near where her new auragonic digs. While moving to place her hand on the creature, Ora nudges her out of the way.

"What are you doing? It's going to drown us if it keeps bringing in more water. We need to go back the way we came, dig through there!"

After finishing her sentence Ani trudges across the waist deep water, passing the swirling pool of spirits seemingly unaffected by the impending liquids, and brings herself to the pile of displaced stones. She eyes the entire wall, searching for any weaknesses to begin at, but only finds scratches or impact marks. Turning her head, she locks eyes with Ora. The dragon holds a firm gaze upon the young woman. Ani's face contorts while processing the situation.

"You tried…"

She watches on as Ora returns to assisting the bladed lizard in tunneling through where the water had broken into the hall. Swiftly she charges back to that side of the hall, shifting her arms high as the water reaches her armpits. While nearing the spectral pool her foot slips, bringing her head underwater. She spins trying to gather her balance again. A spike of panic overtakes the young woman as her hands aren't long enough to touch the bottom. She kicks but pushing up doesn't launch her far enough to breach the surface.

Ani scans under the water, finding stone debris and acrylic glimmers. Her eyes land on the headless body of the grand tamer drifting within the silted water.

If only—

A lump forming in her throat gets stunted as a claw grabs her, thrusting her out of the water with a splash. Ora holds her in its front paw, connecting eyes, then swings her above to place the young woman on its back. As soon as Ani affirms a grip of a protruding spike, Ora rears its neck and unleashes a devastating blast of electrical power upon the weakened wall ahead of them. The young woman covers her eyes with her left hand. Her chin touches the lump of scarred skin, reminding her of the gykeng. She extends her arm, focusing on it. A spectral wisp of grey swirls from the water depths below the roaring dragon and into her arm.

Thunderous cracks deafen the chamber as the wall ahead of Ani bursts, spewing water wildly. Ora brings the pair into the frothing invasion to dig for a moment before diving headfirst into the watery hole. The dragon swims with all of its power up through the jagged tunnel and into the wide and freezing sea.

Ani holds her breath with an agonizing effort as Ora keeps swimming forwards. The light of day dances upon the chopping waves far above. She can see the edges of her sight begin to darken as an entire sea presses down on her while Ora swims upwards with an unbridled power. Breaking the surface, Ani takes a frantic gasp of air. The dragon spreads its massive wings, then begins climbing as high into the sky as it can. While sheer winds nearly absolve her of all heat, the rush forces Ani to twist her head. Her turning sights are placed towards a set of glowing oranges across the choppy waters. She yanks on the spike, bringing Ora into an arc to her right, and opens the horizon to clearly see.

It's real, it's happening right now!

Ani's eyes sharpen as she steers Ora towards the burning peninsula.

Chapter 26
The Opening

The few corrective thumps from their new master keeping the line in a collective silence is all Fylorn hears along the long walk since being taken prisoner.

I understand Elijou being silent, its practically all she is. But Ram, they must have shoved something in that Nhavyyet mouth of his.

Words are words. For some, there is only action.

Brilliant. Should I write that one down when I get to my cell?

Follow the master.

Right, my master.

"Aal-Ivus?"

Each lingering second of the long silence chews on the archaeologist's hopes until a casual drawl enters his ear.

"The same."

"What happened to you?"

"Why are you here?"

"You answer first!"

"Well, young one, I evaded being captured. I figured I would be safe here, but the Legion is led by Saents, and as much as everyone is welcome in Mashar Pelim – This place is no Xelis – I've been… In some ways you've seen me at both my worst and my best."

"I thought you were going to take haven in the Manse?"

"I thought so too." A grim shadow crawls across Fylorn's vision before the hood is swiftly removed from his head and his sight is filled by the Hal-Vagenkar's face. One of the elongated teeth nearly touches the archaeologist's cheek. "Now, why are you here?"

"We need to break into the prison."

Aal-Ivus unleashes a silent laugh before adjusting to seriously scowl as his mind follows through the words of Fylorn. "No. No…"

"Yes."

"Why?"

"I need to break someone out and bring them home."

"I see." The winter green of the Hal-Vagenkar's skin shines through as a beam of light brushes him. "Seems like you should have been there and not at the Manse then."

"What a pleasant observation," replies the archaeologist in a tone dripping with scorn. "Anything else you want to share, you traitorous bastard?"

Quickly and calmly, Aal-Ivus replies, "What makes you say that?"

"As it stands, I'm bound and you're leading me to an endless prison."

"The Gross Prison of Underföld."

"I thought the Saent called it the Endless Prison?"

"He has ideas of… grandeur. But, with my words, there are now many less people being stuck here endlessly. The goddess herself would turn red from the work I've been accomplishing here."

"Ardaelius…"

"Fylorn," the Hal-Vagenkar quickly squirms his bottom lip between his large teeth, "I wasn't lying to you when I said that she's the only one I live for."

"I wasn't calling you a liar, I was calling you a traitor. I helped you return to your work for her, and this is how you repay me."

"I have the Nhavyyet too."

"Right. And how exactly is this going to further her love for you?"

"What do you even know of her?" Aal-Ivus scoffs.

The archaeologist screams in a whisper to his new master, "Look me in the eyes and tell me that what I'm doing isn't of service to her– Tell me it isn't better for her than sitting in some cell until your ugly mug comes to convert me!"

Aal-Ivus lowers his yellow eyes down to glare upon Fylorn. The tiny red veins creeping their way to his iris pulsate with every breath the man takes.

"I need you to help me," the archaeologist slowly and carefully picks his next words, "for her."

"Need me?"

"That's what I said."

A wheezy growl puffs from Aal-Ivus. "I would love to say that I'm busy, but…"

"But what?"

"But what you want is probably the stupidest thing I've ever heard of, let alone accepted an invitation to."

A thick grin slinks across the archaeologist's face.

"We're nearly there. Keep up impressions," the Hal-Vagenkar orders before brushing past Fylorn.

The endless street comes to a close while connecting with an open and angular structure ahead. Reaching walls and even taller watchtowers form the intimidating entrance to the prison. Splotches of grey sit in flagrant opposition to the clean and spectacular state of the rest of Mashar Pelim.

While holding an open-eyed stare, the archaeologist halts his step to still his breath. A firm shove to his back resets his focus and air returns to his lungs. He shifts his glance, expecting a man heavy in silver to be the culprit, only to find the wide frame of a Nhavyyet.

"Keep moving, we're almost there," Ram comments. "I can feel it."

"It looks like the prison is right ahead of us," Fylorn replies.

"How can you see that…" Elijou concludes. "Why are we supposed to trust this green man again?"

"Excellent question," the Nhavyyet rebukes.

"Because he owes us a favor," Fylorn states as he picks up his pace, then his words become an utterance. "And I have a feeling that we'll need the help."

The Pajiado woman scoffs. "Feelings? I don't think feelings are going to be a huge help for this, weak man."

"Yeah," Ram raises his volume, "Elijou here has it all worked out for when we split up and they start torturing us!"

Fylorn turns before making any kind of response to his companions. He marches ahead, steady behind Aal-Ivus, until they approach the wide gates of the prison. After digging his heels in, he watches on at the Hal-Vagenkar silently communing with the nearest guard. Within a moment, the grand lengths of steel open wide, welcoming the fresh prisoners. A flow of grunts comes from behind as warnings to what will happen if anyone fails to move ahead.

The rhythmic stomping begins once more, but the archaeologist's mind is elsewhere. Layers of grime stick to every surface of the perfectly stone-cast walls. The inner courtyard is wider than most dig sites Fylorn had been to. His eyes trail to a battalion of well-armoured guards pacing along predetermined routes as each sling disapproving stares at the caravan.

Amidst the Hal-Vagenkar leading them along the grey gravel, he halts beside a pile of chopped-up wood before casting a low glare over his shoulder. Upon receiving the approval, a shuffling of guardsmen alarms the archaeologist and he turns to view all other bags being removed from heads.

The voice of Aal-Ivus barks, "You will keep your eyes low, and don't speak to prisoners. Do I make myself clear?"

"Absolutely," flies from Ram while Fylorn and Elijou nod to confirm.

The Hal-Vagenkar moves ahead once more, bringing them to a secure door on a small, one-floor structure. He pulls out a personal key to unlock the door, then nods for a stationed guard to open it so the prisoners may enter before him. Fylorn glares at the green-skinned man as he passes. Inside is a simple space dominated by a sturdy staircase descending into blackness. Waiting, promptly to its left, is another guard along with what appears to be the commanding officer of the prison, beaming in a wide grin.

"Master Aal-Ivus, back so soon? I have my doubts that more will be accepting of her word yet, but you have proved me wrong before. Nevertheless, it's always a pleasure to see you." The warden shifts his gaze past Fylorn, but abruptly holds his long stare at Ram and Elijou. "Interesting finds. I trust you have a special place in mind for these ones?"

"They won't be here long," the Hal-Vagenkar coyly responds. "The march over has shed light on how willing they already are. I imagine a few days in the brilliant darkness will bring everything into a clarity for them."

"Excellent, I hope it does."

The slimy smile smeared across the warden's face drives a chill up Fylorn's spine. He suddenly feels a bump into his back as one of the armoured men who led them here barges ahead. He posts himself on the other side of the staircase. As the two men guarding the stairs become statues, Aal-Ivus saunters over to unlock the door of metal wire. He slowly opens it wide before extending a reaching gesture to Fylorn.

"Please, come with me now, or wait for them… if you prefer."

Each hair on the archaeologist's arms rises as the Hal-Vagenkar's words slip out, just as devious as the warden himself.

He's acting, right? This must be a show he's putting on… so they don't suspect anything.

Only she knows.

A soft tap of a boot hitting the back of his shin brings Fylorn back into the moment. He throws a look over his shoulder to find Elijou glaring at him. With one heavy foot, he sets himself forward and begins down the staircase. The steady metal clinking accompanying each step taken plagues the archaeologist's mind. He follows the dark silhouette of the Hal-Vagenkar down past door after door. At one dim metal entry, Aal-Ivus holds his heel while twisting his head.

"In here."

"I can't believe they just let you take us alone," pipes in Ram.

"I can't believe you've almost kept your mouth shut," the Hal-Vagenkar snaps back.

The Nhavyyet rears his head to make his retort, but Fylorn jabs him with an elbow. A grim glare strikes back at the archaeologist, holding on to a stewing tongue. With averted eyes, Fylorn watches Aal-Ivus open the door to the cell block, then once again gesture the prisoners inside. The line of shambled men and women trudge ahead into the blackened space. Row after row of iron bars to his right hold decrepit people.

Long hair. Thin faces. Scraps of bread scattered around their new home... My new home if anyone decides they have their own ideas!

One after another, Aal-Ivus begins placing prisoners into empty cells. As the line thins, the Hal-Vagenkar comes to open a door, and throws only Elijou inside before moving on.

"Aal-Ivus," the archaeologist calls out.

"Silence!" the Hal-Vagenkar barks back.

Fylorn feels the vibrations of the order echo through him. The tall man's powerful voice stirs many of the other prisoners, leading to small but audible clicks of metal upon metal.

As the archaeologist stomps ahead, ready to confront the Hal-Vagenkar, Aal-Ivus swings a cell door open and promptly shoves Fylorn inside. After a loud shuffle, Ram rolls into the cell as well. The archaeologist quickly rises to charge the iron bars, but a click of a key precedes a toothy grin on the other side.

Chapter 27
The Release

"He left us here," flies from Ram. "He actually left us here!"

"A Nhavyyet prison."

"Yes, I see the irony. I can't believe that bastard left us here."

"How many floors did we go down?"

"I don't know. Was I supposed to be counting?"

"Don't the Nhavyyet use a different measurement? A foundation, or structure?"

"Lofts."

"Alright, lofts." Fylorn begins whirling his hands while his mind works away. "And that run thing. What was that called?"

"Shouldn't we be working on breaking out of here? Should we call for Elijou or something?"

"The Blah-blah-blah Run?"

"The Blavovad Run," Ram begrudgingly answers.

"Yes! That one. That never moved through a loft, correct?"

"It did indeed stay on one loft, yes."

"So…" The archaeologist strides over to the door. "Building something this complex, with this many lofts, they would have tried to design some kind of system to feel through the floor."

"My friend…" the Nhavyyet utters while leaning against one of the cell walls. "The only thing I'm feeling is you losing your mind."

Fylorn takes both hands and grips onto the bars of his prison door. He closes his eyes, allowing his mind to settle, then shakes them.

"Can you feel that?"

Ram sighs before replying, "Yes."

The archaeologist does it again, this time hearing a small jingle. He peers down to find a key resting within the lock of the cell door. Twisting his hand, he reaches down to turn the key. A pleasing click shifts the door, nearly sending him through to the solid wall beyond.

"My friend! Wait, how did you do that?"

Fylorn pulls the key out of the hole, then shows it to the Nhavyyet. "I told you."

Ram scoffs before rushing from the cell and looking down the hall along the way they came from. He darts away into the darkness.

"Ram? Ram!" Fylorn lets out in a hushed voice.

At the end of the hallway, the glow of a fire appears. As it nears the archaeologist he slowly backs away, further down the prison block. Before he turns to flee, a stark voice orders out.

"Stop!"

Every nerve in Fylorn's body tenses. He tries to run but his body refuses to move. The torch closes the distance. As it crosses a few cells beyond the archaeologist, a familiar voice calls out.

"Fylorn!"

The light of the torch finally touches the archaeologist's eyes, revealing Aal-Ivus holding it. While his breath slows, Ram and Elijou appear around the Hal-Vagenkar. The Nhavyyet hosts a bow and quiver on his back, while the glint of two simple daggers reflects from the Pajiado's hands.

"Where did you get that from?" Fylorn directs at Ram.

A sword is tossed in the air from the stout man. The archaeologist reaches out to catch it while watching a sharp grin emerge in the Nhavyyet's face.

"You idiot!" spits out Aal-Ivus. "Why didn't you tell me she scampers through walls like a spirit?"

"You're the idiot!" Fylorn argues back. "You put us in different cells! How was that supposed to work?"

"Says the idiot whose plan it was to use a bunch of mystics to draw out a dragon!"

"Draw out a dragon?" cries out Ram.

"Dragons will come when you use too much," Elijou admits.

"How does he know that?" Fylorn argues.

"How don't you know that?" counters Aal-Ivus.

The archaeologist puffs out air. "How's a dragon going to get down here anyways?"

"Give me the key," the Hal-Vagenkar demands while extending his hand out.

"Why? I need to go find the Wöllralt."

"Yes, I know. Now give me the key."

Ram questions, "Why do you need the key?"

"Just let him have the key," complains Elijou.

"What?" Fylorn squawks. "Are you on my side or his?"

Aal-Ivus leans over and snatches the key from the archaeologist. Before anyone can react, the Hal-Vagenkar spins to face a cell, then swiftly uses the key to unlock it. The slow opening of the iron bar door sends a creaking throughout the dormant cell block. As Aal-Ivus returns his toothy face to the others, a round of confusion holds words from leaving anyone.

"I locked them up," the Hal-Vagenkar finally speaks. "Ardaelius let them out."

"Who's there?" a voice calls out. As Fylorn turns to find the source of the noise, another torch light comes rushing down from the end of the hall. In a flash, Aal-Ivus brushes the others to the sides of the corridor and brings his own torchlight nearer his face.

Nearly out of breath, the guardsman screeches to a halt in front of the Hal-Vagenkar. "I heard a riot beginning down here. What have you heard? Did you quell it?"

Aal-Ivus leans to the side, looking behind the guard. As the man turns to follow the Hal-Vagenkar's investigation, Aal-Ivus tilts his head down, then juts his long tooth up and through the chin of the man. A scream of agony and shock burst from the guard before his life quickly fades away. In a resounding echo, the silver-bound man falls limply to the ground. The Hal-Vagenkar spits to the side before leaning down to search the still remains.

"Aal-Ivus?" comes from Elijou.

"Are you alright?" Fylorn calmly asks.

The green-skinned man rises, fully stretching his back to reach his full height. He then holds his fist out before flipping it open to reveal the metal treasure within.

"There's another key. Now, go find that Wöllralt," Aal-Ivus barks. He quickly reaches out to hold Elijou's shoulder before speaking directly at her. "You, come with me. We're going to have some fun while they do the work."

Within the faint light, Fylorn watches a faint grin creep onto the Pajiado's face before the pair bolt away down the corridor. Ram bumps shoulders with the archaeologist to get his attention.

"Alright. I've been thinking about your stupid idea and I'm pretty sure I can feel where this giant guy is."

"Can you really?"

"I mean… Unless they're keeping something absurdly large inside of a tiny cell for their own amusement," the Nhavyyet replies with a shrug.

Fylorn cracks a grin before handing the torch over to his companion. "Lead the way."

The pair charge ahead, deeper into the cell block. They find another flight of stairs that leads them down two more floors to a single door. Fylorn opens it with the key, letting it slowly swing open to reveal the dim black within. Ram steps ahead, reaching the torch out as far as it will go. Flickers of light touch both sides of the corridor as they creep forwards. While passing empty cell after empty cell, they cast glances at each other.

"Are you sure he's down here?" Fylorn quietly questions.

"Should be," Ram answers in a hush.

The Nhavyyet leans one way, then the other before coming to one of the cells on the right. Fylorn shuffles up alongside him to see grey dominating the small space within, making anything in the cell barely visible.

"Need something?" a feral voice growls.

"You," the archaeologist snaps back.

Ram shifts the blazing torch to Fylorn's right side. The illumination elongates to expel the hidden shadows ahead of them. An endless dark beyond confirms the expanse that the archaeologist had been warned about. The simple cell holds only a bench for sleeping on and a pile of hay in the corner. Sitting slouched upon the furthest edge of the bench is the oversized man. Long, wavy brown hair flows from the Wöllralt's head, down past his shoulders. The leather straps encircling each of his forearms are worn and fraying. His shaded eyes glare at the floor of his prison.

"No," Full Giant replies, long and low.

A screaming wail from a man touches Fylorn's ears. The hallowed sound draws itself into a whisper while fading away below the prison. Allowing a sigh to reset himself, the archaeologist slides the key into the lock and turns. A low creaking echoes out while moving the wrought iron door.

"What do you mean, 'No'?" Ram demands.

"There's nothing left for me out there."

"Your village, they want you back. We're here to bring you home."

"My sister will never forgive me."

"I'm sure she might, but we'll never know until we get there."

The darkness within the hollow cell deepens until Fylorn only sees an absolute black. From the edges of the torchlight comes a giant's face, burdened with grief and anguish.

"She will not forgive me."

The Nhavyyet interjects, "How about I forgive you once we get out of here. Then, you can go on your merry way."

"I was merry once," crawls from Full Giant before returning to the gloomy shade of his prison.

We were so close.

"When?" the archaeologist utters.

"We don't have time for this," Ram barks. "Can you not hear the banging outside?"

"When?" Fylorn doubles his question, reinforcing it on this second ask.

"You don't want to know about me. I'm simply the bones of your quest," pitifully crawls from the Wöllralt's mouth. "Go attend to the others."

"Actually, Fylorn. We can't get out of here without Elijou…"

The archaeologist spins around to find Ram holding his face in his wide hand. "Aal-Ivus…"

"Did they actually abandon us?"

A deeply guttural chuckle flies from Full Giant, echoing around the enclosed space. "What a pile of–"

The giant man's speech is cut off as Elijou and Aal-Ivus bolt in from prison walkway. The Pajiado woman shoves the Hal-Vagenkar ahead before emitting, "How did I manage to get hooked in with the two chattiest people in the entire world? If this man would–"

Aal-Ivus quickly interjects, "Where is that guard? Hmm, little woman? Did you take care of him, or did I? Maybe you worry about having the energy and I'll make sure that people aren't suspicious."

"Enough," grumbles from Fylorn.

"You're right," the Pajiado woman spits out. "Is this the giant man? Let's get out of here." Elijou pushes her way past Aal-Ivus and Ram to come face to face with Fylorn. She glares at him as she moves beyond to stand before the mountain of a man still sitting on the stone bed within his cell. "Get up."

A wild racket rattles the hallway outside of the cell. Grinding and pummeling dominate the space as the echoes of closing combat crawl nearer. The hairs upon Fylorn's neck raise, and he snatches the torch from the Nhavyyet's hand.

"My friend!" Ram returns, but it fails to disturb the archaeologist.

Making quick, powerful stomps towards Full Giant, Fylorn brings the light to his oversized face. "You heard her, get up."

"I don't take orders from the likes of you," he plainly replies.

Crashing sounds flood the walkway before shadows of debris being tossed cross the cell door. An unexpected wind graces the nape of Fylorn's neck, playing with his heightened hairs.

"Look, Wöllralt. You're only way out is through those doors—"

"Who said I was leaving?"

"You want to see your sister again, right?" Ram calls out while pulling out his stolen bow and preparing an arrow to be nocked.

"She is always with me."

Elijou leans down, placing her hand upon the giant man's thigh. "I want you to see her again."

The gentle tones coming from the Pajiado woman shift the tension of the cell, sending a chill up Fylorn's spine. Full Giant leans down to bring his face close to hers. One quick glance confirms the fingers of her resting hand to be twisting, while the archaeologist clearly spots the other hand sneaking behind her back while she curls her finger. The world around Elijou and Full Giant melts away, consuming a portion of the stone with them. In their wake is a small valley of rubble. Ram grunts in alarmed response before snapping his stare to Fylorn.

"Where did she go?" Fylorn's words are barely louder than a mutter.

"No time to worry about that," Aal-Ivus calls out. The archaeologist twists his sights, bringing the light to the front of the cell to confirm the Hal-Vagenkar leaning out. "The guards have found us."

"Do we stay here, or make an escape?" Ram asks while tightening the draw of his bow.

"If she comes back, this will be where she returns."

"If? If! What do you mean 'If'?" the Nhavyyet roars.

"Keep your voice down," Aal-Ivus demands.

"Why?" Ram redirects his focus to the Hal-Vagenkar. "If they're coming, then let them. What choice do we have now?"

"Do you want to fight, or do you want to escape?" Aal-Ivus counters while gently pulling the cell door closed.

"What does it look like?" the Nhavyyet snidely remarks. "Aren't you supposed to become wiser in your old age?"

"I'm wise enough to know that you're being an idiot."

Ram spins to face Fylorn. "My friend, can I–"

All power in the Nhavyyet's voice drifts away as a whoosh of winds pelts the back of the archaeologist. Fylorn turns to see Elijou kneeling, then raising her sights to match his.

"Who's next?"

"One at a time?" Fylorn swiftly asks, but Ram bumps his shoulder while passing by.

"You can probably take me with someone else, being…"

"Green man!" the Pajiado woman calls out, completely disregarding Ram's self deprecation. "You and Ram together."

The archaeologist reaches out to grip Elijou's forearm, garnering her full attention. "Are you sure?"

Her somber eyes meet his. "I don't have much more in me."

Fylorn gives a curt nod before backing away to allow her to take the other men. He gazes on as she twists her fingers, but focuses his sights on her pained face as the air encircling the trio is ripped from existence. The trick causes a sweeping rush of wind this time, extinguishing his handheld flame. A cold stillness engulfs the lonely cell. Fylorn returns his sights to the cell door, this time barely seeing anything in the pitch black. His ears perk up as the shifting of stone leads to subtle cracks echoing throughout. He lowers himself onto his knees while keeping his predatory sights at the prison entrance. Another faint crack resounds within the archaeologist's ear. Quietly placing his blade on the ground, he slides his hands along the tacky floor.

Ram would know if this was breaking off or not. Damn woman could have told us that her mystics cut a chunk out of wherever she is…

A light approaches the outside of the cell. Fylorn holds his breath while it halts.

"Giant man? Have you been behaving?" a thick voice calls out.

I can't reply, he'll know it's me…

"Giant man?" the voice asks again.

A creaking of the door assumes the archaeologist's full attention. He bolts ahead to pin himself at the base of the door, denying it to be opened.

"Not funny, Wöllralt. Let me in and maybe I won't accidentally nudge you off that ledge."

Fylorn holds maximum pressure upon the door while the man on the other side begins knocking into the iron frame trying to entice it open.

"Are you dead on the other side… I can't smell you."

A whipping of air splashes upon Fylorn, bringing his face out towards the black beyond.

"Come here," Elijou demands at full volume.

"A woman?" comes from the other side of the door. No further questions are asked before the pounding against the door becomes violent.

"Start your mystics, then I'll jump over there," Fylorn whispers out to her.

"It doesn't work like that."

"Am I supposed to fight him back while you do it?"

A slighted gruff comes from Elijou. Tiny lights evolve into a vivid illumination swirling around the Pajiado woman. Each pulse strengthens while growing. Fylorn had seen it each time before, but now he could see a faint flickering within.

The cast is weak, she wasn't lying…

His somber eyes meet hers. Careful not to test her concentration, the archaeologist shifts his gaze to a crumbling of stone at the gate of the cell. In one foul burst, Fylorn is knocked from his post, tumbling ahead to land alongside Elijou. The open door is slammed hard against the wall of bars that holds it. Jingling from worn guardsman attire precedes the figure barreling towards the Pajiado woman.

Only a darting hand and feral cry fling from the archaeologist before the hulk of man smashes into Elijou. Her startled scream and arching stomach continue to haunt Fylorn while the rest of her body flies ahead, into the pitch black beyond. In between her exaggerated breathes, the simple wisps of her sleeveless coat flapping from her plunging departure claws at the archaeologist's ears.

One powerful fist detonates on the archaeologist's face. Before he can fully stand up, two powerful arms grapple Fylorn from behind. The receding view of a hollow darkness holding the image of his latest failure is all he sees before being dragged from the cell and deeper into the chaos of the prison.

Chapter 28
The Winds

Raging winds claw at Ani's face. Her unrelenting grip of Ora's spikes keeps only her elbows shaking. The long, fixated gaze of the blazing forest beyond the sea nearly dries her eyes out.

The king, that stupid wretched king thinks he can do whatever he wants. Not if I can help it. There is no turning back now, I am the hero they all think I am.

"I have to be," Ani utters to herself.

The air screeches past her as Ora reaches supernatural speeds. While viciously flapping its wings, the dragon gains as much distance as possible.

What happens when I… Am I going to kill the king? That would make me a murderer! And then all of Goromföld shall look upon the girl of perfect spirit as a slayer of the innocent. No! I was brought into this – I didn't ask for it – I am innocent! I will save the people, and prove that we aren't the kind of villains who kill their own… mother…

Ani's eyes slowly descend to watch the waters below. The glistening force of the waves grows more powerful as the pair close in on a middling distance between Millown and the peninsula. When she brings her gaze up, the placid view astonishes her.

"Where did it go?"

The horizon is filled by the natural beauty of a thriving forest, untouched by flames or harm of any kind. A harsh wind pelts her, forcing her to squint as she scans along the shore and back through the rising trees. Ani wretches the spike on the dragon's back, bringing its wings up to slow into a glide.

"Where did it go?!"

Ora tilts into a slow circle, adjusting for the severe velocity they had reached. Ani uses the moment to think while her eyes blankly drift along the coast. Passing the grand delta, she broadens her view to the entire bay of The Mouth of Ardaelius. Her sights then cross the distant forests between the hills and plains.

"Tushma..."

Of course! I've been trying and failing to find my way because I don't know what I'm doing. I need him, now more than ever.

Ani pulls on the spike, guiding Ora back towards Millown. A quick scan ahead provides a majestic midday view of the river's delta, then beyond to the forest between Goromföld's grand hills and plains. As the dragon glides forward, she notices the biting winds of their elevation dried out her wet clothing.

I may need to get warmer clothing if I keep flying like this.

Without warning, Ora dives before spinning towards a low hanging cloud. Ani barely retains her grip when the majestic beast begins oscillating its glide.

"What are you doing?" she calls out to the dragon.

A feral growl rumbles along the throat of Ora, bringing a tension to Ani so powerful she lowers herself on the creature's back. From behind bellows a tremendous wail, one that the young woman had only heard once before.

The mechanical egg!

Ani twists her head around to be pelted by a buffet of winds. Squinting her eyes allows for a mere moment of seeing the colossal tunnel of clouds flying towards the young woman and her spectral dragon.

A scorching sensation engulfs her left arm while she watches the amorphous structure flow towards her. It dominates the sky as a confined continuum. A streaking glimmer reflects from it, nearly blinding Ani. She swings her face, crossing over her stiff arm, and finally sees the emboldened, black hand-mark on her wrist writhe upon her skin. Her breath slows while her face hardens.

I am to be judged…

While trying to deny a tear of pain from rolling out of her eye, she turns her focus back to tracking the coming land. Scanning each way, Ani tries to anticipate where Ora intends to go. The panning shores slow to a crawl. A current of air becomes visible before her, then a force pulls on the young woman's skin so powerful that it threatens to strip her bones. Her hair streams into a dedicated arrow behind her head. She painfully twists her head to see a gaping maw amidst the tumbling clouds of black and grey.

That thing is trying to eat us!

Ora wanes, then droops. Every muscle in the young woman's body resists the tugging upon her, but the dragon succumbs. They are taken by the unrelenting suction. Föld spins around Ani as she is brought closer and closer to the ever-expanding being.

How is this thing more powerful than Ora?

Ani helplessly watches as the pair fly in reverse, and the sky around them diminishes. Each precious moment slips away while her and the spectral dragon are swallowed into the vortex. Trying with every measure of strength she has, the young woman squints as the wind presses into her face.

The intangible sight of violent winds and unprecedented storms within the divine beast challenges her mind. From all corners of the torrent around them come tendrils of spun cloud. They reach out to take hold of Ora's limbs. The dragon unleashes a bellowing cry before defending itself with a potent electrical breath. Wild crackling from the attack overwhelms the numbing noise of the winds, forcing Ani to choose between holding on or being deafened. Finally, the chaos of her loose hair slapping her in the face breaks the young woman and she relinquishes one hand to cover her head and wrap around one ear.

The tendrils take no heed to the vicious display of the dragon. They slowly creep onto and around the dragon's feet, beginning to restrain Ora. Tears flood the young woman's vision as the wind whips upon them. She can feel the tiring grip upon the spike begin to shake. A burning sensation envelopes her, then from her second spirit's wrest plumes the bladed lizard. Mounting the back of its spectral companion, the gykeng climbs towards a secured limb and delivers a devastating blow, forcing the twisting cloud to retreat.

Once again, the pinching scream thunders from the column of cloud, bringing her mind to an apical break. Her hands fall slack. Her vision fades in and out, the darkness threatening to overtake Ani. Colours leave the visage of blurry greys fighting whites as she plummets away. The vortex of the tunnel pulls her into a spin away from her auragonics, dragging her deeper into the beast.

Her eyes blink, she catches glimpses of two intertwined streams of spirit racing to return. They connect, dissolving back to their home within her. Each moment of suspension, the stupendous weightlessness of it all, gives her more time to remember why she's here. She rolls her head back, embracing the fall. The endless rush of air passing her ears creates a volume so loud that her thoughts transcend beyond the noise. Ani closes her eyes.

A gently placed pressure upon her chest brings her eyelids open with a panicked snap. The unsettled maw of the bladed lizard glaring its sights directly into hers nearly collapses her chest in sheer fright. After the faintest flicker of its nose, it guides her arm over its back, spinning the young woman to see over its shoulder. She grips her own hand around its neck, giving in to the request. It streamlines into a dive ahead, aiming towards a wall of undulating cloud. With arms held out forward, the auragonic jams itself into the wall, sinking its elongated blades into the amorphic barrier. As Ani feels the sheer strength of the beast nearly buckle while tearing a hole in the wall, a spray of liquid bleeds from the seam.

Wailing from the colossal creature returns, this time bearing a heightened pitch of pain. Ahead of Ani, the gykeng continues breaching, splitting a clouded door open, then slipping through. Colour engulfs the young woman as the sky bombards her with hues of blue. She spins in a rapid descent. As she tries to orient herself, the emergence of Ora settles her into a mighty dive directly towards the water. The bladed lizard releases itself from its physical form to wisp back to the young woman's arm.

"Into the water!" she booms.

Ani's focus snaps to the corner of her eyes, becoming fully alert to the ever-growing funnels of cloud reaching down at them. Ora sharpens its body. She lowers herself into the dragon's shoulder blades just before they plunge into the surface. Immense liquid pressure strips the young woman from her auragonic. Ani spins in a cyclone, unsure of what is up or down while bubbles rush past. The moment of her holding a breath in the black, choppy water is cut short as her body is pummeled and dragged through the water. She feels scales and claws before being thrust through the glassy surface.

A half-measured gasp is all Ani is allowed before being submitted to Ora's desperate climb through the air. Water screams past the young woman as the gargantuan beast of winds nearly drives a breath into the sea with a booming gust. Waves crack and merge into one another while Ani feels her skin being tugged upon again.

"Dive!" she hollers.

Ora reacts with perfect timing, barely giving the young woman a chance to gather air before being dragged back into the Mouth of Ardaelius. Her steel grip of Ora's spikes holds true this time, keeping her on the dragon's back. The sea serpent worms so fast through the water that Ani can't bring her eyes closed, and bears witness to the liquid around her being vacuumed upwards. A majestic spray of foam and salty water joins the spectral dragon carrying Ani while they are ripped from security and back into the open air.

Each flap of Ora's wings fights to gain any ground. The young woman darts her sights back and forth to try and find a solution, then spots the tear that her and the bladed serpent had escaped from.

"Turn around!" Ani barks.

The young woman feels a rumbling come from within the throat of the dragon. She raises her arm, then flexes to command her second auragonic free. As Ora complies, and twists into a tight arrow using the momentum of the colossal cloud's suction. Ani quickly looks behind to see the gykeng, perching at the ready on the dragon's lower back. Moments before being drawn into the grey maw once more, the spectral dragon veers, using the built-up speed to spin and glide along the outer edge of the colossal, funnel beast. In a joint effort, the bladed serpent raises its arms and slices the pall flesh above it.

Ora digs its claws deep into the underbelly of the elemental being, drawing a thick, plumeous blood, while unleashing a screech that immediately reaches a pitch higher than Ani can hear. The semi-silent wrenching, coming from the dragon's mouth, compels tears from the young woman's eyes.

Ani can't help but grin at the monumentous endeavour. She watches as a mist of the beast's liquids rains behind them. The young woman affirms her grip of the spikes before her, then yanks to bring Ora wide and away from the amorphous torrent of clouds. As they flee, funnels of wind strike out to entangle the dragon and its riders. The moment stretches indefinitely, until the world around her stills. Ani watches in horror as grey funnels form a cage, enclosing her within. She can feel the air gradually being squeezed from her new prison. Unparalleled pressures are laid into her until the bladed serpent dissolves into a wisp and returns to her. Ora casts weak eyes at its Anchor, delivering final words.

A blink of light astonishes the young woman, but she holds her eyelids open while the event reveals a young Pajiado woman centering the anomalous vortex. Energy arcs from the elegant mystic as the colossal beast flares in response. The combat of pressures ahead of Ani brings a complex assault to her chest, leaving it difficult to breathe. Then, the spectral dragon she rides on faults into a stream of spirit back into her. The clouded floor beneath her gives out, and the young woman free falls through the sky. Wind whips past her as her body begins to tumble. Each violent turn ensures that Ani loses sight of where she is or has been.

Finally, she closes her eyes.

Two hands grapple her sides. Her eyes snap open to find the Pajiado woman gripping her. The soft white hair of the woman streaks behind her through the air. Both fiery eyes lock into Ani's as they conjoin into a unified spin within the sky. Nothing the Pajiado says from her bold red lips is able to touch the young woman's ears, but Ani's body senses a realization that allows her mind to settle into an undue ease. She closes her eyes, and smells the salty water approach while the Pajiado tightens her grip. The darkness behind Ani's eyelids is challenged by a bright fila before becoming an absolute black.

Chapter 29
The Whistle

Ram and Aal-Ivus have Full Giant. Elijou is gone.

The toes of Fylorn's boots bounce on every gap of stone while being dragged. An unceasing pressure from two gleaming guards holding either armpit restrains him. Each passing splatter of blood in the hallway fails to tell him where he's going. A blurring of his vision forces the archaeologist to question whether they are turning corners, or his consciousness is fading. The loud bang of a steel door being slammed shut snaps his focus ahead.

Before him stands a tall and thin man. The blacks of his long robe are bordered by a trim of rusted orange. He pulls back his hood to look down on Fylorn, face to face. His grey skin is peppered by aging spots and wrinkle lines.

"This is the one who broke my prison wide open? One man?"

A grumble comes from one of the archaeologist's captors. "No, the others got away."

Fylorn hears the tall man hiss before spitting out, "Go! Find them. Leave him with me."

The floor cradles the archaeologist as he is thrown away. Each fading footstep rings within his ears. His one swollen eye is barely open enough to spot the remaining man circling him.

"Who are you?"

Pain surges through Fylorn's scalp as his head is lifted, but he answers anyways, "It doesn't matter."

"It matters to me," the tall man barks back. A spattering of spit lands on the archaeologist's ear. "I don't know you, and you have no reason to dismantle my work the way you have."

"Your work?"

A scoff shoots out from the tall man. "The work of a saent."

"No," Fylorn utters to himself.

He feels a thin finger hook under his chin to bring his sights directly to the bloodshot eyes of the saent. The sharp bones along the pious man's face present every subtle twitch of his muscles.

"It must be pure luck for you to have managed to worm yourself into here. For a notorious amount of time, the Saent of Retreat has been more than adequate in dissuading lesser men from attempting such idiocy."

"And?" slips from the archaeologist's bloody mouth.

"And now I am forced to prove it." The saent releases his hold while standing to his full height, then casts an innocuous glare upon Fylorn before turning.

Each rustling step the pious man takes sends a foreboding rhythm into the archaeologist's ear. His wavering sights linger on the small pool of his own mortality slowly drying on the stone floor beneath his chin.

"Aren't you going to restrain me?" Fylorn asks.

One warm chuckle shoots from the saent. "In due time. Tell me, are you worried about losing those freedoms?"

Fylorn looks upwards to analyze the puttering of the pious man. He watches for an elongated moment at the saent stoking a vibrant flame on the other side of the room. He blinks a few times while processing the image of rods being rearranged. The clanking of metal on metal assumes the archaeologist's focus until his captor speaks again.

"Feel free to answer at any time."

"Why?"

"Because I've tortured silent men before, and it has yet to sway my actions." The grey skin of the man reflects the warm orange of the smithing flame ahead of him while angling an eye towards Fylorn. "Do try."

"I meant, 'Why do you care what I think?'."

The saent smiles before returning to his heated affairs. "You may not know this yet, but as someone who is quite close with Ardaelius I can tell you that making a grand show before death doesn't change things on this side or the other. She does not judge you for being yourself."

"My self wants to live."

"Live..." the pious man chokes out a scoff before humming to himself.

"Was that funny?" Fylorn inquires.

"For someone who managed to slit the belly of this prison wide open, by means of which I will find out – believe you me – you don't seem particularly observant." A wave of heat circles the room as the saent withdraws a metal rod glowing between red and white. He examines his work, then dips his shaded sights down to the archaeologist. "What we can't do kills a part of us. It's a death that even Our Goddess herself has no power over. It's what you should truly be afraid of."

A splash of heat cascades across Fylorn as the pious man balances the glowing tool within his hand. After resting it at a vertical angle, the archaeologist comes nearly face to face with an elaborate symbol of an eye placed at the end of the poker.

It's a stamp.

"You mean to brand me…"

"So, I ask again. Do you fear losing your freedoms? Certainly, having Ardaelius keep her eye on you will diminish opportunities to act in the ways you have."

Before allowing Fylorn the time to answer, the saent kicks him in the gut. A resounding sensation of agony ignites a fury inside of the archaeologist. He moves his hands to defend but another strike flips him onto his back. One black boot stomps onto Fylorn's collarbone before a thud of the stamp nearly knocks the wind from him.

"The only thing I fear is not being remembered," the archaeologist gasps out.

A breath of reprieve precedes the burning through his robes and melting into his skin. The searing of flesh becomes the dominating scent around him. One feral howl from Fylorn denies the room any silence.

He feels an additional kick to his ribs, forcing him to flip over on his side. Each time he draws air into his newly disfigured chest it sends intolerable waves of pain. Howl after howl, Fylorn's protest continues until he cannot bear to exhale. Finally, the pain becomes senseless, and the hissing of the stamping rod being cooled flushes his ear.

Putting pressure onto his arm returns the pain to his chest, but the archaeologist denies it power over him. He rises to his knees, displaying his drawn lips and bared teeth towards his target. Shifting his weight swings Fylorn forward, setting him on course to impact into the back of the saent.

Without a flinch, the archaeologist's jabs square into the pious man. A startled yelp flings from the saent before Fylorn wraps his hands around the man's head. Fighting through the struggling neck and failing arms, the archaeologist lowers the saent's head into the water holding his work, then holds it there. The violent splashing attacks the mottled skin of Fylorn's chest, challenging his strength. One swift kick from the pious man sets the archaeologist off balance, and puts a moment of room between the men. The saent turns to properly defend himself, but Fylorn charges ahead. Now face to face with the grey-skinned man, the archaeologist musters all of his power to bring the saent's head under water once more, and this time quickly snatches one of the rods within the basin. In perfect timing, Fylorn relocated the rod down into the pious man's mouth. After a few jittery squirms, the saent's body stills.

The archaeologist falls to the floor, landing in a leaning sit. He swiftly pulls his overexerted breathing into check as the intensity of his fresh chest wound returns to him.

"Ardaelius, damn it," falls from his mouth.

He drifts his eyes towards the deceased man, half hanging from the workshop basin. Quickly, he averts his sights to the sole door to the room.

Can't sit around here forever, or until they come and find me... and what I did to their saent.

A step taken that she will be most intrigued with.

Fylorn releases multiple short groans while rising to his feet. He gives one final glance at the man in rusted orange robes, then shuffles from the room. Hallway after hallway, the archaeologist takes his time to avoid rushing patrols of guards trying to return order to the prison. Hollering dictates when Fylorn gambles on moving ahead or waiting a moment. The arduous journey through the gross cell block to the stairwell becomes the archaeologist's own personal Dak.

As he arrives at the first step, he reaches out to grip the railing. A hallowed ring ejects from the disturbed metal. The siren call for the guards to come find him sends a cold sweat down Fylorn's back, but sets fire to his feet. Doubling his pace, the archaeologist climbs the stairs until he approaches the gates within the diminutive shelter on the surface.

No one defending the stairs? Either the prisoners won, or someone is playing games with me.

Once at the final step, he moves to open the wire gate door while swiftly scanning the area. The clutter of swords and spears being sprawled across the ground in a hurried mess brings the archaeologist's hand to a halt.

Are they all down in the prison still? Did I actually miss them all?

Breaking and clattering upon the outside door forces an involuntary shift in Fylorn. He sets his body closer to the concealed corner within the platform while trying to ignore the growing sweat on his brow.

A deep voice trickles in before the door fully opens. "How do we know that he didn't make it out already?"

"You don't know Fylorn," a rhythmically assertive voice whispers out. "He hasn't gone far."

The words take a breath to sink in, reminding him of his chest wound and the complications if he should challenge another fight. He peeks out the corner, only to be met by an arrow slamming into the wired wall ahead of him.

"Dammit, Ram. It's me!" Fylorn bellows out.

"Fylorn?" the Nhavyyet calls back.

"I thought you knew him," comments the deep voice.

The familiar chuckle of a Hal-Vagenkar rings out. "Clearly you don't know the Saer of Scrolls. The man has read–"

A thump precedes a guttural groan.

"We get it," Ram grumbles out. "Fylorn! Get out here."

The archaeologist limps out from the blackened corner, sliding his fingers through the holes of the wired door, then pushes it open. An audible gasp comes from Ram, while the other two become fuzzy as Fylorn focuses on his childhood friend.

"Where did yous come from?" the archaeologist inquires. "I thought Elijou–"

"Your chest…" the Nhavyyet utters.

Fylorn's chin wiggles. His face becomes firm before replying, "I'll be fine."

"Where is she?" the Wöllralt demands, his glare upon the archaeologist darkening.

"She didn't make it," Fylorn slowly explains.

Full Giant instantly barks back, "Why?"

"What do you mean, 'Why'?" the Hal-Vagenkar retorts while shaking his head.

Without looking at the alpine-skinned man, the Wöllralt asks again, "Where is she?"

"One of the guards knocked her out of the cell." Fylorn watches as a shade of grey overtakes Ram's face in response to his grim words. "She's gone."

"But she can go wherever she wants!" the Wöllralt roars.

"Look, Full Giant. She ran out of mystics. She used her last one on me and it failed. She's gone. That's it."

A thunderous thump cracks out into the room as the Wöllralt smashes his fist into the stone wall near the outside door. Broken veins of the impact remain as he reluctantly removes his white knuckles. The other three men all bring their sights to Full Giant. Fylorn can feel the hairs of his neck rise as the oversized man turns his head to face him. The red around the Wöllralt's eyes divulge a well of secrets about the ex-prisoner.

"We need to leave," the archaeologist manages to say.

Full Giant reaches to open the outside door, then solemnly ducks under the frame and out of the diminutive room. Fylorn catches Aal-Ivus slide worried eyes towards him, but silently shakes his head before following the oversized man out.

A twang of pain surges through the archaeologist. He keels over, slow enough that Ram notices before he leaves and rushes to support his companion.

"What happened?"

"I killed the saent…"

"You?" a ring of astonishment floods from the Nhavyyet while beginning to walk Fylorn forwards with him. "Did he do that to you?"

The archaeologist gives a slow nod as they pass through the doorway and the light of day flashes in his eyes. Before he can take a good look at the pitch ahead of him, the solemn words of Ram slip into his ears.

"Well, saves me an arrow or two."

Fylorn chuckles, then looks around at the carnage surrounding him. From one side to the other, blood spatters the green. The tower once warded over by fierce men in silver now lies in shambles on its side. In each direction beyond it, dirt rests in piles of upheaval. A wide scattering of bodies fills the dishevelled scene with the smell of violent rebellion.

They did win…

"Damn maniacs could be anywhere," Aal-Ivus spittles out.

Full Giant thumps as he leads the party through the prison yard. He throws half an eye over his shoulder.

"I'm not talking about you, you big lug," the Hal-Vagenkar defends.

The tension of the Wöllralt's face flickers. He then twists around towards the other three men. His chest blooms as he builds up to speaking, but stops at the crest of his breath. The red of his eyes dissipate as they grow wild, rolling around in their sockets looking to the skies for something.

"Full Giant?" Fylorn questions.

"What are you seeing, big guy?" Ram asks in addition.

The silence of the oversized man brings a definitive chill to the air. Grey begins to darken the sky, blocking out the fila and threatening a storm.

"That was fast," Aal-Ivus utters.

"We have to–" The words of the archaeologist are cut off by a bestial wailing from on high. Fylorn immediately shifts his gaze from the Wöllralt below to the clouds above. Before he has a chance to react, a whoosh of cloud plumes as a dragon breaches from the grey threat. Its fierce, crimson scales glint in the light as it dives towards the ruined yard.

A thud pelts the archaeologist's side as Ram knocks his companion into a pile of wood. Fylorn's helpless, sideways view witnesses the divine serpent colliding into the field of the yard. A tremor vibrates through him upon the beast's landing. The overbearing threat awaiting before them widens its nostril and jerks its head in each direction upon gathering itself. A set of distinguished spikes create a road along its back primed for impalement. In a quick flutter, it snaps its wings out before tucking them in on its sides. The yellow eyes of the creature scour the prison's turret walls before locking onto Full Giant.

"Run!" bursts from Fylorn's mouth.

Action explodes around him. Aal-Ivus rolls to behind the fallen tower, wildly looking around for something. Full Giant leaps aside as a swift lick of flame comes from the dragon's mouth. Out of the corner of his eye, the archaeologist witnesses Ram draw and fire arrow after arrow with immaculate finesse. All connect, but most bounce from the serpent's unparalleled scale defence. A hail of fire crosses the yard, and instinctually Fylorn's body tucks itself into a hole behind the broken wood. Searing heat engulfs the meager wall, and a powerful flame roars while climbing over the peak towards the archaeologist. He swings his sights both ways, spotting Ram's fierce assault and hearing the Wöllralt overexerting grunts.

Please don't tell me that idiot is fist fighting a dragon.

You must leave them or lead them.

A deep singe of pain reminds Fylorn of his chest wound. The agony weakens his muscles, and he falls back into a lean against the burning wood. Abounding shouts echo throughout the yard while the growing heat threatens to consume him. Notes of a heavy drumming cut through the violent cries. A steady rhythm pries its way across the yard and into Fylorn's ears. His eyes burst open with exhilaration. He can feel the heat of his blood as it flows through his veins. With a tense neck, his sights crawl along the battlefield at his feet and find a soiled sword without an owner. His shaking hand reaches out and takes a hold of it. A fine edge that once bore a glint of death now extends from a chipped hilt having dirt, blood, and rust dominate it.

The pulsing of his heart compounds as his body remains stagnant. He rises, then swings his eyes out behind him, over the scorching pile, and out into the display of combat centering the dilapidated prison. Crunching and swearing echo from Full Giant as he delivers the might of his people upon the winged beast. Using a cleaving sword in one hand and a post embedded within stone for a hammer in the other, his onslaught of rage is a beautiful sight. Fylorn's eyes snap to Ram prowling the outer ring of the yard, picking up and firing every arrow he can get his hands on. Then the stark tones of drumming draw the archaeologist's attention. He spots the Hal-Vagenkar standing behind a flipped-over tanning rack, heaving with everything he has onto the makeshift drum.

How do I lead men like this?

You show them that fear isn't an option.

A chill runs down Fylorn's spine. He takes a deep breath, the first in a while, and feels the expansion of his sealing chest wound. The pain fuels him. He digs his foot into the ground, then charges at an angle between the dragon and Ram. Each step he takes is a leap off of some debris to bring him across the field of battle that much quicker. He twists his head to watch as Full Giant punches the inside of the fiery beast's leg, then thrusts his sword up between two belly scales. The resounding roar of the serpent sends a shockwave out from its gaping mouth.

The archaeologist returns his sights ahead, finding his footing wrong and slips. Swinging his weight sideways, he avoids the blade of his sword, only to land in an excruciating roll across chunks of broken stone. He blindly ejects a harsh scream as the nerves of his chest burn. Through the cracks of his eyes, a breathtaking visage looms over him. The mythic creature stands with golden eyes set in rage.

Claws, large and wide. Scales, sharp and jagged. The heat irradiating from the thick throat of the colossal beast buffets Fylorn. Sweat runs down his skin but all he can feel is an unnatural chill. The world stills as the archaeologist watches the dragon breathe.

Once.

Twice.

Three arrows zip past his eyes, plunging into the breast of the creature. Each one punctures between scales.

"Fylorn! Move!"

The sound of Ram's holler rattles Fylorn's head. His sights blur as his face twists to the call but his eyes stay locked on the dragon's vibrating throat. A swell of its muscles precedes a vacuum of air. Intense waves of heat lick at the archaeologist, reminding him of the coming scorch.

His feet scramble. His arms flail. His eyes widen while his jaw clamps shut.

Ram's volume grows until Fylorn sees his body flying through the air and slam into the side of the colossal beast. The impact is so powerful that it forces the dragon's mouth away, casting flames far to the right of the archaeologist. A wild scream of sizzling rock and wood blasts Fylorn while his scramble away becomes a full-blown flee for his life. His heart pounds within his chest. As he makes one flick of a glance over his shoulder, he catches the blink of a moment where his Nhavyyet companion rolls from a stomping paw.

The archaeologist's heart lurches within its confines at his companion narrowly avoiding death. His heels dig into the gravel. He swings his head to find Full Giant nearby. A violent crack draws everyone's attention. Fylorn snaps his sights to the dragon standing over the Nhavyyet, and the crawling of unsettled föld beneath.

"Wöllralt!" The charge, so loud and dominating, coming from the archaeologist's mouth steals Full Giant's focus instantly. "Break the ground beneath them!"

After one breath of hesitation, the oversized man scoops up an adequate boulder. As Fylorn casts his gaze ahead he bears witness to a swift yank from the serpent's head as it rips the flesh from Ram's hand, leaving exposed bone behind. The archaeologist's chest heaves, forcing more pain to spread through his torso. His eyes widen and feet press forward towards his companion. From over his head comes a whoosh of air as the boulder is violently tossed ahead.

Within the blink of an eye, Fylorn helplessly watches on while Ram rears his injured hand, preparing to stab the scaley leg ahead of him with his fresh bone, all while the boulder impacts. As the soil underneath of the dragon splashes, it breathes in to eject another swath of flames upon the men, but instead its head is thrust to the sky. A thunderous crunch waves out. Dust unsettles. Ahead of the archaeologist, the very ground releases and the mythical creature plummets below. As the lethal breath of the serpent scorches the sky above, it lands on the first floor of the prison. At a perfect height, the swinging arm of the Nhavyyet accompanies a surprised but triumphant roar from the stout man as he plunges his superior bone into the fragile eye socket of the dragon.

The following howls of agony and victory send a wash of nerves along Fylorn, until the flailing head of the dying beast threatens to set blaze to the entire prison. A firm grip upon his back nearly tosses the archaeologist, but as he involuntarily speeds towards Ram, he watches a second hand grapple his Nhavyyet friend the same. Heaving breaths from Full Giant splash upon the swinging men as they are swiftly brought from the bowls of death to the safety of the displaced tower.

As the firm grip is lost, Fylorn feels the tough hold of the ground below. He looks over to see Ram holding his hand, and an unending flow of blood pouring from it.

"We have to go," comes from Aal-Ivus.

"I don't think anyone here is in the condition to go right now," Fylorn barks.

"Are you in the condition to be a prisoner?" the Hal-Vagenkar retaliates.

Bells ring out within Mashar Pelim, marking the first sign that the city was coming to handle the situation. The archaeologist's steady breathing brings the world of his pain back into view.

"We can't stay here," Full Giant remarks. "They will kill me on sight."

"Or worse," grumbles out of Ram.

Fylorn's lip quivers while his friend's face winces. His feet trail over to the edge of the sideways structure to find himself in time for the final moments of the dragon wild clawing to escape the hole it sits in. He holds his eyes on the incomprehensible writhing of such a creature; at the building steam coming from the insurmountable life that had to be taken for him to live. After a powerful thrash shakes the ground, the archaeologist holds steady on a nearby broken wall as he witnesses the panicked flee through the smoky air from the prison. His eyes trail down to the mangle hole in the devastated prison yard to find an impacted tooth left behind.

That's as close to a dragon bone as I ever want to be again... I can't believe Ram actually did that; proved to Nhavyyet far and wide that his bones are– His wound!

His tired eyes watch the steam still rising off the abandoned tooth. He turns to the three men behind him, then orders, "Bring Ram here."

"Why?" the Wöllralt complains.

Fylorn catches the Hal-Vagekar's eyes dart back and forth, piecing the scene together before his face lights up.

"Yes, do it," Aal-Ivus says in support.

The oversized man picks the Nhavyyet up, cradling him around the sideways tower towards the others. Aal-Ivus goes towards the dragon's tooth first, then Fylorn lines up after.

"Didn't expect one of those to be left behind…" utters Full Giant.

"Why do you need me?" inquires the Nhavyyet.

"Your wound can't be open that long, you'll bleed out, or get a disease, or–"

"Again, what is your plan?"

"Put it on the tooth, burn it closed," crawls from Fylorn.

Full Giant groans in agreement, continuing to carry the Nhavyyet to the steaming tooth. Ram makes small primal noises of disagreement but ultimately doesn't stop the oversized man from placing him down next to the impacted remains. As Full Giant backs away, the stout man's sights linger on the scorching podium ahead of him. In a swift action, he raises his bloody skin and bones, then makes contact with the steaming tooth. Immediately, the searing of the Nhavyyet's flesh roars. A restrained growl comes from Ram as his skin is sealed. His arm begins to shake before he forcefully retracts it back to the comfort of his chest.

"That's enough…" he whimpers.

"Alright," falls from Fylorn's mouth before turning to the Wöllralt and Hal-Vagenkar. Their eyes set on him, awaiting his next words. "It's time to go back to the village."

Pluming of smoke linger above grand bellows to make a grey forest entrenching the prison. The company bands together, then crosses the destroyed yard to the once fortified entrance. Hobbling through it brings them face to face with the horrors that the city had been dealing with. The mess of blood and broken stone extends in every direction ahead of him, but Fylorn turns to walk past it in silence.

Chapter 30
The Legacy

The long walk from Mashar Pelim is filled with lurking in shadows and hiding in caves to keep Full Giant concealed. Once the party finds themselves within the security of dense forests, they strain to make as much ground as possible during daylight and hunker down for the nights. Finally, they make it to the river. Even with all of Aal-Ivus and Ram's bickering, they secure travel to the other side.

Coming to the monumental pier of the village brings the archaeologist front and center to the gathering awaiting their arrival. Wöllralt young and old stand on the fringes of their home, casting hopeful eyes out at the docking vessel.

"Full Giant?"

"Yes," the enormous man replies.

"Does your village have anything that might aid Ram's missing hand?"

"I need to see the Nhavyyet, not have these big..." the stout man's eyes squint as he controls himself, "people, rig some kind of stone to my arm."

"He's not wrong, it's probably stone." Full Giant confirms.

"Also, it's a great reminder that I killed a dragon... Remember, if anyone asks, that's what happened."

Fylorn groans before disembarking from the stationed boat. He holds nothing back, walking in a straight path to the fortress at the height of the village. Every Wöllralt gazes upon him, some with shock and awe, while others scowl in disagreement. Neither bother him as he brings himself up the flat, stone staircase and to the oversized entrance. Inside of the sommos, the lrotirölt stands awaiting him, and silently allows him passage inside.

One roaring fire presides in the center of the tribal hall. Numerous strings of bones dangle around the room. A moment passes before the mossteev turns to face the archaeologist. The woman's blackened face fuels Fylorn as she speaks.

"What is it you wish to know?"

"Tell me of your god."

"What is your name?"

"I am Fylorn Dagus."

"And it is with this name you shall understand that which you are owed. The one to give us unending fire. The one some call the father of stone. The Wöllralt of this hohrt, and everyone before it, knelt to one known as Togös, a god among men. A being whose true name has been handed down from one mossteev to the next. Ayagog-Dagus."

My ancestor is the god…

Good. Now, say my name!

The strength of Fylorn's legs give out. He braces for impact by landing on his right knee. While raising his head, he finds himself kneeling to the mossteev. Before correcting where he is, words flow from his mouth.

"Tell me everything about Ayagog-Dagus!"

A heavy exhale storms from the Wöllralt woman before lifting her chin. "The great Togös is, has, and was only known to reside within The Perfect Wild. Closest to the

Tonnifin hohrt was his spire. There he died as a man of stone, to remain forever alongside his greatest offenses."

"Where, tell me exactly where."

"We do not know. The Höllron dared not to go—"

A screeching yelp comes from outside the stone fortress. Fylorn rises to his feet while casting his sights outside. The mossteev thunders past him, nearly knocking him over. He follows her outside. The blinding light of day takes him aback, but holding his hand over his brow lets him spot a young woman along the riverbed. She screams again.

White hair, sleeveless coat. Elijou!

Fylorn bolts down the flat and wide staircase. His pace outmatches the Wöllralt woman as he speeds past other villagers stoic to the event downfield. The archaeologist nearly loses his breath while bringing himself to such a pace. He leaps from the lowest step as the Pajiado woman calls out to him.

"Fylorn! In the river!"

His eyes dart around to try and solve the riddle she had given him. There were no signs of anything unordinary.

"What!" he calls back, testing the limits of his stamina.

He diligently watches her swing her arm around to point at a log wedged in the river. Immediately he spots a body clinging onto the frail support. Fylorn propels himself forward to reach Elijou, but sprints pace the sopping woman directly to the water's edge. He trudges deep into the river. Wading up to his waist, the archaeologist comes within reach of the body. A young woman wearing torn leathers smeared in stains of blood shows no sign of consciousness aside from her lifesaving grip.

Is she holding on, or trapped?

He reaches out, extending his fingers as far as they will go while keeping himself from being swept away by the current.

"Take my hand."

The young woman's hand feints, then swings wide. Fylorn watches as her blue eyes explode open while the water tugs on her, bringing her underneath the log and downstream. He plunges his hand in, grasping with luck to take a hold of her flittering cloth. Using every bit of strength he has, he tugs on her. The strain seems too much. His fingers begin to slip, then he feels an enlarged hand grab him by the shoulder and drag him backwards.

The motion knocks Fylorn off balance, but to no consequence and his limp body is kept afloat by what he swiftly understands to be Full Giant. Long brown hairs from the giant dangle onto the archaeologist's face while the convoy of bodies returns to dry land.

On shore, Full Giant steps back to give the pair some space. Fylorn rolls the young woman over to ensure she hasn't drowned, only for her to stick her hand out once more. The archaeologist responds in kind, extending his hand to acquire a hold of her overpowering grip before pulling her to her feet.

The dark, wet hair resting as a mess upon her head flips back allowing a beam of light to cross her blue eyes, and reveal a familiar face.

"Ani?" Fylorn breathes out.

She coughs, dragging her eyes up to the archaeologist, then cracks a smile.

Ani & Fylorn's story will continue in

Her Final Disciple

Welcome
To
Föld

Here is an appendix for the world surrounding Of Perfect
Spirit. Within there is a list of local words and their
meanings, a quick walkthrough of the culture, as well as a
map.

Enjoy!

Words
From
Föld

Alokhevryk (Ahl·Oh·Khev·Rik): A legend among the Nhavyyet, one whose name is used in dire times as a swear.

Arkölox (Ark·Oo·Locks): Six legged feline beasts found in the mountainous forests of Goromföld. Their violet eyes can usually be seen prowling in the dark night.

Auragonic (Aura·Gone Ick): The spectral creature residing within the Spirit's Wrest of a Spirit Anchor.

Bourtaulitanbour (Bohr·Tau·Lit·Ann·Bohr): The native language of the Nhavyyet.

Claven: A grouping of holds based on a long-ago agreement within a region.

Dak: An abhorrent place believed to be where one is sent to in the event of death after an immoral life. It is mainly believed that Ardaelius herself resides here and becomes one's master upon arrival. A place of cold and death, Dak is a miserable end to an improper life.

Droniyagibbpotad (Droh·Nheeyah·Gibb·Poh·Tahd):
Amphibian creature with highly mineralized exoskeleton
that has steam/mist release along the ridges between its
carapaces. It has chelae(claws) on two large limbs, two large
hopping limbs, and two medium limbs for more versatile
use. Likes to sleep a lot. The apex creature is named after the
noise it makes from steam.

Edvekrotinyagach (Edd·Veh·Kroh·Tein·Yah·Gah·Ch):
From unknown origins, these beasts of burden have been
serving their Nhavyyet masters for as long as anyone can
remember. By all accounts they seem to be the breeding
conclusion of a hauling bear, a basic hog, and possibly even
the Nhavyyet themselves.

Fila: The star of this planet's solar system; the equivalent
of Earth's Sol.

Filaash (Feel·Ah·Sh): The cardinal direction equivalent
to north. It is in relation to the fila being high. As in filaash is
the part of the continent farthest up the planet.

Föld (Foo·Ld): The planet on which this story takes
place on.

Földic: The cardinal direction equivalent to south. It is in
relation to the lands of Föld being low. As in földic is the
part of the continent farthest down the planet.

Földwalker: A title given to Nhavyyet that has left the
Sierra.

Goromföld (Gore·Ohm·Foo·Ld): After The Year of
Conquering or The Vilagost, the Hue explored filaash and
discovered a second continent on Föld. Though translated as
'The Harsh Land' it is commonly referred to as 'The Land of
Ardaelius'.

Gykeng: A bi-pedal mystery. This ancient beast has very
little known about it, aside from the peculiar nature of
having forged blades attached to its arms, head, and knees.

Hal-Vagenkar: A half-bred individual of Vagenkar and Hue heritage.

Hellix (Hell·Ix): The core mount of Goromföld. They are canine in nature, though are larger and fiercer.

Hohrt (Who·Art): The Wöllralt word for tribe, and/or the collective of their family.

Hold: A domain of either Diplomacy, Resource, or Defence. In example: A city, tower, forest, or mine.

Höllron (Hoo·Ll·Rohn): A hominid creature of grand size and mysterious descendancy.

Hue: A hominid creature of primate descendancy.

Imperadomanhavyyet (Empair·Ah·Dohm·Ah·Naw·Vee Yet): The dominion title of all Nhavyyet living within the Sierra Ta Nahvyyet.

Kindly Crossed: The customary greeting amongst people of Föld. Intentionally speaking, it is a soft question if the person one meets is friendly or not.

Lrotirölt (Ll·raht·Ee·Roo·Lt): The patriarchal figurehead of the Wöllralt. It is their solemn duty to protect those of their horht.

Mossteev (Mow·Ss·Tefv): The matriarchal figure tasked with tending to the legacy of the Höllron. It is her sacred duty to secure the bloodlines of her people through means of bone-string 'scripture' and influence the Wöllralt accordingly.

Mostern: The cardinal direction for 'Towards the Gire Sea'.

My'To'Tang: A grand bird with a wingspan of over six meters wide. They are predominantly yellow in colour with a red tinge along their primary feathers edge as well as long flowing red feathers on the crown of their head. With an elongated beak in the shape of a wedge the avian predator is known for impaling its prey, then splitting them apart.

Nhavyyet (Naw·Vee·Yet): A hominid of heterocephalus descendancy.

Örum (Oo·Rhum): Also known as the Bitterworm, this large annelid creature will secrete hyper-caustic liquids. To sustain itself, the creature will wrap around tree trunks and melt the biological material before absorbing it.

Ostit (Oz·Tit): A half-bred individual of Pajiado and Hue heritage.

Pajiado (Pahj·Ee·Adoh): A hominid creature of avian descendancy.

Rock Climber: A scaley monster of great power and speed, these lizards hunting the furthest reaches of The Perfect Wild can flex their scales to defend from all angles.

Saent (Saint): The title of disciples ascended to the highest tier of Ardaelic Faith. The limited sect of six saents are individuals who retain control over the faith at large as well as being the Ardaelic Legion's key governing body.

Saer (Say·er): A title bestowed upon an individual who is in ownership of a claven. In example: Saer Jaemon.

Sanctuary: The exact opposite of Dak, Sanctuary is a haven for all who fully embodied the Gods' will. A place of pure bliss, one is rewarded with everything they have ever desired here.

Sea-pigs: A slang term used for pirates.

Söcartya (Soo·Kar·Tee·Yah): Known by some as the Mimic Deer, this hallowed creature stalks its prey while echoing sounds of familiarity. Its soft approachable exterior is the last thing victims see before being devoured alive.

Sommos (Sohm·Mohs): A title bestowed upon the sacred stone temple of which the mossteev tends to the bone-strings.

Spirit Anchor: A designation given to individuals who have the power to absorb the spirit of a dying creature into their own bodies, thereby retaining their essence to later expel back out in a physical form. Colloquial terms include Taker and Tamer.

Spirit's Wrest: Every Spirit Anchor's ability is dependant on a physical manifestation on their own body called a Spirit's Wrest. This malformation comes in a standard vertical scar somewhere on the individual's body. It is within this scar that the auragonic resides.

Teremföld (Tee·Rehm·Foo·Ld): Translated to 'The God's Land', it is the earliest known continent on Föld and is roughly thirty-seven million kilometers squared.

Vagenkar (Vah·gehn·kahr): A hominid of suidae descendancy.

Vastern: The cardinal direction for 'Towards the Kazdim Sea'.

Vheer (Ve·Her): An ancient word among the Hue meaning 'Blood'. It is used by families to establish lineage and value of heritage.

Vidicai (Ve·de·ki): A hominid of felid descendancy.

Wöllralt (Woo·Ll·Rah·Lt): A half-bred individual of Höllron and Hue heritage.

About
The Land of
Ardaelius

Customs

Travel: People don't travel a lot in Goromfold; it's too dangerous. Horses were brought, but were no match for the gruesome creatures of the lands. Instead, the people considered a fiercer mount. Caravan guilds harvested oversized berries to grow native beast into what we now call, the hellix and hauling bear.

Cities: With the dangers present in Goromföld, small towns were not an option. As such, large, fortified haven became the staple of life for pioneers of the land. These cities typically don't have a traditional street design, but more of a widened trail system.

Metals: The distinct metals the Land of Ardaelius is known for are silver and tungsten, or Ardaelic Ardent.

Faith

The House of Ardaelius: These churches to the goddess are the focal point of each city. It doesn't matter how far out you go, you can always find a church without walls, an obelisk out in the wilds, where anything can happen in an embrace to the chaos.

Ardaelic Wedding: Within the Ardaelic faith, there is a particular ceremony that her followers take part in. When two chose to join, they bleed into a vessel before mixing the blood. They then drink the liquid as a sign that they are a match for one another.

Azephyre: A massive soaring creature of pure wind. The being is a direct atonement to the element, and one of the Exalted. It soars across Föld doing Vihara's bidding.

Blue Sisters: Originating from Galiram, this order of women holds worship to Vihara. They have been known to use extreme measures to ensure their vision is carried out.

Seer: A mystic leader among the followers of Vihara. These individuals are often blind to help facilitate the judgements of the goddess and to see her next actions.

Locations of Interest

Underföld: Huge hollow spaces, connected in every direction, that can be found below the surface which remain a mystery to even the Nhavyyet.

Ködiam: The grand school of Millown renown for its etiquette and library.

Lake Barrelwood: Long ago when the world was new, large swaths of land between the sierras filaash and hills földic fell into the underföld. The sunken hole soon filled with water run off and became a grand lake.

Drifton: A bastion of wealth among the forests filaash of Cornon, this city has made its name by collecting rare wood that floats.

Wellias: Once a city brimming with potential, the aftermath of a civil war left only ruins to be reclaimed by the creatures of Goromföld.

Oldston: The grandest city on all of Föld, and spiritual capitol of Teremföld.

Xelis: Capitol of the Ardaelic Legion, this city began from the plentiful minerals and has grown to be a figurehead of Cornon

About The Author

Oh. Hi. You've found me. I'm guessing you would like to know more about the man who wrote this story. Yes, I suppose we can do that.

I still have many of the story concepts that I drafted out when I was young. From the multiple book series I dreamed about, being high fantasy to werewolf epics, the constant of telling stories remained. From a young age I always knew I was going to be a writer, not an author. As it turns out, some of the promises you make yourself as a child have to be broken– What was that? Ah, you want to know about things like where I live and how many dogs I own? Right.

Erik Tucsok lives in London, Ontario. He is a loving father and cares for (the city's legal limit) dogs. He enjoys movies, music, and spending most of his time arguing with himself about things like why the letter Y is called 'Wi' and not 'Ye'. For instance, the word 'Why' starts with a 'Double-u'. Wouldn't the letter W be called 'Wi' and the letter Y be called 'Ye'…

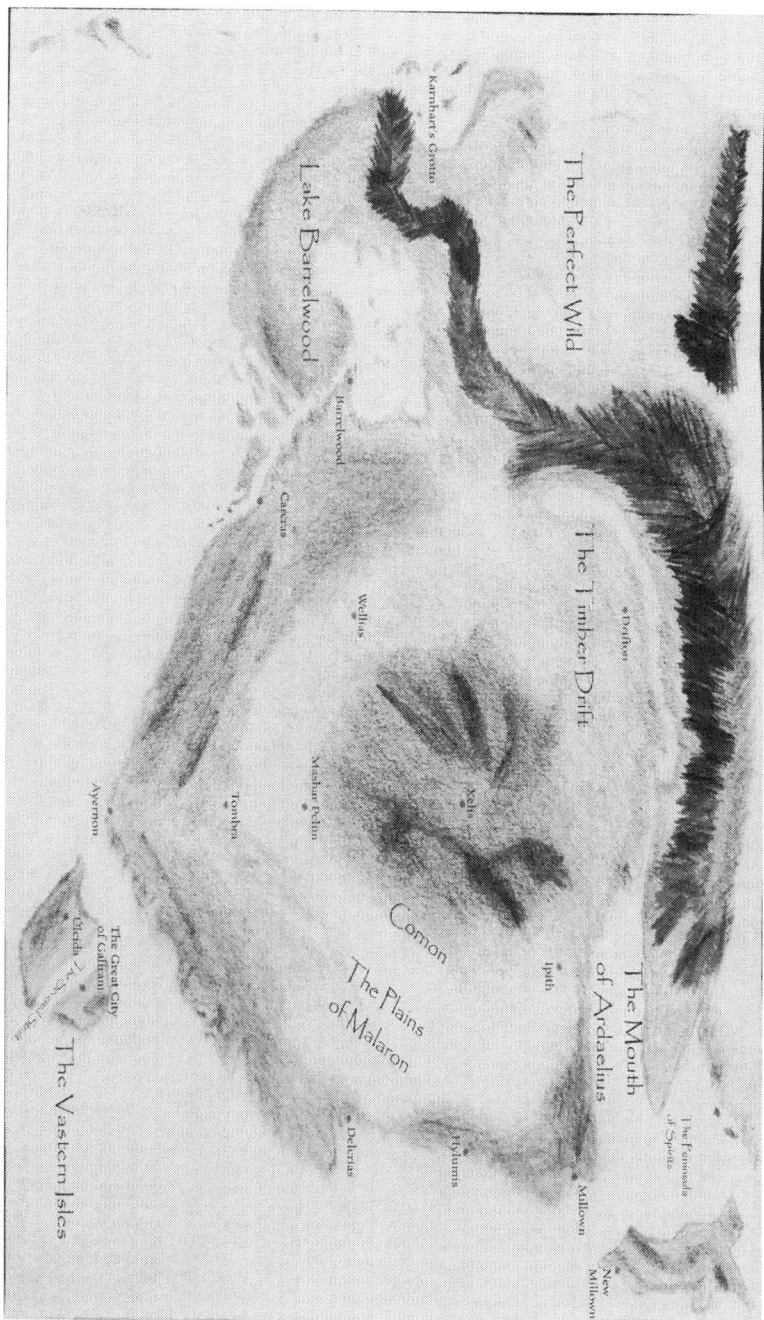

The Perfect Wild

Kambar's Grotto

Lake Barrelwood

Barrelwood

Cheum

Wellus

The Timber Drift

Drufien

Mashar Pelint

Xelis

Ayermon

Tomilrn

Comon

ipth

The Mouth
of Ardaelus

The Great City
of Calfuun

Uceda

The Plains
of Malaron

Hylums

The Peninsula
of Spirelo

The Vastern Isles

Delerlas

Millown

New
Millown

Manufactured by Amazon.ca
Bolton, ON